WOES OF LAVENDER

First edition. April 29, 2024.

Copyright © 2024 Razz Vernicus.

ISBN: 979-8224367535

Written by Razz Vernicus.

CW00927361

Table of Contents

Chapter One: Perfection 1

Chapter Two: Luminous 9

Chapter Three: Ascent 21

Chapter Four: Larceny 31

Chapter Five: Reflection 43

Chapter Six: Assistance 55

Chapter Seven: Inquietude 63

Chapter Eight: Misconception 77

Chapter Nine: Revelation 87

Chapter Ten: Iridescent 99

Chapter Eleven: Encumbrance 109

Chapter Twelve: Confidential 119

Chapter Thirteen: Heist 131

Chapter Fourteen: Blooming 145

Chapter Fifteen: Incandescence 159

Chapter Sixteen: Return 171

Chapter Seventeen: Affluent 185

Chapter Eighteen: Warmth 195

Chapter Nineteen: Stability 205

Chapter Twenty: Adorned 215

Chapter Twenty-One: Nostalgic 225

Chapter Twenty-Two: Vannril 235

Chapter Twenty-Three: Favor 245

Chapter Twenty-Four: Together 257

Chapter Twenty-Five: Pinnacle 269

Epilogue 279

Thank you for picking up this book! I wanted to write this message to anyone who ends up reading it that I appreciate them for taking the time to read this.

The making of this book was largely thanks to Kit Roe's editing, Barbara Galiza's beautiful cover design and the EvoSphere Design team for the title art.

I hope you enjoy the Celegons and all the other creatures you will discover in this book.

Razz Vernicus

Woes of Lavender

Razz Vernicus

Chapter One: Perfection

Naturally, the first thing I did was get caught. Not that this was the first time; as an amateur I regularly found out several ways to mess up on the job. But this time it was different, not only did I slip up, I slipped up on a supposedly easy heist as a professional. The infamous Lox Lavender was immediately discovered as soon as she climbed through an uncovered skylight. To make things worse, it had to be the Celegon with sunset eyes who was made aware of my presence.

My morning started out somewhat great. I'd had food to eat when I woke up, there were no monsters eagerly waiting for me when I left my dome and I'd even been informed by one of my close informants about an easy job soon after I'd ventured into the nearest town. This particular Celegon had proven herself moderately reliable when it came to relaying information about potential heist targets. The past two times I had spoken with her, she was almost completely accurate in describing the risks and rewards of the target homes. Maybe I was a little too confident in what she told me.

"Yep! Even I find it hard to believe, but you can't deny the facts. The place is completely deserted, which is weird because you think they'd assign a few caretakers to keep things in order. I guess they think their filter will be enough, but that only keeps the monsters from entering, not other Celegons. Anyways, these guys live in a huge mansion and it's probably loaded with all sorts of treasures and stashes of orbs. Those Iseirres won't even know what hit them!" she relayed to me in a bubbly manner as I took two shiny blue orbs out of my satchel and pocketed them into hers.

However she was not satisfied with just the blue orbs, as she kept eyeing my satchel and giving me smug looks. The information seemed solid enough at the time so I went ahead and gave her two more. Paying her more now would keep things cordial for our next meeting. Not that I would care to meet her again anytime soon. Now that I had the details, I needed to do a few things in preparation before I infiltrated the mansion.

The morning sun had only just risen into the sky by the time I had learned about the mansion and its whereabouts. So, if I was efficient, which I was, I could get everything done in the same day. The first thing I did was head towards my target. I dashed out of the small wooded town, let my translucent, flowy wings emerge from my back and flew straight there. I memorized the trees that stood out from others so I would be able to easily navigate back. The mansion was in the middle of a particularly dense forest, a smart choice since it made it more secluded from monsters and thieves like myself.

If only it were more hidden than it appeared to be, perhaps it would have been harder to find. Doubtful, as I was given exact coordinates, but it would have made it a little bit harder for me. I landed just a few trees away from the front entrance and clawed my way down. Then I began to scope out the overly extravagant home from the outside to try and pinpoint the most efficient way to enter. After a few hours of checking out the exterior, I realized that it was indeed empty as no one came and went. The only security appeared to be the many so-called "monster repellent" flower bushes which all seemed to be very well cared for.

Once I had decided on my entrance, I flew all the way back to the small town to purchase supplies I would need for a successful heist. While I could have brought them with me the first time, supplies can be heavy and I wanted to know that the information was legit before starting anything. By the time I had returned to the town, it was a bit past noon and I was drained from using my wings. I first took care of my physical needs by purchasing some rather expensive emeri and eating it to relieve some of the pain in my back as well as some of the dizziness I was experiencing. Then I went over to a different merchant to purchase a strong woven rope.

Normally I would make my own rope out of vines and tree sap, but it does not hold together as well as woven rope. I would need that kind of reliability in a tool if I happened to spot a particularly heavy and valuable item and move it to a hidden spot on the roof. I needed to make a mental note of learning to make my own sturdy woven ropes someday; it would certainly save me the orbs. Ropes of any kind were to be discarded after use and stashed somewhere less obvious. Before I flew back to the heist target, I briefly rested and indulged in some emeri so I would have as much strength as possible before I began my quest to infiltrate the Iseirre mansion.

The sun had just started to descend in the sky as I took off. I had always liked sunsets with their beautiful orange and purple colors clashing together across the sky. After an hour or so, the sunset soon faded as the sky began to take on its darker colors. My timing was impeccable. By the time I landed on the roof of the mansion, the sky was at its darkest. While most nights were almost pitch black due to the lack of stars, the twin moons reflected just enough light back on the world in order for me to locate the skylight I was planning to enter.

It was at the mansion's far left in a corner, so I assumed it dropped down into a storage or food preparation room since those specific rooms often had small skylights. I took a bottle of sticky tree sap and dumped a large glob of it close to the edge before placing the end of a rope on it and pressing firmly. Then I pushed the rest of the rope down the skylight hole once I was certain that it was firmly attached to the sap. Once I finished acquiring the valuables, I needed to make sure to find a good hiding spot for the heavy tool.

My heart fluttered as I began to descend down into the dark mansion. I began to wonder about all the treasures and orbs I would gather. Maybe I would finally have enough orbs to exchange for spare lighting parts for my portable dome. My thoughts were short lived however. The rope made a snapping noise. Before I could summon my wings, my back plummeted into an assortment of soft cushions.

Several wax clumps in the room began to light themselves, allowing me to see the interior more precisely. I briefly panicked, thinking this mansion was haunted with some kind of transparent monster. This fear subsided as I turned to my right and was now locking eyes with a Celegon whose eyes bore a strong resemblance to the sunset I had recently seen.

Instead of frantically flying back up the skylight that I came through, I stood frozen in place as I examined the newly lit surroundings. It was a typical wealthy Celegon's living quarters, adorned with fancy paintings, several carved storage units and of course plentiful soft cushions and fine blankets. Though in addition to all that, there were several dirty empty bowls scattered throughout the room. My eyes then slowly fixated on the Celegon laying down in front of me.

I noticed that his dark green fur was stained with the same color that was in the bowls on his paws and face. Considering most of Lixion was starving, this made the event even more off-putting. Likewise, he probably was just as surprised as I was after seeing a thief break into his mansion.

His name was Marles Iseirre; I had met him once long ago. Vibrant orange eyes, dark red tints in the hair tuft on his head and the stone in his tail that shared the same color. It was definitely the same Celegon I had seen before. Only physically his body had undergone some changes through the years. He was now considerably heavier than before which caught me off guard as most Celegons struggled to keep any weight on them at all.

For the first time in a while, I was unsure of what to do. I could most definitely outrun him with ease, fly out where I entered from. For some reason that did not feel like the right thing to do in this situation. After all, he knew what I looked like now. He could hire several others to track me down later. Killing him was not an option either, not that I would ever intentionally try to kill anyone of my species. If I knocked him out I might just about kill him considering the state he was in. While I pondered what to do, the Celegon continued to examine me. He did not appear to be startled anymore; instead his eyes beamed with curiosity. After a few more seconds of silence, words were spoken.

"You're Lox Lavender aren't you?"

I flinched at the sound of his voice. I suppose I was ready to be confronted about what I was originally planning to do, I was certainly not expecting to be asked a question in a calm tone. Telling lies and manipulation were two things I was taught to be great at, but for some reason I could do neither to this Celegon. It was as though I had completely forgotten how which added tension to the situation. So I decided to tell the truth. If things began to take a turn for the worst I could always just run away.

"Yes. What of it?"

He initially seemed surprised by me admitting that I was in fact Lox Lavender, but his expression then began to melt into a relaxed smile. Even though it was brief, that moment of silence was slightly unsettling because I had no idea what was going to happen next.

"Oh I was right! I wasn't completely sure, but I thought you maybe could be because of your colors and that you came through my skylight. I never would have thought that I'd ever meet a real thief someday. Oh and I'm Marles Iseirre, it's a pleasure to meet you!"

He smiled as he began to stand and reached out his paw to me. I reluctantly took it, and as soon as I did I felt a sticky substance on my own. He seemed to realize what had happened, and immediately pulled his paw away from mine to grab for a blanket on the ground. I stared at my palm for a moment—at the yellowish substance before a blanket was rubbing against it.

"I'm so sorry about that. I completely forgot that I still had that mess on my paws. Cheese based soups are quite hard to clean off fur without water, I should go fetch some from—"

Before he could finish, I swiftly took back my paw and placed it promptly into my mouth before licking the remaining cheese off. I only tasted cheese a few times in my life; it was one of the harder foods to safely acquire. I was certainly not going to let the stuff go to waste. It was a little amusing to see Iseirre's reaction, at least until I heard him say, "Ah don't eat that! T-that's poison!"

He really should have said that before I had put my paw into my mouth. My tongue had just finished licking the last bit of cheese stuck in my fur by the time my ears heard poison. My mind panicked for a moment, but then I began to question a few things about what just happened.

"You poisoned your cheese?"

"No, the cheese is poison."

"Well, if the cheese is poison then why are you eating it?"

"B-because it's delicious!"

I thought to myself for a moment as my mind processed what was currently going on. This entire situation seemed off somehow and I could sense that he was lying about something. Maybe this was a sham, he was using conversation topics to stall for time until another Celegon living in the mansion realized what was going on.

My instincts told me to leave, and whenever they tell me to do something, I always listen. As quickly as my body was able to, I turned around and ran towards the nearest wooden door and pushed it open. I dropped down to run on all four of my limbs as my eyes darted across the dark hallway looking for an exit. Almost immediately after I left the room, I heard Iseirre call out to me.

"Sorry Iseirre! I'm afraid my thief policy doesn't extend to rich Celegons!" I called back to him as I continued to run through the hall.

He continued to call out to me, but his voice grew fainter. I could only assume he was trying to chase me down; luckily for me I still had enough energy to fly. Just a few seconds later, my ears began to pick up strange sounds back in the direction that I came from. I began to slow my pace and listen more intently to the sounds. They sounded like someone was choking, struggling to breathe and shortly after I heard something drop to the floor. My mind began to panic as I frantically sprinted back towards the noises.

Before too long I approach Iseirre, who was practically drowning in his own vomitus and seemed unconscious. Without thinking, I took hold of him and dragged him back to his room. Doing so was a little hard, but somehow I managed. I propped him against one of the cushions before grabbing a dirtied blanket and using it to wipe his face off. His eyes began to open and flicker a bit before they focused on me.

"Are you alright? I thought I heard choking so I came back to see if- "

Before I finished my sentence I remembered that I was supposed to be making my escape. He was safe and therefore no reason for me to still be there.

"There, now I owe you nothing. I'll be taking my leave now," I huffed as I turned around and walked towards the door.

Then I heard him faintly mutter, "Celegons are cheese intolerant."

I froze in my path. Was he still trying to stall for time?

"What—What does that even mean?" I ask without turning around to face him.

"Celegons can't digest cheese. It doesn't give our bodies any nutrients for energy or magic, so the body rejects it. I just thought you should know so you aren't tempted to eat it anymore, it's really bad for our stomachs. I know in your line of work it's best to stay as healthy as possible," he replied as my mind began to think of more questions.

"So, knowing that, why have you been eating so much of it?" I questioned as I turned around to face him. There was a little pause before he began to awkwardly smile.

"I already told you, I love the flavor of it," he laughed lightly before staring at me directly in the eyes. I was not sure if it was the color, but his eyes had a way of sucking you into them. I was not sure exactly how I felt about it. "Also, thank you Miss Lavender," he said as his eyes began to glisten; small flames in the room appeared to reflect off them. For a brief moment, I wanted to smile and tell him that there was no need for thanks.

"For what? Dragging you back to your room? I don't need any 'thanks'. If you really want to pay me back, give me some orbs or something actually useful," I scoffed as I began to tug on my satchel to make sure it was secure.

"Oh yes, thank you for that too, but I wasn't finished. You made me realize something," he went on and I waited anxiously for him to finish so I could hurry up and finally leave. My mind blanked out for a moment, ignoring most of what he said aside from the last sentence. "And that's why I want you to take me on as your apprentice," he finished. I almost started laughing because I was sure he was not serious. It was not until I looked into his eyes again before I realized he was.

"Simply put, no."

Chapter Two: Luminous

For some reason I told him that he could come with me. This was roughly ten minutes after him practically begging me to. Granted, I was being a little sarcastic when I'd accepted his request. So I devised a plan to have him stay with me for a few days. Once he saw how bland my living situation was compared to his mansion, he would regret coming with me and beg me to take him back. I could also make a profit off this since there was little chance he could return here alone in his current state. I would offer to escort him back safely and in return get paid a few orbs for my trouble. Unfortunately for me, plans that you make up in such a short time have a way of failing you.

I was currently waiting for Iseirre to pack up a few things to take along with him. Well, waiting as in exploring the dark halls of the mansion. If it were a little lighter outside, looking around might have been more enjoyable. While it was hard to see everything, it was clear that the mansion's interior was quite sizable. It certainly made the insides of my dome look very miniscule in comparison. Iseirre's room alone was easily quadruple the space of my little dome. Not that I was envious; big open spaces always made me tense, so living in a mansion would probably make me feel insecure and paranoid.

My feet walked over the plush rugs that adorned the floors of the hallway as I began to make my way back to Iseirre's room. The softness of them was noticeably more so than the ones I often found in inns and shops. While it felt nice on my feet, getting accustomed to it would be an issue since I often traveled through thick forests that boasted rocks, branches, and other sharp things. Just another reason why Iseirre would be begging to go back home after a few short hours of walking on forest grounds. As I approached his bedroom, I heard him rummaging through his belongings. He was definitely packing things that he did not need. Then I heard a bit of shuffling and soon enough he emerged from his room's doorway.

"Alright, that took longer than expected but I'm all packed and ready to go!" he beamed as I resisted my urge to sigh aloud.

The first thing I noticed was that he was wearing a long red scarf that was wrapped along his neck and fell down almost past his upper legs. The obvious display of wealth felt a little tacky for wilderness travel. He also had a bag that was slightly larger than my satchel that hung right down the center of his back. I always thought packs like that to be inconvenient as they got in the way of flying, among other things. Not that these concerns of mine mattered since I was not planning for him to stay with me for very long.

"You're really going to wear that thing? Oh nevermind, we've lost enough time already. Hurry up, let's go," I stated as he pulled at his scarf for a moment before following me.

Shortly after walking down the hallway together, I was slightly surprised when I started to see some of the unlit wax clumps on the walls suddenly light up with small flames. It occurred to me that the same happened when I first fell into Iseirre's room, which could only mean that one of his talents was fire oriented magic. This would prove useful on certain occasions such as traveling the dark forests at night. Perhaps during our short time together I might be able to learn a few things myself.

Of all of the talents Celegons can learn, fire magic was certainly one of the more useful ones. I have heard difficulty wise that it is easy to pick up, but hard to fully master. All talents are hard in their own ways however. Most Celegons are only able to learn one or two before meeting their ends. As a thief I only know a modest amount of the ice talent, if only for self defense. While it would be beneficial to learn as many types as I can, mastering them takes time; time that I could use for more important things.

Since the wax clumps illuminated the halls, the paintings and decorations were much more interesting to look at. Additionally, the rugs bore unique patterns and symbols that caught my gaze. While looking at the extravagant rugs, I happened to notice that same spot where Iseirre had practically vomited his stomach out. I did not pay much attention to the color before, but in the mostly yellow mass I saw that there were traces of blood. Apparently I was examining this a little too intently and Iseirre caught on.

"O-oh don't worry about that, I'm sure one of the caretakers will get to it eventually before it leaves a stain," he tried to laugh in an attempt to mask his obvious embarrassment and divert my attention from his mess.

I had never felt more reassured that my plan would work out; he's spoiled, had some sort of illness, was quite unfit for travel, and relied on others to do his cleaning. I wondered if he would even be able to survive outside for a short amount of time. Of course I was not about to let him die on my watch. I needed that travel fee after all.

While it was still quite dark outside, the moons reflected just enough light to see the surrounding area. The windy outside air briefly rushed over my fur before suddenly coming to a halt. It seemed as if the moment we stepped outside all wind currents vanished. This was very odd since there was always a breeze flowing through the outside air, even if it was very faint. My eyes flickered around until they landed on the rightmost side of the mansion rooftop. It was almost as if something was there, watching us. But by the time I'd looked at it, it had already vanished.

"Iseirre, you were the only one here tonight aside from myself, correct?" I asked as I began to examine the rooftops more carefully.

"Yes, that's right..." his voice trailed off as he looked at the roof and then at me with a concerned expression.

I could only assume that either he was lying or he was so sheltered he had not developed his senses enough to know something seemed off.

"Oh! You're probably wondering why I'm here alone and where everyone else is," he smiled and his eyes seemed to tell me that he really wanted to share such important details.

"No, not re—you know what? Why not, just be quick about it," I stated as I continued to monitor the rooftops for any signs of movement.

It was not that I was completely disinterested in why he happened to be there. It just wasn't fun openly conversing when it felt like something was stalking you.

"Well," he started, clearly excited to tell me about this amazing story. "To answer that, they have all been away at a social gathering for about two days now and our caretakers have been sent on their own excursion. I believe everyone was to return this morning, if I'm not mistaken. There's also a magical barrier set up around the mansion that's supposed to ward off monsters, so it's perfectly safe to be here alone for days at a time," Iseirre explained with much more detail than I was asking for.

I did not know much about magical barriers, also known as filters, mostly because only Celegons who possessed powerful psi talents were able to create them. Obviously the barrier did an awful job keeping thieves out. So monster proof or not, there was a fair chance that there was something out there watching us.

"Let's just hurry up and get out of here," I huffed as I began to expand my wings out of my back.

It never seemed to get any less draining every time I did it, though I had done it countless times now. Arguably, the hardest part of flying was extending a pair of thin but efficient magic wings from your back. If you think about it too much it's honestly quite painful, but I suppose all magic comes with a price. I glanced over towards Iseirre and noticed he was simply staring at my wings in awe instead of summoning his own.

"Come on, we're flying out of here. I don't want to waste too much time and risk any chance of the other inhabitants returning early," I stated as I eagerly awaited for him to get to it.

Only, he laughed a little and said, "Well, actually you should know that I can't really fly."

This was shocking to say the least. I mean he was quite fat, probably the heaviest Celegon I had ever come across. Even so, Celegons wings were able to adjust so they could ascend into the sky no matter how light or heavy they were. So, why could he not fly?

"So this is kind of embarrassing but," he looked over at me, almost as if he was asking me to feel sympathetic. "I've never been able to extend wings from my back. Everyone else makes it seem so easy, but no matter what, no matter how hard I try, I just can't seem to do it," he said, his voice sounding quite bleak at the last few words.

I was about to feel sorry for him. Not being able to fly is like losing a piece of freedom from the soul. Seeing as how most other Celegons could fly, it must have been especially hard on him. Despite the depressing undertones, he came back with a very unsettlingly positive outlook on the situation.

"But that's completely okay! I heard flying's quite overrated anyway. Walking is far more scenic and doesn't use any magical energy to keep you going," he smiled with a giddy look on his face which nearly made me roll my eyes.

Well, he was not exactly wrong. Flying did use a substantial amount of magic energy, especially if you were going fast and over a long distance. As inconvenient as this appeared on the surface, this disability would prove useful. The longer he stayed at my side, the more I would charge for the return fee. This would make it harder to keep him alive, so with that in mind, I decided I might as well double the rates. Retracting wings was thankfully a bit easier than extending them, so it was done quickly and with little pain.

"Alright, we shall walk from here then," I said as I began to quicken my pace in the direction of the forest.

Originally my plan was to run back to my dome after I had robbed this place, before Iseirre squeezed himself into the equation. With Iseirre in his current state I doubt he would be able to run for ten seconds before vomiting or wheezing. We would have to walk as briskly as he was able to.

As we approached the thick forest that surrounded the mansion, I felt my fur rise slightly on the back of my neck. That same feeling, the feeling I got when I first stepped outside had returned.

"Um, Miss Lavender? Something tells me it's not safe to go outside the barrier right now," Marles' voice sounded much more serious than his previous statement, and while I knew something seemed off, I could not stay here any longer.

"So you're suggesting I stick around until there's daylight and those affiliates of yours show up? I'm a risk taker, but I'm not an idiot. Look, you can turn back now if you aren't up for a little thrill, tell them all about how you actually met the infamous Lox Lavender and maybe they'll even believe you. That would most surely guarantee your safety, at the sacrifice of you becoming my apprentice," I could feel my mouth forming a smirk as I confidently strutted my way into the forest.

Guess I would not get anything out of this after all. Backing out at the first sign of danger, how typical for a spoiled and pampered Celegon. Of course, my amusement was short-lived as not a moment later he was walking at my side.

"Huh, so you can sense the danger, yet you are still following me," I sighed as I heard him giggle a bit.

"Well I can't exactly be your apprentice if I stay home. Plus, with the two of us we would be able to protect each other against whatever danger that lurks outside the barrier." He smiled gleefully as I began to question his common sense.

Protect each other, who was he trying to fool anyway? He would be dead in seconds if a monster showed up. If anything, I was concerned for his mental health as well as my own safety; his positive outlook was far too bright for him to see things clearly. *Yes, I will protect you Iseirre and then get that sweet reward from you once you realize you have taken on too much.*

My inner thoughts were cut short as my senses detected a change in the atmosphere. It suddenly began to feel warm and the surrounding ten feet of darkness was illuminated by an orangey light. I glanced toward the source to see that the top of Iseirre's tail was coated with a thick fluffy layer of orange flame.

"W-what are you doing! Do you not see how thick and close these trees are together? Are you trying to start a forest fire and get every monster within a five mile radius on our tails?" I exclaimed, only slightly panicked as the thought of burning down a forest did not rest easy on one's conscience.

He began to giggle again, much to my annoyance as clearly preserving forests was not a concern of his. He was definitely strange. From the short time I have known this Celegon, I noticed he seemed to laugh a great deal more than anyone I had met. The laughs that came from him felt quite genuine as well. They made me feel all fuzzy inside, but at the same time really irked me. Perhaps because he was laughing about the thought of massacring an innocent, beautiful forest which made me feel uneasy.

"Don't worry, I'm quite good at containing my fire to myself. I can assure you I have never caused any forest fires during the time I've been alive." He beamed as he began to swing his tail around playfully, almost as if he was attempting to torment me.

I could also tell he was holding back more laughter too. Honestly, I was quite surprised how he was even managing to hold it in at this point. The flame on his tail looked quite painful, but it did not appear to be causing him any harm. I could only assume Celegons who could control their fire talent possessed some sort of immunity to the flames they controlled. I did not really know much about the fire talent, much less any others save my own, as talents are not the primary tools of a thief. He certainly made for a good torch though.

I must have been glancing at his tail too often as I could hear him faintly laughing again.

"Would you like to touch? I promise I won't burn you," he smiled warmly as he casually grabbed a hold of his tail and stuck his left paw into the flame.

I stared at it blankly as I observed how the flame was not burning his paw before turning my head away as if I was uninterested. He was a bit quiet after that, hopefully taking the hint that I had no interest in more casual talk for one night. Until he asked the question I had foresaw coming from the moment we walked outside.

"Also—I'm a little curious, where are we headed, Miss Lavender?" I winced. Him calling me that would simply not do.

"Right now we are headed to my dome which is situated about two hours of walking distance away from here. Mind you, it would have taken us only fifteen if we could fly. And could you do me a favor and stop referring to me as 'Miss Lavender', Iseirre? It feels odd using my thief surname in regular conversation," I shudder as the thought of him potentially calling me that around other Celegons could be life threatening.

"Alright, but only if you refer to me as just Marles from now on," he chimed in amusement.

I guess it was a fair trade off, but referring to him by first name this soon and after everything that just happened seemed a bit too friendly to me. Still, if it was to get him from unintentionally alerting other Celegons that I was Lox Lavender, I guess I had no choice.

"Okay *Marles*, please refer to me as Lyla Sky—I mean Skyli from now on," I stated, only to realize my mistake only after I had said it. My fears only intensified when I saw his eyes light up with delight.

"So Miss S-hold on, Lyla?" His brain appeared to be processing it, much to my dismay. "Ly-la. Sky-li. Lyla Skyli! Wow you have a very lovely name Lyla. It's so pleasing to say," he said to me with a happy grin, seemingly clueless as to how I did not want him to use that name.

Perhaps he simply wanted to torment me. Either way, it did not matter since I was not planning on him sticking around me forever; for now I would just have to deal with it. Even so, I could not deny that his name was also quite pleasing. Marles Iseirre. Marles, not quite a Charles. Though 'icy air' was quite an ironic name for him.

The rest of the trip to my dome went fairly well. Iseirre, or Marles as he wanted me to refer to him as, had stopped attempting to strike up meaningless conversation; which was a mental relief. That meant I could finally listen more closely to the sounds of the forest and pay more attention to the roots under my feet so I would not trip. Another thing I was actually quite surprised with, was how well Marles did on this journey. He only stumbled over branches about thirteen times, which was way off from the minimum of fifty times I thought he would fall. Despite all of that, he did not vomit once—which honestly shocked me.

There were parts in the forest that were challenging for the both of us, but luckily those made up a small fraction of the entire journey. This forest was quite dense and some trees grew so close together that we had to either squeeze through or find another path. As a thief, I was constantly slipping into tight spaces to hide, so I was somewhat used to it; however, and unfortunately for Marles, he lacked my skinny body and flexibility. So it took him a bit longer to get through those parts. Then there was the monster shriek I'd thought I'd heard out in the distance. It'd forced us to lay close to the ground, surrounded by the darkness, for about twenty minutes until we were sure it was safe to move again. I would never admit it aloud, but Marles' flame really helped make me feel more secure. Whenever it had gone out all of a sudden, I'd feel a chill go down my spine.

Eventually, we finally reached the small clearing where my dome was located. Which was good, because Marles looked like he could barely walk a few more steps. It would be only a matter of time before he would ask me to escort him home, and I would be getting a sweet reward for doing so. My estimated time of arrival had been only a little off; it had taken us a good two hours and thirty-three minutes to get here. We would have arrived sooner if Marles had not slowed us down. Really, I should be grateful we were able to get here at all; I could finally let my guard down a bit since home was near.

I reached into my satchel to pull out the small roundish remote and gently pressed the top right button. With a bit of delay, the once empty clearing was now filled with my small dome; which had become visible to us and potentially every other living thing watching.

"Alright, now get in quickly so I can invisilize it again," I said as I waited for him to crawl through the small door.

Once I saw he was inside, I slid under the doorway myself and immediately pressed the same button; which caused the door flap to seal shut and make the outside invisible again. As I got up from the ground, I was hit with the sudden realization that I had not properly cleaned the place for the past two weeks; meaning it was a massive mess. An organized mess, but to anyone who was not me it would probably just look like a regular mess. I glanced over at Marles, who looked a bit fazed after seeing the place—my tiny, compact, but still livable dome that was probably *not* up to his standards.

"Seems quite... homey." Marles smiled as I stared at the space in disbelief.

Yes, 'homey' was definitely the word to describe the atrocity I was looking at right now.

There were blankets and cushions in the cooking area to the left, cooking utensils in the bedding area to the right, and my whole study area in between was a complete disaster with paper and books scattered across my desk. Of course I was not actually bothered by it; I was just visualizing what was probably going on inside his head right now. For Marles' sanity, I quickly cleaned up the majority of the mixed up items and put them in their proper designated areas. I didn't bother organizing the papers and books as I did not care to sort them all right away. As long as they were out of sight, he would not be tempted to read through my life logs or past targets of mine.

The thought then occurred to me that Marles' room back at his mansion was far filthier than my moderately messy dome. With the empty bowls of cheese soup strewn across the room, he was certainly more a slob than I was. My mouth curled up into a prideful smirk when I thought about that.

"Sorry about that. I wasn't exactly expecting any guests anytime soon, or ever in fact," I huffed as I attempted to seem annoyed even though cleaning took very little time and effort. I expected to get a reply but instead he simply just stood there motionless.

I gazed into his eyes, which appeared to be half closed and had lost a bit of their sunset vibrance. Was he asleep with his eyes open? I gently poked him with my tail, but he was unresponsive and did not make any noise other than to breathe. Since he was still standing I assumed he was only half asleep, but I was confused as to why he did not at least sit down to do so. I mentally sighed as I used my tail to guide him to the bedding area and gently pushed him down onto a small pile of cushions. Then I took off his bag and tossed a blanket over him.

Alright. So he fell asleep here and is staying with me for the night; lodging is kind of expensive so I will definitely charge extra for that.

Definitely. Tomorrow.

I quietly exhaled as I nestled myself down into the blankets and cushions away from him. Then I fiddled with the remote so that the lights inside the dome were dimmed down just enough to still be able to still see everything. Then promptly took my satchel off. My blankets were a bit scruffy, but they were still decent at retaining heat. My cushions were a bit too soft, and I felt the dome's floor under them, but I greatly prefer them over cushions that made me feel like I was sleeping on rocks. I kept trying to find things to distract my mind with, but nothing was working. Sighing, I turned to look at Marles and thousands of thoughts raced through my head.

What am I even doing?

I shuffled a bit under the blankets as I tried to think about this logically. There was another Celegon who I knew next to nothing about sleeping just a few feet away from me in my personal dome; that is subjectively crazy to a lot of Celegons and potentially dangerous. If he woke up before me he could smother me to death or worse, kick me out and steal my dome and everything in it. And I keep telling myself I will get a reward out of this, but will I really be that lucky to have things turn out that way? Or was I just perhaps, lonely? I mean I definitely get my fill of social interactions with shopkeepers and rumor-spreading Celegons, but did I want something a little more personable, more real? No, of course not; especially not after what happened with *her*.

I stretched into a more comfortable position in the hopes that I would lull myself to sleep; unfortunately, when there are so many things on one's mind, sleep can be hard to accomplish. Thus began the impossible battle, my attempt to silence the noise so I could get some rest. However, no matter how hard I tried, these thoughts would not cease. So I gave up and attempted a different approach. I accepted them and began to focus on the more pleasant ones. Soon, before I knew it, memories resurfaced and I found myself lulled into a peaceful slumber.

. . ⤜ . .

"Lyla! Come over here, look at what I've snagged!"

I heard a voice call out to me from across a tall grassy field. Curiously, I moved towards it without a second thought. There was a grey-furred Celegon with bright sky-blue eyes who possessed a smug, yet happy expression on her face. It was Alise, my best friend who had just returned from some epic heist and had a sack full of treasures.

"What did you get? I wanna see!" I exclaimed as I rushed toward her and attempted to peek into the sack; she playfully snatched it away from me.

"H-hey now you little brat, you know the rules! I'll only show you my spoils if you've done something for me in return. Now I wonder what that could be," Alise grinned widely as I started to think a little.

"Oh of course! I tried making something new today with water nymphs and kimberis," I smiled as I turned around to see the meal I had prepared for us in the cooking area in the dome.

After I went over to grab a serving I turned around again; Alise is sitting at the desk looking over potential heist targets.

"Hey Alise? When can I go with you on a heist? I've been practicing so much and I-I think I'm ready now," I asserted confidently as she continued to research targets.

"Oh Lyla, I'm sorry but you'd just get in the way as you are now. Just keep practicing and one day your skills will even surpass mine." She chuckled and I found myself beginning to feel a bit down.

"Okay, if that's how it's going to be then I'll just practice until I'm finally good enough for you!" I stated confidently as the area around me faded to black. *"Alise? Alise where are you?"* I shouted out into the darkness.

I looked to the left and to the right and there was nothing but darkness. I tried to move, but no matter how hard I did so my limbs would not budge. Then I looked down and finally saw something come into focus. It was a piece of paper with many words on it. Maybe I should read it while I waited for Alise to come back. The more I read it, the more it hurt and eventually I could not take it anymore and dropped the paper, watching it float into the dark abyss. Then I looked up as it felt like my neck was being pulled to look at whatever was up there. My eyes teared up, but it seemed as no matter how many tears were in my eyes I could still see it all so clearly.

"A-Alise?"

Chapter Three: Ascent

Annoyance. This was the simplest way of describing how I have felt for the past three hours.

Celegons as a species always seemed to have weird sleeping habits, myself included. At least compared to monsters, who most think have an inability to dream, and are thus able to get a good night's rest without any internal disturbances. Dreams, for the most part, seem to plague unlucky Celegons who just want to sleep peacefully through the night. Not that all dreams are bad, but they can be inconvenient as a Celegon can just as easily wake up from a great dream just like nightmarish ones. My dreams were probably the worst of all, a sickly combination of good and bad.

The worst part was I was in the unlucky portion of Celegons who have multiple dreams in one night. Meaning, everytime I try to go back to sleep after waking up from one dream, my mind would either continue from the last dream or just end up starting up a completely new brainwave created mess. If dreams actually meant something, like possibly predicting the future, maybe it would not be so bad. But instead I get tormented with blobs of meaningless skits. All of them seemed to blend my past memories and mix in random eerie stuff that I have never seen before. The scariest random one I can remember was the one where I was drowning in a giant, deep endless pond full of salty water.

Here I was, ranting internally about these awful dreams that were not even real before the sudden realization hit me. Marles was here in my dome, sleeping on my cushions and blankets without a care in the world. Why I was even the least bit okay with having him in here with me escaped my mind. The cost of inns at towns varies, but averages out to a value of fifteen orbs. With that in mind, it should bring his estimated total debt to around forty blue orbs, almost the worth of a singular gold orb. For some reason, maybe because I did not sleep very well, my plan on extorting orbs from Marles made me feel somewhat squeamish. Gazing up at the ceiling, I saw the small glass covered hole at the top of the dome was emitting a faint glow of daylight telling me it was early morning.

Turning over to my side, I could see that Marles was sleeping peacefully, presumably without the disturbance of dreams. Stretching my limbs, I got up knowing that trying to rest more was pointless. Everything appeared to be the same from before I drifted off; which was good, because I was not in the mood to confront Marles about tampering with any of my valuables. Not that he seemed the type to do so, which only proved how ill-equipped he was to be a thief. At the same time, he showed no sign of giving up on learning how to be one. Rather than worry about my future troubles, my stomach had other needs that required catering to.

As I made my way over to the cooking area, my hunger induced thoughts were diminished briefly as I remembered Marles would need to eat as well. How simple it would be if his body could eat itself for nourishment, if only Celegons were like monsters in that regard. Monsters were able to eat parts of themselves if they grew desperate enough, while our bodies simply grew weaker until starvation. Since I was not planning on being unnecessarily cruel, I would spare him some of my berries and roots for the time being. More specifically, the most bitter and sour of the bunch. No one would beg to be taken home if spoiled with delicious sweet berries after all. In my cooking area there was a crate and two jars next to the counter. The crate was almost always empty as its primary use was for storing surplus food—which I rarely had—while the jars were always a little full of foraged roots and berries.

Gently opening the lid of the ceramic jar, I slipped my paw in to scoop out some berries. I soon met with the gritty insides. Perhaps I had forgotten that I already ate everything in that jar? I quickly moved on to the second to find that it was seemingly barren as well. Before my mind turned savage and tried to blame Marles for stealing, I thought really hard trying to see if I could remember eating the contents of the jars.

Possibly from hunger clouding my mind, I had indeed forgotten that I had run out of my supply of forage without paying it too much thought. Not that I had ever been accustomed to being satiated for extended periods of time. I was just a little hopeful that I would maybe have something small to eat for breakfast today. Though my stomach was disappointed about the prospect of no breakfast, I was sure Marles' would be even less compliant than my own since he did not ever go through such hardships back at his mansion.

While I waited for him to wake up, my dome called for some much needed cleaning and organizing. I began to gather up all the books and papers around my desk and place them into slightly organized stacks. As I shuffled through some of the papers, I came across the one that labeled all of the different orbs and their values. Even though it had become useless to me the moment I memorized it, I just could not bring myself to dispose of it. After I lazily shifted the paper under a stack of books, my ears began to twitch at the noise coming from behind me. My head whipped around to see Marles briefly stretching before promptly burying his face into the cushions.

"Marles? Are you awake?" I call out to him; no way I would be allowing him the privilege of sleeping in. His body sluggishly moved to a position so he could see my face as he gave me a weak smile.

"Good morning Ly-Ly," he yawned as if he was still half asleep.

He appeared to be a little battered; it was especially noticeable by looking into his eyes which seemed as if a bit of life was drained out of them. Their color had dulled and they seemed quite puffy. Since he was obviously not feeling his best and appeared to be slightly delusional, I decided against calling him out for saying "Ly-Ly". He was probably too dazed to realize what he was even doing.

Part of me was concerned since he had been doing just fine the other day. But then I realized he'd also eaten all that cheese and this was all likely a side effect. I lost any possible pity that had been forming. Therefore, going outside and experiencing some cool crisp morning air would only do him more good than harm.

"Alright, now that you're awake we need to start moving," I stated as I reached for my satchel that had somehow gotten itself buried under the cushions. Marles sluggishly stood to his feet and absentmindedly went for his bag before I spoke up.

"Oh you won't be needing that. Feel free to just leave it there unless you'd rather burden yourself with carrying something," I lightly snickered as he gave me a tired smile.

My eyes trailed to his neck. He had not removed that scarf, not even to sleep. On closer inspection I noticed that it was slightly dirtied from the night before, when we were navigating through trees and bushes. Since we were already in here I should tell him to leave it as well, no use worsening the quality or having another thief notice its value.

"Oh and leave the scarf. You wearing it once we reach a town might cause us to attract unwanted attention."

Once we were both outside, the damp early morning breeze washed over our faces. It seemed to be rather peaceful at the moment, but danger could find us at any moment. While it would be ideal to give Marles a near death experience so he would beg me to take him home, I was hungry so the plan would have to be slightly improvised.

"Okay, so here's the plan. We are heading to the nearest town, Oakurrow, which would probably take us at least two days if we walk. Additionally, it just so happens that I have conveniently run out of food, so it is a priority to search for some on the way to town. Given these circumstances, I completely understand if you're ready to give up and want to be escorted back home," I say that last part with a slight bit of desperation as I was hoping that maybe I would finally get what I desired.

I may have exaggerated the travel times slightly, only because I knew running was not an option in his condition. Naturally, I only set myself up for more disappointment.

"And leave you alone to fend for yourself? Of course not, not after how far we've come already! Also if you are out of food, I wouldn't mind sharing some of mine," he smiled generously as I looked at him with skepticism.

Regardless if he was trying to act loyal or cheeky, whatever he was trying to do irked me; considering he seemed plenty awake now I was not going to let this slide. I took this as an insult that he was implying I would not be able to survive without him when clearly it was the other way around. Even though my stomach was rumbling in delight at the thought of being filled with food, my mind spoke its thoughts.

"Food? Oh please don't tell me you brought more of your yellow poison with you," I sniggered as he began to make a horrified face.

Just the fact that I mentioned it felt as if I was about to get a reenactment of what happened in the hallway. Though he looked disgusted, I did feel a slight sense of relief that he seemed much better than when he had first woken up.

"N-no, not ever again," he shuddered briefly before turning his focus to my dome. "Also, you are taking your dome with you right? It's awfully big and definitely extremely heavy. I'm sure I've heard domes are portable, but nothing about this looks portable in any way," he stated with a confused look on his face as I stared at him dumbfounded.

Considering domes were brought to our planet over twelve years ago by the Malyspi, I would assume every Celegon would know about them by now. Especially with them being classified as luxury items and all. Marles is failing at being a wealthy Celegon; well—a *previously* wealthy Celegon. Assuming he was not being sarcastic about not knowing how domes worked, I gave him a simple yet genuinely annoyed response.

"Yeah, moving this is clearly impossible," I smirked as I reached into my satchel for the remote to press that ever so convenient button.

We then watched as the dome quickly folded in on itself until it was nothing more than a small metallic cube. Marles stood awestruck as I went over to pick up the dinky cube and slid it into my satchel.

"T-that's how? And somehow whatever's inside doesn't get crushed in the process, that's amazing! My guess would have been some type of teleportation process." He smiled awkwardly and I was briefly amused at his ignorance of the technology.

After packing up the dome, we began the trek through the forest. It was much easier than the previous night since we had daylight on our side. The first part of the morning walk was oddly relaxing. Partly because of how the morning sun shined brightly through the tops of trees, and partly because the constant breeze felt almost perfect with how it coursed through my fur. Additionally, Marles had not yet pestered me with the idea of conversation on this lovely day. Maybe he was simply too tired since it was still morning, but regardless of the reason for his quietness my ears were delighted to be filled with all the early noises of nature.

If we were really lucky, I might pick up the sound of a stream. Streams were the only constant viable safe spots to acquire water, which always meant I was constantly running out no matter how much I stored in my dome. How I envied Celegons with water talents, being able to take water out of clouds and plants and then selling that water at an absurdly high price. As uncommon as streams were, rivers were even more rare and elusive. And unfortunately, unlike streams, rivers were almost always crawling with monsters. In addition to being overrun with the dangerous creatures, rivers were far deeper and wider than streams; I have heard far too many tales of Celegons drowning in the deep water.

Just thinking about water was making me more aware of how dry my mouth was, so I tried to distract myself with other things. First thing to come to my mind was another way I could bait Marles into letting me take him home.

"So Marles, I was wondering since you can't fly, are you also unable to climb? As thieves it's a vital skill to have; if you can't, well—it's just not practical. You at least know how to climb, don't you?" I began to smirk as I saw the uncertainty in his eyes.

"W-well it's been a while, but I'm sure I'm still able to!" he let out a weak laugh as my smirk widened.

"Is that so? Would you mind demonstrating for me? Pick any tree and climb it." I smiled devilishly as I continued to examine his anxious behavior. His eyes told me all I needed to know as his pupils contracted with worry. "We aren't exactly in a hurry to get to town, so feel free to take a minute to see if you're still able to climb. If you can't, that's alright, but I personally don't think you'll do too well on a heist."

My smile grew to a wicked state as it felt as if I could just see the pile of orbs practically materialize in front of my eyes. My body planted itself down onto the soft grassy dirt as I motioned for him to climb a tree. The trees in this forest were fairly tall but by far not the tallest. While I might be able to climb the trees with ease, this would most certainly be no easy task for Marles in his current state.

As expected, he did not immediately give up but he did give me a confused look as if I was joking. Once he saw that I was serious, I watched as the anxiety that plagued his face vanished and was replaced with a glimpse of confidence. He began to examine the trees, possibly searching for the easiest one for him to climb before picking one. Then he took a deep breath and dug his paws into the tree's dark base. I watched intently as he began to slowly pull himself up the tree little by little. Though his mind was determined, I could tell that his body was struggling heavily since it was not conditioned for this level of activity.

It was only after what seemed like barely twenty seconds his arms were shaking and his lungs were struggling to breathe. He was not even a fourth the way up the estimated twenty-six foot tall tree before he lost his grip and tumbled to the ground. Since he only fell a few feet, I was not too concerned. However I was interested to see how he was going to respond to this. Eventually I moved to help him off the ground, earning me an embarrassed smile from Marles. Pulling him up by grasping onto his paws, it felt as if my heart began to ache, probably because I pitied his circumstances. I then made the mistake of looking directly into his eyes; which made me think back to when I was in a similar, but vastly different situation.

All I could think about was what a strange predicament this was. As much as I wanted him to give up so I could potentially get a sweet reward, seeing the hope dry up from his normally glowy sunset eyes just made me feel plain awful inside. This must have been what my eyes looked like all those years ago before I saw the most beautiful eyes I had ever seen. Through harsh treatment, I knew it was possible to make even the most beautiful eyes go dull and hopeless. While I would never say this aloud, all I could think was, *"With eyes that shine as beautifully as yours it would be a moral disgrace to let their warm embers extinguish, Marles Iseirre."* Now, without saying that sickeningly sappy line, how was I going to give him the needed boost to keep going?

"So with that demonstration I think you made it quite clear that you are a shoddy climber," I began as Marles' eyes appeared more sullen by the second. "But you must have some potential?" I paused as I briefly thought of a good way to phrase my words.

Giving him too much hope might make him egotistical and arrogant, but not giving him enough would make him return to his previous lifestyle. Whatever changed my mind so quickly in the spur of the moment, it was surely not my amazing conscience.

"You are like a high quality monster pelt that is stained with blood. While blood can be hard to clean off, it's still manageable and the results are worth it. As long as you put in effort to improve your skills, I think you have what it takes to be a thief. But I'm not going to sweeten anything; you are going to have an extremely tough time the way you are now and it will only get easier for you if you put your all into getting better," I explained as I argued internally with my thoughts over whether what I said would be taken well or not.

His eyes were like traps, even when not glowing their brightest they still somehow lured you into them. It did not take too long for them to react to my words though; in just a few moments they began to shine valiantly with joy, radiating with clashes of pink among the orange hue. It almost hurt to resist, but I refused to let even the most persuasive eyes sway my emotions. Maybe that worked once, but I never wanted to feel that pain again. When I was trying to have a serious discussion, emotions could be so galling at times.

"So you really believe that I have potential?" he asked almost impatiently as his eyes continued to sparkle.

"Y-yeah, I mean no! You *might* have potential if you work hard, but nothing is guaranteed." I smirked as I skillfully averted my eyes from his. "With that said I have a little task for you. I want you to be physically able to climb to the top of one of the trees in this forest before we reach Oakurrow. That gives you a fair bit of time. Feel free to ask me for advice or try to figure it out on your own; ultimately it's up to you. If you can accomplish this, you may be receiving something useful for your efforts. And if you can't, well let's just hope that you aren't faced with a life or death experience where you need to climb to save yourself." I nervously laughed as many memories where I would have been caught if I was not able to climb fast enough resurfaced.

"You'd really do that for me? In that case I'll choose to be mentored by the professional." He beamed as my tail began to sway back and forth with interest.

So he picked the 'force bonding' option; I guess it could not be helped as no way would he learn how to climb a tree that fast on his own. As long as I assumed the worst would happen, I would not be set up for the inevitable disappointment. In a way, I was also strangely excited to get to train someone the same way someone had once done for me at barely thirteen. Still, it seemed a little weird to be teaching a fully mature male Celegon, though it might be insightful in a way. The rare chance that I would actually be able to pull this off could be mutually profitable if executed correctly. I was sure that if she knew, she would be proud of me for trying at least.

Thus, I began to rigorously train Marles on how to climb a tree. It seemed like a truly impossible task for him to accomplish the more he practiced, but I tried to be supportive in my own way. My initial goal may have diminished, rather quickly at that, but I still had hope that somehow I would benefit from this arrangement. Of course it was mandatory that I should not let myself get any more attached than necessary, as he could easily die before we reached town.

There was a rare chance that he would make a potentially good ally, but I already knew that I worked most efficiently alone. I would be doing a vigorous amount of improvising for as long as this was going to play out, however long that will be.

After three days, we had reached a certain cleared area of the forest, Oakurrow. Against all odds, not only was Marles still alive, but somehow had finally managed to climb to the very top of a tree. The events that followed were, well, more expected.

Chapter Four: Larceny

Unlike some of the small flying nymph species, Celegons did not traditionally learn to fly under pressure. Typically, learning to fly first starts with the young becoming curious about the area above ground. As it was increasingly more common for Celegons to hatch orphaned, a Celegon's own independence was furthermore influenced by the thought of flight. For myself, I felt the inclination to ascend after watching someone I once admired speed though the clouds. This all goes to say that falling out of a tall tree is a really redundant way to learn.

While I did not have too much time to react due to the speed he was falling, my brain was fast enough to think level-headedly. The fall would not kill him, but it was possible that if his skeleton did not have time to react there would be a chance of severe internal bleeding. The other option would be for me to fly up and try to catch him, only that would be a pretty dumb idea. If I did that we would both end up getting hurt, as the best I could do was—possibly—soften the landing. Sometimes it seemed as if I could barely support my own weight; no way I would be strong enough to do thrice that.

Within a few short moments, I felt my wings emerge and a breeze in my face. Trying not to think about the oncoming pain I will be in, I focused on snatching Marles' limbs. As expected, the very moment I took hold of his legs I felt myself being dragged down by gravity. No matter how hard I pulled, nor how vigorously my wings flapped, could I get us to stop falling. Gritting my teeth and bracing my bones, I made it so I was below Marles when we plummeted into the grassy ground.

Though my bones were hardened, the amount of pain from the pressure was building up. In hindsight, maybe I should have been more selfish and let Marles hit the ground first; he had more padding after all. Upon impact with the ground, I could feel my organs getting squeezed and bruised. Though I was in a lot of pain, I was at least grateful my satchel was not underneath me when I hit the ground. Shortly after we landed, Marles quickly got off me and I began to take deep pained breaths. My lungs felt as if they were slightly damaged from the fall. Though they would heal, breathing was not my favorite pastime at the moment.

"L-Lyla are you okay?" Marles panicked and started frantically checking me for external injuries. Even though being in pain agitated me, I had to remember I put myself in this position; lashing out at him would not be reasonable or deserved.

"I'll be alright. I've been in worse scraps than this, after all," I groaned. Truthfully, this was not the first time I had gotten injured. Nor would it be the last.

Marles seemed relieved until the moment came when I coughed and a moderate amount of blood came along with it. While I was not too worried over a little internal bleeding, it was entertaining to watch Marles worry over something so trivial. So typical for a sheltered Celegon.

"Lyla, do you have any emeri on you?" His expression and tone became serious and was, admittedly, giving me further amusement.

"Of course I do. I always try to have at least three in my satchel at all-"

I paused as I watched him start searching through my satchel. Before I knew it, he was holding one of the smaller emeri just barely above my mouth. A part of me was reluctant to eat it. I did need it, but at the same time I could have just grabbed it on my own. Which would definitely have hurt, but accepting it this way would also be accepting his odd gesture of kindness—something I did not ask for.

"This happened because of me; if I had been more careful then it wouldn't have come to this. I-I know it's not much, but I did bring a few orbs with me. I'll buy you three emeri to make amends for my actions," Marles declared as my eyes lit up with delight.

That was all I needed to hear before gleefully biting into the emeri in front of me. This offer was at least treble as good as the sweet metallic taste filling my mouth. Though, I realized I should not get my hopes up too high; Marles had been isolated after all. Part of me wondered if he even knew how much just one emeri could cost. I also wondered how many orbs he had brought along with him. As I consumed the emeri, I could already feel its powerful liquids seep through my body working on repairing the damage. Before too long, I was standing on two feet again and full of vigor from the fruit.

"Now that that has been dealt with, let's hurry it up and head to Oakurrow. It's not much further; you can see it just beyond the trees. Oh, and aside from your falling performance, good job on scaling that tree," I remarked as Marles faintly smiled.

After going past a few more trees, we came to a clearing in the forest that housed the small village of Oakurrow. Even though many referred to it as a village, I always thought it to be more of an outpost; this was mainly because of how miniscule it was and how few merchants there were to rob. The village itself was surrounded by tall log posts, presumably to help keep large monsters at bay.

Aside from the intimidating, but useless wall of wood, there always seemed to be Celegons on top who were constantly scouring the surroundings for approaching monsters. Luckily, it always seemed the surveyors were always more worried about monsters over thieves. And rightfully so, as monsters caused far more damage than thieves like me. Along with the walls, everything else in the village was made entirely out of wood aside from bits of cloth here and there. I decided to take Marles into a small area with the few market stalls first to see if he was up for a little classic thievery. Now, while I did not expect him to succeed, I was hoping to get some worthwhile entertainment out of it.

"So now that we're here, I'd like to see what you're capable of. Go and pick a target." I smirked as I motioned over to the three stalls in the market, all stocked with a variety of food, emeri, other trinkets and—of course—*orbs*. Marles seemed initially caught off guard, but there was no way I was going to make things simpler for him.

"You mean, now? You aren't going to show me the ropes first?" he asked, probably assuming I was joking.

"Nope. Try to weave your own ropes. I'm sure you'll do great," I said with a big smile on my face. My grin widened as I watched him slowly go to the stall with a particularly stressed looking Celegon in charge. They must not have made many sales so far. Street merchants always had it a little tougher than those who operated in buildings. It adds to the struggle when potential customers have a possibility of robbing your stall.

It might have seemed cruel, making him attempt to steal without any guidance; however, I was taught that this was the most proficient way. Essentially, the new thief would have to figure things out on their own, often inventing their own techniques. While observing him, I could also pinpoint his weaknesses; which could be corrected for future thieving attempts. Even though I was considered a prodigy and seldom got caught, my mentor had used the same methods on me; which helped me further hone my skills. With that in mind, my expectations for Marles to succeed were river bottom, but at least I would get some joy from watching it all fall apart.

Since the village was small, there were hardly any Celegons passing through to check the stalls and shops. This typically meant the shopkeepers were more observant and harder to steal from; unlike in the more populated towns, where there is less worry since the customers have a chance of ratting out thieves in hopes of compensation. I watched him from afar as he started a casual conversation with the previously stern-looking Celegon, who now looked as if she was thoroughly enjoying their chat. A part of me was curious if he completely abandoned the idea of stealing; he did seem a little too nice. The first time I was ever tasked with stealing, not *only* was I not caught, but I had managed to reap three gold orbs from an unsuspecting merchant. Marles was definitely not 'thief material'. Perhaps I should tell it to him straight after it all played out.

"Oh it's Lavender! Fancy seeing you here again, so soon too!" a bubbly voice called out to me.

I turned to my left a bit to see a sky-blue furred Celegon with beaming dark blue eyes skipping towards my direction. Her body was skinny, like most but was a few ounces more well-fed than mine. She practically radiated with giddiness as her long tail often bobbed from side to side. The worn satchel that hung from her side was also stuffed with papers and various orbs.

She went by the alias of Blubelle, which was quite obviously based on my own. She also had been the one to relay information to me about the Iseirre mansion, so I had mixed feelings about her at the moment. Apart from that, she had always been fairly amicable towards me. Well... aside from that *one* time I had initially stolen from her. If this town was not so empty, I would not waste a second scolding her for referring to me as Lavender so openly.

"Hey Blu," I greeted her with friendliness as I masked my irritation with her.

"So, how did it go? Come on, you've got to give me the details. I mean, I did get you the lead after all," she smiled in an obnoxiously cute way as I tried to resist berating her for the situation I had gotten into because of her.

"Well you see," I started, trying my best to mimic her cute mannerisms. "*That* happened," I huffed as I pointed towards Marles, who still appeared to be talking to the vendor. She seemed a bit confused at first and then came to a sudden realization.

"Ooh, you made so much from your mission that you were able to afford an overabundance of food resulting in your mate to become all fatty-like. Speaking of, I don't recall you having a mate before and why didn't he share with-"

"Blubelle, come on be serious," I interrupt, not afraid to express my annoyance.

"Lavender. What am I even supposed to say? What am I even looking at right now, I mean that has got to be the fattest Celegon I've ever seen!" she exclaimed. I prayed for Marles' sake that he was so caught up in conversation his ears were oblivious to her loud statement.

"You don't have to point out the obvious, especially not so loudly. But do you know who he is? Anyone come to mind?" I asked, hoping she would figure it out for herself. The puzzled look on her face said otherwise. "Really? No clue? Well then I am proud to present to you, Marles Iseirre!" I proclaimed almost in a sarcastic way as I watched her eyes light up with shock.

"*He* is Marles Iseirre? That can't be. I thought he was assumed dead years ago! Of course, I never got the chance to actually see him in the flesh, only heard rumors. Apparently back in the day he was very handsome. I vaguely recall all the mateless female Celegons gushing over him when I was little.

Hey, you were around when he was right? Don't tell me you were swooning over him too!" Blubelle laughed as I began to feel a mix of emotions swell over me. Was she implying that I had feelings for him back then?

It was such an odd thing for her to presume of me. Well, perhaps not so odd; I do remember several others having such symptoms. Truth to be told, the first time that I had carelessly gazed into those sunset eyes was not in his mansion. It was around ten years ago when I was barely thirteen at the time, quite different than I am now. Not only was I vastly different in personality, physically I looked different as well with changed coloring attributes. Considering I never got an actual chance to speak with him back then, I doubt he would remember such a small flicker of white fur.

But just why did Blubelle of all Celegons have to know about him? While she was an informant, old news like Marles was not going to get her any business. Even if he used to be quite fetching, there was no use in—

"Uh, Lavender? You're kinda spacing out a bit. So I'm guessing you did have a thing for him, lame! Let me guess, you were so fascinated by him then that you still see him the same now? Was he the real treasure of the Iseirre mansion?" She smiled mischievously as I snapped back out of my thoughts.

"You got it. It's hard for a female to resist those charming sunset eyes, that long perfect hair tuft with red stained ends, not to mention that well kept body he used to have. Seriously Blu, you are completely missing the point I'm trying to make," I sighed as I started to explain my problems in detail without any misinterpretations.

I briefly told her about our encounter: him wanting to be a thief, and of course my initial plan to get orbs out of the whole ordeal; which was failing miserably.

"I see. Okay, I have a few questions. One, what did this cheese stuff taste like? Two, did you steal any of said cheese stuff? Three, why are you making him your apprentice? *I* wanted to be your apprentice first!" Blubelle bawled as I felt once again she had completely missed my points.

"I told you before I had no interest in taking on any *apprentices*. This is different because it will hopefully net me some orbs when it's all said and done. And no, cheese is poison and I advise you to not seek it out and only eat it if you happen to be starving to death!" I snapped as Blubelle wore a dejected expression on her face. This quickly changed into a more curious one as she pointed behind me.

"He's coming over here," she chimed. I suddenly realized I was so caught up in talking to Blubelle that I had forgotten to keep an eye on him.

Sure enough, he casually trotted on up to us with a suspicious grin on his face. Looking back towards the stall vendor, it appeared as if nothing had changed; she appeared neither angry or surprised.

"Someone looks awfully happy after failing a task. Don't worry not everyone ca-"

I stopped talking as he revealed that his bag was filled to the brim with a small variety of fruits and roots, as well as three emeri on top. Did he really expect me to believe that he stole them, he could have easily just bought them while I was not watching.

"W-well how do we know you didn't just buy them, huh?" I questioned as a loud sound filled the air.

"Thieves! Thieves in the market!"

Without a moment to waste, I took Marles by the arm and bolted. Out of the corner of my eye, I saw Blubelle fly upwards as she was just as much at risk. I could only run so fast on two legs, so I let go of Marles and began running on all four limbs hoping he would follow. Dashing out of the village and into the forest was an easy task for me, though I wondered how Marles was faring. I could still hear him behind me, so at least he was not lagging behind.

Though food was valuable, I had doubts that the vendor would track us down into the forest; this was especially since they would be leaving the rest of their goods unattended. While the adrenaline rush was not as pronounced as when fleeing from monsters or powerful Celegons, it still distributed an exhilarating feeling throughout my body. We would be safe once we were far enough that Oakurrow would no longer be in sight through the trees. This would only take a minute of running. I could only hope that Marles would be able to make it. Even though I did not look back, my ears picked up the sound of his paws hitting the dirt.

"Alright, it should be safe to stop now," I reassured Marles as my feet stopped in their tracks. I swiftly stood back on two legs and turned around to see he had collapsed onto the forest floor. His body was trembling all over and he appeared to be struggling a lot with breathing. "A-are you alright there Marles?" I ask, not quite knowing how to ease whatever pain he was in.

"Yeah, I-I'm," he began as he struggled to stand up. Then I watched as he suddenly darted behind the nearest tree and began to hear gagging sounds.

Covering my ears to avoid hearing the grotesque sound of bile being expelled, I knew that something had to be done about this. If he would be staying with me for the foreseeable future this would not be ideal for either his sake or my sanity. He might not be compliant with it, but I would have to inquire about his obvious health issues. I doubted I would be able to help very much since I lacked professional medical expertise, but I could try to enforce a more beneficial lifestyle for him. Coincidentally, my stomach reminded me that neither of us had eaten during our time together. He had offered me food earlier, which I declined, but I hadn't seen him snacking on it either. After the noise was over, I uncovered my ears and watched as Marles stumbled out from behind the tree, body still jittery post-vomit.

"Marles, come sit down over here, we need to have an honest and open discussion with one another." I gently sighed as I plopped down onto the grassy soil. Marles seemed a bit worried as he forced himself over across from me. "I hope I don't come off too harsh but-" I paused as the look on his face was practically begging me to let him get a word in before I finished. Feeling slightly guilty, I motioned for him to get whatever he needed to say off his chest.

"I-I'm sorry. For getting us caught back there, I understand if you'd want to drop me as your apprentice here and now." He tried to keep a pleasant expression on his face, but all I could sense was discontentment.

Out of all the things I could do, I started to laugh. Not that I was trying to make him feel bad, but I was just too amused and also a bit relieved. I was lucky that Marles' reaction to my sudden outburst was simply surprise, rather than anger or despair.

"Are you really apologizing right now? First, you would know by now if I was upset already. You didn't fail or get us caught, we just didn't leave the scene quick enough. But that can be corrected in the future. So nothing to feel down about, no worries." I smiled as his expression softened.

He pondered to himself for a minute before coming back with, "Ly-Ly sure has a pleasant face when she smiles genuinely."

It is ever so interesting how just a few words can completely change the disposition of a conversation. I had half the mind to berate him for insulting me, at least that is what I assumed he was doing. But I did not want to risk putting him in a foul mood with me. As long as I ignored it and acted like the name calling did not faze me he would tire; that was the hope anyway. Perhaps I should have come up with a name he would find as equally antagonizing as I found mine before moving on the conversation.

"Well then *Marley*, let's get to talking about what I really wanted to discuss with you." I grinned in hopes that he would find that irksome.

"Aw that's adorable! We have code nicknames for each other already," he chimed as I swore to myself I would never call him that again. At least he was in a cheery mood now, though at my expense.

"So to start off, have you eaten nothing aside from that cheese soup in a while?" I asked bluntly. He seemed confused as to where I was going with this. At first he appeared hesitant, his eyes dulled as he bit his mouth shut. Then he began to smile awkwardly, since he figured out he would have a hard time navigating this gracefully.

"Well that was direct. Yeah, for quite a while now actually," he openly admitted to which I was surprised by.

So he had eaten nothing but delicious poison for who knows how long. This had to definitely be the source of his stomach issues. Not to mention all the nutrients he was lacking; even though most Celegons are malnourished they still often manage to find different meals.

"So tell me, do you find me repulsive?"

For a moment I thought I misheard him. But when I saw his bleak face, I knew I had heard right. Why even ask me that? This conversation was meant to be about health, not keeping up appearances. Though if this was about him vomiting, I admittedly found the activity unpleasant.

"Where is this coming from?" I asked, worrying that he had overheard Blubelle earlier. He had a sullen look in his eyes, complimented by a weak smile; it was easy to tell he was not joking around.

"Just a hunch is all, though your friend was fairly loud too." He grinned awkwardly as a moment passed where I took in what he said.

"Well first of all your *hunch* is completely wrong. Maybe in Blubelle's mind you are, but that doesn't change how I think about you. What's got you so worked up about one Celegon's opinion anyway? You think I loathe being around you because you look a bit different? As long as you are alive, I could care less on how you look so long as you prove to be useful. What I do care ab-" I stopped, then corrected, "What *I am* concerned with is your health. There is no way you got all of your essential vitamins from *poison*," I began lecturing ; which, oddly enough, appeared to improve his demeanor drastically.

From there, I decided it would be best to set up my dome so we would have a safe space to indulge in the food Marles stole. I went to work on cleaning and organizing the cooking area while I had Marles store the excess food items into the appropriate jars. It still surprised me that he actually managed to steal them. There had to be at about twenty items that he had stuffed into his bag. That would last me at least a week, but since Marles was here I assumed they would diminish much faster. Still, I was impressed. I could have stolen much more myself, but this was really good for his first attempt.

"Marles, you still haven't told me how you were able to procure the goods," I stated after I finished wiping down the wooden counter.

"But a true thief never reveals their secrets," Marles replied, clearly trying to sound mysterious before starting to chuckle when he caught me glaring at him.

I watched as he put the lids back onto the jars, which were a tad overflowing as they did not make their usual ceramic noise when the lids were added. Perhaps I should look into getting bigger jars if Marles was to be staying for a while.

"Well, I bought the emeri, but for the rest of them I sort of just started tucking them into my bag when she wasn't looking," he casually explained as I decided not to pry further to see if it was really true or not. He stole them and at the end of the day, that is all that really matters.

On the counter I had laid out an assortment of roots and fruit for each of us, three for myself and five for Marles. While my pile consisted of two fruits and one root, Marles' had four roots and one fruit since it is common knowledge that roots are packed with more nutrients than fruits. Though I seemed pleased to be able to eat, Marles for some reason seemed less than enthusiastic.

"Don't tell me you're going to act all picky now," I sarcastically groaned as he shook his head.

"No, that's not it. I'm actually tolerant with most of these, even the renroot which I find a bit bitter. It just seems like a lot," he told me as I could not believe what he was saying.

"You think this is a lot? Well by average Celegon standards I guess it is, but coming from you it's a bit odd. You shouldn't feel bad about eating what you stole; you earned it after all. Or if you feel that way because I'm not having as much as you, it's because I don't need it. Right now it's really important to see if we can solve your health issue and a surefire way to do that is to regularly pump your body full of nutrients," I told him confidently; in reality, I had no idea if this ideology of mine would work for his issue.

At least this seemed to make him feel good enough to start eating his portion. Though things turned chaotic when I caught him trying to burn the renroots with his tail fire.

"H-hey! Put that out, you're going to burn my precious dome to the ground!" I demanded as he simply just smiled at my clear anger.

"Don't worry, as I told you before I have very good control over my fire. If it scares you it will all be over quick, I'm just going to lightly roast these roots to bring out the good flavors a bit," his eyes gleamed as he lowered a renroot into his fire before I quickly snatched it away.

"If you burn them then they lose most of their nutrients! Fine, you can do one but I can't just let you burn all of them." I sighed, handing it back over to him. He then pouted and remarked, "Ly-Ly's no fun." To which I wholeheartedly agreed with.

Though the time we spent in Oakurrow was short, albeit eventful, we certainly would not want to return there anytime soon. Getting caught was one thing, but having the target see you was a whole other deal that usually ended with the thief paying to get a pardon. Since I certainly did not want to give up any of my orbs anytime soon, I thought it would be best to set our sights on a bigger, better town. Possibly one much further away to give Marles some time to heal. It might finally be time to revisit where I was left by *her*.

Chapter Five: Reflection

There I was again, in that dark room. Why was I here again? It is all such a blur. My lungs felt exasperated from screaming; though, no matter how much I exerted my voice, it seemed no one could hear me. No, no one cared. When someone did hear me, it only led to trouble. So I quickly learned that screaming never solved anything, and turned to crying quietly. Cry all you wish, little Celegon, just stop before mother sees you.

· · ✤ · ·

Clenching at my stomach was not my favorite way to wake up. It appeared to be a side effect from having that recurring dream, then accompanied by phantom hunger. Or perhaps I was simply hungry. Normally, the longer I went between meals, the less pronounced my hunger became, and in turn the weaker my body became. Though, after having a meal my stomach always seemed to reset and I would become revitalized.

Groggily, I shook off my nightmare induced headache as I trudged over to the fruit-filled jar in the cooking area. Grabbing a mostly pink fruit out of the jar and placing it into my mouth, it was only moments before the sour-sweet taste flooded my tastebuds. Welons were my favorite of all fruits in Lixion, not only were they tasty, but they were also very cutely shaped and had green juices. It was a sharp contrast to the outer pink flesh. While they were not as common as other fruits, I still managed to find—on average—at least one every two months.

Soon after devouring the fruit, I began to feel more awake—my hungry stomach sated. It was then I realized—after gazing over the other cushions and blankets—that Marles, nor his bag, were anywhere to be seen. At first I dismissed it as a symptom of tiredness and hallucinations. I could have been imagining him being gone, or perhaps I was still dreaming.

My immaculate sense of time told me that it was still early in the morning. Dewdrops still glistened on leaves and mist hovered just a bit above the ground. I also could not comprehend why he even wanted to leave, especially not without a bit of warning beforehand.

Stretching my limbs, I skipped around the bedding area to do a double take. It seemed as if only cushions and tattered blankets remained. For some reason I was having trouble comprehending that he left; I did not want to accept it. Perhaps things had not ended with a happy conclusion the other day and he had given up on being a thief entirely? Unless of course, he had seen through me from the very start?

Initially, I had been expecting him to find the life of a thief too hard, but now I guess my mind had been warped into thinking he was committed to staying.

Regardless, he was missing. And since I had gotten involved with him, it partly made it my responsibility to find him. After slinging my satchel across my back, I promptly left my dome in search of the missing Celegon. The ground was cold and the air was moist; though, there was plenty of daylight to illuminate my surroundings. I decided that it would be best to leave my dome stationed in its current spot for the time being; it would stay well hidden as long as I kept it invisible.

The cool air helped snap me out of my tiredness more as I started to examine the area. Though, a part of me wished that I had stayed in the marginally warmer confines of my dome. It may not have been heated, but at least I would not have had to deal with the outside wind currents. While a Celegon's nose was not as keen as that of a monster, our eyes were quite good at picking up small traces and details. This is, of course, good for thieves when looking for valuables; however, it is useless when it comes to tracking something down. Having a good memory meant you would be able to find places you had been to before; unfortunately, it does not entail finding things that have yet to be discovered.

This meant that my chances of finding Marles were surprisingly quite low, especially since he had not left any clues of where he would be going. I was not the biggest fan of aimlessly wandering around, but since I had a goal in mind I hoped it would not be too redundant.

It was then, suddenly, that I began to feel very strange and uneasy. Almost like a dizzy spell had come over me, yet I could still see and hear fine. It also felt hard to breathe, almost just like in those dreams I occasionally have where I am suffocating. Then my ears began to flinch as I heard the unmistakable sound of a thick liquid splattering on the ground.

There was only one thing that came to mind when I heard that sound; monsters. More specifically, the sound of a monster clenching down on its prey in a violent fashion. Though my feelings were a mixture of distraught and terror, I still decided that I would cautiously scope it out. Crouching down, I gradually trudged towards the noise as long grass patches began to tickle my stomach. My ears began to pick up new sounds as I approached, ones that alluded to a monster dragging their prey along the ground.

The closer I got, the more cautious I had to be with my feet. Stepping on a branch or leaf could be potentially life threatening since I would draw immense attention to myself; monsters could easily hear the slightest of noises. The surrounding forest had gotten slightly thicker too, which meant there were more trees and brambles I had to navigate around. Though my goal was close, taking the stealthy approach always made it seem like it was an eternity to reach it; the same was true of heists at times. As I neared I heard yet another splatter, a familiar shade of dark green caught my eye through the trees.

My heart nearly stopped.

However, as I carefully adjusted my view, I could see that he appeared completely fine; no blood or injuries to be seen whatsoever. Relief washed over me as my strained nerves relaxed. Allowing myself to breathe again, I then tried to see what he was even doing. He appeared to be facing in front of a tree looking at some sort of white cloth that was wrapped around the base. Said cloth looked to consist of more colors; though, it was hard to get a good look at it since I was examining it from the side.

Eventually I realized, as I watched him work, that he was, in fact, painting something. This was further confirmed when I saw that his paws were covered in different colored pastes; though, it was a little different from the norm of using one's tail to paint. The splattering sound that I had heard, it seemed, was when he had been mixing the pastes. Though I was not able to see his full progress on the painting, I was quite curious to see what it was. Turning my gaze a little past the tree he was at, I found my answer.

My eyes had found themselves being locked into cold, pale white eyes. The chills that ran through my bones pierced all my senses and filled me with fright. How long it had been there I had no clue, but it was now aware of my presence and undoubtedly Marles' too. Neither of us were anywhere near safe and that beast needed to go. Though my body had begun shivering, I knew what had to be done.

It was a lone monster, easily quintuple my size. Its roundish head was coated with black fur, as was the rest of its body aside from its white underbelly and dirtied feet. Unlike Celegons, these creatures stood on all four limbs at all times. Like all other monsters I have come across, this one's fur was scraggly and unkempt. Though no emotion was shown, there was a glint of malice in those pale eyes.

In no time at all, my legs were sprinting towards the direction of the monster as a clear thought appeared in my mind. This monster was bigger than average and most likely faster too, but it would not stop me from trying to injure it to the point it could no longer harm us. From the moment I had started moving, the monster quickly did the same—charging in my direction and gnashing its sharp teeth for all to see. At this point I was certain that Marles was now seeing these events unfold; however, as I was so determined on not dying, I paid him no attention as I faced the monster.

I could feel the stone in my tail getting cold as the monster quickly approached. I swung it in front of me full force as a blizzard of ice was cast upon the ground beneath the creature. As expected, it was smart enough to avoid the blast, but was completely unaware of what I was actually planning on using my ice talent for. I sprinted faster before jumping onto the ice covered ground, causing my body to slide at an alarmingly fast speed. So fast that I was able to get underneath the monster without it grabbing me, sliding right under its matted white belly.

I quickly jabbed my sharpened claws deep into its soft underside. The monster blood burned on my paws so I could only leave them there for so long. When I retrieved them, the black blood quickly evaporated, relieving the burning sensation. Though in a lot of pain, the monster did not lose any swiftness as it quickly repositioned itself to snap at me. Stunning it temporarily had done nothing in stopping it from performing a counterattack.

It lunged for my torso; while I was able to avoid the fatal bite, I did not come out unscathed. Its teeth had scraped against my back. The pain made me wince, but the adrenaline in the moment dulled the sensation. I was lucky to have escaped greater damage caused by the monster's powerful jaws. As my tail sharpened, I attempted to hit one of its legs in the hopes of toppling it. Unfortunately, it somehow foresaw that; instead, it used its heavy leg to pin my tail to the ground. Since my tail bone was already hardened in preparation for the attack, the pressure the monster put on it was not painful but rather uncomfortable. I felt my body tense up as the monster's teeth lunged towards my face.

Then everything started to feel, really warm. Not hot, but warm enough to make me feel a tad overheated. Since I was pinned to the ground, I could not get a view of the source, but I had a theory. The smell of singed fur filled the air and it was only a matter of time before the monster leapt off me, howling as it fled deeper into the forest. I immediately turned to where Marles was, only to see him rushing towards me with a panicked expression.

"Lyla w-what were you doing?" Marles questioned as he frantically dashed to my side. For some reason I was actually pleased to see him concerned about me; this was despite the fact that I knew I would have done just fine on my own.

"Well I was looking for you, saw that monster and..." I trailed off; I could tell by his expression that something seemed to be upsetting him. "Is something wrong? I don't think that monster will be back anytime soon," I reassured him as he continued to look unimpressed.

This was strange. I watched in confused silence as he briefly mumbled something to himself that was incomprehensible to me before averting his gaze and sighing.

"Forgive me, I'm just a little disappointed. More importantly, are you hurt anywhere? Ah y-y-your back is bleeding!" he exclaimed with worry as he went behind me to examine the teeth marks. It did not feel too horrible; though, I could feel blood seeping out, which was not ideal.

"Hey Marles, if there's blood still coming out would you mind licking it for me? I can't exactly bend my head back there and it would be a waste to have that blood perish," I remarked as I casually waited for Marles' response.

For as long as I could remember, Celegons had been able to share their blood with one another. A Celegon's blood was one of the key things that kept them alive, as well as one of the things that could cause them to perish. Celegon hearts, unlike monsters or nymphs, only produced a very minimal amount each day. Hearts also needed blood to function. If a Celegon did not have enough blood in their system their hearts would fail to function. The only way to keep them beating was to share blood with other Celegons or have emeri, which is also referred to as the blood fruit.

"You want me to lick it? A-ah, but isn't t-that what mates do?" he stuttered as I shot him an annoyed look, but was laughing on the inside over how flustered he was.

Marles was both correct, yet incorrect simultaneously. Mates did share blood, but in a much more intimate way than what I was offering him. Celegons would even barter their blood at tight times. In this situation, I was generously offering a lick or two of spilled blood that would go to waste otherwise. Now, would I clarify that with Marles? Of course not.

"I'm fairly sure that's only when mates intentionally draw blood. You have my permission, no need to be shy." I chuckled as I could only imagine the look on his face. "*Just don't bite into the wound.*"

I then felt as my back became damp as he hastily licked my wounds. It felt oddly nice in a way. Despite the area being injured, this seemed to make it feel better. When he finished, he went to face me. He was clearly still embarrassed. I could not help but smile at him in amusement.

"That wasn't so bad now was it?" I asked, cheeky smile still in place.

"T-thank you," he replied awkwardly as he brushed his mouth with his paw for a moment. "Now I know it wasn't your intention to disrupt my painting, but well now I'll just have to scrap it." He let out a resigned sigh as I stared at him in confusion.

Surely now with the monster gone he could go back to painting, albeit with much less tension in the air. I suddenly bolted towards the tree to see the artwork Marles had been working on.

Naturally, I felt a great mix of emotions when I saw that Marles had been, in fact, painting the monster. Though I was briefly caught off guard at the level of detail in the painting, I quickly grew upset that Marles was willingly putting his life in danger. If he had decided to paint a harmless nymph that would be different, but this was completely foolhardy. But instead of exploding at him, I tried my best to be calmer and more considerate.

Marles had joined my side and was initially silent as I viewed his art before saying, "It's awful, isn't it?" This was soon followed by awkward laughing.

"No! I think it looks great, especially the details you did with the background," I half-lied as I did not think the fact that he painted a dangerous monster up close was great at all.

"I know you're lying Ly-Ly. To be fair, she was quite restless and it has been some time since I last painted," he stated as he turned his attention to his paint covered paws.

"A *she*?" I questioned as I was not aware Marles could tell a monster's gender. Most did not care to know such details about them, let alone specify them.

"W-well I assumed it was. Aren't the ones with mostly black fur females?" he asked as I nodded in response.

My attention then focused below the painting where a variety of colored pastes were on the ground. I would be lying if I said I was not curious about how they were made. But as I did not want to appear dumb for not knowing such a simple answer, I pushed that aside.

"Is there a reason you paint with your paws instead of your tail?" I asked as Marles began trying to peel the now dried paste off his paws. He effortlessly disposed of it all and began to sigh.

"I don't really know myself, to be honest. It just comes more naturally than using my tail. I do use my tail for precise details, but not very often. Hm, do you mind doing a small favor for me?" he asked as his mood perked up a bit. I was not sure what this favor was, but—assuming it would not be difficult—I agreed. "Oh good! Do you mind sitting down over there for a bit?" he asked, pointing in the direction where the monster used to be.

Knowing full well why he told me to do that made me feel oddly ecstatic. While I was confused that I felt this way, I was sure that it was because—for the first time—I would be able to evaluate and critique a painting of myself. It would also be nice to see what I looked like again; it had been a while since I had seen myself clearly in a reflection. So I trotted over to the area he wanted me in and sat comfortably in the grass as I began to watch him.

I saw as he reached into his open bag to grab some peculiar looking ingredients. They were inedible herbs by the looks of it. I assumed he had brought them from his mansion. Though they were small, as he crushed them up, they produced quite a lot of liquid. Soon, his paws were drenched a dark purple color. My fur was not that dark at all by any means, so I was eager to see how he would incorporate it into the painting. While he was mostly behind the tree, I could tell he was being careful and gentle with his painting techniques. This was in contrast with earlier when I heard him being slightly more aggressive as he'd applied the paint to the cloth.

Being still came quite naturally to me, probably because of how I was raised and from my training as a thief. Still, there was something oddly eerie about casually sitting out in the open like this. Even if that monster did not return, I just felt too exposed. I began to wonder why I was even doing this. Did I feel bad for Marles? Regardless, I had agreed to sit here and I would see it through.

After watching him pluck grass and smear it on the painting cloth for about twenty minutes, I knew it was only a matter of time before it would be finished. When Marles stopped touching the cloth, I patiently waited for him to call me over to see. Only instead, he hastily started untying the cloth from the tree.

"I'm sorry Lyla, it's too bland to let you see, I-I really messed up," he stammered as I quickly shot up from the ground and sprinted towards the tree.

"N-no you can't!" But it was already too late.

In front of my eyes was indeed a portrait of me. Light colored fur that was tinted slightly darker purple at parts and lavender eyes accompanied by an emotionless smile. It was very much me. But at the same time, something felt off. The way it was painted... it made me look as if I was more beautiful than I really was. Now I did not consider myself to be unattractive by any means, but I knew my looks were not quite this extensive.

"You really know how to bring out the beauty in things." I laughed lightly as Marles looked at me in confusion.

"B-beauty? I completely messed up! I should incinerate this, this painting's quality isn't half the quality it was supposed to be. Lyla, look at the eyes. Yours are far more glowy than the painting's and-" I stopped listening as he continued to rant about how awful a job he did of painting me. Maybe he was being sarcastic, but hearing that made me feel genuinely happy. This blissful feeling was short lived however and it was only a matter of time before he said, "Maybe this painting just makes me feel weird since my suitresses all had forced me to paint them."

That would make sense. Vain and wealthy Celegons would of course want paintings of themselves. At least I was not someone who pressured him into painting me, but I still felt a little sick to my stomach.

"Sorry, I shouldn't say things like that. Just some bad memories from my past." He forced a smile as his eyes began to look sullen. As much as I would like to keep it for myself I knew that it would not be right of me, especially since this would most likely trigger him more.

"Alright then, let's burn it!"

With the help of Marles' fire talent, the painting was soon reduced to ashes on the ground. There was a small part of him that seemed reluctant to do so at first. Although he was the one to bring it up, it was not until I spoke up in agreement did he go through with it. Perhaps he thought I would be saddened by the only portrait I had of myself being lost to the flames. Even if I was, it mattered little if it made him recall his unsavory past experiences.

The grass had long lost any dampness by the time we relocated his painting supplies back inside the dome to keep them safe. The remainder of the day we spent training. That included sharing some basic thieving advice with Marles that he could build off of as well as light exercise. His body was quite sensitive and I did want to avoid him losing any more meals because of overexertion. It was a slower day, but the hours would soon ween into the last few minutes of sunlight.

Marles, exhausted from the day's activities, was now snoring comfortably inside the dome. As for myself, I needed a moment outside where it was quieter to think easier. With him around my quiet days and nights would be filled with more noise. At least his chatter was not as overbearing as that blue Celegon's. I could live with it once he learned to sleep quieter.

The fur on the back of my neck twitched as I could sense someone approaching from up in the trees. The light weight of the footsteps was either of a nymphs or a small Celegon's. As it got closer, I was able to tell more and narrow down who it was based on how they limped over the tree branches. It had to be him.

"Little Lavender, it has been far too long."

Up on a thicker branch stood the emaciated body of a male Celegon completely black in color. Celegons that boast a singular color tone in their appearance were quite a rarity, I should know, but his dark appearance was unique in that it helped him blend in effortlessly under the night's elements. For a thief, it is a good trait to have. But the Celegon I spoke to was no such thing. Something much worse.

I did not know of his name, only his alias which was a single character: Z. Even my mentor, who knew him better than I, had only spoken of him using that letter. It most likely was a fragment of his actual name, if I had to guess. Like his true name, he mattered very little to me. He was only a still living reminder of someone I had lost years prior.

"Quite the contrary, not enough time has passed since our last chat. Not that I even care to. Why waste my time talking with someone who doesn't even give me decent information?" I responded bitterly as I stood my ground, glaring upwards at him. While he looked weak and was a bit sickly with some illness unknown, he was more than capable of using his talent to rough me up if he saw fit. "I suspect there's a reason you've made yourself known tonight?"

I noticed something flicker in his dark eyes as he stared down at me. He always looked at me with this judgmental stare. Though I knew my eyes never looked kindly back at him either. Then he took a pained breath as he clutched his side. Somehow his sickness never impaired the smoothness of his voice whenever he spoke to me.

"I had seen you emerge from that mansion with another at your side. I found my curiosity peaked. Why would complacent Lavender burden herself with taking care of that bloated, pampered shell of a Celegon?" he inquired as his mouth bore a mocking smirk, teeth gleaming in the night. However I did not let it stir me as I answered him.

"So it was you watching us leave the Iseirre's. Should've known. Explain to me how that impacts your way of life?" I questioned while flicking my tail in annoyance.

"It matters little. I just did not realize you longed for companionship so much. I would tell you not to ruin his life like you did hers," Z told me somewhat nonchalantly as his mouth smiled but his eyes remained rather expressionless. They were fixated on me as they waited for a reaction they wouldn't receive. When he saw I was not going to give him an enlightening conversation, he shook himself a bit before peering down closer to me.

"Farewell, Little Lavender."

I then watched as the black Celegon slipped effortlessly deeper into the darkened forest. Not caring to follow him or wonder wherever he would end up next. Even if I had no preference if he lived another day, he always exceeded my expectations whenever I crossed paths with him. For someone that frail, it was a miracle he was even alive at all. His outstanding luck made me feel that I would see him again several times before whatever was affecting his body consumed him entirely.

It was late and he had robbed me of precious moments better used resting for the next day's activities. Marles, if he were still awake, would be wondering where I was by now. My ears carefully listened for any movements before I started to make my way back to the dome. Occasionally I would feel eyes lingering on me after my conversations with Z, but they were not present this time. All the more better for my mind to forget that he was even here.

Chapter Six: Assistance

Nothing happened. Well, nothing really noteworthy happened during the past two months at least. No deadly monster attacks, no thrilling heists and no stalkers; just traveling through the wilderness and occasionally finding small targets to rob. It all seemed a bit too peaceful; which felt unnatural. Though I knew the peace would not last long. My ideology was that long terms of peace meant something catastrophic was just around the corner. At least Marles seemed to be faring well.

Marles Iseirre, formally pampered Celegon was still with me after all this time. At this point, I had given up that he would eventually return to his lavish lifestyle; though, I would not say I was bothered by his constant presence. I admit that I had grown used to him, and for some reason was able to sleep easier at night with decreasing nightmares. He had also improved his thieving techniques moderately, though he was still not nearly as good as I was. His health had also gotten better after becoming more adjusted to the harsh environments. He still had some stomach issues here and there, but much less so.

In addition to this, he had also become much slimmer; though, he had not lost all of his initial chubbiness. While he was in a healthier form, there was something I was not too fond of. Much like in the past where he was admired by female Celegons, some started taking notice of him again. Even though he was not becoming arrogant from the positive female attention, something about it irked me. Maybe I was a little bit worried that he would take an interest in one and decide to quit being my apprentice. Regardless, it was agitating having to witness him being fawned over.

Currently, Marles and I were on our way to Tarrina Town, a larger Celegon establishment that was surrounded by nothing but treeless tundra for miles. It was a place that held lots of memories for me; unfortunately more bad than good. But the past was behind me, and hopefully I could make better ones with Marles by my side. Perhaps I would even be able to cover up those I wished to forget.

Tarrina Town was ripe for thieving and decently safe from the surrounding monsters thanks to its thick stone wall. The only bad thing about it was the exposed surrounding area; travelers could be easily spotted by monsters from miles away.

The tundra areas of Lixion were always more windy than the forests since there were no trees to help obstruct the breeze. There was also a slight chill in the air that would make me briefly shiver every ten minutes or so. It did not help that the sun was setting and with it would go the heat.

Thinking about shivering made me shudder a bit prematurely. Shortly after, I felt a warm wave of heat wash over me, knowing exactly what its source was. "Put it out, Marles," I sighed as I turned to look at him and his flaming tail.

"You just seem cold is all. Why must you be rude and always reject my offers of kindness?" He smiled as his tail fire grew brighter.

"Always? I'm not that cruel. But you know that using talents for unneeded tasks is wasteful. What if we're attacked by a monster in the next few minutes and all your energy is drained because keeping warm was so important?" I asked matter-of-factly, watching as he disheartenedly extinguished his flames.

In silence, we continued to press on to Tarrina Town. Before long I started to second guess what I'd said to him. Yes, it was beneficial that we conserve our strength, but it was not my intent to make him so gloomy.

"I'm sorry, Marles; this weather must be making me more bitter. It's your choice to use your flames or not; I'd just prefer it if you'd conserve them more. You wouldn't want to be helpless during a monster attack would you?" I laughed as Marles shook his head.

"So I'm useless without my talent now? The cold's not made you bitter; it's your ice talent that's freezing over your heart," he said, trying his best to sound sad, only to fail and smile in the end.

Marles and I, we were not exactly close per say, but we had become accustomed to each other during our time together. It was simply an unrequited friendship situation.

He was after my friendship and I was after his, well... *nothing*—really. Not that being friends would be bad; just that, friends tended to engage in physical things like hugs. Hugs as a generalized idea seemed okay with me, but not with him. Still, we enjoyed an amicable relationship nonetheless; which I was quite content with.

Gazing out into the empty rocky tundra, which was illuminated by the beautiful orange and pink sky, I could spot the large town far off in the distance. If Marles could fly, we would be there in a matter of minutes; unfortunately, as that was still not an option, on the ground we went. Despite dropping some weight, I knew my small body would still not be able to support us both in the air. Though, if I had to catch him again, no one would suffer damage—unlike before. I was surprised I was not sour about having to walk everywhere; it had toughened my limbs slightly, and allowed me to conserve my magic. Sometimes I got the urge to soar in the open skies, but I resisted for Marles.

I winced as a small pain made itself known on the bottom of my foot. A sharp rock had neatly wedged itself into the sole. Shaking it out, I noticed a very miniscule trace of blood. I ignored it as it appeared to be but a drop, but someone else thought otherwise. The sound of many heavy feet scratching against the ground filled my ears.

Judging by the sound vibrations, there appeared to be three monsters heading in our direction. The pressure they put on the ground sounded quite weighted too; they were above average in size. Even one large monster alone posed a significant threat; there was no way we could take on all three and live. In the tundras, Celegons typically evaded monster attacks by flying away; however, as this was not an option, we had to improvise.

The two of us bolted towards the far off Tarrina Town. It would still take us a while to get to. Though the ground was mostly flat, it was also quite rocky and rough on my feet—especially now that I was using all four limbs. Monsters had toughened bulky feet, so the harsh ground was of no consequence to them. However, while the monsters were running with the intent to kill, we were running to survive. No matter how much strain our bodies were going through, we would always be faster if it meant our survival.

The monsters were fast approaching us from behind, but we would only let them get so close. Then we would hit them with everything we had. I quickly glanced at Marles who was sprinting just a small distance to the right of me. While neither of us could risk looking back as that would slow us down, our ears would tell us just how far back the monsters were behind us. As of now, I could hear their feet, their ghastly breaths, and the wind rushing through their fur. By the time I could hear the drool dripping off their teeth, it was time for countermeasures.

Without looking back, I heavily concentrated on the stone in my tail as I kept running as fast as I could. As my stone grew colder, I began to direct my focus on the bottoms of my paws and feet. Then, with a quick burst and a slight strain in my tail, the ground below became frosted over with a thick layer of ice. Beside me, Marles was also using his fire talent to temporarily melt the ice he passed over before I iced it again. Though my radius was limited, this would certainly hinder the monsters in speed.

As much as I desperately wanted to continue, my magical energy was already quite drained. I was exhausted. My limbs, too, were weary from the consistent fast-paced running. But we absolutely could not slow down. We had to survive this. I glanced to my right; Marles also seemed tired, but he looked nowhere near as strained as I was.

If I could only grab an orb from my satchel. Ingesting it would certainly give me a boost to keep up my ice talent. To do that though, would require me to stop running; which was not a safe option. Because while my ice slowed down the monsters, they would tear me open if I did so for even a moment. Marles would be killed too if I stopped producing ice, or maybe he would survive if the monsters were satisfied with eating just me. No... they *always* wanted more. My head was pounding and my heart raced violently as I felt the cold energy from my body dropping by the second.

Panic arose in my heart as the next few sprints I took had less and less ice underneath. When my feet touched the rocky soil that was when I felt a warm—no—*smoldering* presence to my right. Out of the corner of my eye I watched as Marles stopped in his tracks and turned to face the monsters, tail ablaze. I attempted to stop as well, but instead I tripped over a large sharp rock. It sunk semi deep into my left thigh and I had to resist yelping in pain. Which was difficult as I removed it both carefully and quickly. I then staggered towards Marles, hoping that I could still fight.

Next thing I felt was my body being sharply pressed against the uncomfortable ground as my eyes locked with Marles' in fear. Sharp claws dug into my back as I struggled to breathe under the increasing pressure. No matter how much pain I was in, I would not stop struggling until I broke free from underneath the nasty beast. A shriek filled my ears as a burning sensation washed over my body. While very hot and somewhat uncomfortable, it did not hurt me and seemed to only cause harm to the monster. The smell of singed fur filled the air. Soon the pressure was relieved from my back, allowing me to breathe one more.

I managed to roll over onto my back, only to see the monster's ugly toothy face. It looked ready to strike at my head before it was hit with another blast of fire. It started to hiss in pain as its attention was drawn to Marles. All three monsters had begun to corner Marles as he attempted to ward them off with his fire, but I feared there was only so much he could do. Pain sprawling across my body, I made my way over as quickly as I could only to get grabbed again. The sound of wind filled my ears. My body was quickly lifted upwards as I felt multiple arms wrap around my stomach. A flash of orange and indigo sped past my eyes as I watched two Celegons grab and swiftly take Marles out of reach from the dangerous monsters.

While I could not get a good look at my rescuers, I cautiously decided to speak to them.

"T-thank you for helping us. We'll be sure to repay you once we're safe in town," I politely told them with hopes their intentions were mostly noble.

"Aw, how sweet of you! You know, I wasn't even going to ask for anything this time, but if you're offering that sounds just grand!" a bubbly voice chimed in a way that I instantly recognized from the first word.

"Glad you're still alive Blu," I casually replied before our conversation was briefly interrupted by the screeching of monsters below.

"Yeah! Yeah! We hear you. You guys are awful and want to choke on our guts, but sorry that's not happening today!" Blubelle taunted at the monsters as they continued to howl in disgust.

Seeing them so far below gave me a sense of relief; though, being held in this position was quite uncomfortable. Both my back and leg were in a lot of pain from the aftermath. Still now that the danger had subsided they would recover soon enough once I got around to eating some emeri and cleaning the areas.

"So you're probably wondering who I'm with. Well, a few days ago I happened to be in a bit of monster trouble too! These lovely Celegons came to my rescue just in the nick of time and splattered my monster perpetrator before it could get to me. They aren't the most talkative. Well—except for Basion; he's really nice and super sweet on Ariele," she cooed as I felt someone's paws dig into my body a little. "What's the matter, Ariele? I think you'd make a great couple!" Blubelle continued to talk as the paws began to feel like they were crushing my organs.

"E-excuse me Ariele is it?" I gasped. "Please don't mind her. She's a bit of a nuisance when it comes to the topic of mates. She's just overly prying because she hasn't found hers yet," I managed to choke out. Soon, and much to my relief, I felt the pressure leaving my stomach.

"Thank you. Dealing with this idiot's consistent blabbering has put enough of a burden on my team's backs," a raspy, yet slightly feminine voice bluntly stated above me—which I presumed was Ariele.

Blubelle quickly resorted to pouting and over exaggerating how upset she was, but luckily for us it lasted all but three seconds. As per usual, I ignored her and refocused on the wellbeing of my would-be apprentice. As my view only consisted of the ground and a bit of what was forward, I was slightly concerned about Marles' whereabouts.

"Those other Celegons, did they take Marles somewhere else?" I ask, hoping that this would not turn out to be a scheme where they had us separated and demanded a fee for reuniting us.

"Marles? That your friend's name? He's being carried by my other team members Basion and Soeki. Though, for some reason, they are struggling with such an easy task and are lagging a bit behind us," Ariele griped as I let out an awkward sigh.

The rest of the flight went fairly smoothly; though, there were a few more times when Blubelle annoyed Ariele to the point I had to harden my ribs in fear of having them crushed. Only an estimated twelve minutes of fast flight led us to the destined Tarrina Town. Being picked up by mostly strangers had both saved us a lot of time and our lives. When we landed, I was still a bit weakened by the loss of blood I experienced thanks to the monsters which made it slightly hard to stand up. My back hurt the most, but the wound already felt as if it was closing up after being exposed to air for so long. When Marles came around I would ask if he could clean it and possibly rub some emeri juice onto it if needed.

As for now, I focused on tending to the injuries I could easily reach. After licking clean my front wound on my thigh, I turned around to face Ariele for the first time. She was mint green with dark blue eyes that matched her tail stone. Her hair tuft was also uniquely curly in that it curled upwards.

"Thank you again for being our rescuers." I politely bowed my head; though, after I looked back up I did not see the other Celegons on the ground with us anywhere. Looking back in the direction we came from, I could see the orange and indigo Celegons hauling Marles through the now darkened pink sky.

They arrived with us rather shortly and not two seconds after they landed, Ariele spared no time at all in lecturing them about their incompetence. While they conversed, Marles walked over to my side. He appeared a little woozy. Before he could tell me about his experience with his rescuers, Blubelle practically threw herself in between us.

"So about your rescue fee—how about a gold orb for each of us? I mean, you two would be dead after all if we didn't save you," Blubelle chimed as I tried to keep my cool in the presence of Ariele.

No way I was going to just fork over that much. Sure we were not dead, but I would rather be dead than without orbs as those without orbs tend to end up the former regardless. Plus, my gold orbs had a special value to me; I was not going to just happily hand them over to strangers.

"Listen, we're a little short on gold orbs right now. Would it suffice if we instead treat you and your friends to a hearty meal at one of the inns here?" Marles politely suggested as Blubelle's eyes transferred from me to him.

She seemed to briefly be at a loss for words as she examined Marles; which was off-putting because there was not much that could silence that chatterbox. With the way her eyes were focused on him, and the slight tint of pink in her light blue fur, it was painfully obvious that she was attracted to him like so many others. I was, of course, annoyed by this; especially since she'd made fun of him the last time we'd seen one another. The nerve of her liking him *only now* that he'd lost some fat.

Thankfully, the moment was cut short as Ariele interrupted with a reply to dinner. "Yes please, we're starving after that flight."

As much as I did not want to put up with Blubelle, it was better than being dead. Marles would have been gone too if not for them. For some reason that fact bothered me more than losing my own life. I was probably just tired.

Chapter Seven: Inquietude

Tarrina Town was fairly large and notably quite difficult to navigate at night for travelers who were passing through. Luckily, having been here before, I already knew that an inn was located just past the large stone walls at the town's entrance. That meant our group did not have to waste any time wandering aimlessly. Unlike the majority of towns that were spread across Lixion, this one had roads that were paved with mostly smooth rocks. While dirt roads got incredibly muddy during rainstorms and wooden roads often pricked my feet on the occasion, the rock roads had to be the best to grace my feet overall. Well, except at night; if one was not careful it was entirely possible to trip over a loose rock and get scraped.

As one of Lixion's biggest towns, it was no surprise that it was pleasing to look at even at night. In addition to almost everything being constructed with stone, there were pretty wax fires stuck all over on the sides of buildings. This special substance was made by certain species of nymphs in copious amounts. Just a few decades ago, one Celegon first used his fire talent on a sizable amount only to be surprised when it began to burn continuously for quite some time. The wax quickly became very popular and used by most Celegons who lived in non-flammable areas. As much as I adored the pretty flames illuminating off the wax, having them in my dome would be potentially deadly.

Of course, even in Tarrina Town the wax could still be harmful to others. Having hot wax drip on fur was a great way to turn an otherwise okay day into a miserable one. Or stepping in a cold wax puddle; not painful, but quite gross. I could only hope Marles would never ask me to keep wax inside the dome. Other than the wax, there were many buildings that would be great for heists. Though our current goal was to find the inn and there would be plenty more time to explore later.

The inn's exterior was mostly carved stone and rocks carefully and neatly compressed together like the other structures in town, but the insides were covered with wood and rugs that gave it a nice comfortable atmosphere. Since it was later in the day, the inn was naturally bustling with other Celegons who had arrived to eat a hearty meal or get a decent night's rest. No matter how full an inn's entrance area was, it seemed there was always room for a few more. I told the others to find an unclaimed area to sit at while I went to search for someone who was in charge. From the corner of my eye, I thought I caught Blubelle looking at me with a certain glint in her eye before the group left, but I decided to ignore it for the time being.

Innkeepers were pretty easy to spot, mostly because of their demeanor; they always seemed quite cheerful and carefree. This was probably because they were living the best lives under the wealthiest Celegons since they always had a safe place to sleep and a plethora of food available to them. After spotting a relaxed hazel furred innkeeper, I got into a brief conversation with him about inn and food expenses. At the end of our talk I ended up forfeiting my six white orbs in exchange for two rooms and an assortment of delicious foods.

I no longer had any white orbs in my possession now. Sure, I could have given two gold orbs instead as that would be worth the same amount, but I always seemed to have a hard time giving up my precious gold orbs. It has been quite a while since I had eaten in an inn. I had never once actually slept in one; I did not need to because of my dome. But I guess it is okay to treat oneself every so often.

Passing by crowded tables as I made my way back to the group, I was oddly pleased to see Marles enjoying himself amongst the rescuers. He seemed to be wrapping up whatever he was talking about as he noticed me approaching.

"But aside from that, being with Lyla has been a very pleasant experience," he finished as he nervously stared in my direction when I began to eye him suspiciously.

For some reason, I had the overwhelming urge to know exactly what horrible thing he may have said about me. And why he said such things as he did not seem the type to pass on secrets.

"Lyla! Sit here next to me, I have the perfect spot for you!" Blubelle smiled wryly as she motioned to the cushion between her and Ariele.

It took me no time to notice that she was sitting next to Marles, albeit quite snuggly too. Though I could not say that this bothered me as now Marles was too absorbed chatting with the orange Celegon—who I believed to be Basion—sitting across from him. After comfortably seating myself on the brown cushion, which had a slight thin layer of dirt across the top, I rested my paws on the wood block of a table.

"Skyli, right?"

The voice that spoke to me was that mint green Celegon from before, Ariele. Her deep blue eyes studied me for a second before speaking more.

"Ariele Thorne, nice to make your acquaintance," she said somewhat formally, which came off a little awkward and almost forced. However, she almost instantly went to a more casual way of speaking which suited her more.

"This here is the rest of my monster hunting team. There's Basion, my most trusted," Ariele gestured over to the orange Celegon with reddish brown eyes. He looked over at me and gave me a slight smile before Ariele continued.

"The quiet one over there is Soeki. He's been with us for a few months now. Doesn't really say much, but he's been great with helping us locate monster dens," she pointed out as the Celegon in question gave a simple nod in response. Ariele then looked over to the light blue annoyance next to me.

"And our most recent addition, Blubelle, who you were already acquainted with," she finished as I turned to look at the Celegon in question. Not only had she joined them, but was having them refer to her as her alias? From my understanding, 'Blubelle' was just an alias until now. A little odd.

"With my addition, the team is now a solid number of four!" Blubelle smiled with a prideful glint in her eyes. Seeing how the others grimaced, I wondered if her presence was actually a hindrance for them.

In a world where monsters were climbing in population and Celegons were falling, monster hunters were to be admired. However, the effort sometimes seemed fruitless. Monsters could reproduce faster than us and have multiple spawn at a time. But at least they were brave enough to do something and try to make a change. Marles seemed especially intrigued at the idea as he looked like he was taking everything Ariele said seriously.

"Hunting monsters?" Marles spoke those words as if he were puzzled by the profession.

Surely he couldn't have been *that* oblivious. Hunting monsters was an activity dating back before he was born. Of course, it was still uncommon to see hunters as not many were wanting to willingly fight monsters.

"For some I suppose it is a little odd to hear. But yes, I—with the help of my team—slay the beasts that prey upon us Celegons," Ariele explained as she shifted a bit on her seat. It almost seemed like just the thought of fighting another monster excited her.

"Ariele is really amazing. Until I met her, I didn't even think it could be possible to wipe all monsters out completely. I want to stick by her and her team until they accomplish the dream of a monsterless world," Blubelle gushed as her tail began to bob back and forth. A monsterless world would certainly be ideal. But a goal like that seemed far too impossible for a few Celegons.

I continued to be surprised that Blubelle herself volunteered to join up with them. Despite not being more than acquaintances; I knew her type. Cowardly. Suited for the life of the common thief and swindler. The only reason I could see her sticking with them was for protection.

"Since monsters began hunting us, they've steadily increased in numbers," Basion sighed, leaning forward on the table. "I'm sure you already knew, but it was not always like this. Something happened to make them switch from nymphs to us as their favorite meal."

I remembered hearing things like that from others before. Those claims could easily be true. But from only living in a world where monsters ate us, sometimes it was hard to believe. Many of the oldest Celegons had long been eaten by monsters themselves.

"I wonder what could have made the change. I wonder if in the distant past, Celegons and monsters once got along. Maybe even understood each other," Marles wondered aloud, causing some Celegons not at our table to peer over at us with interest.

An uncomfortable feeling tugged in my chest. That was what Alise thought. It was something that she could never convince me of. That feeling left as quickly as it came as my attention was directed to claws digging into wood.

"Out of the question."

That low voice came from Ariele as all eyes locked on her. Her calmer tone was now filled with hatred and her eyes sparked with malice. Even not directed at Marles himself, the words he spoke had ignited something inside her.

"I've lost many to those beasts. Seen them brutally gutted before devoured by them. To be able to communicate with creatures like that is unthinkable," Ariele growled as Blubelle quivered next to me. All but Basion seemed to be avoiding her eyes for the next few seconds.

A part of me was sympathetic towards her. She formed bonds with others only to have them be taken away time and time again. A strong Celegon. But forming relationships like that was foolish.

She seemed to pick up on the fact that the mood had now turned sour after her comments. But her face twisted into a confused grimace as she wondered if the conversation could be salvaged. Basion took notice and it appeared like he had an idea on how to change the subject. However, Ariele beat him to it.

"So, are you and Marles mates?" she asked me bluntly with a casual expression on her face. It was definitely one way to divert the topic away from monsters.

"A-Ari, you can't just ask that of them like that!" Basion exclaimed. She simply looked at him in confusion.

"Can't I? It's just a simple yes or no; no need for them to be complex about it. I only want to know if my hunch is right. Oh I know, I'll tell them you and I are on our way to becoming mates so they'll feel more obligated to respond," she replied to Basion who opened his mouth to protest before hesitating as his orange fur tinted red.

I was quick to respond to this as I was worried things could potentially escalate to make others feel uncomfortable.

"No, we aren't mates," I stated in a more serious tone as I glanced over in Marles' direction to see his expression.

He seemed a bit startled at the notion but otherwise not visibly uncomfortable which was a relief. It was then Blubelle began to have that same mischievous look from earlier that I did not like one bit.

"So that means Marles' future mate is currently unknown?" she smiled wickedly as she inched towards Marles before suddenly hugging onto his left arm. This surprised everyone at the table, even Soeki who had been rather quiet this whole time.

At this point I was ready to be done being cordial as Blubelle was crossing a boundary that I was certain Marles wanted no one to cross. My insides burned as I watched Marles' fur slowly rise and his body stiffen as Blubelle continued to embrace him. Though he forced a smile that may have fooled others, I knew by the mere look in his eyes how much this was hurting him inside. She may not have ill intentions, but she had to stop. Could she not feel how tense he was?

However, before I could say anything, the quiet Soeki spoke up. His pinkish red eyes sparked with the slightest bit of irritation as he observed the scene.

"That's enough Bells; he's clearly not enjoying you doting on him like that." The indigo Celegon paused for a moment as if he was nervous about being confrontational. Bluebelle's eyes certainly lit up when he spoke, though she quickly averted her eyes from his. "Well, you've got my attention. Now will you let poor Marles be?"

After his short speech, Blubelle immediately retracted herself from Marles and turned a little red. Something about how he called her "Bells" made me think back to something. Someone I once called Belle on occasion. In the midst of thinking back, two large wooden trays full of fruits, roots, and even some delicious looking water nymphs, were placed down on the wooden table for us.

"Oh, look all, the food has arrived," Basion pointed out nervously, clearly trying to direct everyone's attention away from the past conversation.

"That was more than obvious, Basion. But thank the Sacred Spirit, let's forget that arduous conversation and eat this food." Ariele smiled as she grabbed a roasted water nymph before shoving it into her mouth.

"The conversation that you initiated," Basion muttered as he began eating some fruit before Ariele could get into an argument with him.

The rest of us quickly followed as we began to indulge in the mildly delicious meal, but I am certain it would have tasted better if we had not had that talk to begin with. I reminded myself that I should not be upset with my rescuer. Ariele downed most of the water nymphs before I could get a bite, so I was a bit sour about that. Again, do not be mad at your rescuer.

After the very filling meal, the group of us headed to the not-so luxurious rooms I had paid for. My stomach felt a little bloated, which would not be good in the long run. I felt good now, but when food was more scarce, I would be really feeling the pain. The rooms at inns were plentiful, but to achieve that they were always small and cramped. My initial thought was that the two rooms would be divided between myself with Marles in one, and Ariele and her party in the other. However, since four Celegons would overly crowd a room, Blubelle was to stay with us. Somehow I doubted we would get much sleep tonight.

The wooden floors in the hallway that housed the rooms were noticeably old, but well cared for in a way that splinters were a low possibility. The hallway consisted of twenty guest rooms, ten on each side; it was most likely that the entrance to a bigger, nicer room was at the very end. The room I would be staying in was the seventh to the right, while Ariele's group would be staying at the eighth. We made a brief good night parting with one another before our groups divided and we made our way into the separate rooms. Pushing open the flimsy wooden door revealed to us our temporary lodging.

Needless to say, I was not surprised to see the tiny room provided minimal comfortings. A small singular monster pelt spread thin over a third of the room while the rest was simply firm wooden flooring. There were also two slightly worn grey blankets accompanied by three tattered browning cushions strewn across the room in an disorderly fashion. The only light that lit the small space, as with most buildings, was from a small opening high above the back wall that moonlight flooded in from. While a bit less hygienic than the confines of my dome, I was sure I'd be content with my sleeping conditions. If Blubelle was not here.

"Ooh, only two blankets! You know what that means, someone's going to have to share," Blubelle chimed as she joyfully paraded into the room, followed by Marles who was not near as dramatic as she was.

I decided there and now would be a good time to stop her nonsense, so instead of entering I stayed at the door for a moment. Soon enough, they began to eye me curiously.

"Blu, may I have a word? Let's chat outside for a moment. And Marles, please don't burn down the inn while we're gone," I smirked briefly at his mild reaction as Blubelle cautiously made her way over to me.

After closing the wooden door, we made our way outside the inn. It was here I began to swiftly climb my way to the top of the structure, carefully avoiding the wax that was stuck on the stone walls.

Once I made it to the top, I gazed up at the night sky and was distracted by its beauty for a moment before Blubelle's expectant eyes entered my vision. She seemed quite carefree, clearly having no idea why I brought her up here and what we would talk about. Before striking up the conversation, I stared at the streets dotted with many glowing balls of wax. While the inn was not too high up, I could see about a third of the town.

"So I take it you're pretty mad, huh Lavender?" Blubelle laughed nervously. I felt quite surprised that she picked up on my emotions so easily, though I was not exactly hiding them.

"I-I'm not mad. At least, I don't think that's the right way to put it. But this is meant to be a serious conversation, so I'd appreciate it if you took it that way," I stated as Blubelle's eyes began to brighten with curiosity. She repositioned herself so that she was sitting comfortably on the roof and closed her eyes for a moment.

"I hope this isn't an advice talk. You of all Celegons should know I give the shoddiest advice for 'serious topics.'" Her body seemed to be resisting the urge to laugh before shaking it off. Though she soon turned her head towards me with a less manic smile.

"Not in the slightest. I just want to be heard, is all. While I'm not currently angry, I was quite upset with your actions earlier. Do you have any idea how uncomfortable he was?" I sighed as she began to smile suspiciously like she always did when she was amused.

"Dear Lavender, I was just being an icebreaker, though maybe I went too far and broke you too! And it was Ariele to start that chain of events, so don't put it all on me." She paused briefly, that smile looking more suspicious than before. "So... does this mean I actually succeeded in making you jealous?" she chimed as her tail gleefully started moving from side to side.

My calm mind was quickly converted into an emotion I did not want to be in. As much as I wished her playful banter would distract me in a positive way, this was not the time for it.

"Blu, you shouldn't joke about that anymore. I know one of your favorite things to do is make situations seem funny and exciting, but I need you to really listen to me on this-"

Before I could finish she casually interrupted me with, "But Lavender! Since you like Marles, what's the harm in teasing if what I do just ends up helping you get closer?"

Since she was not going to take me seriously, I felt as if I had no other choice than to be even more firm with my tone.

"Blubelle! You can't keep doing that anymore. Maybe to other Celegons, but definitely not to Marles. He-" I paused as I tried to recollect myself. I did not want to tell her everything I picked up here and there. Some things were better left unsaid. "He was forced into courting these other no-good wealthy Celegons in the past. I try not to pry or ask about it, but it is clear that the experiences have worn him down. You can pick on me all you want, Marles too, but I'm begging you to stop treating him like some object you can flirt with. He has feelings. And though he's strong, I don't want him to feel awful and dread the past more."

When I finished, she looked as if maybe she finally understood the importance and how her actions were hurting Marles. Her eyes were widened and her previous cheekiness had diminished from her features. There was even a slight pause before she said her next few words.

"Lavender, you're in love with him aren't you?"

My emotions began to sprawl all over from the depths of my brain to the tightness of my lungs. Did nothing I say get through to Blubelle, or was this just another one of her teasings? Her facial expression did not bear her usual mischievousness; her smile seemed quite genuine and understanding for once. I wished she were joking; I wished she did not have to ask a serious question—one that only obligated me to give a serious answer in return.

"What does it matter if I do? I've already told you his experiences and how he wants nothing to do with a mate," I stated firmly as the slightest tears began to form in my eyes; I hurriedly blinked them away.

"But Lavender, so what about all those other Celegons he was with? You know as well as I do you can only match with one mate in life, and I strongly believe that you are to be that Celegon for him!" she chimed as I continued to contemplate what she was saying.

My mouth began to tremble slightly as more and more mixed thoughts and emotions clashed in my head. The idea of meeting your mate, becoming immensely attached to them, and having someone who would always care for you sounded like a blissful fantasy. No matter how alluring the prospect, I had to give everything in my power to ensure that never happened between Marles and I.

"Listen Blubelle, I do care for Marles a lot, so make no misunderstanding of that. I've grown attached to him in the time we've spent together and he has proven to be a valuable ally. I know you like to tease and overcomplicate even the simplest of situations, but please don't initiate or even encourage any notion of Marles and I being more than work partners. I-It doesn't only affect him, it hurts me as well," I explained as I tried my best to keep the countless feelings from escaping to her view.

Her dark blue eyes glimmered beautifully in the moonlight, but were stained with concern that did not suit them. She could only softly say Lavender one last time before we both drifted into a state of silence. In that silence we watched the flames of the countless wax clumps dance below.

The two of us sat on the rooftop for a while longer, just staring at nothing. Eventually, Blubelle told me she wanted to go back and promised not to inform Marles of our talk before she left. At that moment, I could not care less if she held true to her words or not. As I continued to look at things,

I noticed that my vision was starting to become blurry. Soon, there was little I could do to keep these emotions from flooding out.

Out of all the times I could have, why now had my body chosen to do this? I felt weak and helpless. I used to be so much better at holding it in until now. It was quite common for this to happen to me as a child years ago, but I rarely partook in the activity after I matured. My mother had even gone to great measures to make sure I never cried, deeming it socially unacceptable. Maybe she was right about that. Other Celegons seemed to be emotionally strong; I rarely saw tears shed even by ones who had gotten wounded by monsters. In moments like these, I wished I were stronger.

I just wish I was better at holding back these uncomfortable feelings as well as others. At least I was alone when I released them; how awkward it would have been if I had done this at dinner. Though, I suddenly picked up a sense that I was no longer alone on the roof. After blinking my eyes clear and briefly rubbing them with my paws, I cautiously listened with my ears to sense if it was that Celegon again.

There were few who would sneak up on me without announcing their presence. As I was not carrying my satchel with me and in the confines of a town, no robber would have any reason to prey upon me. Which is what led me to suspect it was *him* yet again. A little too early to be seeing him, but I had a gut feeling that it was not anyone else I knew.

"Is that you Z? Isn't it a little early for you to be stalking me again so soon?" I said as I continued to have my back towards the presence. "But please correct me if I'm wrong. I don't want to look ridiculous in front of a stranger by assuming you were someone I know."

They made no comment to my words, which was a bit off since the Z I knew would usually have spoken up by now. My ears alerted me that they were getting closer by the softness of their feet becoming faintly louder with each step.

"Are you attempting to frighten me by staying all silent or just too dimwitted to come back with a decent affront? Surely there's something you have to say to me. Or is it just that time of the season where you blame me for her death?" I scoffed as I turned around to face the Celegon who had long resented my well being.

My fur began to raise at the sight; not out of anger but out of fear. The very sight of the black Celegon had briefly shut my thoughts off.

"Little Lavender, nice to see you again too." He wheezed a bit as he spoke, clearly struggling to stand.

His gaunt body was considerably battered and worn. It was quite obvious to see several gashes in his right side so deep that I could only assume he had just barely survived a monster attack. While I still felt conflicting emotions, I gravitated towards anger—angry at him for being so foolish and careless. He was always in poor health, an illness he never publicly disclosed with me; seeing him this injured made me feel sick to my stomach.

"Z! Wh-what, how d-did," was all I could barely sputter out.

Without a moment to waste, I ripped open my satchel; thankfully, I had not stashed it in the room. I pulled out one of my emergency emeri. His dark eyes looked considerably more dull when he saw what I was holding.

"Eating is not my favorite pastime, you should know," he droned as I cautiously approached him and stared at his open wounds in greater detail.

They seemed remarkably fresh, so whatever did this could have been just a bit outside the town. I was admittedly relieved that he had made it here without dying. With wounds like these accompanied by his abysmal condition, it was a miracle he was still breathing.

Sitting down with him on the rooftop, I held the emeri up to his mouth—which he reluctantly bit into. He seemed to be in pain with each swallow and began shivering slightly the more he consumed. Whatever health issue a Celegon could have that made eating delicious emeri a chore must be by far the most horrendous; I pitied him for it greatly.

After that, I paid attention to what I assumed were monster bite marks on his side. The scent of the blood that dripped from his body was so foul smelling I gagged a few times, but I still tended to his injuries by taking a second emeri from my satchel and rubbing the juices on the open wounds. Although his body had no negative reaction to the emeri juice, I still wondered if it was a painful process for him.

"Sometimes I wonder if you are truly the most reckless and ignorant Celegon I've ever had the displeasure of meeting," I muttered as he began to eye me suspiciously.

"I have similar notions about a certain Lavender Celegon as well," he replied, his voice trailing off for a moment.

He shook himself a bit as his body processed the effects of the emeri. As I waited, I began to grow impatient while he simply sat in silence.

"So that's it huh? You just come here all wounded and expect me to fix you up? With not an ounce of gratefulness in sight, I might add," I huffed as I awaited his response. Instead, he gave me a half-effort glare before staring up at the night sky like I was non-existent. "Where did all your famous quips go? I know better than to expect polite conversation with you, but you ought to at least have the strength to tell me what happened," I went on as he still continued to remain silent, which irked me.

I gritted my teeth in irritation as he continued to act like I was less than him; it amazed me how someone so weak could remain so arrogant.

"Were you attempting to die the same way she did?" I started, somewhat startling myself in the process. "Do you think letting those beasts tear you apart would give you closure?" I continued, terrified of the words that were coming out of my mouth. Why was I feeling compelled to say this? Everything in my conscience was telling me to stop but my mouth kept on speaking. "Is this what Alise would have wanted?" I went on as my entire body began trembling.

He then stood up and turned his head towards me with a cold glare in his eyes. "It wasn't the monsters that did this."

I swear I heard him say that it was not a monster that hurt him, but I must have misheard. There was no way another Celegon would have attacked him. For one, he carried nothing of substantial value on himself as he wore no bag or satchel. Any Celegon to have assaulted one of their own like that would be the most cold-hearted Celegon to exist—attacking him in his already weak state.

"You haven't changed at all. I was hoping you had matured more from our last meeting, but you're the same Little Lavender. Telling you won't solve anything." As he spoke, his voice began to trail off as if into a whisper; he shakily stood up, and it was obvious the action took much effort. Not that I cared about him leaving that much, though I was wondering if he could even manage to fly.

"Are you sane? You shouldn't be flying right now—you should be resting!" I lectured as he gave me a bored look that made my fur flare up in anger.

"I am *not* weak, Little Lavender. I will endure. I have survived while watching newer generations perish because they are too weak to survive in these hard lands. Flying will not be pleasant, but I do not care to rest among those who live in towns. They'll be the first to go, after all," Z told me while straightening himself as if he were in no pain at all.

He yawned out as he began to stretch his back. I had half the mind to continue conversing with him, but I knew he was too stubborn to tell me what really happened. Soon two glossy black wings emerged; he used them to ascend off the ground.

"Z... just who or what have you angered?" My mouth gently clenched as I watched him soar off into the darkened sky. Even if I disliked him, I trusted what he said to a degree. No weak willed Celegon would have been able to survive for as long as he has.

My mind tricked me into seeing a faint smile on his mouth, but I knew it was only my imagination. He never smiled, at least not for the many years that I had known him. Probably not since she'd met her end, anyway.

Alise... I still miss her.

Chapter Eight: Misconception

Pessimism aside, sleeping at the inn was hardly ideal. The inn itself was decent enough; though the blankets and cushions were slightly scratchy. Marles occasionally made odd noises in his sleep, but as of late has been more quiet and far less disruptive. The main issue was none other than Blubelle herself. I was debating if I could do anything about it. As the two of us were sharing a blanket, sharing a close space was a given; but I had certainly not been expecting her to latch onto me in her sleep all clingy-like.

She was very much asleep, something I envied the pleasure of doing. In addition to clinging to me uncomfortably, she was also murmuring barely recognizable words. Her sleepy tone was grossly affectionate; that much I could understand. While I was sure she did not intend to direct this behavior towards me, I did not feel any less creeped out. It did make me wonder, however, if she was dreaming about having a mate, or if there was someone more specific on her mind.

Semi-grateful that at least my stomach was not getting crushed, my mind tried to wander to other things. Particularly things that would not cause me worry or stress. However, that was not made easy when there had been so much as of late that sought to plague my mind rather than ease it. I forced myself to imagine welons in all their delicious glory in detail. Soon enough, I was able to coax myself into sleep once again.

• • ⊷ • •

"Mother?" A little Celegon of all white meekly approached an older Celegon who bore a mostly dark violet color scheme. The more mature Celegon studied the

little one with cold, but interested blue eyes as the white fluff attempted to get words out.

"What is it, Pura? Don't tell me your sister harassed you again. You both know the punishments if either of you get damaged," the violet Celegon mused in a scornful tone as she scanned over the white one's currently untarnished body. The little one shook her head and began to smile delightedly before she told her mother what had been on her mind.

"I've thought about it a lot and I've decided that you don't need to give me rewards for doing good anymore. I promise to do my best even without receiving them, but please continue to reward my sister since she deserves them much more than I do!" the child beamed as the mother's eyes grew colder.

"You ungrateful brat!" the violet Celegon suddenly yelled as her tone seethed with disgust. The movement of her paw was so quick and precise, something the child failed to notice as her eyes were locked into her mother's.

• • ᕬᕔ • •

My eyes snapped open while the right side of my face burned with pain. Quickly, I lifted my paw to brush it away, to ease the unwanted sensation; it was then I realized it was only phantom pain caused by a dream. Internally groaning, I then looked around to see that Blubelle was missing and that Marles was still pleasantly asleep on his side of the room. Blinking my eyes a little bit, I glanced at the opening at the top of the rock wall to see the faint gleam of daylight shimmering in. While my mind craved more sleep, my body seemed rested enough and ready to take on the challenges of the day.

As I began to stretch myself, my brain briefly wondered where Blubelle snuck off to. My eyes drifted to the sleeping Marles. He seemed to be breathing softly; which was good, though I wondered if he was secretly awake. I cautiously moved myself over to Marles as my heart seemingly grew stiff in my chest. His dark emerald fur was quite relaxed across his backside; he was either still peacefully asleep, or pondering something trivial. It was easier to look at him this way. While he was certainly more entertaining when awake, it was also much harder to keep my thoughts straight.

When it came down to it, it was easy to see why he was so beloved by female Celegons. Not only was he charming, but his general demeanor helped him get along with pretty much anyone. And while having him around constantly had made his flaws, the ones that inconvenienced me the most, more prominent, I found myself unable to wholy ignore the lingering pesky feelings that refused to cease. Perhaps I thought keeping him around for as long as I had would help me realize that I was simply kidding myself into thinking it could be more than the initial partnership he had sought, one I had tried to get out of and had now warmed to.

Though I had to admit, I had gotten pretty good at hiding it even from myself at times. Still, I knew it would not be healthy to hide this information anymore, especially if it was in fact the real deal. Strangely enough, the thought of rejection was somewhat relieving to me. After the awkwardness we could continue to be allies. It was the thought of returned affection that chilled my core. Having him as a mate, in particular, seemed unrealistic and I was not even sure how compatible we would be. They say mates are predetermined by the Sacred Spirit, an unseen force that was said to bring life to everything in our world. Would that be the case for Marles and I?

Life was just simple the way it was now. Everything I hear about mates just seems too complex for my lifestyle. Like how if one partner dies it—

My body flinched as Marles suddenly rolled over to face me. His orange eyes blinked a few times before he flashed me a lopsided smile and began to stretch. For a moment, he simply laid on his back as his tired eyes adjusted to his surroundings. Pushing away whatever thoughts I had been bearing previously, I grinned at him as I began to get closer to his face.

"Marley," I asserted in a soothingly soft voice. His eyes lit up with curiosity, and I knew he was considering my motives.

I seldom referred to him as this because I knew how much he preferred being called this to his whole name. Since he adored the name so much, it would never fail to get his undivided attention after I had spoken it—especially in such a kind tone. One might think that he acted in awe out of endearment towards me, but his other actions told a different story. He was indeed caught off guard with eyes lit up and all, but there were no other signs of excitement or fur tinting red in the face as Celegons often do towards their beloved. Knowing this put me much more at ease as I was finally able to let the awful notions escape my mind before I began to act.

Briefly slipping my arms underneath his back, making it so our noses were almost touching, I used all my strength and jerked my head backward, flipping him over in the process. He fell quickly onto the wooden flooring as I heard him squeak in shock after the event. The sound he made caused me to start belting out with laughter; a few happy tears clouded my eyes while my whole body shook with giddy. His response to this was a bit of moping, so I crawled over to where he was sulking.

"Why do you take so much pleasure in humiliating me like that? So early in the morning too," he whined as he refused to look me in the eye with a massive pout spread across his face.

"Really, Marles? You can't tell me you weren't anticipating something was going to happen along those lines. I think you should be thanking me for helping you get a head start on waking up; you looked exceptionally shiftless today," I remarked as a grin made its way to my mouth. He tried his best to act full of resentment, though I wondered if he knew how see-through he was.

"Why not be sweeter for a change? I'm sure it would be just as effective in waking me up, possibly even more so! Imagine—Ly-Ly waking me up with a surprise hug instead! Just the thought of it fills me with enough energy to take on the day!" he beamed with enthusiasm as I stood beside him trying to hold in my laughter.

As I playfully started to pat at his head, he eyed me intently with a confused smile.

"But doing that sounds positively boring, not to mention quite strange. Very *strange*," I paused a moment to add a bit of dramatic emphasis. "Things are better this way. And don't you dare say you don't enjoy my antics because we both know that's untrue!" He sheepishly agreed by nodding his head as an awkward smile made its way to his mouth. However he soon appeared deep in thought. Perhaps I did go a little too far this time.

"You know you're allowed to tell me off right? If I'm being too cruel you just need to say so!" I forced a laugh as his face suddenly snapped back into reality.

For a moment his gaze appeared quite serious; though, that quickly disappeared and he began to grin and avert his eyes from mine.

"O-oh no, you should know by now how lax I can be. Plus you did help me wake up faster, so there's really no issue there! I was just thinking about something else last night. You see, Blubelle..." he began as I hesitantly braced myself for what was to come. Blubelle had come to the room before I did, giving them plenty of time to talk about things Blubelle would say.

As someone who enjoys gossiping and inciting chaos, she could have given him multiple subjects to stick in his brain. Despite me being firm before, it was possible that she had leaked the entirety of our last night's conversation to him. A shred of hope made me wish it was just typical Blubelle nonsense.

"She asked me for love advice."

My mind briefly went blank after hearing what came out of Marles' mouth. Suddenly millions of thoughts began to mix in my mind and soon I was filled with all sorts of uncontrolled emotions.

"Wha- why in the world would she ask you that?" I found myself blurting without thinking first. He seemed equally surprised as I was after realizing I had lost my composure. I started to laugh, trying to recover, but I could hear my own hesitance in the sound. "I-I'm sorry," I stammered next, as I desperately grasped for the right words, "I'm just so upset that she had the nerve to. I j-just, I know she probably didn't mean anything bad, but she could have hurt you!"

My limbs felt a little shaky and my eyes began looking anywhere but at him, unable to focus on a single object in the room. Feelings of distress still lingered from the night before. Judging by the worried look on his face, explanations were needed.

"I know how uncomfortable you can be when the talk of mates and affections get brought up. I feel upset with the fact this happened while I was out and you having to hear her talk about it. Sorry for overreacting like that," I apologized as I dropped my gaze to the floor, scratching the back of my head.

I'd stopped shaking, but my head was still spinning; I felt as if I was unable to fully comprehend what was happening around me. Then, paws cradled my cheeks and gently inclined my head upward, pulling my gaze from the floor. This made me tense up further. Marles' eyes looked even more stained with concern; I watched as he appeared to force a tight smile.

"You don't have to worry about that Lyla, I'm perfectly fine. It may have bothered me more in the past, but I'd like to think that I've healed now and can listen to others talk about their mates and feel happy for them. But I am worried about you right now, did something happen last night?" he asked in a reassuring tone that coaxed me into feeling safer.

Giving him a vague summary of what happened would not be too risky I suppose.

"I had an encounter with a Celegon called Z. Though he was the one who was injured, nothing fatal happened between us but..." my voice trailed off as my mind began to clear. "May I give you more intel later? I don't want our morning to start off sour."

In a very swift movement, I felt myself being held in a way that I was not used to. My brain and body were both overcome with a mix of feelings because of the gesture. One aspect of it was quite nice, warm, inviting and soft. Though my heart was beginning to swell with the emotion I disliked so much. Both enjoying and despising the feelings, I ultimately allowed him this.

The physical tremors had ceased and I was content that this was not as bad as I thought it would be. He lingered a little longer before eventually pulling away from me with a weak smile, one which I returned.

"We should see if Ariele and the others are still here," I stated as I collected the last of my bearings before standing strong on my feet. Marles heartily agreed before standing beside me with what was a much happier and more natural smile. "Let's hurry on then!"

We quickly gathered our things from the room and I opted to search through my satchel quickly; one never knew with Blubelle. Then I was heading out the squeaky wooden door. The hallway was slightly dimmer than before as it was early in the morning and there were no wax clumps to illuminate the surroundings. Luckily there was only one direction to go and that was to the entrance area that we dined at last night. Glancing over at Marles for a moment oddly refreshed me as it seemed he was back to being his usual carefree self. It certainly gave me the motivation I needed to really push this day in a positive direction.

After a quick trot to the entrance area, we saw that none of our rescuers from yesterday were anywhere to be seen. While it was still quite early and some Celegons would prefer to sleep a little longer, the fact Blubelle was absent from the room could mean they had left already. I felt a slight frown forming on my face before shaking it off; partings are best kept brief anyways. Since there was nothing for us at the inn, I bid one of the working innkeepers farewell before we exited into the faint glow of daylight.

Stepping outside onto the rock paved ground, I looked upwards to see that the sun had not yet risen over the tall stone walls that surrounded Tarrina town. Slightly saddened that the wax flames that dotted the stone roads and buildings had burned away, I turned to Marles who looked like he was ready to fall back asleep.

"Come on Marles, you seemed plenty awake earlier," I smiled as I nudged him gently in the side with my tail.

"Oh I am! Just taking in the scenery," he yawned as I continued to maliciously poke him.

"I have a fun idea that will sharpen you up for the day!"

The fresh morning air greeted our bodies as we began to wander towards the market section of town. Even towns with the thickest and tallest walls were subject to giving their inhabitants a cool, constant breeze due to it drafting down from above. Without a worry of stepping on wax, we both gazed upon the many stone structures in town. While certainly not as stunning to look at during the day, the grey atmosphere provided us with a sense of security. But there was also an uneasiness since there could always be someone watching. The stones underfoot were also refreshingly cool from the morning dew. I loved the simple pleasures in life.

Soon we approached the part of town that had a more interesting infrastructure. The surrounding buildings were curved in such a way that it formed a large circular open area filled to the brim with various merchant stalls. It was still quite early in the morning, but there were plenty of Celegons, merchants, and travelers alike. There were dozens of good targets; however, as I was scanning the market, a particular large flash of green sped past my eyes. The figure darted into one of the many buildings that surrounded the market stalls and I felt insanely compelled to follow it.

"Did you see that creature, Marles?" I asked as he too seemed enamored by the majestic being.

"Y-yeah, do you know what it could have been?" he questioned me as I started smiling wryly.

"Sometimes I forget how sheltered you used to be. Well Marles, that was your first time seeing a Malyspi. They come from an entirely different world. Strange, I know. And currently no Celegon has been able to go there yet! Just think of all the new experi- riches! Riches and treasures that there are to steal, wouldn't that be great Marles?" I tried to grin convincingly as I corrected myself, and he gave a concerned smile.

"You always seem to have a hard time admitting what you really want, Ly-Ly," he let out a discontented sigh before shortly following it with, "So, would it be rude to follow this Malyspi?"

Completely disregarding our approaching hunger, our curious minds directed our feet to scamper towards the shop the Malyspi went inside. The shop's doorway was adorned with lots of green foliage that helped it stand out from the other many structures in the circular plaza. This was, undoubtedly, a herb nursery. Marles seemed to be especially ecstatic; it was written quite clearly on his face. And given what I had learned about him recently, that wasn't much of a surprise.

Marles would often paint when we had nothing scheduled to do for the day. Naturally, he eventually had begun to run out of the special paints he had brought with him. That was when he revealed that he crushed certain herbs to create paint. The full-grown herbs he used were often rare in normal circumstances, but he had shown me a special method he had learned a few years back. Marles was able to use plant talent magic to help the herbs grow from seeds at an alarmingly fast rate, in turn allowing him to make more paint much more quickly.

His plant talent was next to useless in fighting, especially compared to other Celegons with better mastery of it. But he was content in it being useful enough for his hobby. It was quite amusing to see him so happy whenever we saw a herb shop, so I made sure to keep track of which towns had one.

We quickly entered the shop, which smelled strongly of several clashing herbs. Amongst the greenery we saw the Malyspi; they were examining a particular cerulean plant near the back of the small store. Thankfully this shop in particular was spacious enough that the being did not have to hunch over too much. It was hard not to stare; the Malyspi quickly caught on and they were quick to face us with a certain glint in their sharp yellow eyes.

A Malyspi's appearance used to unnerve Celegons when they first arrived. This was because they looked similar to monsters. Though, they were a bit smaller, had fluffy ears, a refined snout, and their eyes sparked with a certain intelligence. Compared to Celegons who varied in diverse shades of colors all over their bodies, Malyspi always seemed to consist of the same color scheme. Males always had short emerald fur all over their bodies and bright yellow eyes; they also all bore a small feathered "cape" that draped across their backs. Female bore no capes, and had softer colors such as cyan fur, light blue feathers, and sweet magenta eyes. The Malyspi that stood before us consisted of male colors as well as having a moderate amount of firm muscle over his legs and chest.

I suppose a lot of Celegons still found them to be intimidating, since they were twice a Celegon's standing height while standing on all four legs. For myself, I was fascinated with the race; this was especially since if not for them, Celegons would not have access to domes. From what was known about their world, it seemed like a place that was very warm all the time; which would be a pleasant change from how unforgivingly cold Lixion can be. Soon my mind was filled with thoughts of one day traveling there and seeing all of their wonders.

"Are you two just going to gawk at me? Shouldn't you Celegons know by now that it's rude to treat outsiders this way?"

My mind had been completely unaware that I had been staring at him the entire time. Panic arose in my chest as somehow I felt as if I had just angered the entire race of Malyspi. Feeling a little tongue tied, I looked to Marles for help in the off chance he had a good explanation.

"Apologies sir, we were just admiring your strong physique! As Celegons it's quite hard for us to build muscle so we quite envy you," Marles declared while flashing a pleasant smile in the confused Malyspi's direction.

The Malyspi stared at us for a moment before tightening his stance and raising his head slightly higher.

"I see. While your admiration is understandable, it is unnecessary. Especially something expected of us by our emperor. Now if you'll excuse me

I have this trade I need to fulfill," he firmly stated before taking his clump of herbs to the nervous shopkeeper who stood behind a small wooden counter.

They always seemed to have a lot of power behind their words. Even the way they spoke was as intimidating and as firm as their outer appearance.

"Well, it was a pleasure meeting you, sir Malyspi!" Marles beamed. But right as we were about to sneak out, the room began to fill with a tense aura.

My ears picked up the sound of a low growl that briefly echoed in the Malyspi's throat before he whipped around and began walking towards us in a menacing way. That was when I realized my mistake far, far too late.

"*Malyspi?* Calling us that is an insult to our race and therefore insulting our great emperor. The Celegons like you who mock us, the sheer audacity of it! We are the Malypsi and don't you dare forget it. Now run off before I do something everyone will regret," he barked as he put his nose scarily close to Marles' face.

Not wanting to risk inciting violence, I quickly pulled at Marles' tail and bolted out of the shop. We ran, and continued to run until we were out of the market area entirely and in a cramped and secluded alleyway. Within moments of stopping, I felt compelled to let out the loudest laughs I had in a while. Marles joined in too and we both laughed until our lungs got tired.

"That Malyspi, was really something," Marles giggled as I tried to repress my laughter.

"No Marles, it's *Malypsi*! You shouldn't dare insult them like that or we will endanger the trades!" I jokingly scolded him as I began to wheeze from laughing too much.

It seems I had forgotten how prideful Malypsi can be too, which was a surprise to both of us. Regardless, I knew I wanted this gleeful feeling to last forever. I did feel like the day was off to a great start. At least, until I remembered I owed Marles that explanation.

Chapter Nine: Revelation

We were temporarily split from one another as we each sought different targets to procure our breakfast. Mine was a poor distracted merchant; my efforts had landed me a rather hearty and large welon—my favorite of all fruits. In the alleyway we had promised to meet back up at, I held it in my paws as I waited for Marles' return. It was torture on my stomach.

I caressed the soft, pink flesh of the fruit as I envisioned the moment I would sink my teeth into it. It was all I could do to distract myself from my growing hunger as Marles acquired his own meal. Hopefully, he had not run into any trouble, but the thought of him getting into shenanigans made me crack a smile. He had grown progressively more skilled in his new crafts, especially in the art of persuasion due to his attractiveness. I knew he would be fine, but I could not say the same for my stomach.

I had half the mind to tear into my fruit without hesitation as it rumbled impatiently. Mindful of conserving food as I was, I desperately wanted to eat this gem as soon as I could. Finally, my ears began to pick up a familiar walking pattern approaching. Though, I was not expecting him to return with such a sizable sack in his possession. He gleefully placed it down in front of me as I began to scope out its contents.

"Someone sure was hungry," I remarked as I curiously peered into the sack. It was jammed full of a variety of roots, mostly consisting of spicy torus. "So I guess you chose quantity over quality. None of these can compare to this majestic creation," I smirked as I held up my prized welon.

He simply shook his head and sat across from me as we began to fill our stomachs. Unfortunately, my hunger was greater than my will to savor every bite and my welon was gone within seconds. So I began to watch Marles as he awkwardly chewed on a hard, uncooked toru root.

"Are you not going to roast them?" I questioned as it would certainly make it more easy to eat. Not only that, but when cooked they lost some of their spiciness and melded into something slightly sweet.

"Well, they do have more nutrients like this," he replied as he continued to nibble on the thick root. "Did you want me to roast one for you?"

"They are very tasty when roasted," I started as I wished I still had more of my welon left. "May I request one roasted?" I asked as his face lit up with a warm smile.

I watched as he held a new toru root in between his paws and ignited it without singeing his fur. Watching a root shrivel under the heat was always an interesting display. But at the moment my attention was gravitated towards Marles' eyes. Seeing the flames dance in them made me appreciate the fire talent even more.

"I'm surprised you've become so health centered as of late. N-not that it's a bad thing. Just ironic since you seem to be doing much better these days. Haven't had an *incident* in a while either. So glad those aren't frequent anymore." I smiled cheekily as his face began to redden.

I would never tell him this under normal circumstances, but he always looked really adorable when embarrassed. Though, normally, he would turn away from me when he was, so I tended to treasure these rare occasions. He was quick to recompose himself though and handed me a freshly roasted toru root. It was quite warm, but thankfully not hot to the touch.

Sinking my teeth into the softened root felt quite refreshing. While certainly not as good as the welon, the spicy-sweet flavor of the toru root was delicious. On top of that, it also warmed my mouth and throat when I swallowed. Why Marles would not roast his escaped my mind. After scarfing down my second food item, my stomach was filled enough and I would be good for a while. Marles seemed to be fine with only eating one thing, which I was a little skeptical about but I concluded he was probably still full from the night before.

Before we got ready to leave the alleyway, thoughts from earlier filled my mind. There was no need to drag them out; it would be best to just get them out and over with.

"Hey Marles? I think I'm ready now. You know, to fill you in on some things," I stated as his ears perked up with curiosity. "But not here. There's a place, it's a little high up but I think we can manage," I stated as the both of us began to stand to our feet.

He sealed up the sack best he could and slipped it inside his backpack, though it was too full to completely close. After he was sorted, I led him down a few familiar alleyways we passed on our way to our destination. These alleyways had a reputation for being dangerous for lone Celegons, but that would hardly be an issue with Marles by my side.

As we continued down the narrow passageways, we came across a certain open space that was surrounded by the stone walls of buildings. It had not changed from the last time I saw it. I was a little surprised that someone had not found a use for it by now. Marles had caught me gawking at the empty area, so I quickly resumed walking towards the real destination to avoid confusion. It was not long after that we arrived at the base of the tall tower that sat close to the edge of Tarrina town's thick wall. I glanced over at Marles as he examined the rocky structure.

The tower was slightly taller than most larger trees. Though because the rocks stuck out in such a way, climbing should be somewhat simpler. Still, I was a little concerned. While I was not worried for his safety as his climbing skills had improved drastically since meeting me, the fate of the vegetables was not looking too good on his back.

"If you want, I could fly your bag up with me," I offered with a smile as he shook his head and grinned. My smile stiffened, but then I simply let out a resigned sigh and extended my wings. "Just know that I will hold you accountable if any of that food splatters on the ground," I scoffed before making my ascent.

With a quick burst, I began running up the side of the tower with my wings outstretched. The wind rustled through my fur as my feet scampered along the rocky wall. In just a few moments I was already at the top, with thankfully no other Celegons to greet me.

I sighed in relief as I retracted my wings and went to peer over the edge to watch Marles climb. He was a little slower than usual, most likely from the extra weight from his backpack, but he would soon be up here in a matter of seconds. His eyes seemed to be unusually determined at the moment; it probably took a lot of effort to make sure he did not drop his backpack. When he approached the siding I debated offering my paw in assistance, but my stubbornness forbade it. Soon we were both able to gaze over the entire town and the vast, mostly uninteresting surrounding area.

"This would be a great spot to come during the night," Marles remarked, clearly hinting at the wax clumps that would be undoubtedly scattered all over the town by then.

It would be almost ideal, if the wind did not insist on being so rough at higher altitudes. Even now it was quite windy, though at night it would be significantly colder. My paws briefly ran over my arms in an effort to warm them.

"Maybe if you don't mind freezing. There have been rumors that another cold year is coming," I stated, hoping that it would not come true.

Around every ten years or thereabouts, the weather would gradually become frigid and remain that way for a little over a year in time; though, they were mostly unpredictable. While they typically showed up every ten years, they sometimes came a bit sooner and would sometimes last longer than a year. Food would become even scarcer and monsters hungrier before the first icefall; it was a very dangerous time, indeed. Marles had yet to deal with the hardships of a cold year, so for his sake I hoped that the weather would simply stay cool.

"Well they are just rumors; plus, I'm certain my talent will do us well in keeping us warm. Even in this wind!" he smiled delightedly as a flame began to emit from the tip of his tail.

"N-no I'm good! Perfectly warm at the moment. Don't need your flames swirling around with these currents," I muttered that last part, but it was obvious he heard what I said.

Still, he respected my wishes to not be engulfed in his fire and extinguished the bit on his tail. While I was certainly aware that he was careful to avoid burning others with his talent, I did not want to get sidetracked on why I brought him up here in the first place. As much as I wanted to just go along with the day normally, I knew that the longer I waited to say what has been bothering me, the harder it would be.

"Now the reason I brought you here, it's regarding something especially important. I'm honestly not even sure if I'm 'ready' but I feel it will be easier on me if I get it over with now," I started as Marles' eyes began to focus as he slipped off his backpack.

The both of us positioned ourselves somewhat comfortably on the mildly warm roof of the tower. Even before I had started talking, I could feel my throat tighten with anticipation.

"I think it's time I filled you in on this part of my past, more specifically about *her*."

As I recollected my thoughts, I began to tell Marles a fragment of my history. Things I assumed I would have kept buried otherwise.

"I met her when I was barely thirteen—my mentor. She went by Alise, although I'm quite certain that it was an alias and not her true name. Through her, I was taught how to make a living through thievery. Learned a few things, some useful, some forgettable. Like how Tarrina Town is great for picking up the most recent information from informants and that the towers—just like this one—are the best places to be when the sky darkens," I explained to him as he nodded. I then quickly added, "We will not be up here after nightfall unless you want to become frozen stiff."

"She sounds like someone worthy of your admiration," Marles chuckled and I was quick to counter that statement.

"False. She was a crooked Celegon who wanted nothing more than to use me for her personal gain. Especially when we discovered my innate skill for entering places undetected. You should be lucky that I let you off so easily, she would have never considered a Celegon such as yourself to mentor," I dramatically declared as I puffed out my chest with a bit of pride.

"You say that, but you seem to be happy about it," Marles pointed out as I quickly corrected that by relaxing my facial muscles. "But Alise was someone you had respected?"

"Naturally. Meeting her was the first step I took onto the path of true freedom," I said as a grin found its way back to my face. Although, there was an unsavory reminder of what I went through to get to that point. "I did not willingly become her apprentice. When I was rushing through the forest, she found me and pinned me against a tree," I continued as Marles leaned closer as his eyes brimmed with cautious interest.

"All I wanted to do was get away—I wasn't thinking clearly. Initially she tried to calm me down, but I kept fighting and flailing about. So... she cut into a blood vessel on my neck which caused me to pass out. When I came to, I was in the dome and she was treating my wound and scolding me for making it so difficult for her, Since I had nowhere else to go, I ended up assisting her in her crimes until my 'graduation.'"

"W-wait, so she attacked and then kidnapped you?" Marles sputtered as I tried my best to resist laughing as this was to be a serious conversation.

It was a truly terrifying experience when it happened, since it was right after I finally grasped onto wanting something in life it was threatened to be taken away. Violence among Celegons was something of a rarity, but I suppose it was slightly less rare years ago. Murder was completely off the table entirely, but threatening did exist and would seldom occur.

"Yes, she certainly was *unique* in her recruitment. But aside from that, I can safely say no bludgeonings or kidnappings happened again. My neck has long since healed though, so no need to look so worried," I smiled as he appeared to calm back down a bit.

Alise was certainly not the best mentor. Other than vaguely telling me what to do or bragging about her accomplishments, there was not a lot of teaching in our relationship. Still, I vastly preferred her company to anyone else at the time. So I did everything I could to stay useful as her apprentice. She rarely praised me when I did well, made sure to pick on me when I did mess up; still, even after causing her obvious inconveniences from time to time, she never told me to get lost.

"Honestly, she was a no-good Celegon at her core. Only really out for herself. Wanted nothing to do with her last living blood relative. But I was someone that proved useful to her. That's why I was kept around. And in the very end I was..." My voice trailed off as I failed to pronounce the final word.

Abandoned.

Thinking about her in detail like this made my heart feel heavy. Even the good memories with her were painful to remember, probably much more so from telling Marles bits and pieces about her. Eventually, I got to the point where that sour memory resurfaced at full force which caused me to clench my jaw. I rose from my sitting position and made my way to the edge of the tower and propped my arms up on the short stone railing. The images in my mind were clouding my brain, almost preventing me from thinking coherently.

Marles soon appeared at my left, leaning slightly over the railing, briefly gazing at the horizon before focusing on me. His presence was calming and warm, especially when he gave me a reassuring smile. Moving onto the next topic certainly would not be easy, but him being like this did help.

"Well anyways, she's long since dead now as you probably suspected. It's been about six years since I last saw her. She had left Tarrina town for a while to supposedly go on a solo heist. There were times I didn't trust her, but I really believed her that time. I never wanted her to go on that heist, especially since in the days before she left she seemed so sad about something. It took around a week to pass before I heard of her death."

My voice began to tremble slightly and I was worried about carrying on, but I needed to finish what I started.

"But it wasn't just the news of her death that hurt me. Alise died because she trusted monsters. She wasn't leaving to go on a heist, she left to go see the monsters she assumed were her friends. They're monsters after all, so of course they devoured her. For one of the cleverest Celegons I knew, how could she be so trusting?"

Tears began to streak down my fur as I internally berated myself for it. For the second time today I found myself being embraced by Marles. Though, this time I felt less confused and more relaxed. Marles was really rare indeed; he made me feel that crying about it was okay.

"You don't have to say any more. I don't want you to have to relive this pain," he said in a soft, comforting tone as he held me in a firmer grasp.

As kind as he was at the moment, he was wrong. I was not reliving pain, but finally letting it out after years of keeping it bottled. It felt freeing to be able to express those emotions without worry of getting reprimanded or ignored. To share these feelings with someone who actually seemed to care, was pure bliss. As I gently pulled myself away from him, I saw that his eyes appeared to be wet but without any tear stains in his fur.

"Alise's grandfather, a Celegon who goes by Z, showed up last night after my talk with Blubelle. His body was covered in injuries that could have only been from a monster attack. I have no idea why, but that lineage, they sympathize with monsters and they've suffered for it. Marles, I want you to promise me that you'll never try to befriend a monster. It already worries me enough that I'll lose you by other means. I already know very well that you'll sneak away to paint them sometimes, so don't get any ideas!" I cried as I put all the energy I had into not stuttering over my words.

"You... worry that I'll get killed? Lyla, I-I promise you I won't."

My teary eyes widened as they bore witness to something they had not seen before. Streams of thick, heavy tears were rushing out of Marles' sunset eyes. Seeing him like that only made me cry harder and then it was me who found myself embracing him. His tears began to drip down my backside as his head rested neatly on my shoulder. We remained like that for a good while before either of us shifted away.

It was very refreshing that I had no feelings of regret sharing these things with him; it made me slightly more optimistic about sharing more with him in the future. There were many details that had been left unsaid, but for now I was just grateful to have the initial conversation over with. Right now I just wanted to be like this, in a vulnerable yet comfortable position. Though in time I would give more information if needed.

My emotions were still a little frazzled, but I had never felt more secure than I did right then. Continuing to hug him could cause my emotions to fluctuate into something less stable, so I decided to get out of that position once I had calmed down enough. As I pulled away from Marles I noticed that while his eyes were now only damp, his downcast expression still lingered. I quickly blinked my remaining tears away before sharing a warm smile with him. My heart flickered a little as the slightest spark became apparent in those twin sunsets.

"Come on Marles, lighten up a little. There's still plenty of daylight left, Celegons to rob and-" I lost my train of thought as he began to smile very genuinely towards me.

"Lyla, it means the world to me that you could open up to me like that. I know it wasn't easy, but I want you to know that I care for you and will always listen to anything you have to say. I'll also be more careful when I venture out to paint." He smiled as my body began to feel pleasantly warm.

I could tell the direction he wanted the conversation to go in; it was painfully obvious. As much as I would be okay with a friendship evaluation, I just wanted things to go back to normal for the time being. And what better way to do that than to mess with him a little?

"Yeah it sure was. Hard to trust someone who used to eat poison, but you seem alright now. Though I can't be too sure if you'll ditch me to run your own plant shop at some point," I said in a joking manner as his expression changed.

Maybe I should have been more direct with what I wanted instead of sacrificing Marles' sanity. His tail started twitching in an irritable way and his eyes lost some of their softness.

"I don't take back what I said, but you are really quite-insincere. Even so, I still—" he stopped short as his eyes caught mine. The stark contrast between his usual relaxed and not relaxed glowy eyes was quite striking, making me feel a bit nervous. I felt it all the more as his expression changed into a devilish smirk; which was not at all common on his usually soft face. "You're right," he went on slowly, "we shouldn't waste daylight. So instead why don't we do something *fun*, something perfect to do while in a secure town like this? Maybe we can see what brings out your inner romantic," he grinned cheekily as I stared at him in confusion.

My stomach twinged a little at the possible implication, but his expression and tone hinted at something else entirely.

"Romance? What exactly is it that you are going on about?" I asked as his suspicious smile remained.

"Why Lyla, you've never been on a romantic excursion have you?" His grin widened as my confusion grew. That confusion then morphed into agitation as I questioned his motives.

"Of course not; I'm more focused on keeping us alive than trying to find out who my mate is. Are you trying to make a point here or just insult my lack of suitors?" I almost growled but refrained from doing so until I uncovered his intentions. His tail swished back and forth aggressively before he stopped and began to sigh.

"It's just that since you've never been on one and I have been on many, it only makes sense for me to share my knowledge since I'm quite experienced." He grinned before staring into my eyes again.

My emotions still were not under control and I could feel tears finding their way back to my eyes. His expression softened and he appeared to be drowning in guilt as he covered his face. Then it hit me—I was not the only one who felt emotionally vulnerable at the moment. That sort of made sense for his odd behavior.

"F-forgive me Lyla, I don't know what came over me. I felt that my feelings were disregarded and I really didn't mean to come across as arrogant." He turned away from me as I suspected he was quite embarrassed over the whole ordeal.

I was no longer frustrated with him and instead empathized as I knew where he was coming from. He wanted to have a longer, more meaningful conversation with me afterwards and I just wanted to move on by doing something spontaneous. Since I was not being serious, he probably decided to do the same with me before thinking it through.

"Listen Marles, we're both clearly under a lot of stress right now, but I promise to talk more about that stuff later. Saying what I did took a lot more out of me than I imagined. I cherish your feelings, honestly. I feel like I somehow transferred my grief on to you, so I feel like I'm to blame for that. So, you know what? I accept your offer. Teach me everything there is to know about courting." I grinned as he removed his paws from his face and turned back to face me. He seemed to have calmed down a bit, but nonetheless looked bewildered at my wanting to know.

"Well to tell you the truth, I only really said that to catch you off guard. As you know, I was forced to court while living as an Iseirre. That knowledge is wasted on me though, since I'm not sure I'll need it anymore. But that's not to say you won't. I think it could also be fun to have you as *my* apprentice in romantic gestures." He smiled and I could not help but double over with laughter.

Thinking that I could use that advice one day was amusing on its own, but adding that I would be his apprentice took it to a whole new level. The prospect of it certainly seemed interesting, and with Marles being an instructor it did promise to be entertaining.

"Alright, I shall be your apprentice for the rest of the day. You have until the sun goes down to demonstrate these 'romantic gestures'," I giggled a bit as his eyes lit up with delight.

He seemed a little taken aback, but otherwise elated at the situation. Marles straightened himself up a little and smoothed out a few bits in his fur as I waited in anticipation.

"Apprentice Skyli, your first task is to simply wait here. Lay on your back and gaze up at the sky, then imagine you are talking to your future mate," he instructed before he left my sight.

I sighed and stared up at the infinitely blue sky. So his plan was to leave me alone on the tower and not be aware of my surroundings; perhaps he was setting up a prank. Still I did agree to be his apprentice and hoped that I would not be staring at the sky all day. Thinking about what I would say to a future mate was hard though, since I would not know much about them anyways. Suddenly a thought came into my mind that seemed much more appetizing.

"You have the most beautiful eyes I have ever seen. Always glowing so brightly and only rivaling the most beautiful of sunsets."

Chapter Ten: Iridescent

Only one thing was on my mind: how long had it been since I had fallen asleep in the middle of the day like this? I was a bit surprised and unsure of how it happened, but I did know for a fact that I dozed off. My body would not have felt so relaxed and stress free otherwise. Well, at least until I remembered why I never sleep out in the open.

Springing up from the warm stone surface, I frantically scanned for my satchel. An uncomfortable feeling arose in my chest as I began to panic at the loss of it and everything inside. My orbs, my emergency emeri, and—most importantly—my dome had been snatched away from me because I had been foolish enough to fall asleep. If Marles found out, it would definitely put a taint on our trust; especially since it meant I had lost some of his valuables as well. I had to do everything I could to find this culprit. If I was lucky they may not have left town yet.

This feeling of suspense was thankfully short lived as I heard a chuckle coming from behind me. I quickly whipped around to face the culprit himself, perched on the thick stone railing. A sense of respect washed over me; I was impressed that he was able to take my satchel from me while I was helplessly asleep. Before I could express my admiration of his skill, a little realization had just kicked in. He had only managed to acquire it because I had been foolish enough to put myself in such a vulnerable position.

Saying I was merely embarrassed would be putting it lightly. I was a hypocrite; I had once explained to Marles that Celegons who sleep out in the open were either suicidal or prime targets. And yet, here he was, catching me in a nap. It was a small consolation that the needed sleep had helped me regain my level-headedness so I could solve this situation rationally.

"How long?" I questioned as he eyed me curiously. "If you don't answer, it could become very tempting to push you off that ledge."

His eyes widened before he began to pout. Though, his courage was in full form, for he continued to remain on the ledge despite the empty threat. Soon enough, he began grinning at me, his tail twitching in an annoyed pattern as a brief chill went down my spine.

"Aren't you being a little unkind, talking to your date like that? As I recall, you agreed to be my apprentice for the day," he said in a somewhat sulking manner as he turned his head away. "But to answer your question, I've been gone for a few hours. As you can see, there's still a bit of daylight left."

My head turned back to the sky. It was beginning to turn just slightly pink, which meant that the evening would soon be approaching. I felt a twinge of guilt for being asleep for so long, but also curious about what Marles was doing during those hours. This also meant that he would have left me here alone all this time regardless if I had slept or not. I stepped towards Marles as my tail twitched aggressively.

"Aren't you being a little cruel, leaving your date alone like that?" I started, mocking his words from before.

Hold a second—he'd said the word date. My mind was a little puzzled at the situation, but I continued to make my point. I gently thwacked the top of his head with my paw, my smile playful. I felt a small sense of satisfaction as a guilty glint appeared in his eyes. He quickly shook his head and began to show me a warmer demeanor.

"Sorry for that; things took a lot longer than I expected, but I suppose that's no excuse. I'm relieved that nothing bad happened. Well, except for this," he said as he handed me my satchel with a slight smirk. I quickly slipped it back across my shoulder. "Forgive me for being so inconsiderate," he smiled hesitantly; guilt still lingered in his eyes.

That was when I noticed something else that was a little different about him, something I should have noticed the moment I saw him. Not only in how he was acting, but that his appearance was a tad off from how he normally looked. The most notable change was that he'd donned his red scarf, which explained why he'd taken my satchel—aside from purely tormenting me. His fur seemed well groomed—more so than usual, especially his hair tuft. That seemed especially glossy and soft. He also smelled as if he had been rolling around in pleasantly scented flowers. Though these were minor improvements to his usual appearance, part of me felt like saying something I would regret.

"Alright then, so what's your plan?" I asked and Marles' smile grew brighter.

Instead of outright explaining it to me, he instead gestured for me to follow him as he started to climb down the tower. I went after him, but instead used my wings to glide down to the bottom and waited a few seconds for him to join me. The scarf hindered him briefly by getting swept up by the breeze and obstructing his view, which made my mouth curl up into a small smile. Once down, he began leading me through the same alleyways we had passed through to get to the tower.

The destination was a place I remembered quite fondly as it was where I first used my ice talent. Though Marles had no idea about the nostalgic value the place had for me, bringing it up now was furthest from my mind. The space had been made over, and was hardly recognizable.

"Marles, you spent those hours solely working on this?"

My mouth fell slightly agape as my eyes rounded at the sight. It must have taken a lot of effort; in fact, it was quite impressive he was able to muster enough energy to do this in a full day, let alone a few hours. Green and flowery foliage was spread unevenly across the surrounding stone walls while some was strung way over the ground giving it a canopy effect. The ground was now mossy and refreshing to the touch, and the entire area was pleasing to my sense of smell. But the most eye-catching thing was in the middle of the quaint area: a giant mass of various flower petals.

Though I was a little worried about all the energy Marles had used, I still smiled delightedly at his efforts at putting together such a lovely scene. This would be a more preferable memory of the place I got mugged at.

"Marles you really didn't have to go through all this trouble but-"

"I did!" Marles interrupted with a bright grin on his face. "It's easy to always be on edge in nature, when danger could be lurking at almost any corner. You deserve a chance to be in a beautiful environment that you can feel safe in," he stated as my eyes stared at the scenery, taking it all in with a sense of appreciation. My tail had started to sway back and forth with excitement, and it was hard to contain it.

"Well—as I was going to say—I really appreciate the effort you took to transform this place. What you did here, it's amazing Marles." I beamed as his eyes lit up.

His tail, too, began to sway with excitement. He then trotted over to the flower petal pile and took a few of the purple colored petals in his paws. He then approached me with a grin as he began to place them in my hair tuft. I flinched a little as I was not expecting it; it was certainly a silly romantic gesture.

"And now I look ridiculous," I lightly laughed as Marles' smile faded for a moment. He then brushed my fur gently across my head and removed his paw.

"Actually, you look very ravishing. The petals especially draw attention to your eyes. They're really beautiful. Iridescent even." He paused for a moment as he stared into my eyes as his sunsets appeared to gleam. I suppose romantic gestures really can be captivating. Though, he very quickly became flustered and replied with, "A-and that is a perfect example on how to flirt with a love interest!" He then smiled triumphantly and gave a slight bow as I could not help but chuckle. Since it was a technique, I suppose it would be natural for me to demonstrate it back to him.

I went to the pile of petals and began to gather orange, yellow and pink variants in my clutches. Then I approached Marles and placed the assortment neatly into his hair tuft. Even with the dark red tint at the ends of his tuft, the colors did in fact put most of the focus back on his eyes. Though even without the petals I never had any trouble getting distracted by them.

"You truly have the most remarkable eyes. They're always so vibrant and whenever I see them glimmer, I'm overcome with happiness. Because of them, I've grown to appreciate sunsets even more than I had before," I stated as I stared into his eyes. The eternal sunsets were as glowy as ever, but they soon appeared to have sparks of worry in them.

"V-very good, my apprentice. Making compliments personable is far more appealing than just saying a common phrase. Not that there's anything wrong with those either! But what can be an even more romantic gesture is-" he paused mid sentence and skipped on over to the petal pile. "Pleasant surprises!" he exclaimed as he whisked hundreds of petals into the air.

I watched as the many petals gently floated down on their way back to the ground in various places, now separate from their mound. Seeing them all briefly dance in the air definitely caught me off guard. It was something so simple, yet the effect was incredibly powerful on my senses. What caught my attention afterwards was a small banquet of roasted goods, which were formerly hidden under the petals. In addition to the flowery breeze that tickled the inside of my nose, I could now smell the scent of a delicious meal.

If it were not for the flowers masking the scent, other Celegons would have undoubtedly caught a whiff and stolen it for themselves. So not only was it a nice surprise, but very clever on Marles' part too. Still, I considered us lucky that no one had come by during Marles' brief absence. I quickly joined Marles by the food and looked at it in delight. It appeared to consist of the same toru roots Marles had stolen earlier as well as a singular water nymph.

Water nymphs were especially tasty and filling, so it was very nice to see one in the mix. The limbless creatures were quite elusive and hard to capture for those even with water talents, and hence have had a consistently rising price. When alive, the flesh was coated with hard scales. Cooking them makes those inedible scales peel right off. For a creature with no eyes and only a swimming tail, they were surprisingly hardy and fast swimmers.

My last efforts at eating a water nymph were demolished by a certain Ariele, so it was fulfilling to get another chance. Though, given how small it was, I assumed Marles and I would have to fight over it.

I joined Marles' side as he plopped himself on the soft, mossy, petal-covered ground. My eyes watched as he went straight for the water nymph; I wondered if I had already lost my chance. But instead of devouring it for himself, he took the roasted water nymph that was in his paws and handed it over to me.

"It's typically tradition to present a gift on a first romantic outing. Though in your case, you'd be on the receiving end." He smiled as I took the nymph into my paws.

While I certainly would not mind gobbling it up for myself, I felt compelled to share the tiny thing with Marles. So I thanked Marles for his generous gift and began to nibble at the delicacy as an idea began to brew in my mind. After all, as his apprentice I should be showing I could be capable of doing the same. After roughly a third of the water nymph had been consumed, it was time to enact my plan. It was almost tortuous to my taste buds to stop gracing them with this flavor, but it had to be done.

"Marles, I happen to have a gift for you too," I grinned as his eyes sparkled with curiosity. "But to give it to you, could you please close your eyes for a moment?" I asked as he cautiously began to close his eyes.

I stared at what was left of the water nymph sadly, briefly lamenting that I would not be able to enjoy anymore of its savory flavor. Then I got closer to Marles, water nymph in paw, before I stopped briefly to examine his features once more.

He looked especially radiant today, perhaps due to the atmosphere we were currently in. Possibly from the extra grooming he had put into making his fur smoother. No, Marles always had a certain charm to him I could not describe so simply. Even with his exuberant eyes closed, I had this conscious desire to hug him again. Hugging him would definitely make for an interesting surprise "gift", and as a bonus I could eat the water nymph.

As gutsy as I was, that would be hard to cover up. Sure he was attractive, but I knew by now it was something else. As much as I would not mind to stare at him a little longer, it would be cruel of me to keep him like this. I began to inch the water nymph closer and closer to his mouth. Out of all situations that have definitely been more stressful, this was one that got my heart pumping.

This ultimately led to me aggressively shoving the water nymph into his mouth, definitely not as gently as I planned. Naturally, his eyes snapped open the moment it had passed the barrier of his formerly closed mouth. They locked into mine briefly filled with shock before the taste of the water nymph began to kick in. After a bit of chewing, he swallowed the portion with a refreshing look on his face. He then stopped to glance at the lower part of my face for a moment before shaking himself a little.

"T-thank you for sharing. It was delicious and a nice surprise," he said as his voice trailed off a little towards the end. He seemed a little out of it for some reason.

"You're sure about that? I probably could have thought of something better." I sighed a little before locking eyes with him again. He seemed to be studying me intently, but he quickly caught on to his behavior and looked away.

A wicked grin found its way to my mouth. He was expecting something different. Once he saw the glint in my eyes, he visibly tensed.

"Was Marley expecting a hug? A sweet, tender embrace as some would describe it?" I asked him, mockingly as I wanted to see if it would get under his skin. As expected, he went wide-eyed and jolted in response. The nickname always seemed to rile him whenever I used it.

"O-of course not!" he retorted as he crossed his arms. "Although if you had wanted to, I would be fine with it," he continued as my chest started to feel a little warm after hearing it. At least until he rambled on with, "For the sake of the lesson! I could even demonstrate how I—"

"Please spare me. I have no interest in hearing of how you hugged others you weren't really interested in," I cut him off as a sick feeling began to brew in my stomach. "That aside... would you really accept any type of romantic advance from me like that?"

He seemed to ponder on that question for a good few seconds. It was hard for me to decipher what was going on in that head of his. But soon one of his usual, calm smiles emerged on his face.

"Y-yeah. I mean, anything coming from you will be special to me. I'm happy to share things I know just as you have been with me these past few weeks. You're a good Celegon and I've come to think quite highly of you," he said, causing my stomach to behave strangely again. He really meant those words?

"Are you that certain of that? I don't believe I am the best role model. But... Thank you. Now, shall we finish our meal before others are drawn to the scent?" I suggested as Marles happily agreed. It was clear that he did not seem to want to prolong that topic either. Food filling my stomach would surely make me think clearly again.

The two of us began to partake in the lesser, but still good food options. The sweet flavor of the roots definitely was not as good as the savory water nymph, but I loved being able to eat them roasted at all.

Marles' fire talent sure was convenient. Without him, I would never be able to enjoy roasted vegetables as much as I have been. And his plant talent, while unhelpful in combat, has helped me appreciate nature so much more. Even without his talents, Marles was a truly fine companion to have by my side. There would be no one better to have as my trusted friend.

He would be a fine mate.

That was what I really thought. Something I had actually considered telling him during our courting lesson. But things were fine like this. We could stay. Just a little longer.

A piercing scream filled the air. The formerly pleasant atmosphere was decimated as my fur began to stand up. The sound most certainly came from the other side of the wall, where monsters were bound to be. A protective instinct suddenly washed over my senses and I had an overwhelming desire to help the Celegon in danger. One look was all it took to convey that to Marles, and he hastily stored the rest of the remaining roots in his pack before we rushed to climb to the top of the wall.

Completely forgetting I had wings, I clawed my way up to the top with Marles tailing close behind. Soon we pulled ourselves over the top to examine the source of the commotion. There were two monsters in sight, though they were much smaller than the normal beasts. Even so, the two of them had ganged up on a lone Celegon who had been backed up against the wall. The outer wall was quite smooth, so climbing in from the outside would be difficult. Unfortunately, it seemed as if they had no strength left to fly.

The monsters had them cornered, bearing their ugly fangs uncomfortably close to the still breathing Celegon. Suddenly, one of the monsters lunged forward and its teeth pierced the Celegon's leg. At that moment, my mind went blank and my body reacted. I had leapt off the wall and dived down onto that monster's back. Panic hit me only after I realized what I had done, but now was not the time to lose focus.

A rush of adrenaline began coursing through me as I dug my sharpened claws into the monster's ragged white back. For extra support, I made sure to latch my tail firmly into its side as it began to try and throw me off. It roared violently and shook quite hard, but I stayed firmly in place as my claws dug deeper. My eyes briefly caught sight of the Celegon; they were bloody, but appeared to be living, no longer the focus of the monsters. My eyes scanned quickly for the other, which was currently being ridden by Marles.

As my claws went under the monster's tough skin, the monster's black blood slowly began to ooze out. A tingling feeling began to form in my paws, and I knew I needed to do something else fast. Concentrating on bringing out my ice talent, magical energy began to course through my body. My paws and tail grew cold. A blast of ice began to emanate from my claws and tail. They slowly started to freeze the monster's blood. This caused it to become briefly immobile, which gave me enough time to slash deep cuts at the side of its neck.

I began to hear my own heartbeat resonate in my ears. What in the world had even come over me? This entire situation was unnecessary; I am no monster hunter. Yet I was fighting this creature like my life depended on it. Alise would have disapproved on several notes. But I was in too deep to back out now.

It let out weak, but angry cries as I hacked away at its tough and vulnerable neck. The process was frightening and exhausting, and close to the monster's mouth—which could regain movement at any time. Wincing a bit as a bit of blood burned my fur, I managed to do enough damage to be sure it would not survive. But this was far from over. I quickly raced to where Marles was, only to see him being thrown off the other monster. He landed well enough, but his backpack had slipped off during the process.

The monster eyed his backpack and roared before tearing into it and destroying its contents. While I was sure he had nothing valuable in there other than food, it enraged me to see the monsters obliterate something that belonged to him. Joining his side, I used more of my ice talent as I focused on the monster's head. He followed by climbing back up on its back and forcibly shoving his claws into the monster's skull. It looked painful, but I continued to use my ice talent until the monster finally dropped to the ground.

Exchanging tired but relieved glances, our eyes checked each other for signs of injury. Other than a few minor burns, messied fur and a dirty scarf, the both of us were fine. We then made our way to the injured Celegon. He was thankfully still alive, but in a lot of pain as he clutched the bleeding leg. He was vaguely similar to Basion from Ariele's group in appearance, but differed in that he had ruby colored eyes. A forced grin appeared on his pained face as he looked up at Marles and I.

"Thanks, I'll be sure to pay you back for the rescue." He winced as I took out the last emeri that was in my satchel. I began to use its juices to treat the open wound.

"You better. Emeri is not cheap, you know. But right now let's focus on getting you to a safer place," I stated after using up the last of the juice.

I then extended my paw to him to help him stand up. Only after he grabbed it, it was clear that even with the emeri's help he could not walk on his own. His big red eyes were filled with a pleading stare and I could not help but feel obligated to assist him.

"I can carry you on my back if needed," Marles suggested as the orange Celegon happily nodded.

With no backpack to carry anymore, it was easy to have the slim ruby eyed Celegon sit neatly on his back. Marles moved to stand with ease on four limbs. It was such a shame that he'd lost his backpack, but at least he was still alive and uninjured after the attack. We glanced over at the monster carcasses briefly, and the backpack's remains that were scattered across the rocky soil. While monster pelts and materials were valuable, we simply did not have the time or energy to drag them into the town's entrance, which was a decent walk away.

Our priority now was to take this Celegon to safety and get a reward out of him. A task that would prove to be far more difficult than it seemed.

Chapter Eleven: Encumbrance

From the moment we had decided to assist the injured Celegon, things were only bound to become more chaotic. Though, since there was a reward in it for us, it did not seem all too troubling to simply take him into town. There was a reason that Alise told me time and time again not to do what she referred to as "honest work".

Within the first few seconds of turning our backs to the carcasses, several gusts of wind blew through my fur from overhead. My head turned around to see five Celegons slowly starting to gather around the monsters we had slain. They were lowly scavengers. While scavengers certainly had a place in this world, it was downright disrespectful to scavenge while the original subduers were still in eyeview. It was true we were starting to walk away, but I was not about to let them simply take them without any sort of compensation.

I gave Marles a signal to keep moving which he seemed a bit skeptical about, but still kept going. Then I promptly trotted up to the excitable group as they eyed me curiously. One of them started to approach me; they had light brown fur and eyes that matched Marles' fur. I was not picking up any vibes of hostility at the moment, but it never hurt to be overly cautious.

"Hey there! We saw what happened from above, you two did awesome work taking out those uglies. Even if they are on the smaller side, pretty impressive." He grinned as I eyed him curiously. His demeanor was upbeat and friendly, but that meant nothing if he was simply trying to take advantage of the situation.

"If you saw what was happening, then why didn't you help?" I questioned as the green eyed Celegon put up his paws.

"Hey, hey, there's no need for any hostility here. You two looked like you had things covered, if needed I'm sure some of us would have swooped in," he smiled; though, I was not certain of how truthful he was being. But he was right, there was no need for things to get tense.

"Those monsters, are you willing to pay for their parts? We did the killing after all as you all saw," I stated as I firmed my stance.

I could tell by the looks in their eyes that they were well aware that I would not be able to take them back on my own, especially not with Marles already carrying an injured Celegon. Still, it is always worth trying to get a payment if possible. He cocked his head slightly as he eyed his fellow Celegons before turning back to me with a coy smile.

"Hm, well since you asked respectfully I suppose there's no harm in giving you a cut. Is a white orb satisfactory enough for ya?" he asked as he pulled a singular white orb from his satchel.

I nodded my head and he tossed the orb over to me. While I would vastly prefer one white orb per monster, at least I managed to get something out of the ordeal. I bid good tidings to the other Celegons before rushing back to Marles, who was still carrying the Celegon towards the town's entrance.

After running up beside him, I flashed him the white orb with a grin as he returned a pleasant smile. The orange furred Celegon was in a far less content mood as he let out a pained groan. He seemed to be anemic from the loss of blood; if only I had an extra emeri to spare. Though I was positive he would not die during the short trip back, especially since the emeri I used had done its job in sealing the open wound. Glancing back towards Marles, I noticed that there was a slight frown on his face.

"Marles, about your bag," I started as we continued to walk beside the outer wall of town.

I felt partly responsible for the backpack's demise, as it would have never met that fate if not for me rushing over the wall. He had that same backpack since we met in his mansion, so it would not be far-fetched to say that he had sentimental attachment to the thing; though, before I could say anything further on the subject, Marles flashed me a hearty smile.

"Lyla don't tell me you're worried about that of all things. Though if you are, I appreciate your consideration. I had nothing valuable in there aside from the leftover roots anyways. And my scarf is still in one piece!" he chimed as I felt less guilty about the situation. At least now I knew that he had no sadness from losing the backpack itself.

"Ah- sorry if I'm interrupting your conversation, but could I humbly ask for another favor?"

The voice came from the orange Celegon, who I had wrongly assumed was now unconscious. He had his head slightly hanging over Marles' right shoulder so his eyes were not visible to either of us.

"We're going to take you into Tarrina town, no need to worry," I said trying to be reassuring as the Celegon began shifting on Marles' back. He tilted his head towards me so that I could now see his ruby eyes, which stared at me with a pitiful expression.

"N-no! There's no time. Please, I beg of you, take me to the forest nearest to here! I have- I need to get there before sundown!" he cried out of desperation as his body began to quiver.

While it was true that Tarrina town was essentially surrounded by nothing but tundra wasteland, there were forests noticeable from a distance. The forest he wished to go to, with a raw calculated estimation, would take at least two hours of walking time. By then it would surely be dark, most likely before we even reach the edge of the forest. The monster density in the area was also fairly high, so getting attacked beforehand was also very probable. And running there was no longer an option because of the injured companion we picked up.

"What's so important in this forest that's worth dragging us along into it? Surely it can wait until you are feeling well enough to make the trip on your own?" I questioned as Marles glanced in the general direction of said forest.

"I-it's my baby, my child. Not even very old and all alone at the edge of the forest. I had to leave her there because of the monsters, though she was small enough to be safely stashed away in a cracked tree. I don't trust that she'll survive much longer, a-and her mother will be so distraught if she finds out I lost her," he bawled as Marles and I looked at each other with different expressions.

I was feeling skeptical as usual and a bit pessimistic in thinking there was a good chance that the child was already devoured by monsters. Assuming the child existed at all. Marles looked especially sympathetic towards him, which was charming in a unique way but a little incautious.

"I don't mind carrying him," Marles smiled as I let out a sigh.

"Marles. It's at least a two hour walk at minimum. I'm not having you carry him all that way on your own," I stated as I caught the ruby eyed Celegon shooting me an apathetic glance.

"Fieres, not *him*," our orange acquaintance huffed before putting on a smile.

For someone desperate for help, he sure was quite uppity. Though I did not fully believe his reason for wanting to go to the forest, I did suspect there had to be something of value there. Perhaps a stash of some kind.

"Fine, we'll take you there. But I expect some sort of compensation for the trouble, otherwise feel free to be left in town until you recover," I told him as he began to contemplate his options. Marles seemed to be in agreement with me until Fieres spoke his next words.

"Even though my darling child's life is at stake you extort me like this?" he sulked aloud as I began to glare at him. If there was solid proof there was a child perhaps I would be more sympathetic. Marles looked worried, but if everything went accordingly, Fieres' "child" would be safe and we would get paid. "Such is the way of this world I suppose. Fine. My child's life is quite invaluable, so I'll give you two white orbs *each* as an act of good faith." He cracked a wide smile. "How's that for a down payment?"

While four white orbs would be a reasonable price for fetching his "child", there was a bit of a problem here. I sensed no sarcasm in his tone, but something felt off. My instincts told me that something very unpleasant was about to happen.

"B-but Fieres, you don't seem to have any sort of bag with you," Marles said as the orange Celegon indeed possessed nothing of the sort.

Fieres then tumbled off Marles' back and landed not so gently on the tough ground. He slowly stood himself up as his weakened body struggled to be supported by only three limbs. What happened next was realistic, but nonetheless horrifying to watch.

The sound of hacking filled the air and I ultimately covered my ears and turned away. Celegons possess a second stomach of sorts, though it is ultimately useless for digesting food. Instead it acts as an empty sack that has debatable uses. Like Fieres here, some Celegons used it as a way of storing small items like orbs. To me though, the idea seemed quite uncomfortable and unsanitary.

Marles appeared as equally disturbed as I was when Fieres finally stopped coughing up objects. The look in his eyes was probably the most fearful I had ever seen him. This must have been the first time he had seen something like this, given how dramatic his reaction was. At least he'd learned something new today, even if it was grotesque. Once that was over, four white orbs, six blue orbs and two red orbs laid out across the ground. There were also various herbs that had been coughed up as well, though they paled in value compared to the orbs.

"Here, take them. It's all I have left after the sepe-" He coughed a bit more, "Separation. Just take them and help me get to the forest."

His tone became serious; a sharp contrast to his earlier disposition. Though that seriousness quickly faded as he dumped the somewhat slimy orbs into my satchel. The condescending grin I caught made me want to cringe. Then he promptly hobbled his way back to Marles and climbed on his back.

At least he had the decency to pay extra after making us bear witness to that atrocity. Or he could have just not wanted to swallow those down again. The process in doing so seemed like it would be painful, though I had no experience myself. I glanced back over towards Marles who still looked a bit shaken and gave him a reluctant smile. Though this was clearly not the romantic ending I had been expecting, at least our day would be financially productive—provided we survived.

The sun that had been warming the cold, dry tundra was now low in the sky after we had been walking for a while. It would most certainly be dark by the time we reached the forest edge; still, we had Marles and his fire talent. Though I would rather Marles not be used in Fieres' search for his precious child. He already seemed quite worn from having to carry him and we were not even halfway in our trek. Not to mention, he should have been tired before now from all the other things he had done on this long day.

"I can carry him for a while if you want Marles," I offered as I crouched down on four limbs. Marles smiled weakly at my suggestion, but Fieres almost immediately objected to this idea.

"No thank you. In all fairness, I should choose who carries me; I did pay you two after all. Besides, I refuse to be carried by any female except for my mate," he chimed as my tail twitched in irritation. "And I'm pretty sure I've already told you that my name is Fieres, so stop referring to me as "him"."

This Celegon had proven to be more of a burden than we initially thought. Marles was clearly struggling from carrying him for so long without a break, yet this stranger chose to be inconsiderate of that. Somehow I doubted that a Celegon like him could have a mate, as I heard that paired Celegons try actively to improve themselves for their mates. It made me wonder what type of Celegon he was before he found his mate, though the idea did not last long. It was pointless to believe anything he said as factual.

"It's fine Lyla, don't worry," Marles huffed; he still managed to smile even though it was clear he was running out of stamina. "So you have a mate? What's she like?" Marles asked as he attempted to make friendly conversation. While Marles' intentions were good-hearted, there was no way it would go smoothly.

"Hm? What's she like, well let's see. For starters I can say that she's easily much better company than you two," he said almost as if he was annoyed by Marles asking. "But," he spoke again, this time with a hint of interest in his voice. "She's also surprisingly open minded. A little wacky, but oddly serene. Very strong, but reserved in her talents. She's my gem." His tone became so soft that it was almost touching.

"By the way, the pair of you aren't mates are you?" he abruptly asked, abolishing the brief nice air to the conversation. Not wanting Marles to use any more energy to talk, I took hold of the conversation.

"No. No we are not," I said rather sharply as I was not in the mood to chat with him.

"Really? Well thank the Sacred Spirit for that. Seeing lovey stuff between other mates while mine is not present grosses me out," he half whined as I repressed saying something both cruel and witty. The redundancy of his words irked me, and I wished he would be silent for the remainder of the trip.

"It would be shocking to see someone like you find a mate at all, now that I think about it. Your figure is neither elegant, nor graceful. I suppose I should at least praise you for being a good cushion," Fieres moaned as he mindlessly made his comment. Seeing the downcast look in Marles' eyes was the worst crime.

Now that. That was completely uncalled for and unnecessary.

"That's it. Marles. Drop him," I growled as I looked Fieres directly in his red eyes. His ears drooped and he seemed completely pathetic. How could he have the gall to say such awful things like that to someone who was trying to assist him?

"Wha- no! We promised we would take him so we can rescue his child," Marles protested as I stared at him in disbelief. Even after being shamed in front of me, he still wanted to do the righteous thing and follow through all the way till the end. "Really Lyla, it's okay."

"But you can't just let him—"

"P-please forgive me. I was only making an observation," Fieres whimpered before squeezing his eyes shut. I could only look at him with disgust. It made me very grateful that I was not the mate to this Celegon. He muttered something about doing better to keep his opinions to himself, but that lasted all of a few minutes.

Unfortunately the meaningless conversations only grew from there. He acted akin to a spoiled wealthy Celegon that never got punished by the harshness of the world. Yes, most Celegons were not overwhelming with kindness, but most at least respected each other to some degree. Fieres was even worse than Blubelle when it came to getting on my nerves; at least she had never gone on about what type of fruit she wanted to be.

"So do you two slay monsters for a living?" Fieres spoke up yet again as I internally groaned. Considering Marles was doing most of the work carrying him, I was the one who answered most of his questions.

"No, we do not," I answered bluntly, hoping it would not lead down an unending pitfall of more meaningless questions.

"I figured. I suppose I will have to accept my death if any spot us before we reach the forest," he said in a despondent tone. While not a direct jab at us, hearing it still tested my patience.

Just a little longer. Then we would ditch him in the forest and leave.

Darkness soon enveloped our surroundings and now only a bit of light lingered on the horizon. Marles' legs were shaking, but thankfully it was just a few more paces until we were under the forest trees. While I was glad we had finally made it to them, there was no telling how much deeper we would have to go. Moreover, I just wanted Marles to finally be able to rest a bit after carrying another Celegon for so long. It was not long after we entered that Marles' limbs collapsed onto the leaf covered dirt.

"So that's it then," Fieres sighed in a disappointed tone as he hopped off Marles' back and stood on his unharmed three limbs.

He began hobbling off into the forest on his own with a look of discontentment on his face as he passed me. Disregarding him, I quickly turned my focus on Marles who was panting and shivering from exhaustion. If I only had more emeri in my satchel, the healing properties would help eradicate his fatigue.

"Easy there, Marles. Just take a minute; you've more than earned that right," I said as I crouched down next to him and began to gently rub his—more than likely—sore back.

He looked up at me with tired eyes as a faint smile appeared on his face. His heavy breathing began to stabilize to a more normal pace and he eventually stood back up on two legs. Everything seemed like it was getting better until Fieres suddenly stormed back on the scene.

"Gross. I thought you said you weren't mates." He sighed as displeasure rolled off his tongue. I removed the paw I still had on Marles' back as he looked at us with a scowl. "Now if you'd stop wasting time, I have a child that needs finding," he asserted with a hefty dose of sourness in his tone as I was filled with resentment for ever helping him.

"Give him a moment, why don't you! He selflessly carried you for over an hour. Certainly he deserves a small part of your precious time for a brief rest!" I spoke up as Fieres narrowed his eyes at me before scoffing.

"Well maybe he should have done a better job at building up his endurance then. Honestly, I have no idea how you could have survived so long being like that," he jeered as he eyed Marles' stomach.

A familiar coldness began to form in the stone of my tail. Thoughts of putting a bit of ice in his fur would be perfectly fine as long as I did not kill him. Shaving off a bit of his ungratefulness would be well deserved.

Luckily for him, a high pitched shrieking noise filled the air which caused me to lose focus. He quickly dashed towards the source almost as if his leg had already healed. My tail flicked back and forth as I turned my attention back to Marles. I saw a short flash of distress in his eyes before they locked with mine. A glint of hope sparked in them as he started to smile.

"We should hurry and help him." He grinned as I nodded in agreement.

Even though it was clear he was lacking energy, he *still* wanted to help the rude Celegon who insulted him just moments ago. Seeing Marles motivated like that, I could not help but go along with him on this. As we started to rush in the direction that Fieres had gone, another eerie sound echoed throughout the forest.

Chapter Twelve: Confidential

A dying howl of a monster sent chills down my spine as I quickened my pace. Marles and I practically flew through the trees to come across a somewhat morbid scene. There a lifeless body of a monster laid with all its intestinal glory oozing out of a massive gash in its stomach. I briefly gagged at the sight before examining my surroundings more. Soon the monster's corpse became a distant thought in my mind.

Cream colored fur, exuberant brown eyes, a blue tail stone, and a black spot on the back. Even though it had already gotten decently dark I could make out those colors. This had to be one of the most beautiful multicolored Celegons I had ever seen before. While it was more preferable to be born with two or three colors, this Celegon's colors all complimented each other in a brilliant way. Though not even the most radiant colors could take my mind off a corpse for so long. Marles and I cautiously walked around the spilled black blood and went up to greet the new Celegon.

"You two, were you the ones who helped Fieres get back here?" she asked as her brown eyes showed signs of wariness. Her calm and relaxed tone of voice almost made me second guess that she had been the one who'd ended that monster, quite vigorously so.

"Yes, is he alright? He came running this way and..." Marles paused as he took another look at the open monster and shuddered. She glanced over at the monster as well and began to sigh.

"Don't worry, I took care of it so it won't bother anyone again. Still, it did hear Fuery. She panicked and now Fieres is probably calming her down as we speak," the cream Celegon explained in a softer tone as Marles sighed in relief. I was, admittedly, relieved as well; for the child's sake, not for Fieres.

"But Fieres, he had an awful wound on his leg. The monsters tailing him got lucky; though, if it were not for him leading them away from us, I'm not sure if Fuery would have made it. As you can see, I can hold my own against a monster. But when facing a group, there's no way we could guarantee her safety," she said, beginning to cover her face with her paws almost as if she were getting ready to cry.

Even though Fieres had been an unpleasant experience for us, it did make me feel slightly better to know his heart was set on protecting his child. Things seemed to be secure now with their reunion, but the forest was dark enough that traversing it at this time would be dangerous. Marles and I were lucky enough to have a dome, but most Celegons lacked the imported device in their possession. It would be a waste to have the Celegon family I had brought back together be torn to pieces the following night.

"Do you have a safe place to set up for sleeping tonight?" I asked as her brown eyes lit up with curiosity.

"No, we do not. The plan was for all of us to get into Tarrina town by evening; unfortunately, plans changed. But the trees here seem moderately safe depending on which ones you choose. And, unfortunately, Fieres had to toss our tent while leading the monsters away," she stated as I glanced at the surrounding trees. They were quite short; a monster would have no trouble detecting a Celegon in one before knocking it down.

"Well, while I don't care to help strangers for free-"

"What my partner means is that it's too dangerous for you to sleep out here in the open and that we would humbly welcome you into our dome," Marles interrupted in a cheery tone as I stared at him a little perplexed. Though seeing her lovely brown eyes light up uncovered my buried kindness.

My ears picked up the sign of something small quickly scampering across the ground. The way it weightlessly glided across the fallen leaves and sticks, it was far too little to be a Celegon. Whistling noises came from the source and as it got closer the whistling dissolved into hissing. Now in my line of sight was a pink skinned nymph noisily approaching us. Though since there were no monsters corralling it this way, it was very odd that it was coming near Celegons like this.

The tiny naked thing eyed us cautiously as its limber body crawled up the cream Celegon's back. It then propped itself upon her head, messing her blue tinted hair tuft in the process. Beady black eyes rapidly passed between Marles and it before it bore its small roundish teeth and hissed. My mind almost went blank to what I was witnessing. Obvious aggression to us aside, this was a nymph that was domesticated by Celegons. Such a thing was unheard of as nymphs were incredibly skittish creatures that most Celegons would not waste their time on.

"Easy there Fuery. These two have offered us shelter for tonight, no need to be so aggressive," she said soothingly to the nymph as it flopped off her head and into her arms. While it still seemed cautious, it was a lot calmer than before.

"A-are you able to communicate with that nymph?" I partially gasped the words out; the experience was surreal. Her brown eyes practically twinkled at my words.

"Well in a way, yes. She can understand a few basic words, but we mostly communicate through emotions. Nymphs are incredibly sensitive to other's feelings. There is a lot we don't know about them though; you two certainly seemed surprised to see Fuery run up to us, after all." She smiled almost whimsically as I simply stared at Fuery in awe.

Though I was not at all thrilled at the prospect of having a nymph loose in my dome, I could not help but be fascinated at this situation. It was astonishing to see nymphs as anything more than food for monsters, or in Marles' case exotic things to paint. Though this nymph Fuery had no fur, three stubby legs spread unevenly along her skinny body, and wide frilly ears, she was a little cute.

"I-is it alright if I touch her?" Marles suddenly asked as her brown eyes lightened.

She nodded her head and held out Fuery towards Marles. Fuery stared at Marles intently as he moved his paw very close to the nymph's hairless back. Soon his paw made contact with Fuery's skin and his eyes sparkled with excitement. Then Fuery quickly whipped her head around backwards and bit him. Marles quietly yelped, but refused to move his paw from its place. Instead of biting down viciously like a monster would, Fuery began to nibble at Marles' paw in a seemingly gentle fashion.

"It doesn't hurt or burn, kind of tickles actually." Marles began to giggle as the nymph began to lick his paw with its bluish tongue. The cream Celegon and I exchanged happy smiles as we watched Fuery begin to chirp with delight.

The sound of another three-legged being alerted my ears, one much heavier than the one already with us. Fieres quickly trotted back into the picture, now donning a sizable satchel of his own. His focus seemed to be entirely on the other Celegon, almost as if Marles and I were not even present. Her attention as well was almost immediately stolen by him.

"Fieres, you're back. What was keeping you away from me for so long?" she asked as if she were scolding him, all while having a bright grin on her face.

"Just retrieving our valuables and getting distracted by a bush full of delicious berries. I'll share some with you if you'd like," Fieres chimed as he walked closer to her.

He stood himself up using his uninjured leg as a support once he was barely a few inches away from her. Fuery then made a high pitched whistling noise and bounded out of her "mother's" arms and onto Marles' head, which briefly surprised him.

The thing that happened next was certainly of intimate detail. Even though it was now fully dark outside, it was easy to see what the two of them were doing. Not only had they begun to embrace, I saw as their mouths became awfully close. My stomach jolted as they made contact and I knew I had to get Marles out of there.

"The two of us are going to find a good spot to set up the dome! C-come on Marles!" I declared before forcefully grabbing him by the paw as we began to dart away from the lovesick pair.

Fuery let out an affirmative shriek before hopping off Marles and scampering up ahead. My heart raced as I pulled Marles behind me as we made distance between them. Him seeing that after everything else he had been through today was the last thing he needed.

Once we were out of earshot, I stopped holding onto his paw and let out a relieved sigh. I almost started laughing at the situation we witnessed until I saw the somber look in his eyes. Worry began to eat at my heart and I felt somewhat guilty I had not taken him out of there sooner. Though, instead of apologizing for something that was not my fault, I gave him a smile and gently rubbed at his head.

"Look, we don't have to take them in if you don't feel comfortable with them being there." I sighed as the look in his eyes persisted.

Fuery trotted over and laid down next to him almost as if she were completely out of energy. His eyes blinked a bit as he noticed her presence, then looked back to me before shaking his head.

"No, it's not that. Well... how do I say this?" He fumbled on his words as heaps of thoughts seemed to be at war with his brain. "Actually, it's alright! Nothing to be concerned over. Fieres and his mate are probably exhausted and just look at Fuery here." He smiled as he failed at cleverly diverting the subject. Fuery seemed to give him a look as if she could tell he was not being genuine.

"You're terrible at hiding that there is something wrong, so why not just get it over with and say it? Or is our friendship one sided?" I asked, hinting back to much earlier in this chaotic day. He seemed a little taken aback at my statement and quickly shook his head.

"N-no of course not! I'll tell you if you want to know, but could we first set up the dome? I feel like this discussion would be easier to have in a lighter and less breezy area." He laughed lightly as I smiled in agreement.

"Then, could you please light up our surroundings a bit so I can find a good spot for the dome?"

"Well, about that..."

Marles' red stone lit up, but very faintly. Only the tiniest flame came from his tail very briefly before it faded into nothingness. He had used all his magic reserves, no doubt from decorating that area in Tarrina town with all the flora. Without an emeri in my satchel to spare, Marles would be magicless until he got some proper rest. Luckily, even though I was used to Marles being there for these types of situations, it was not too terribly hard to find a decent spot to set the dome.

With the peculiar cube placed neatly in a secure spot, I backed away and pressed a button on the remote. The dome then began to glow before enlarging to its full, roundish form. Though it had only been two days since we had last gone in, it certainly felt like we had been away from our home for quite longer. Marles and I quickly entered into familiar surroundings. Though there were a few changes I had still not gotten fully used to yet.

Once inside the dark dome, I pressed a button along the wall to turn on the internal lighting which washed a bright light over my cluttered surroundings. While not exactly messy or disorganized, it had certainly become fuller since Marles had arrived. The once empty space between the place where we took meals and the entrance was now occupied by three well cared for bushes. Two being berry bushes and the other a supposedly hard to come by herb, flecci it's called. Originally, I was against the idea. But now I was happy to have a semi consistent source of food, even though it was unsustainable on its own.

Another change, which was more noticeable when first entering, was—of course—Marles' paintings. He had blank canvases and cloth neatly stacked in the same area I kept important papers and my desk. Thankfully, he kept all his herbs and paint mixtures in the cooking area, safely away from staining anything. He had several paintings put up around the dome's walls, mostly consisting of monsters, nymphs and landscapes. Still, I could not let myself be distracted as there was a needed conversation to have with Marles.

"Now that we have the dome secured and working, what was it that you needed to get off your mind?" I asked him with a coy smile only to see his attention was drawn to the bushes. It was clear rather than intentionally avoiding the conversation, he was genuinely curious about the wellbeing of the plants he had parted with for two days. "Remember, you're wiped out of magical energy," I say as my comment brought him back to focus.

"I-I know that. Just checking to see if they need any water," he smiled as he started to examine the soil. He gently stroked the soft leaves of the flecci bush before hesitantly facing me, aware of what was to come. "To be honest, I guess I was feeling a little jealous."

I stared at him a little confused as my mind began to make assumptions. Those assumptions multiplied at an alarming rate to the point it strained my brain. Still I tried to keep my cool as I attempted to tone down my thoughts.

"What do you mean by that? You can't possibly be implying that you are interested in *her*, are you?" I asked as confusion spread over his features.

"No, not even. I mean she certainly seemed interesting, just not the definition you're thinking of. Um, but Lyla, why was that the first thought that came to your mind?" he questioned as I felt relieved in knowing that it was not the case.

Still I felt a bit worried over his question, telling him the obvious answer would put me in a vulnerable spot. I would simply have to squirm my way out of this and make it so I would be the one teasing him.

"Oh I just thought it seemed like a safe bet. Though since she has Fieres as a mate after all, there could only be one reason for this "jealousy". Marley must finally want a mate of his own." I grinned cheekily as I watched his expression slowly change. He seemed a little surprised at first, though then began to avert his eyes as he covered his mouth with his right paw. His fur then began to faintly tint red in his face, darkening further when I continued to stare. "Ooh I was right then! You should see your face, it's all red and adorable. Ah but don't worry Marles, I'm sure you'll find your mate," I stated as my heart began to flutter after I patted his head.

In the midst of my many thoughts, one in particular jumped out at me. What would happen if I suddenly kissed him, right now, without any warning? Perhaps this thought was revitalized by recently seeing other Celegons kiss, but this was something that crossed my mind every once in a while. What would happen in the aftermath was always an interesting thing to think about. Though there were many possibilities, there would always be one outcome.

All thoughts dropped as a certain sound clinked near the cooking area. It had just occurred to me that Fuery had mysteriously disappeared from our sights once we came in. My heart sank as the noise devolved into crunching sounds.

"She's after the reserves!"

After capturing the elusive nymph, we decided it was time to go retrieve Fieres and his mate. Fuery had only devoured barely half of a root, thankfully due to her small mouth. Still we made sure Fuery knew we were upset at her rummaging through the jars. Not sure how well she understood us though. She continued to make high pitched chirps as she followed us back to her adoptive parents.

When we made it back to them they were conveniently not still kissing, but relatively close. We let them know that the dome was set up and they eagerly followed us back. Once we were all inside, they briefly gazed around before loosening up the tension that built up in their bodies as they entered. Fuery decided that she wanted to wrestle with the blankets and cushions as the rest of us proceeded to sit down near the entryway. When we were all situated on the slightly cool floor, the cream Celegon spoke up.

"You two have a pleasant home here." She smiled as her gaze met a few of Marles' paintings.

"Yes, it would be a shame if someone stole it," Fieres remarked with a smirk before being gently jabbed by his mate. "Easy, I know we wouldn't get away with it anyhow, Cairy," he muttered as he was being judged by her piercing brown eyes.

Cairy, so that was her name. It was quite beautiful and suited her. They both sat silently next to us for a moment, probably uncomfortable to be in a stranger's home like this. Domes also came off as a bit intimidating to Celegons who were not used to being inside them. Then a thought popped into my mind; one that should have sooner. There was a fair chance our guests were hungry.

"I'll go see what food is left," I said, breaking the silence.

Soon after I walked over to the cooking area, I began to hear voices chattering. Knowing food was coming possibly lowered the stress they were feeling. I started opening jars and pouring out the contents. We did not have many fruits or roots, but considering Marles and I had already eaten a decent amount today, it would be enough. I scooped the contents into my arms and made my way back to them.

"Which is exactly why you can't overlook arbosis," I heard Fieres finish as I set the pile of berries and roots down next to them. Their eyes piqued with interest at the sight of the meager amount.

"I know it isn't a lot, but feel free to eat whatever is in this assortment. You all must be tired and hungry after all you've been through today, that includes you too Marles," I eyed him as a surprised expression made its way to his face. Fuery, who was formerly intrigued by the bedding, came rushing over to the sustenance chirping loudly.

"Are you not going to eat any Lyla?" Marles asked as I continued to stand above the group. I certainly would not mind eating more as my body would make use of the energy, but it was obvious I would just be taking away from those who needed it more.

"No. I already had plenty to eat today, remember?"

"As did I-"

"Just eat the food, Marles."

Fieres seemed a bit hesitant with eating the food I provided unlike the others. He looked at me with a skeptical expression before turning back to the berries.

"I assume this isn't free. How much are you charging?" He sighed as I thought to myself for a moment. A crucial detail resurfaced in my mind.

"Oh, nothing more than the rest of that payment we were promised," I stated as I tried to contain my pleasure from watching his expression change.

The payment he had promised was not explicitly stated, but I was eager to see it nonetheless. Cairy seemed quite surprised at this as well, as she should be as she had no idea about this until now. Even so, there was no way she assumed that this would all be completely free of charge.

"Fieres, how much did you promise them?"

Cairy's eyes began to fill with worry and her calm composure dissipated. Just by looking at her face, I could tell that they had practically nothing at all, or nothing they could afford to spare. Noticing her mother in distress, Fuery stopped eating and rested her small head on Cairy's legs. Instead of letting guilt cloud my judgment, my brain proposed a new idea.

"Sorry about this Cairy, but we made a deal prior to your involvement. How about we all come to a mutual agreement on what we receive for our efforts?" I suggested as I looked towards the satchel that was around Fieres' waist.

The two Celegons looked at each other nervously before nodding their heads. Marles seemed a little anxious as well and Fuery's body began to shiver for a moment.

Fieres began to empty out the contents of his satchel in a separate pile close by to the remaining food. Several blue and red orbs clinked before rolling on the smooth floor of the dome. Though there were many, their value was low and it appeared as if he had paid more in the down payment than what was in his missing satchel. In addition to the orbs, several herbs, a few berries and some papers decorated the dome's floor. Curiously, I picked up one of the papers.

Before I even started to read, I could sense Fieres and Cairy tensing up. With what I was reading, their stress was understandable. I however was delighted by the content of the paper. There was no reason to have them worry in suspense, but it was amusing to see Fieres so worked up.

"So you two are informants." I grinned as I looked over towards Marles whose expression relaxed. The other two exchanged meek glances before Cairy piped up.

"I suppose there is no denying it. We gather information, sometimes we sell it, sometimes that information is... private." She tried to keep her calm, but her mouth was quivering slightly. Fieres placed a paw along her back in an attempt to comfort her, though it was obvious that he was far more nervous than she was.

"*Lyla.*"

I glanced back towards Marles who had a slightly firm tone in his voice. He was right, it would be better to just reassure them. Sighing, I quickly gathered all the papers and put them neatly in a stack.

"Ease up a bit, everything's fine. We just so happen to be investors of this particular type of information you carry," I stated as I felt the tension in the air waver off.

"So you two are..." Fieres stopped himself before continuing with, "Oh, nevermind that. Take whichever location you want, but please leave the rest to us."

The first one I had picked up already seemed ideal. Located near Rimereach, a forest town in which homes and shops were constructed far above in the high, thick sturdy trees. Though this mansion was said to be built of stone and on the ground, undoubtedly surrounded by a psi barrier like Marles' former home. It would take us a little more than a week to reach the nearby town if we traveled southwest of Tarrina town, but the rewards would surely be worth the trip.

Still curious about the other papers, I handed the one I was set on over to Marles while I skimmed over the others. Most of the other locations were much further than a week's walk away. The few that were closer was what I considered meager information; they were only about certain shops resupplying their goods. It must have been fated that I picked up the best one of the bunch without having to look at the others. Until I came across one completely inapplicable to potential thievery.

It was a rumor, written out on the confines of the small, crumpled paper. Informants attempt to sell them occasionally, but I had yet to buy one from them. In my experience, the only rumors I needed to know came to my ears freely by other Celegons. Though that did not mean I was not intrigued to find out what rumor had been collected onto this paper.

New Information Gathered!

Malypsi have been noticeably withdrawing from Lixion. The friendly positive beings seem to be disappearing with no clear explanation of their sudden removal from Lixion. We are to believe that they are returning to their home planet Mhiva, where their Emperor currently resides. Malypsi and Celegons have had a mostly good relationship, with them bringing their technology to trade in exchange for Lixion's abundant flora. No Malypsi have explicitly stated a reason for their abrupt departure at the time of writing this.

Some Celegons say that remaining Malypsi have been giving them certain glances. Sources say these glances consist of uneasiness, bleakness, and worry. Celegons who read this, please go out of your way to be hospitable to any Malypsi you encounter. Please do anything you can to prevent driving the Malypsi out of Lixion.

I had not really noticed much since I had been busy with other matters, but the rumor appeared to be accurate. There had been less Malypsi, even in larger Celegon towns like Tarrina town. It was almost a bit hard to believe as we did happen to meet one just earlier today. But before that, it had been a decent while since I had seen another.

"That's the one about the Malypsi right?" Fieres asked as he gazed at my expression. "We traded that with another rumor bearing Celegon a few days back; weird isn't it?" I quickly put it down with the other papers that had been organized in a neat pile.

"We'll be taking that one there," I gestured over towards the one Marles was holding before handing Fieres the other papers. Marles seemed a little concerned about the Malypsi rumor, but it would do no good to tell him now. It was quite late and, after all, it was only a rumor.

The food was soon diminished after that, and we decided it was in everyone's best interest to get some rest. My bedding area was a little small for four Celegons and a nymph, but we made it work comfortably somehow. It was also a logical excuse to sleep more close to Marles than I normally did, which was not all that bad. As the night grew on, I sensed one by one as they each drifted off to sleep. All but me. I could always rest after the strangers were gone.

I was plenty entertained by the thoughts clouding my head to avoid being swept up with weariness. Malypsi leaving Lixion being the most prominent. With them home, there would certainly be more monsters lurking. Lixion would start to regress to how things used to be years ago.

Chapter Thirteen: Heist

Sneaking through the mansion's dimly lit passageways was easy, aside from avoiding countless Celegons that also happened to be there. Though I was too proud to admit it at the moment, I had gotten the dates mixed up.

The mansion was due to be empty eleven days after I first read the information from Fieres. Today would be the tenth—one day off. Little did I know that on this specific day the inhabitants would be holding a massive social gathering.

Our prior escapade was unfortunately just as stressful as our current. After our farewell with the nymph's family, we had to make the trek back to Tarrina town to resupply ourselves with some of the most overpriced emeri. That had been lost thanks to the monsters who had managed to land a few fatal blows before we had run them off. When we finally made it to Rimereach, I had planned to do the heist solo. But Marles reassured me he was ready.

He was less than not.

Currently we were both cramped into what appeared to be the mansion's food store room. The hiding space was quite limited with little room to stretch, but being uncomfortable was far better than getting caught. Moving even a little would be a dead give away. The caretakers that were tasked with collecting the food for their guests were getting quite close.

"Herb pastries? Seriously? How could they ask for *herb* pastries?"

"I know, fruit pastries would be a far better treat. But I suppose the guests want what they want."

"Tange filled pastries would make my stomach melt. But no, they want bland, spicy pastries. Working here gives us the perks of uneaten leftovers, but what's the point if they are just awful?"

"At least they'll be free."

The two voices continued to banter back and forth as the caretakers began to rummage through the storeroom. My body was frozen in place as they drew nearer and my eyes locked onto Marles who was crammed inside the toppled crate across from me. His hiding spot was worse than mine, but we lacked better options. Both of our selected crates were empty, save for us, and there was far less food in the very back. We could only hope they could not see us from where they were.

"Hey, where are those flecci leaves? I almost forgot we needed some for the seasoned water."

"Are they not with the rest of the herbs?"

"They don't seem to be. Do you think they were put further back somewhere?"

"Possibly, you should check. You know they'll upset without-"

"Yeah, I know. We'll make their seasoned water."

One of the two began walking closer. I held my breath once I sensed that she was just behind the crate I was in. My fur began to stand up as I heard sharp claws harmlessly brush against the wood. The vibrations almost made me shiver. Soon I heard a crackling noise come from overhead.

"Found 'em! Any idea why they were just randomly put here atop this crate?"

"Nothing I know of. Let's just hurry and bring these to the cooks so they can prepare it."

With that now taken care of, the two voices slowly faded away until there was a pause of silence. Once I was sure that there was no one else in the room with us, I released my held breath with a sigh of relief. Then I began to breathe normally again and stretched my body outside of the crate. Marles did the same and he seemed a little shaken from having to be in that uncomfortable position for so long. I stood myself up slowly and peered over the crate as I cautiously examined the room's entrance. There did not appear to be any signs of movement which put us in the clear.

"Alright. Plan. Let's relocate to a more secure hiding spot and discuss further strategies there," I whispered as Marles shot me a confused glance.

"I don't object, but wouldn't it be better to just leave the place entirely?" he asked as I shook my head.

We were in a bad position here, but leaving? It would be practical, but it would also be admitting defeat. Even if the odds were not in our favor, I was not ready to yet call for retreat.

"We can certainly try, but have you considered how hard it would be to leave this place undetected? Most of the guests have relocated outside by the sounds of it. But we'll discuss this later, somewhere safer," I told him as I started to carefully navigate myself around the crates.

I was very careful to avoid stepping on any stray berries that had gotten lost from their crates. Though, most likely the caretakers would face the punishment instead of us. Soon we approached the large open wooden doorway and I could finally breathe air that was less musty.

No sounds of footsteps filled my ears, but this mansion was padded with plush carpet. I dared to poke my head out further to see no Celegons coming from either way. Other than the low flicker of the burning wax clumps that rested on the stone posts that clung to the walls, there was silence. Soon my feet began to glide across the brown carpet until they reached a split in the hallway. Looking down the path to the right, I saw it was just as clear of Celegons as the path forward.

The emptiness only made me more cautious as we started to make our way down the right passageway. I expected that we would at least see a caretaker or so roaming the halls, but it was possible they were all outside with the guests. Still—I wanted to find shelter immediately as these hallways had no spots to take cover in. While it would be okay if a guest or caretaker caught a passing glance at us, it would be bad if one of the mansion's residents laid their eyes on the fellow intruders that we were.

Further down the wax lit hallway, my eyes caught sight of a closed wooden door. Seeing as there were not many other options, I cautiously approached it and gently pushed it open to reveal a small gaudy bedroom. Marles and I hurried in and I quickly, but carefully pushed the door shut to prevent it from creaking. Only when we were in the room did we discover it was not as empty as it appeared to be.

"Reene? Is that you?" a voice yawned as my eyes quickly locked onto the source.

There was a large, wooden table structure that was pressed against the room's left wall. It was covered with cushions and blankets on top, along with a small presence shifting under the covers. I then noticed a very sizable gap underneath the wooden frame that could be of instant use to Marles and I. Before the Celegon could uncover themselves, I grabbed Marles' arm and directed him under the structure with me.

While I tried to be as silent as possible, the act could have been quieter. As we repositioned ourselves under the frame, our feet slid on the carpet just enough to make a bit of noise. We froze immediately after that to prohibit more, but this Celegon was quick to notice that something was off.

"Did you go under my bed again Reene? It's never very funny," the same voice said groggily as a bit of creaking was heard from above.

Then with a light slip, I stared in silence as I watched two yellow legs plop themselves down on the brown carpet. Quickly, I rolled my body away from the yellow legs to end up on the other side of the wooden bed. Marles followed my motions and soon we both hid behind a blanket that was dropping just enough to cover us out of view from the other side.

"Oh, Reene's not here," the voice sighed before climbing back onto the bed. "But you two are! Heya!"

My heart jumped out of my chest as I was now locking eyes with a yellow furred Celegon. Her orangish eyes sparkled as she smiled at the two of us. This was it, this was the end for us. This spoiled child would rat us out for sure. Then I took a moment to reassess the situation.

Child.

I glanced over the yellow Celegon's body. She was certainly small, if I had to guess only a few years old. Most likely between three and five years. The naive look in her eyes told me she had yet to know the harshness of the world outside the wealthy Celegon assemblies.

"What are you two doing in here? Do you find social gatherings boring too?" she asked with a delightful smile on her yellow face. Saving me from the trouble, Marles was the first to speak to the young Celegon.

"Yup, we decided to ditch it. Honestly, I always found them to be dull. Especially when you have to pretend to be six times happier than you really are," Marles said with a confident grin which seemed to greatly please the child.

"You really do know! I just dislike them so much! Oh, what do you not like about them?" she asked, beaming violently in my direction. I still felt a little tongue-tied, but I was grateful I was asked a question I could faithfully answer.

"Me? Well what I don't like is," I started as I thought back to myself for a moment. I did have experience in this after all.

The last social gathering I went to officially was a little over thirteen years ago, but my memory of them is still sharp as ever. My mother would always make a fuss about going to them and how important it was to make appearances. Conversations directed towards me were always the same, bland topics that I was educated to respond to in an equally unexciting way. I suppose the food was nice, though I was very restricted to what I was allowed to eat.

"The ribbons and the lace never felt good being wrapped around my ears; such a dumb requirement. Having the same conversations with everyone felt like slow torture too. But as he said, I think the worst part is trying to stay in a good mood the entire time when you aren't enjoying it." I felt a small smile forming as I began to reminisce about the times as a child that I counted down the seconds it would be over.

Our opinions seemed to please her very much and she opened her mouth to say something else, but then a knock came from outside the wooden door. Marles and I retreated underneath the bed as the door began to creak. A groan came from above us followed by a prolonged sigh that originated near the doorway.

"I was hoping you would be ready by now Anna," a new voice gently whined in displeasure as the bed shook a little. There was something familiar about it. Could it really be Reene?

"I'm not going! No one's going to notice if I'm there anyways," the child protested, earning a low growl from the other Celegon. I watched as the ends of two larger yellow legs approached the wooden frame.

"Come on now, is showing up really that hard? Your parents would want-"

"Well they aren't here!"

There was a bit of silence between the other two before the other Celegon sat herself on the bed. More shifting was heard from above before I could hear the faint sound of sniveling.

"You're right Annazie, they aren't here. But their spirits have entrusted me and the rest of our family to look out for you. Being a part of this family isn't easy, I know, but I really only want the best for you. These social gatherings? They'll become easier with time and you can have fun if you let yourself. Why don't instead you focus on the outing we'll be going on for the next few days?" she asked gently, her voice soft as she attempted to comfort the child.

Her kindness kindled a spark of jealousy. It was something I had lacked when I had been a child going through the same thing. Annazie seemed to be a little quiet after that, but I then heard a muffled "alright". Soon, the larger of the two yellow Celegons slid off the bed and began to walk somewhere else in the room that my eyes could not follow.

"Let's get you some ribbons. How about pink?" the older Celegon chimed as sounds of wood being slid tickled my ears.

"So I'd match with you Reene? No thanks!" the child chuckled as an exaggerated gasp was heard from across the room. Frantic shuffling of soft objects came from the same direction.

"You brat! Fine, we don't have to match," Reene whined as the shuffling came to a halt. "You know, orange would be a nice look too," her voice trailed off as she began to approach the bed.

The wooden frame began to creak slightly and I heard the familiar sound that sleek ribbons make when being fastened. A few pained yelps filled the air, but they quickly softened down. I could only hope that Reene did not tie the ribbons on her as tightly as my mother did. Soon the sounds had ceased and before I knew it, the two of them had hopped off the bed and began to approach the door. I was a little wary that the child would alert Reene about us, but my chest eased when I heard the door shut behind them.

Peering out from under the bed for further inspection, I sighed in relief after discovering that we were alone once more. I slid my body across the carpet and came out from under the bed. Now would be the time to come up with a short term plan.

"She was rather adorable," Marles said as I gave a nod. "And you're much more knowledgeable of social gatherings than I thought you were."

"She was. Anyways, there will be plenty of time for these conversations later. We need to focus on coming up with a strategy while we're here," I stated as it was a priority we were not found by adult Celegons.

"Why don't we just lay low and stay here until everyone leaves tomorrow morning?"

That was a pretty solid idea for the most part. Staying here did not have many risks, unless the Annazie child decided to check her bed again and turn us in. If we were quiet and still, it would not be an issue otherwise. It was past evening now so waiting it out a couple of hours would not be too outlandish. Then Marles' stomach began to howl which annihilated the initial thought. Through all the training and preparation in the past two days, neither of us had eaten as much as we should have to keep up our strength.

"That's a good start, but we need to refine it a little. If Annazie comes back here to sleep tonight, which she undoubtedly will, you'll need to eat some food beforehand to silence your stomach. I propose we split up temporarily. I'm sure you can find your way back to the storeroom to acquire some food. And while you're doing that I'll scope out the mansion a bit more," I explained as Marles smiled sheepishly. Still, he wasted no time in following my suggestion by heading to the doorway. But then he paused and I waited, brow arching in question.

"Don't get yourself caught now Ly-Ly," he teased. My body felt a surge of energy.

"Don't get caught by any ladies, lest they fawn all over you Marley," I shot back only realizing after what I had just said.

His eyes widened for a moment before that awkward smile returned. Without another word, he carefully made his way out the door. My shoulders slackened for a moment, my whole body practically drooping before I shook it off and collected my bearings. Why must these feelings be so potent?

I made my way to a large, wooden container in the room, which I assumed to be full of ribbons. I opened up one of the compartments to find an array of the aforementioned as well as a few full-bodied outfits, though they were not for adult frames. Ribbons alone were quite pricey due to the material and how time consuming it was to make them, so I could not even imagine how much a full outfit would cost. Pawning them off would be useless however, as it would be worthless to the average Celegon. So I settled for a few light blue ribbons since they reminded me of the ones Alise once wore.

I began to fasten them firmly around my ears, almost as if past memories took over and did it for me. Then I added a third to the end of my tail and made my way towards the door. The ribbons were already making me feel hindered, but I ignored the tightness and pushed my way outside the door. Once again, no Celegons in sight in the hallways.

Since I knew that going left would lead back towards the food storage room, I opted to go right. As I walked down the hallway lit only by the dancing flames of wax, I came across several doors that were very close together; they were similar to an inn's. This would either be where the live-in caretakers slept or extra rooms for guests. I continued down the long hallway until it soon began to curve to the right. From the outside the mansion seemed intimidating in size, though it was surprisingly smaller on the inside. It was not long before I heard Celegons chatting from just beyond barely cracked doors that led to the garden.

Since I had no intention of inviting myself, I promptly turned around and began to make my way back. Curiosity begged me to check at least one of the rooms I had passed, so I allowed it temporary control. Before pushing a door open, I pressed my ear to see if I could hear any noise on the other side. To my surprise, my ears detected noise from outside of the room—directly behind me. I pushed on the heavy door just enough to allow me to squeeze inside before it closed itself shut.

The voices grew louder and my eyes quickly scanned about the room for yet another hiding spot. The wooden bed in this room was full of clutter underneath so I had to improvise. Just as the door began to open, I shoved my body into a messy ribbon enclosure. If I dared slip on any of the silky ribbons Marles would probably not see me for a while.

"Come on, let's hurry up and find it then! I know it's somewhere in here," a feminine voice with an exuberant amount of haughtiness hollered.

"We would have already had it if you were more collected and organized," a more masculine voice grumbled back.

"H-hey! That's no way to talk to your employer!"

"Y-yes, Miss Clain."

Loud shuffling noises were then heard throughout the room. My body stiffened as I felt the vibrations of a set of paws on the other side of the double doors I had shut myself in.

"Is there any chance you placed it in here, Miss Clain?" the Celegon who I assumed was her caretaker asked as he opened the doors slightly. I held very still as the slightest sliver of my body would soon be exposed for him to see.

"Of course not! I only put *my* presents in there. The one for Lady Reene has to be under this obscenely small bed!" the other voice barked. The doors were eased shut and I soon felt as the caretaker's presence moved away, footsteps soft.

The tension in my body eased, but I was still on high alert with the two Celegons in the room. This was especially true with one of them likely to be one of the homeowners given how they sounded very familiar with the room, and with how they acted like the typical spoiled and wealthy type. The *worst* sort.

"Finally, here it is. No thanks to you," she scoffed as the caretaker apologized in response. Instead of immediately leaving to deliver the gift, they chose to linger.

"Is something the matter, Miss Clain?" the caretaker asked as his voice quivered just barely.

"With the gift? No, Lady Reene will enjoy it for sure," she paused a moment before continuing. "I'm just preoccupied with the social gathering we're scheduled to go to in four months."

"The one at the Iseirre's I presume?"

I felt a little tinge of guilt pull at my heart. Marles probably had no idea. Sure—he proclaimed to detest social gatherings in general, but a part of me wondered if he missed his family at all.

"What else could I mean Osric?" she huffed, next pausing. I could hear the frown even if I couldn't see it. "You know, that Marles and I, we used to court," Clain said. My interest was instantly piqued. "Before he got really fat that is," she finished, voice dripping with disappointment.

There was a dramatic sigh before she continued. I really wish she would just finish her point. So I could hear it and so she could leave, meaning I could get out of the cramped closet.

"Miss Clain?"

"Well," she went on, "it's just that I've heard that he's gone *missing*. Just up and disappeared from the Iseirre mansion one night," she sighed again as I heard a sliding noise.

"Having lingering feelings?" Osric asked and she began to chuckle in response.

"For that fatty?" I could just imagine the pompous spoiled female rolling her eyes as she spoke. "Can't have lingering feelings if there weren't any there to begin with. Still, he was *quite* handsome in his prime; I won't deny that. Just a shame to have one less beautiful Celegon in the world," she said, her voice sticky sweet. "At least there will always be *you*, Osric," Clain chimed as I heard more movement.

"T-thank you Miss Clain?"

Finally, it seemed as if they were progressing towards the door. Soon I would be reunited with food, shelter, and Marles. My legs could almost taste the freedom of being able to stretch out again. Unfortunately I had one more short conversation to overhear.

"Oh and Osric," Clain started as I waited for her to hurry it up. "If you ever get fat you'll be dismissed from your position as my aide."

"I don't think we have enough food in our disposal for that to even happen, but understood, Miss Clain."

With that, they were finally gone and I escaped from my enclosure. My eyes widened at the state of the room, which was somehow even more cluttered than when I had first come in. I had done enough scouting for the day and Marles was waiting for me. My mouth frowned as I thought back to that Clain. It must have been awful for anyone, much less Marles, having to court someone like her.

From there I carefully navigated my way back to the room and was extra cautious checking for Celegons. Once I got there, I gently pushed open the door to see Marles organizing a small variety of food. His head immediately turned around—likely out of caution—only to smile when he saw it was me.

"Ribbons, huh?" Marles grinned.

For a brief moment I was confused. It must have shown because he pointed to his own ears.

Ribbons. Right.

I quickly pulled them off and undid the one on my tail before stashing them where they belonged. Afterwards, I joined Marles who seemed quite proud of the small spread he'd acquired. There were two bowls of soup that had a greenish reddish mixture, most likely made with specialty vegetables. And there were various berries. But what really caught my attention were the muffin pastries.

"Are these for dessert? You have good taste." I smiled as I gently nibbled on one to test the flavor. Quite sweet as expected, and with just a hint of tartness.

"Well... I got them for you. Feel free to eat them now if you like; I'll just have some soup and berries for myself," he said before holding a bowl of soup to his mouth. I placed the muffin back down and decided to try my own bowl of soup. It was full of savory flavors, but lacked the sweetness of the muffin.

"Are you sure you don't want one? There are three after all." I gazed at the muffins. It confused me why he would get three and not even eat one for himself.

"I really shouldn't-" is what he was able to say before I put the corner of a muffin into his open mouth. His face lit up at the sweet, spongy texture before pouting after realizing what it was. As he reached for it, biting down the rest of the way since the deed had been done, I pulled my paw away with a grin.

"Y-you're mean Lyla. Now I have no choice but to eat the rest," he said as he sulked. Even so, while he appeared upset, I knew he was enjoying it. I could hardly feel bad about it. He probably had not eaten a muffin since back before we started traveling together.

"You know Marles, handsome as you are, I don't think you have to worry about what you eat too much." I smiled and yet again, only realizing after that once more my mouth had moved faster than my brain.

My stomach began to feel like it was full of air when my thoughts caught up to me. Marles' face had immediately flushed to red and quickly swallowed the remaining bit of the muffin before covering his face. I forced myself to appear calm on the outside, but my insides were a bundle of a squirming jumble of unwanted feelings.

"H-how can you say something like that so casually? It's not a very funny joke Lyla," he whimpered as he averted his now uncovered eyes from mine.

"I'm not joking!" I exclaimed as my brain pondered the multiple outcomes of this conversation. I always had this urge to playfully toy with him, but I also wanted my real meaning to be clear regardless of how I truly felt about him. "You have gotten thinner over the weeks; which isn't surprising since we burn so much energy in our line of work. So I think it's perfectly fine for you to be able to eat what you want—to treat yourself. Besides, it's not often that we get to eat this fancy stuff." I grinned before tickling at his side until he started laughing.

The tickling took our minds off of other things and soon we were able to eat our meal in peace. Before long though, the door decided to creak open and we were forced to retreat under the bed once more. No footsteps were heard, which meant it was likely Annazie since she was so small. Light grunts came from the young Celegon as she quickly pulled off her ribbons and tossed them to the floor.

"Well that was a bust," she sighed, small feet padding their way to the bed and then disappearing from my sight as she climbed in. After cozying herself under the covers, I thought it was only a matter of time before she drifted off to sleep. "You guys? You two aren't still here, are you?"

I tensed at the possibility of her knowing. Then relaxed once logic kicked in. By her tone of voice, I could tell she barely had enough energy to keep awake. Social gatherings could be especially draining for any Celegon.

"If you are, it's okay. But it would be nice to talk to you again before I... pass out," she yawned the groan of words as I heard what sounded like her wrestling with the blankets.

I turned my head towards Marles, who nudged me a little with his paw. He smiled at me reassuringly once I had caught his eyes. He then turned his head up towards the wooden bed frame and had his mouth agape. At this moment, I could honestly not tell if he was being serious or messing with me. Instinctively, I used my paw to prohibit his mouth from making a sound.

His eyes widened slightly as his mouth closed back up. He then carefully began to remove it from his face. At least, that was what I thought he was doing. All he did was simply slide it down to his upper chest and grin. Was he seriously planning on holding it there so he could speak freely?

Moving as quietly as possible, I shifted myself so that I was crouched over him and facing him directly. It certainly caught his attention away from speaking up. Wait—what was I thinking. This position... It was too close!

Not only that, but it was also very cramped. With the bed above us, that gave little room to sit upright; hovering above Marles did not leave much room either. But if I were to lower myself, I'd be pressed into him. Marles was not dense with that knowledge himself.

Although it was dark, I was still able to see parts of his face vividly. Especially his eyes, which even now seemed to glow like low burning embers. I found myself leaning just a little closer than I had before. My paws repositioned themselves so that now they were each on the sides of his chest. This staring contest between us lasted a little longer before I felt his arms gently stroking my back.

One thing led to another and I took my gamble.

Soon our mouths met and my heart began fluttering vibrantly at the contact. Thoughts raced through my mind a mile a millisecond and a warm feeling bloomed in my chest, the heat of which spread outward to the tips of my ears all the way to the tips of my feet. Goosebumps danced along my skin. My eyes were closed as I let these amazing emotions take over, as I let them put my body into a state of unconditional warmth and security. When I broke away from his mouth finally, I opened my eyes to find him staring back.

While no words were spoken, his eyes seemed even more fluorescent than ever. The paws that once gently touched my back had started to pull me closer again. I was soon in a *much* more comfortable position, no longer craning over him. His soft body was warm, inviting and astonishingly soothing.

I found myself incapable of staving off the considerable amount of heat that rushed to my face. Even though we were under the shaded bed frame, I was completely positive that the light lavender fur along my cheeks had become *a lot* darker. Though, it seemed like there was not a need to worry about that anymore. My heart began to flutter harder as I had the desire to relive that new experience once more. I planted a softer kiss on his neck before silently shifting even closer.

I made it so we were as close as could be without becoming uncomfortable. I could not—even if I tried—force myself to stop grinning, but eventually I was able to loosen up enough to drift off. Never had I felt more relieved to fall asleep while trespassing.

Chapter Fourteen: Blooming

After another dreamless slumber, my mind began to stir with thoughts. We were at the mansion near Rimereach, stowed away under a child's bed until morning. Though time could be difficult to track when one was stuck inside a mansion. Under a bed and in near complete darkness.

I started to stretch out my body and yawned a little. My eyes slowly opened as they began to adjust to their dark surroundings. I saw Marles close beside me with his eyes still closed, looking very much at peace and tranquil. My mouth smiled as I reached over to wake him up. Then my body locked itself in place as I remembered the events that happened before we'd dozed off.

My heart jumped as I began to recall the details. I had kissed him. Under a bed. A child's bed. On a job. It was completely unplanned and was entirely on impulse. I studied his features a little more before I detected some movement on his face. Soon his orange eyes were wide open and looking directly into mine.

I stared back for a moment before breaking the hold we both had on one another and then listened carefully for any noise other than Marles' quiet breathing. Once I was certain that no other noises were present, I made my way out from under the bed. Carefully crawling across the carpet, I turned myself around once I was no longer underneath it and inspected the rumple of blankets and sheets. Not even the tiniest lump was present. A grin grew across my face now that I knew we were alone. Marles came up from the other side to investigate what I was looking at.

"It's morning, so I'm sure everyone has already left by now." I grinned as Marles walked closer to me. He seemed slightly nervous, probably confused about what happened at night.

"Ah, Lyla if now's a good time I—"

"Yes, it's finally time to get some work done! You can start in this room, I'll check some others in a different area so we can cover more space faster," I stated gleefully before bounding off towards the door.

Before he could say another word to me, I pushed myself out and began to race down the hallway. My heart was pounding, but I could not let myself be distracted by my feelings at the moment. There was always later and later would be better.

The empty halls were exhilarating to run across, knowing that there was little chance anyone would hear me no matter how hard my paws hit the carpet. Soon—once I was far enough from the room Marles was in—I slowed down and started to walk back on two limbs. I felt my mouth in reminiscence as my stomach fluttered. If I had stayed I would have never left the room. Sighing, I tried my best to empty all of that out of my mind as I continued by the hall, now only lit from the light peering in from the outside. Eventually I found myself in a guest room, hoping that things of value were left behind.

The first thing that popped into my mind were the blankets and cushions that adorned the wooden bed. The blankets were soft and heat retainable with a pretty bluish hue while the cushions were firm but quite cozy. The bedding that was back inside my dome was starting to get a bit ragged and was becoming dull in color due to overuse. Surely they would not miss one of the guest room's beddings too much. If the hallway was just a little wider I would be able to set my dome up, but for now I would focus on gathering the smaller valuables before coming for the bedspread.

I began my search and started looking underneath the bed to see what I could find. Empty. Then I started to look in the various storage compartments and wooden containers in the room. All of which were also empty. I thought to myself for a moment before I remembered the particular cluttered guest room. There had to be something that disorganized Celegon had left behind.

I quickly left the room and approached the one I previously hid from the Clain Celegon. Pushing open the door revealed a very clean and presentable room quite like the one I was just in. Still I did not lose hope as there was a high chance something was forgotten in the once messy room. This time I checked under the bed, which was previously jammed full, to find a few stray red orbs just there for the taking. Not what I was expecting, but I slipped them into my satchel with contentment.

Next I found a few ribbons, a small pouch with blue orbs, and a couple of containers holding mysterious powders I would examine later. I placed everything in my satchel before heading to the next room. It took a bit to repeat the process for each room, but soon enough I had searched them all. My finds were mostly stray orbs, forgotten ribbons and powders but it ended up being a decent amount. My satchel was far from full though and I wanted to check the garden to see if they happened to be growing vegetables or fruit.

Walking up to the two large, wooden double doors, I opened the latch that held them together so I could pass to the outside. My mouth pulled itself into a grin as the semi cool afternoon air washed over my body. Mansions were always so stuffy and usually I could not wait until I went outside again. Though I suppose earlier events caused me to forget that until now. Shaking my thoughts, I turned my attention to the well kept garden that was quite the sight.

It was quite a delight for my eyes with all the greenery and flowers, though it lacked the raw untamed look of the wilderness. Everything here seemed orderly and symmetrical. So many sweet scents tickled at my senses, almost a little too much. Marles would probably love to have a look at all the plants here before we departed.

Dozens of flowery plants of yellows and blues were lined up close by the stone pathways; those led to the plaza centerpiece of the garden. That area was where all the guests had gathered the other day; it looked quite peaceful without them there. The caretakers did an amazing job to ensure not a trace of the previous night remained. Wealthy celegons didn't care how messy they were during a night of socializing, after all. While I could stay and marvel at its beauty for an hour or more, my goal was to look for food bearing plants. Thus I continued on deeper into the garden. As my eyes checked around, I eventually caught sight of a few berry bushes that had been planted into a neat row.

Happily rushing over to pick some, my eyes caught sight of something much more valuable. I couldn't believe it as I approached, yet there it was. A healthy emeri tree stood before me in all its glory. The blue leaves glistened in the sun as the red stems were virtually see-through in the sunlight. As I looked closer, there seemed to be a line of emeri trees, five in total.

In the wild, emeri trees had been growing incredibly scarce due to monsters disliking them. They would tear down saplings without a second thought and destroy any fruit they found. What was worse was they could smell the trees from far away, so most towns were not able to grow them if they had no barrier.

No one knew why the monsters had developed a hatred for the trees, but because of that the emeri price was constantly rising. This was not always the case, however. The change was rather recent. But no one knew why this was, nor how to quell the situation.

There seemed to be quite a few emeri in the trees, I counted ten in total that appeared ready to harvest. Out of respect for the trees I only took five of them and hoped that they would remain healthy and strong. Thanks to the plump emeri, my satchel was now full. I probably needed to check back in with Marles now, something I did not feel entirely ready to do.

"Why, if it isn't Little Lavender."

My body froze at the sound of that voice, but relaxed a bit once I recognized it. I must have been more in my head than I thought if I could not detect his presence.

"Isn't it a bit too early to be stalking me again, Z?" I asked, my voice tinted in mild exasperation as I turned to face him.

He was perched in one of the non-emeri trees looking down at me. His previous wounds had healed, but he looked just as sickly as ever; malnourished with unkempt fur. As he descended from the tree and walked closer, his gaze found my own and held—heavy with the usual disinterest, as if he couldn't be bothered to care about anyone or anything, much less me. I often wondered how much of that was true—that he didn't care. Especially given how often he deigned to seek me out.

"You seem to be in a better mood than usual," he stated as he turned away to examine the emeri trees in front of us. He put his paw on one and briefly scratched the black bark before turning back to me. "I take it you and the Iseirre fellow have become mates?"

I glared at him for a long moment. Then sighed and broke his gaze briefly. There had to be a reason other than this that prompted him to speak to me.

"I don't believe that's something you should be concerned with," I shot back as a suspicious glint appeared in his eyes. He almost seemed hurt, but I knew him well enough to know he was feeling apathetic.

"You don't know how wrong you are. Having a mate can be... a pleasant way to pass time. But don't misunderstand me, it's not something I'm too thrilled about," he went on as I felt my fur bristle.

"If that's all you came to say, leave. I want nothing to do with you if you simply came to chastise me for having a mate," I growled as I turned my attention to the base of the tree he climbed out of.

When he started walking closer he took his normally uneasy steps. I refused to look him in the eyes at first, but when I finally did I saw something I did not expect. Soon my body was too paralyzed to even move, my mouth too shocked to protest. Z was hugging me. At least I *assumed* that was what he was doing.

His body quivered slightly as it always did with his condition, but it felt surreal to be feeling the shivers up close. I could hear his irregular breathing patterns more intently, the faint thumping of his weakened heartbeat for the first time. For him to hug me like this I knew something was wrong. Terribly wrong. He gripped me as tightly as he could with his poor body as he began to speak the words, "It's all my fault."

My ears flinched in surprise as I heard water droplets hit the firm soil below us. Soon his grip loosened and I stepped back; not far, but just enough to keep about a foot between us. A comfortable distance. I was still processing what to feel after his sudden action as I looked into his eyes. And while it was hard to tell, they were definitely more watery than usual. What was more, instead of the usual smug or uninterested look in his eyes, he appeared like he was about to break down into tears.

"Z? What is it? You know I can't read your mind." I sighed as his head tilted down slightly.

If he hadn't appeared shaken to me before, he definitely did now. And unrelated to his illness. We were far from blood related and bore a mutually unspoken disrespect for one another, and yet... I felt obligated to listen to whatever was eating him up well enough to show this kind of weakness in front of me.

"I-I hurt her. Badly. She'll come after everyone now because of my actions," he started, every word laced with regret and a real fear. "She's going to die and cause unspeakable things to happen to our kind."

I could feel my insides tremble at his words because of that spoken fear. I had no clue what he was talking about, and perhaps that made the anxiety and trepidation I felt worse. I tried to calm my nerves until I knew exactly what was going on.

"Is this about a Malypsi? You hurt one and think if she dies that they will be out to get us Celegons? It's true that their emperor seems to care a lot for his species, but I don't think he'll punish every Celegon for something that could've been an accident. And you don't know if she's dead, to say you killed her would be—"

"Who said this had anything to do with those Malypsi?"

My pulse rate rose as I looked at him in confusion. If it was not Malypsi, was it monsters? While it was true that monsters were good at killing, Celegons had managed to survive among them for as long as anyone can remember existing in this world. For a moment I thought I would figure out a possible reason for the Malypsi leaving Lixion. Z seemed to regain his usual emotionless demeanor as a serious look gleamed in his eyes.

"I have no clue what those Malypsi are planning, but I assume it is nothing hostile. Perhaps they are leaving because they are aware of what's to come. I wouldn't expect them to tell Celegons about it; they are in this for themselves after all. You've never heard the word Pythera, have you?" he asked as I tried to think back on my memories. Though no trace of it before now had crossed my mind.

"No I haven't. What does it mean?" I questioned as he started edging closer to me. I suddenly felt an uncomfortable sensation from him, almost as if he was a monster himself.

"It's the name of the species that will end the Celegons."

I was suddenly taken aback by all of this, wondering if he'd actually lost his mind out alone in the forests. Part of me felt compelled to laugh at how ridiculous this all sounded. Coming from a Celegon who trusted monsters, it sounded unreal. Still, Alise trusted monsters, to the very end. Even if I could not fully believe him, I had to at least hear him out as a precaution.

"Why must Celegons taste so delectable?" Z spoke in that monotonous tone as he looked over at nothing in particular. I had no clue what led him to say that of all things. Was he implying that they, like monsters, would also like to eat us? Regardless, I pushed it aside as I had a more interesting topic I wanted to pursue.

"Pythera huh? And what makes you so sure that they will be able to end us so easily?" I asked as I waited for him to speak again, curious as much as I was anxious for the information.

Whatever his response, I would not be too vexed by it. After all there had been no proof that Pythera did exist other than his mention of them. Still... I was eager to know the story he would come up with either way.

"You seem as if you don't believe me," he began, "But you'll find out soon enough even if you do not. They are much bigger than Malypsi, but slightly smaller than the largest of monsters. Incredibly sturdy and heavy, but when needed can outspeed you in moments. More importantly, Pythera have these 'vines' that emerge from their sides, though more grotesquely than how Celegons emerge their wings. When they touch you, it shocks the body in a way that keeps all senses intact aside from the body's mobility, making movement impossible for a few minutes." As he explained, my stomach lurched.

"How will I know if I see one, Z?" I asked as he turned his head to an approaching noise.

He gave me a quick nod before ascending to the sky, removing himself from the scene and leaving me with more questions than answers. Part of me wondered why he had told me anything at all. Of the creatures he described, I could only assume that they were unique in appearance and I would know immediately if I happened to run into one of them.

Marles must have started looking for me; I guess a fair amount of time must have passed since I'd retreated from the room. Guilt and the fluttering feeling returned to my body as I heard him approach. Though I was a little worried for Z, I pushed him out of my mind as I made my way towards Marles. Upon seeing me, his face instantly lit up and he happily walked over. His attention was diverted to the emeri trees behind me almost immediately.

"I was wondering where you went off to. Wow, just look at these emeri trees! It's been too long since I had last seen any," he said as he marveled at their appearance. "Oh! I also managed to scrounge up a few things of value and put them in a pile in the little Celegon's room. Though I think the food will be worth more to us than the things we can pawn off."

"You must have really liked the muffins huh? Missing the perks of luxury?" I grinned as I found myself hugging him from behind.

It sort of shocked me how my body reacted like that on its own. My heart started to beat faster on impact, so much so that he could probably feel it against his back.

"Hey that's not—"

He paused mid sentence as his mind caught up with what was happening. His body tensed slightly and I could now feel his heartbeat in addition to my own.

"So I wasn't dreaming about what happened last night after all?" I heard Marles ask as my heart began to beat faster.

"I was a little impulsive, I know. Sorry for that," I replied as I loosened my arms from his chest. I looked towards the ground, only looking up once I heard him chuckling. He turned around to face me with his usual happy smile, his eyes damp.

"I'm just so glad that it's you." He grinned as he pulled me into a hug. I returned it, now feeling his heartbeat sync up with mine. We continued that way in silence for a little longer. I don't really know how long it was, but I was the first to pull away; we couldn't stay here forever, as nice as that would be. Once I did so we just stared at each other, perhaps for a bit too long—as if waiting for the other to do something. I could feel the heat creeping up my neck and, given his silence, assumed he must have been feeling the same nervousness. Then Marles spoke up again, words only a little broken, "S-so, what do we do now?"

"Well we—" I started as I thought of the usual activities that mates partook in together. "We help each other to make sure that neither of us leaves any clues that we were the thieves that robbed this place!" I stated proudly as his eyes beamed in agreement. "And I'd like to ask your help in moving some bedding materials outside, I'm not sure if I'm strong enough to do so on my own."

We then went straight to work on transporting the cushions and blankets to the dome which I had set up in the garden's open space. It was quite a challenge to not drag the heavier blankets across the dirt when we carried them outside, but we managed somehow. Once the bedding was securely in the dome, we made our way back to Annazie's room to gather the items Marles collected and then proceeded to make multiple trips to the food storage and take as much as we could carry. It was surprising how much would have gone rotten if we had not taken it; wealthy Celegons can afford to waste, indeed.

Our efforts rewarded us with a decent supply of fancier food, a comfortable bedspread, and a few items we could sell to a shopkeeper. While all the work was tiring, we would not be finished until we had successfully relocated far away from the mansion's perimeter. Though coming here had not been the most profitable, it had certainly not been a waste to get more food to prolong our survivability. The emeri especially would be useful to have more of, which was my favorite thing to have acquired from there.

The two of us had started the trek into the deep forest to find a suitable spot to set up the dome for the night. It had been quiet between us since we had last talked in the garden, other than instructing him on things to do back at the mansion. The silence was comfortable, but also lonely. I could hear the many leaves rustle in the trees above, one of the only sounds to break the quiet from time to time when a breeze blew by. Occasionally I glanced at Marles, checking on him; it seemed as if he were perplexed by something, but not enough to speak up about it. The sounds of the sleeping forest continued on for a little longer until I decided to disrupt it.

"After going through everything, I'm sure you'd never want to go on another heist again am I right?" I chuckled softly as I spoke, as I looked towards Marles who had snapped out of his thoughts. He looked away nervously before he started to fidget a bit with his paws.

"N-no, quite the opposite actually. I was a little more underprepared than I originally thought I was, but I'll practice more for the next time." His smile wasn't wide or confident. I let out a happy sigh. His aptitude for wanting to improve was admirable. I was also impressed that things went as well as they did, no matter his own assessment.

"You did great."

"Really? That means a lot coming from you. It makes me happy to hear you say that."

"You're making it seem like I never praise you, but yes I do. It got tight in there a few times, but you always pulled through. You kept your cool and didn't stress, arguably the most important factor in going on a heist."

"Even though I almost gave us away near the end?"

I had almost forgotten about that detail. That moment where I was not certain what he was about to do and what was going through his mind. But now that this information was out in the open, it was hard to resist going off about it.

"You were actually going to do that? What were you thinking?" I practically spat as I stopped in my tracks.

Though I was thankful everything turned out okay, the fact he was planning on giving us away was baffling to me. Marles seemed completely caught off guard when he saw that I was fuming.

"She seemed like she was lonely," he said softly, possibly hoping his compassionate views would lower my agitation.

"So you're saying that if I hadn't kissed you then—" I started and then stilled as my body continued to boil with frustration.

Though once the word 'kissed' left my mouth, the anger I felt was replaced with something else as the memories flooded back. It had only been a day and I was trying so hard to suppress last night's events. My stomach began to tingle as I turned away from Marles. Maybe this was a reason I had avoided acting on them sooner.

"W-why don't we continue this line of conversation in the dome?"

"I agree. I-it's getting dark so we'll have to set it up soon."

Despite the large amount of thick tall trees in the area, we managed to find a spot just big enough for the dome to nestle into. I was quick to set it up. Soon we were inside the compact, but also familiar and comfortable surroundings. Even though I was hungry after all the work we had done today, I practically flung myself onto our new bedding and stripped myself of my satchel. I buried myself in the comfortable mass and began to relax. My relaxation ended when a blanket that was shielding my head was removed.

"L-leave me be, Marles. I'm tired," I told him before snatching the blanket and then covering myself once more.

My face began to feel warm as I heard Marles sigh. I hugged onto one of the nearby cushions. As expected, he was not set on letting me avoid him and soon joined me under the covers. I rolled over so that I would not see him, but that did not stop my heart from beating faster. Soon, I felt a paw press against my back, causing me to squirm uncomfortably.

Once again, I felt myself acting on impulse. My body flipped itself around so I was now facing Marles and soon my arms wrapped around his waist. I held him tightly and laid my head close to his without saying a word. I felt my mouth curl into a smile as I heard his nervous heartbeat, before frowning when I realized mine had begun to mimic.

"You know, by the time I assumed I would receive this level of affection from you, I thought I would be thinner." He chuckled the words awkwardly before I pulled myself closer. After a short quiet pause, he asked softly, "When did you realize it was me?"

"Well, I don't mind being affectionate with you now. W-wait that's not-. Nevermind that. Your question, I'll answer. All I'll say is that I knew longer than you," I replied in an attempt to sound serious as I looked into his eyes.

Unfortunately, this made it harder for me to look at him without feeling fluttery. How could we have a serious discussion if my mind kept getting sidetracked? Still, I felt a little pleasure in knowing he was under the same influence.

"Then it must have been painful to keep it in for so long. I know you had your reasons for waiting—as did I. I know that I'm far from the ideal mate right now, but I will put in the work to get there." He smiled as I moved my head into position to kiss his nose. "L-Lyla! I'm trying to be serious here!" He visibly sulked, his fur reddening on impact.

"Heh, this really is a double-sided pain." I giggled as I continued to plant light kisses on his red fur. His face grew into a deeper pout, as if he was undecided as to whether or not he was enjoying the attention.

"Pain? Is me being your mate really that bad?" he whined the question only slightly as I continued to chuckle.

"N-no, that's not what I was getting at." I smiled. I was trying my hardest to hold back laughter. I did not want him to think I was laughing *at* him.

"It's just that things will be much different now. This vulnerability. I suppose all mates experience it with one another, so it can hardly be classified as an exclusive feeling to just us. But it is still new to me. The prospect of something new does scare me a bit," I admitted as I leaned my head against his.

It all felt too safe. Marles made me feel safe and secure, now more than ever. For as long as I had ever been alive, I never truly felt like I could be at ease. Even alone in the confines of my dome, I was always anxious that something bad could creep up unexpectedly. But when Marles became a constant in my life, everything started to feel more animated.

"In short, you terrify me," I chuckled, causing him to back away for a moment to look me in the eyes. He appeared a bit perplexed as a bitter smile overtook the rest of his features.

"Is that... supposed to make me feel good?" he asked, shaking his head briefly. I shifted closer to him again before putting my paw against his face. A smile broke across my mouth as I stroked his soft fur.

"Let me finish," I spoke up before rubbing his head. "It is true that you make me afraid. But what worries me is the prospect of losing you. I love living life with you by my side. This life is far from easy, but having you around makes it bearable. I'd rather not—I don't want to go back to how it was before you," I confessed, my paws suddenly becoming shaky.

Marles looked down at them as his eyes seemed to emit a soft glow. He placed his own paws over mine and within just a few seconds, the jitters were eradicated completely.

"Well, until then—if such a thing is to happen—let's just enjoy our time together. I'm content with just being here with you like this. Even if you aren't the most sincere at times," he said as I felt my stomach twist a little. "But... I'm very grateful that you still manage to say what's on your mind when it counts. And I'm sure that this will gradually become more natural for the both of us."

His sentiments were a little overbearing, causing my heart to swell in my chest. I was about to lean in to kiss his cheek before I felt my tail being grabbed. The action caused my eyes to grow wide, but I did not stop him. Instead I let him carefully examine the violet stone embedded into it.

"You've always had such a beautiful stone. I suppose that would make sense since stones are said to be a reflector of one's personality," Marles remarked as I scoffed in response.

"That is just a rumor, you know. But you aren't wrong. It is a pleasing color to the eye," I said, watching as he continued to examine it. I liked the purple much better than the white it used to be long ago. "You are... also quite pleasing to look at too," I commented, averting his focus from my tail.

The night continued to go on with a pleasant atmosphere between us. He seemed more than okay with the situation we found ourselves in, which was good. Truthfully, I had never heard of any Celegons who had been unhappy when they had found their mate; it was difficult to call his present mood unhappy, at any rate. Provided we stayed alive, it could be a good thing for us. As they say: when one mate perishes the other will soon follow a similar fate.

Any obstacles seemed non-existent at this moment. Anything and everything to worry about could wait till morning. Morning, where things would surely start to make sense.

Chapter Fifteen: Incandescence

Another night had come to pass and I awoke in a very comfortable state. I vaguely remember dreaming a bit, something awful, but it was so brief I could barely recall the details. Not that I wanted to try, I had more important matters to focus on.

Marles was snoozing peacefully close by, which made me smile. I moved myself closer so that I was nuzzling into his warm soft body. The feeling was so blissful and calming that I practically had to fight myself to stay awake. I continued to do this for a while longer until my stomach began to nag at me to eat something. Regrettably, and after a few moments, I let go of him and began to trudge over to the newly stocked food storage area.

My eyes blinked a few times before I shook my body awake. Eventually I opted to drink more of the soup. While not my favorite of the items, it was filling and would revitalize my senses quicker than anything else we had. After quickly slurping down a bowl, I made my way back to Marles and rejoined him under the blankets. While I tried to be subtle, he had already begun to stir from my movements. Soon, twin sunsets began to gaze tiredly into my eyes.

"Good morning Ly-Ly," he started to yawn out as my chest tightened with excitement.

I simply inched myself closer to him as his senses began to sharpen. My mouth grew to a smirk as I kissed his chest, causing the expected dramatic reaction.

"L-Lyla w-what are you," Marles stuttered as he started turning red almost immediately. I chuckled as I began to comb my paws through his head fluff, causing the already present bed head to appear more floofy than before.

"You're adorable Marley. Sorry, I can't help it; you're just so fun to tease like this." I giggled as he shook himself awake. "Here let me make it up to you. Wait here just a moment." I smiled as I removed myself from the mass of blankets.

I skipped on over to take out a muffin that was stored in one of the jars and then walked over to present it to Marles. Upon seeing it, he immediately turned away from the treat and began to scowl to the point of pouting.

"I have no interest in eating any more of those," he snarked as I continued to hold the muffin. My smile grew as I decided to down the muffin myself. Once he saw the muffin was no more, he turned back to me with a skeptical look.

"You know if you kissed me right now, you might still be able to taste it." I grinned as he grimaced.

"W-we should probably get a head start on the day," he stated nervously as he scampered into the cooking area, where he promptly began to stuff his mouth with berries. The day certainly promised to be interesting.

We were currently starting out in the outskirts of the forest that surrounded Rimereach. This would normally be a little nerve-wracking, seeing that Marles could not fly to safety and running would be tough due to the giant trees, but we were under the state of perpetual infatuation—euphoria. Thankfully, I managed to put that aside temporarily to formulate a safe plan to get out of the forest. As with all plans, no matter how certain they are, they have a chance of failing.

The dew on the trees was quite thick, which made the water roll off the bark in large amounts. We made sure to get our fill of it before we progressed further; morning dew only stuck around for so long and was a good source of fresh water. The ground was slightly muddy, but thankfully covered in many leaves; which meant we did not have to worry about getting our feet too dirty. Though, one did need to be mindful of one's steps. My foot happened to come in contact with a particularly slippery patch of leaves, which caused it to slide out from under me. In turn, this caused me to propel backwards into Marles.

"You okay there Lyla?" he asked as he helped me stabilize myself while he kept his own balance in check.

"Yes I'm f-fine," I stated as I found myself locking eyes with him mid sentence.

Why did it have to be so hard to avoid the fluttery emotions when it was not ideal to have them?

The trees eventually began to spread out and reduce in number, creating more room to navigate and made our traveling easier. This pattern continued until we came across a rare sight. My eyes widened at the large portion of still blue water just up ahead. Marles most likely had no idea, but this was an incredibly unlucky sign. Staying level-headed was key in this situation as there was no reason to frighten Marles.

I used my tail to tug at his to subtly ask him to follow me in a different direction, hopefully leading him away from the stillwater. From the corner of my eye I could see that he seemed a little confused, but his trust in me thankfully prevented him from saying a word. There were not many twigs to step on in this forest, nor were the leaves dry and crunchy; as long as we had stable quiet footing we would be alright. I should have known from the moment I saw that water that luck would not be on our side today.

Low growls resonated in my ears, causing Marles and I to slowly lower ourselves to the damp ground and crawl. Even though no devastating howls filled the air—ones that would emphasize they were on our trail—hearing non-threatening growls this close was still very frightening. Monsters were known to pick up scents at an alarmingly fast rate. As we crawled on the forest floor, my heart twitched impatiently for when we would eventually hear the shrieks. Soon, we started to crawl through a bush as I took the lead and began clearing a path for Marles.

My pulse stopped as my body fell out from under me; it happened so quickly I could barely tell what was going on. The wind was immediately knocked out of me as I tumbled down a wet rocky hill that went on for an eternity. Likely, it was the only thing that kept me from initially screaming in reflex. Once I stopped It took a moment for the pain to catch up and a whimper escaped my mouth. I could feel that I had landed on a rock; it had definitely pierced my left side. I wanted to scream then, but I continued to resist as my eyes watered.

Blinking away my blurred vision, I tried to move as my eyes scanned upwards for Marles. Though I could not see him in my current position;

instead I saw a different life form. While not immobilized, it felt incredibly painful to move and it was agonizing trying to get myself to an upright position. As I did, the creature stared me down motionlessly. Unable to look away, even if I wanted to, I got a good look at its white eyes. Eyes that, even as they lacked color, were filled with life.

It was different from any other monster I had seen, but still so similar. One of the larger ones who was completely black except for the eyes, but still as menacing as any. This monster kept its mouth closed, while most I had seen kept them hinged open hoping to snap down on a Celegon. The fur on this monster was also surprisingly well groomed, though still slightly unkempt. If I had any strength, I would have tried to run away; however, I knew I would never escape in my condition.

A large tongue extended from its now slightly open mouth, though it bared no teeth. My insides felt sickened as it approached my body. The smell was far more pungent up close. It began to lick at my wounds, slightly burning at the contact; it was very different from the soothing effect from Celegon tongues. Still, it was not as bad as touching monster blood; the burning was only temporary and started to lessen the more it licked away my blood. The monster stealing away my blood like this was torture, as if it was trying to slowly torment me until it finally decided to devour me.

The licking continued for a little more until it decided my body was no longer leaking blood enough to its liking. It then retracted its rough slimy tongue and peered into my eyes for a moment. I saw the slightest spark before seeing all of its many teeth emerge. A deadly howl emerged from its lungs before it began to approach my body again. Now it seemed no different from any other monster.

I spat as much ice as I could on its nose before forcing myself on my feet, agonizing each step I took. It let out a shriek before bounding towards me, shaking the ground with each heavy step. No matter how much pain I was in, my body fought to survive as I used everything I had to get it moving. Even if there was no means of escape, to just give up?

I would not stand for that.

The monster's claws soon smacked hard against my back, shoving me down into the mud. I tried to cry out, but the pressure on my lungs was suffocating me. Even though my bones were sturdy, it felt as if my insides were fit to burst. If I let myself die here, what kind of awful Celegon would I be? The only solution was that I do whatever I could, no matter the cost.

My teeth found their way onto the monster's foot. The black blood burned my tongue and started to drip down my throat. Even though it hurt, I had to. I bit down further until I reached what seemed like the monster's bones. If I bit hard enough, they could snap.

Soon I felt myself being flung over the ground and then tumbling further across the muddy clearing. As I laid on my side, my cheek flat on the ground and my head turned towards the creature, my eyes adjusted to see it glaring at me before charging. I only had enough strength left to spit out the remaining black blood that had not yet burned into my mouth. I no longer had the energy to even wince afterwards. My senses had dulled, so I was not sure if I could feel anymore; however, my vision was suddenly filled with a beautiful sight.

Sunsets. Fire. Light.

If my eyes had the energy to sparkle they would have. Flames overtook everything I could see; they quickly engulfed the monster. It was a power unlike I had ever seen from Marles. The intensity of it made me feel warm, but it was difficult to tell if that had more to do with the pain than anything he had done to save me. Still, I liked to think it was the fire.

The monster was quick to escape, but not without strands of singed fur. The fire soon dissipated to reveal Marles. He looked weakened and battered. I felt agonized that there was nothing I could do to aid him. My heart sank; I watched as the monster began to swipe at Marles.

A wave of dizziness overwhelmed me. From my loss of blood or ingesting the black blood, I did not know, but my life force was slipping away. My lungs too, were ceasing to function. I could only watch the fight as I felt my other senses begin to shut down. To conserve what little energy I had left, I shut my eyes to try to keep living just a little longer. Even if it meant I couldn't see him, I hoped he was alright.

Focusing on breathing, I strained to listen even as the world began to go quiet. The tiniest bit of Marles' voice began to fade, the monster's roars a distant hum. Anything and everything beyond that was gone. As the embrace of life faded from me, I could no longer tell if I was breathing. The last to go was my mind. It would not be long before that drifted away too.

. . ❧ . .

I'm sorry Marles, for leading you down this path. If not for me you would have been alive and well back with your family.

Is that really what you think, that you brought him to his end?

Of course. If I never met him, things would not have turned out this way.

Maybe so. Or he may have met a much worse fate if he had not met you.

Maybe. I guess I'll never know huh?

You tell yourself that. Farewell Skyli.

. . ❧ . .

A slight tingle tickled at my nose. It continued to pester me until it was all I could think about. My body let out a sneeze, which stopped the issue. I then felt content that the problem was no longer present until I began to feel more tingles in various other parts of my body. My ears, eyes, limbs and even my tail were all begging to be moved in some way.

Soon, I felt my heart pounding in my chest and a familiar sweet metallic taste in my mouth. My heavy eyelids forced themselves open, but in that moment everything was blurry and I could barely make out colors. Muffled sounds began to pass through my ears, agitating me. I had no idea what was happening around me and my senses were too dull for me to tell. Drowsiness soon took over and compelled me to close my eyes.

"Lyla?"

I stirred around a bit and blinked barely, not fully opening my eyes. Before I even opened them I realized my body had serious dull aches coming from all over. The pain in my left side hurt the most, but my body was also still battered from having been thrown by the monster. All of my muscles seemed to be waking up and coming to terms with how tender they were.

My teeth were clenched before I breathed heavily; my lungs were in a lot of pain, perhaps even more than before. I felt my mouth being opened up before special fruit was being squeezed inside. The metallic juices rushed down my throat; I bit into it with meager strength.

I tried opening my eyes again after swallowing the small emeri to see if things were clearer now. Things were still slightly blurry, but after a bit more blinking my vision cleared to a satisfactory level. I was back in the dome and nestled in the new bedding we recently stole. Marles was sitting in front of me with reddened eyes that looked overcome with exhaustion. Upon closer examination, I saw that he also suffered from plenty of wounds, most notably the gash on his torso. Even though they appeared to be healing, seeing him like that hurt me.

"Marles, I-I'm so sorry. It's m-my fault," I sputtered out before pain kicked in. Even though it felt like the wound at my side was reopening, my heart was aching more in this moment.

My vision had returned to being blurry again as I cried. I was right; because of me Marles was hurt. My mistake for falling down like that.

"L-Lyla, wait a moment. It's no one's fault. Things just happened. Everything's going to be fine now, I promise. We're both still here and able to recover from that incident safely," Marles reassured me as he lightly touched my paw.

I could barely feel it, but what I could feel felt quite nice. I took a breath to calm my nerves as I tried to convince myself there was no reason to panic.

"Still, you ended up hurt as a result of my slip up. I'm grateful that we're both still alive after that though, so please don't misunderstand. Thank you for saving us back there." I tried to smile, but I was unsure if I was since my mouth felt numb. Marles eyes began to look downcast after my statement.

"I wouldn't have been able to save us if it were just me." He sighed as he looked over at me with a bitter smile. "A Malypsi of all things happened to be nearby when I started to get hit pretty hard. More monsters had entered the area too. He managed to take them all on by himself while I was lying on the ground. If not for him then..." Marles paused before looking over at me. "I'll have to do a better job in the future to protect my mate from harm."

His face had brightened up, which in turn made me feel lighter. I tried to move my paw to touch him, but unfortunately was still too weak to move properly. Even with us both ragged like this, he managed to smile and try to make me feel better.

"I'll work on using my talent more effectively. I never really saw a need for it when I was on my own, but practicing will help both of us avoid death in the long term. Let's stay alive together for as long as time allows us," I stated before coughing a bit.

He then smiled at me before suddenly leaning over to kiss gently on my mouth. Despite being numb, I could at least feel the pressure. The warm scent of him overwhelmed me in that moment as well, and I took solace in that. My face flushed as all of the pain in my body dissipated for a moment. When he pulled away, he held my gaze for a few beats before suddenly becoming flustered.

"Something wrong, Marley?" I began to chuckle before realizing it would hurt my lungs.

He shook himself before scooching his way beside me and laying down. Then he lightly pressed his body against my side, but not too much as our wounds were still quite tender.

"Let me know if this causes you any pain; I'll move away if I'm hurting you." He let out a tired sigh before leaning his head down on the cushion in front of him.

On the contrary, his presence seemed to have a healing effect. A comfortable silence took place as we rested in the warm bedding. Until a specific question arose in my mind.

"Marles, did that Malypsi give a reason as to why they helped us? They are quite strong, but it's unusual for them to casually help Celegons they do not know in danger," I stated as Marles turned his head towards me.

"Oh right. After he drove off the remaining monsters, he made a comment that he was lacking in training and wanted to get a bit more practice before he left Lixion. He was a strange blue fellow, but much less uptight than the other Malypsi we met," Marles explained.

"You said he was *blue*?" I asked as I tried to think of any Malypsi who were not green furred. Perhaps the Malypsi's fur looked bluish due to the lighting in the area.

"Yep, blue fur and had these piercing yellow-green eyes. He also had this long red blanket-like thing that draped over his back. It looked a bit feathery in texture," Marles went on as I tried to picture the Malypsi in my mind.

There was a chance he could have misremembered things; he might have been more hurt than he seemed. As I could not check in my present state, there was no way for me to know then. Even so, I definitely believed him when he said a Malypsi came to our rescue, just not a blue one. There was indeed a singular blue Malypsi like Marles had described, but that would mean Marles had seen the Emperor. Everyone knew that the Emperor was always accompanied by at least one other Malypsi—one of the few he trusted implicitly.

Marles let out a yawn before wincing in pain as he began to gently rub at his wounds. Even though I felt less guilty about the turn of events, it was still difficult to watch while he was in pain. Knowing he saw me in a similar state was also painful in a different aspect. The both of us were almost too weak to care for each other. Marles appeared barely mobile to me, though he was putting in a good effort to hide it.

"How is our emeri stock looking?" I inquired. He looked at me with nervous eyes.

"Well we had to use up the ones from Reene's family garden..." He sighed as I looked at him, shocked. "No more than that as of yet, but we will need more soon."

I was bewildered at that fact. Not that we had used the ones we had just acquired, but how many we had needed to recover. Then I realized it was more likely that we had not eaten or used what we actually needed to recover.

"How many have you used for yourself, Marles?" I asked, hesitantly awaiting the answer.

"Let's see, I've given you two to eat and used one for treating your outer wounds. Though it's probably time to use another to treat your outer wounds again. Oh right, you wanted to know about my intake! For myself I've had one for my insides and one for my outsides," Marles said and I began to worry.

"That's not nearly enough! You need—" I was cut off as I began to have a brief coughing fit. Once I could speak again I continued to scold him. "More than that, Marles! Please eat at least one more and don't worry if we run out of emeri. We can always get more later when we're better," I demanded as he reluctantly began to walk over to where we had the emeri stored.

One emeri would be fine for minor injuries, but certainly not enough to heal wounds of his caliber. If he was worried about not having enough to treat me that would be different, but I knew well there was enough emeri stocked for both of us to recover. Marles quickly returned holding two emeri in his paws and instantly devoured one of them for himself. The pleasant look on his face after he did so, and knowing that the emeri would go right to work, made me feel warmer.

"If you're feeling up to it, I can start reapplying emeri juice to your wounds." Marles smiled as I gave him a weak nod.

I could feel every drop of emeri liquid as it seeped into my sores. It made me feel incredibly relaxed and comfortable, and a bit of an energy boost towards recovery. My limbs were still weak, but the emeri gave them some encouragement to get moving. I waited patiently for Marles to finish as I began to stretch and flex my arms and legs.

Afterwards, Marles ate the emeri pulp per my request and laid next to me. There was not much to talk about as our bodies relaxed. The both of us were quite weak even after ingesting emeri; so it was no surprise when our exhaustion consumed us and we both fell into a peaceful slumber.

· · ∾ · ·

After another day had passed, I awoke with sore, but much better limbs. I turned around almost unconsciously and found my head nuzzling into a texture softer than the blankets. Instead of opening my eyes, my face instinctively snuggled further into the object until my brain consciousness caught up with instinct. I wrapped my arms and legs around his body and pressed my ear up against his chest to hear a slow contented heartbeat. Moments later the heartbeat picked up in pace, signifying he was awake.

"Sorry, did I wake you, Marles?" I asked as I began to hug tighter. The heartbeat increased in speed and mine soon began to follow, mimicking it.

"Y-you did, but it's f-fine," he stated as his arms began to gently find their way around my back. "How are you feeling?"

"Well... as you see I can move, but still a bit sore. Are you feeling better?" I asked, finding I had little interest in moving from my current position.

"Yeah, so much better," he said; I could practically hear him smile.

As I smiled as well, I realized my mouth was dry and slightly parched from lack of emeri or water consumption. We must have been asleep for a lot longer than a few hours.

"Marles, I'm going to pop outside for a moment to see what time it is. Hopefully morning so we can get some water to drink off the trees," I stated before pulling my body up to a standing position, wincing slightly as my legs wobbled beneath me. Marles looked up at me with surprise before standing up on his own with a smile.

"I'll come with you. You still seem a bit hurt. You can hold onto me for support if you'd like." His smile remained as he extended his left arm out to me. I took hold of it, but was not sure how much it would prevent me from losing my balance. Still, the gesture made my heart warm.

"Thank you, but before we go there's one thing I need to do first. It's important that I do this in case death is waiting right outside for us," I explained before reaching to kiss him on the mouth.

He returned my affections before pulling himself back from embarrassment. I grinned before tugging his arm along to the dome's door. We soon emerged from the dome's comfortable confines to the crisp air of the outside. The first thing I noticed put a damper on my previously chipper mood.

Ice flurries. They playfully flickered down from above as the wind carried them to their final destination. As a Celegon who could concoct her own ice using magic, I had grown to be quite fond of their beauty. But seeing this many all throughout the air caused a chill to roll down my spine.

It was the start of another cold year.

Chapter Sixteen: Return

As time went on, a powdery ice began to pile up all over Lixion. It was a gradual process, and after around four months there did not seem to be a single spot left that was untouched by white. This was still considered early in the cold year with the worst left to come, though Marles and I were adapting quite well to the changing environment.

While my ice talent did next to nothing to help in the ongoing cold year, his fire talent had proven to be useful once again. From melting the frigid ice piles into usable water, to being a consistent source of warmth, he really was helpful. Though I had long since gotten past merely being appreciative of his talent's benefits. He had remained so kind and hopeful throughout this awful climate as we continued to figure each other out. Still, there were a few things I had yet to become used to.

"Lyla, come here for a moment would you?" Marles smiled as he clasped his arms around my waist and pulled me close to him.

Additionally, in these four months his figure had become more refined; which emphasized his handsomeness to other female Celegons. While not inherently an issue, this seemed to give him a bit of an ego boost and bolstered his courage in being affectionate with me. Though I greatly appreciated the attention, he only seemed to have the confidence to do so when we were in a town. Which of course meant plenty of Celegons around to eavesdrop.

"M-Marles! Can you quit it already? You know how I feel when you do those things so openly," I complained as my body grew warm all over.

As expected, a few Celegons in town had already begun glancing over this way. His grip soon loosened and I quickly squirmed my way out of his arms. He sported a happy grin on his face; it irked me that he never seemed the least bit nervous about doing that. However, when we were alone, his behavior contrasted greatly with how he was acting now.

The two of us had wound up back in Oakurrow after traveling around to other towns in Lixion. Since the cold year started, other Celegons had been more wary of losing their items to thieves, making our work that much harder. I supposed all Celegons were having a rough time, aside from the wealthiest few. Still, we scraped by with what we could; I had little to complain about as our quality of life was far from being the worst. Additionally, thanks to Marles' optimism, it was not as noticeable when things were going downhill.

The last time we were in Oakurrow was when Marles had been caught *procuring* a bag full of goods from a stall merchant, which meant a proper payment to her was necessary if we were to stay here. We'd only be losing a gold orb to cover the fee, so nothing too outrageous. Of course, losing any orbs in a time like this was downright awful. Still, it was worth it to make sure we could walk around town freely without looking over our shoulder, or trying to use disguises and making ourselves look suspicious in the process.

Most of the stalls had become covered with monster pelts in effort to block out the cold, so we had to be sure to peer carefully into each one. Since there were very few in the tiny town, it was easy to locate. Her stall was cloaked in pelts, and she was also using a blanket to keep herself warm in the more than chilly weather. As we stood in front of her stall her sullen eyes briefly squinted in our direction. They blinked with apparent curiosity at first, and then lit up in recognition once they landed on Marles—widening briefly.

"N-no way, it's," she started as Marles handed her a gold orb with a smile; which she quickly accepted. She looked at him and then back at the orb, smiling in turn. "Th-thanks for paying up. No p-problem about the delay," she stuttered a bit as her fur tinted slightly red. Marles gave her a nod before we left her stall and continued on. Once we were far enough away I let out a snicker.

"If I had known that would have been her reaction, we'd have been better off giving her a white orb instead." I grinned as he looked at me, one brow arched in question—as if he didn't fully understand. "Well, what's done is done. So, want to hit up some other unlucky—"

"Is that Skyli and... Iseirre?"

We turned a bit towards a familiar voice to see it coming from a mint green Celegon with an orange one at her side. I smiled a bit as they approached us.

"Ariele and Basion? It's been a while; glad you two are holding up alright." I grinned as I scanned my surroundings a little more. Curiously, I did not see either blue Celegon nearby. An unpleasant feeling began to lurk in my stomach.

"Blubelle, has she—"

"Run off on me along with Soeki? The nerve of them, splitting up our team like this," Ariele growled as I sighed quietly in relief. At least she was alright for the time being. Ariele quickly calmed down as Basion began to speak up.

"The two of them will be fine, don't worry. We have plans to meet up at the Iseirre mansion a few days from now," he explained as my heart almost stopped. I looked over at Marles as he seemed just as taken aback as I was.

"The Iseirre mansion? You're going there?" Marles questioned as I began to recall a detail I had kept from him.

"Ariele's been getting quite a reputation for her monster culling, so they invited us as a group to be at their social gathering. Wait, hold on," he said next, looking at Marles, brow knitting. "Aren't you affiliated with them?" Basion asked and Marles shook his head.

"N-no, not anymore at least," he said as he began to smile awkwardly, as his tail flickered about. Basion stared wordlessly at him for a brief moment before turning to Ariele. It was clear she had been listening, but her mind seemed to be wandering to other thoughts.

"That's unfortunate then," she said. "Though if you do end up there, do me a favor and distract that Blubelle for a bit." Ariele said this with a dash of irritability in her voice, before quickly brightening at the both of us. "Oh and, congratulations. You two seem happy together." A cheeky grin appeared before she began to walk off with Basion. He quickly trailed after her while bidding us farewell with a wave. Thus leaving me alone with a slightly anxious Marles at my side.

For now I chose to ignore Ariele's bait, too distracted by Marle's reaction. It seemed justified; he had not seen his family since he'd run off with me months ago. I had often wondered if he had a longing to return home to them, despite never bringing them up to me. Even though he was so open with me about various other subjects, talks of family felt almost forbidden. Perhaps it was only fair as I had never felt the inclination to tell him about my own past and family aside from Alise. Regardless of how he felt, I did want to make sure he was alright.

"Marles, if you want to we could- h-hey!" I sputtered as he began to pull me behind him by interlocking his tail with mine.

Aside from the initial surprise, I did not protest and allowed him to lead me. We continued briskly until we were just outside of town and the ice was coating the bottoms of our feet. His tail soon unwrapped from mine and he began to collect together a pile of fallen twigs. I quickly pitched in and soon we had enough for Marles to ignite.

Marles used the tip of his tail to set the supple pile ablaze before melting away the ice and snow around the flames. We then sat on the slightly wet dirt together and began to stare at the glowing embers.

"It's a little sad, you know?" he said before reaching to grab a stray twig to toss into the flames. "Since this cold year started most of the plants have gone to sleep. Even the plants in our dome have been affected by it despite my best efforts. I miss all the wild greenery that's now enveloped in ice and being able to use my plant talent more effectively," he continued before finding something else to fuel the fire. My heart sank a little as he said that.

Though his skill with his fire talent was incredible and resourceful, he was happiest when practicing his plant talent—which he was far less adept at. When one considered that most harvestable herbs had become quite scarce, he also had a lot less painting materials at his disposal. Even though he was good at keeping up a cheerful attitude, not being able to practice two of his favorite hobbies had to be eating away at him in some way. With our environment becoming quite monochrome, I worried about how he was handling the loss and the lack of color in his life.

"But you know, they'll wake up eventually," he said.

Marles began to smile as he moved himself slightly closer to me. I could not help but smile too at his unshakeable optimism. Though, I did frown when remembering what Basion had said back in town. Marles must have seen something in my expression and caught on to what I was thinking. Or it might have been that he planned to talk about the next topic anyway. Regardless, he sighed before continuing.

"It's been a while since I've seen them. I wonder if they think I'm dead?" He let out a half-hearted laugh. "Or think of me much anymore."

"Do you think of them often?"

He seemed to tense up for a moment before relaxing again. His mind began to ponder words before a small grin appeared.

"Not often, but occasionally I do. They are of my blood and contributed to raising me, after all. Just as you think of your late Alise from time to time. Though, much less than I used to as there's someone else prioritizing my thoughts." His fur reddened and he turned away in embarrassment. His attempts at being suave were appreciated, though I wished he felt less awkward after doing so at times. "I-I feel like I'm more of a Skyli than an Iseirre these days; it suits me don't you agree?"

I leaned closer to him and gave him a brief side hug. I was elated he felt that way, though I still had other things that lingered on my mind.

"It hasn't crossed your mind that you might want to see them again?" I asked as my tail began to fidget back and forth. "Seeing how close we are and all," I went on as he flinched at my sudden touch to his thigh. He quickly shook himself free of the jitters and met my gaze. It was almost as if he was testing me—to see if I was up to no good.

"I suppose seeing them again wouldn't be so bad, especially if you tagged along. Is my Ly-Ly curious about meeting the ones who raised me?" Marles grinned cheekily and I closed my eyes for a moment.

It would be a lie to say I had no interest in the slightest. Still... they *were* wealthy Celegons; I would also be lying if I claimed I held no prejudice towards that class. Though, when I considered how well Marles had turned out, I decided it was possible for them to not be too unbearable despite this flaw.

"N-no, not particularly. Meeting them sounds quite daunting. I did take you away from them after all," I said as I wondered how they would react to finding that out. Marles began to chuckle softly before moving in closer.

"In all fairness, *I* decided to leave. If that was an issue, or if they needed me for something, they would have sent someone to find me. As we've encountered no such Celegon, my presence there is clearly not required. Wait, hold on Lyla," he paused for a moment before thinking to himself. A curious smirk found its way to his mouth and his eyes gleamed with wonder. "You were thinking of robbing them, weren't you?"

A chill ran down my spine that was *not* induced by the falling ice flurries around us. The thought had definitely crossed my mind, but I would have never mentioned it to Marles; it was his former home, after all. The Iseirre mansion was surely stacked in terms of valuables, not to mention the social gathering would attract more wealthy Celegons with their own valuables in tow. Marles had grown quick to catch on to my more devious thoughts, but I did not expect this. Guilt began to wash over me as he probably assumed this was the reason I brought seeing his family up in the first place. My eyes flickering away from his certainly did not help paint me in an innocent light either.

"Sounds like an interesting idea."

I stared at him, a little confused on what he meant. Not many Celegons would be willing to rob their blood relatives, even in dire situations.

"Are you implying that you would be okay with stealing from your family's mansion? For the record, I was not even going to bring up the idea but... since you did..." I paused as I gazed into his mischievous eyes. They were just as entrancing as ever, but seeing that extra glint tightened my chest. Soon I began to shudder a bit and realized that the branch pile Marles had lit had almost gone out.

"Oh so it was on your mind after all," he said, his voice sounding playfully amused. He tapped my nose before continuing with, "I'd be on board with it. Our survival is important and I know however much we take my family would be just fine—even in this unending cold. So why don't we do both? You can meet them. We'll use that to get in the front door. And then we'll rob them; sound like a plan?" He smiled as I continued to find myself surprised at how okay he was with this course of action.

If he was not my mate, I would have suspected that this was an elaborate scheme to get me caught. No, Marles would not have been capable of coming up with something so fiendish even if we were simply allies. Though, seeing him plotting this made me think otherwise. Perhaps my crooked ways had finally started to taint him. As the fire's cooled embers blew through the air, I figured it was worth a shot.

"Alright, it's a plan then. But... about the social gathering...," I started as I began to grimace at the idea of attending one by choice. He also seemed a little hesitant when I mentioned it and must have sensed how I felt; a bright smile soon found its way to his face.

"Well as long as we're able to endure it together it can't be too bad," he reassured me as I began to nuzzle gently into his side in hopes of sharing some warmth. "Y-yeah, everything will be fine." I kissed his neck a little before he eventually sprang up from the ground quite flustered. I chuckled quietly as I stood up, watching as the last bit of heat faded from the ashes.

"If we're really set on this we should get moving. It's already past noon and it will take us a bit to travel to Iseirre mansion," I said as I wrapped my tail around his. He nodded as his embarrassment faded away and we began to make our way in the direction of the mansion.

As we walked through the icy forest, I thought about returning to the mansion and actually being able to steal from it this time around. It was also almost nostalgic looking at all the trees just outside Oakurrow. If only I could remember the exact one Marles fell from months ago; it was a shame they looked so different covered in ice. Beautiful, but unrecognizable. I wonder if my mother could see me now, would she think the same?

The ice flurries had begun to sprinkle down from the many trees. It was quite noticeable when they dotted Marles' dark green fur, while it made mine look slightly whiter. Though their presence meant death for many Celegons, I had a hard time not finding them enchanting in a way. It also felt positively refreshing to have them land on one's tongue. When Marles was not looking of course.

After a while our feet had begun to grow numb from trudging in the thick layer of fallen ice flurries. Unlike most situations where a Celegon could adapt and grow used to a situation, the more we walked in it the worse it seemed to get despite having to deal with it on the ground for days. Marles used to melt paths for us, but that was a quick way to drain his magical energy. As much as it would be nice to take breaks, it was best to not waste any daylight; this was especially true during a cold year. Traversing at night when it was coldest would be detrimental to our health at these temperatures.

Time slowly passed as we continued onwards, but soon enough it was too dark to continue and we needed to set the dome up for the night. The outside air was beyond frigid, made worse by the ongoing breeze; there was only so much comfort Marles' flames could bring. My paws were shaking so much from the cold that it was hard to press the right buttons on the remote. Soon, I managed to hit the correct one and we quickly squeezed our bodies inside once the dome had enlarged itself. While not drastically warmer, I took solace in the blankets and was happy that the dome's walls shielded against the wind. I spent no time snuggling up to Marles as it was beneficial to share body heat.

In mere moments, exhaustion began to take over my senses. The colder temperatures really did have a way of tiring our bodies. Time seemed to speed up rapidly during our slumber and eventually it was time to rise again. The cold also made waking up considerably more difficult.

Waking up and breathing in the cold air alone almost immediately put me back to sleep. It almost felt as if my nose had frozen over; I quickly began to rub it in hopes of warming it up. My eyes opened up and I frowned. Even though we were in the dome and underneath blankets, it was still dreadfully cold when the sun had not risen much yet. Thankfully Marles was close and getting closer would make getting up much more bearable.

As I snuggled closer hoping to share some warmth with him, I felt him begin to stir as well. Though I was sure he appreciated the contact, especially with how much warmer he felt by comparison. He began to squirm uncomfortably as my body temperature synced with his.

"Y-you're very cold you know," Marles groaned while his body momentarily shivered. I nuzzled myself against his chest and began to gently brush against his fur with my paw. Soon I planted a deep kiss on his lower right cheek. "H-hey! Your mouth is cold too," he whined as his fur became dusted with red. Ignoring his protests, I climbed on top of him with a smirk and stared him down.

"Aw come on, you're hurting my feelings saying stuff like that. You know, back when you were fluffier I never recall you having a problem with being cold." I sulked as he stared back in confusion.

""Fluffier"? I don't think I've lost any fur- wha. L-Lyla! You can't possibly mean you preferred me like that!" He began to pout as my grin grew.

"I don't see why you're so upset over it. Having that padding would definitely help you now with how cold it's gotten. Not to mention how adorable you were! I could just feed you muffins all day," I teased as he continued to show a sour, but not hostile mood.

He then closed his eyes for a moment before proceeding to get out from under me. After standing himself up he shivered a bit before looking back and giving me a weak smile.

"I'm going out for a little bit, but I'll be back before too long," he stated before abruptly leaving the dome.

I straightened myself up and sighed. While I did not mind him going out on his own occasionally as he often went to paint, his alone time outside had increased quite a bit in the past two months. He used to leave an average of once per week or less, now it seemed as if he went every morning for a little while. He wasn't painting much either, given the lack of materials. Ultimately I never tried to stop him if he wanted time alone, though I worried for his safety.

I may have felt the tiniest bit lonely too; I already missed his presence. He must not have been bothered by it much. Otherwise would he not rush back? I made myself shake off those feelings as I moved to prepare for the day.

Our food stores had almost run completely barren. This was one of the main hardships of the cold year and was to be expected, but that knowledge didn't make it any easier. There was still a small number of roots in a jar; not much, but enough to last a few days. I pulled out two, quickly devouring them. It calmed my stomach a bit. I realized then that Marles had left without eating anything again, and I could only hope he would find a bit of forage during his time outside.

I began to tidy up the different sections of the dome. There was not a lot to do, with it being fairly small and regularly cleaned, but doing so made it easier to upkeep. Once the cleaning was finished, all there was left to do was wait for Marles to return. And what better way to wait in comfort from blankets. Though with the cold, it was hard not to fall back asleep instantly.

"Ly-Ly, I'm back."

I felt my body being pulled into something warm. My mouth instantly curled into a smile before the rest of me had time to react. Soon my eyes were open and I flipped myself around and nuzzled my head against his face. He seemed to be reciprocating without hesitation, which excited my pulse for a bit.

"I-I don't think I was asleep for too long," I mumbled, as it truly felt as if just moments ago I had drifted off. He chuckled a bit which made my face grow warmer.

"Don't worry, it's perfectly fine if you had slept a bit more. You probably need to conserve more energy in this weather. I wasn't gone for long and there is still plenty of daylight left to travel," he reassured me as I stretched. My paw began to trail from his chest all the way down to his stomach, which tensed on impact.

"Did you find any berries or roots to eat during your excursion?" I asked as I began to caress his sides.

"N-no. I didn't s-see any today unf-fortunately," he stuttered as I moved my head up to kiss his nose. His face had grown completely red and he had trouble looking into my eyes all while having a big awkward smile on his face.

"Then go eat some of the roots. You should at least have a little; it's easier to get sick when it's cold like this. Up you go now!" I instructed as I playfully started to push him upright.

Per my request he ate some before the two of us resumed our journey. The ice flurries had come once again and were falling heavier than usual. They were thicker; which was not a good combination with today's strong winds. It had only been flurrying lightly earlier, but the weather had taken a nasty turn the moment we packed up the dome. This only further fueled my determination to reach our destination, as then we would not have to worry as much about the atrocities of the cold year for at least a little while.

Hours soon passed as we witnessed what felt like a colder and windier repeat of the previous day. Our feet were dripping wet with frigid water and our fur coated with a layer of white. I'm sure the white had covered my purple coloring quite well, enough to make me look almost completely white again. That is, aside from my eyes and tail stone at least. We'd had to shake off the buildup several times to avoid being caked in a freezing mass of ice. The sun gradually went down until the sky was a fair orange and soon we could see glimpses of the Iseirre mansion through the trees.

"Well, h-here we are finally," I said as I shivered. Marles appeared to be worried as he gazed at the ice covered mansion in the distance, so I quickly nudged at his side. "Hey, I bet your old female caretakers will be excited to have their sweet Marles to attend to again. They'll be so thrilled that they won't remember your little farewell gift to them before running off with me," I joked as his fur turned as red as his tail stone.

"You'll never let me live that down, will you?" Marles sighed and grew a slight smile as I began dusting off more clear crystals that found their way onto his fur.

As we approached the entrance, there were already a few Celegons scurrying about outside. My first instinct was to find a stealthy way by, but I had to reassure myself that would not be necessary. They seemed hard at work trying to clear the entrance of white; though, their efforts would be in vain as the ice would simply pile up once more. Still, however focused on their work they were, once we got closer their ears were alerted to our footsteps. Their eyes lit up once their gazes were set on Marles.

In no time at all, the five of them that were outside instantly took to swarming around him. Though I was given a few confused glances, it was clear Marles had become the center of attention. Some of them seemed to be on the verge of tears seeing him again.

"M-Mars, it's really you! You've finally come back home," one cried, choking on her words as she could barely contain her excitement.

It was honestly a little heartwarming to see them all gushing over him after not seeing him for so long. That is, until I found myself excluded from the circle as they huddled around him. I had to take a few steps backwards to excuse myself from being shoved by the others; they were too fascinated with Marles to recognize my presence.

"Where have you been all this time, handsome? I should scold you for running off without saying goodbye to us, but I'm just so glad you're home again!" another spoke up as the others agreed with her statement. "And just look at you! You're looking like your old self again and seem just positively radiant. Though I hope you've been eating enough, food has been scarce for most after the cold year began. Oh! Who am I kidding? A physique like that needs to be well fueled to maintain." She smiled mischievously as she placed her paws on Marles' waist.

The others soon began feeling all over his body, giggling as they made contact. My chest twinged a bit at their antics, though it seemed mostly harmless. Marles himself seemed quite embarrassed over the whole ordeal and shot a glance over towards me that almost seemed as if he was begging for help.

"O-okay that's enough now, all of you! Sorry I made you all worry, but as you can see—I'm still alive and well. You see I've been with Ly-"

"And just *who* is this?" another caretaker suddenly blurted as she locked her green eyes on mine.

The others soon followed suit and began staring me down intently. Though I did not pick up any hostility, it felt like quite a change in atmosphere to when they were chatting up Marles. Still, they were rightfully cautious of me, especially someone in close proximity to Marles.

"She's the one who lured our Mars away!"

Now I felt I was about to be pummeled by verbal threats. There was a bit of a mixed reaction to who I was, which was oddly enough a little humorous.

"No that can't be right, she must have retrieved Mars from the wilds and brought him back to us!"

"If that's the case, then I bet she's expecting a reward. Celegons like her all do."

"Then she's no good! Can't be trusted and shouldn't be allowed to associate with someone as upstanding as Mars!"

They began to argue amongst each other briefly before Marles moved his way over to me. He nuzzled himself close into my side before brushing his nose gently against my neck. They quieted down real soon after that. While my body was stiff in shock and my heart was a fluttery mess, he at least made it known to them who I was to him. I hoped the ice had coated my face well enough to hide the fact that I was blushing like a fool; I did not want Marles' caretakers' first impression of me to be that of a red-faced speechless idiot.

"While I find all of your concerns endearing, Lyla is my mate. I know this is sudden, but I would appreciate it if you all treated her nicely and not judge her too soon. I'm sure you all have many questions to ask, but at the moment we're a bit tired from traveling today. Could I trouble one of you to spare a room for us?" Marles asked as my heart continued to flutter.

His direct, but not stern demeanor was quite an attractive side of him I did not see too often. Despite them still seeming cautious, for the most part it appeared as if they trusted Marles. One immediately started racing to the mansion's entryway while the others began to chatter again.

"Mars has finally found his mate, this is great news!"

"But if she's not someone of high standing then..."

"Look at how happy he seems though! She has nice colors too."

"But the Sir and Lady..."

"Forgive the others for rambling, Mars. I would be delighted to escort the pair of you to your room. We've been keeping it nice and fresh in case of your return, which you have—so if you both will just follow me?" a caretaker chirped as she began to usher us over towards the mansion's large fancy wooden doors.

With daylight illuminating them, they seemed quite impressive and uniquely carved in a way that added elegance to the mansion. Though my eyes were intrigued by their design, I was more interested in what was within when they began to open up. Not ten paces away from entering the mansion ourselves, a forest green Celegon with intense yellow eyes hastily made her way out of the mansion. I instantly picked up a haughty vibe seeping out of her, though hints of distress were also in the air.

She immediately locked eyes with me before turning her attention towards Marles and then the caretakers who were still socializing. She took a deep breath before storming a bit past us, which intimidated me slightly. Marles seemed unfazed however, so I assumed everything would be alright. The caretaker who was at our side simply nodded her head and made her way inside the mansion before the other Celegon could speak.

"You all have a lot of nerve! I do not shelter and feed you creatures so you can sit around slacking off. Your only task was to clean up all this white trash before the guests arrive. Was I not clear enough?" she barked at the group.. They quickly resumed their efforts in no time at all as the Celegon beside us sighed and turned her attention back on us.

"So you've finally decided to come crawling back, is it? Well, at least you've finally gotten around to improving your figure, so that should help with your courting arrangements—which will be scheduled accordingly. And you, scurry off now. This is a private conversation," she said sharply as her gaze shot to mine. Instead of doing what she requested, Marles pulled me close to kiss at my neck. The expression in her eyes dulled as she continued to stare into mine.

"I see. Very well, if that's how it's to be."

Chapter Seventeen: Affluent

The forest green Celegon continued to stare at me with discontentment until she finally turned her back on us. While her gaze no longer lingered on me, the intense presence she held still remained. Her eyes gave off the opposite effect Marles' did, striking and imposing without a hint of softness. My body stiffened a little as she spoke again.

"I'll notify your father immediately. When we are ready to see you, we will send a caretaker to fetch you both. While I wish your return would have come with fewer complications, we'll make do. As for *you,*" she said with emphasis, pausing long enough to narrow her eyes on me, "Cause any trouble on my property and I will dispose of you *myself.*" Then, without another word, she swiftly turned on her heel and went back inside the mansion. When her presence could no longer be felt, it was then I felt myself relax. I released a sigh and closed my eyes. .

"Your mother seems quite... formal?" I awkwardly smiled as he nodded in agreement.

"One could say that. She didn't seem as furious as I thought she'd be, all things considered. Still, I wish her tone with you could have been a little more respectful." He frowned and I quickly took hold of his paw.

"Her reaction was understandable and, honestly, I'm not too bothered by it. It's not like she forbade me to set foot inside her home, so no need to act so worried," I reassured him as I gave his arm a squeeze. Then I began to shiver again. Standing still did little to ease the bite of crisp air. I glanced over at the caretakers, who were still struggling to get rid of the fallen ice flurries. "Seems like they could use a little help," I remarked as Marles' eyes lit up with surprise.

"Is Lyla Skyli suggesting we help others without gaining something in return? Goodness, you really have changed. Oh," he said, pausing. I could see something had just occurred to him. Briefly, he looked put out. But I knew it wasn't one of his real pouts; I had seen enough of those by now to tell when he was being silly. "I should've known. You want to get in their good graces." He sighed with very obvious exaggeration before flashing a wicked smile. I playfully hit his arm as we continued walking.

"There's nothing wrong with building a little positive reputation here and there on occasion. Though I'm not sure where you pulled the *we* from, Marley." I rolled my eyes, but the action was playful rather than antagonistic. "I was *merely* going to suggest your fire talent would prove very effective in this situation." I smiled as we neared the caretakers.

Their eyes met mine with skepticism, but they were more mollified once they realized Marles and I would be assisting in the clean-up. Well... they were probably more receptive *because* of Marles presence more than mine, but I would take what I could get.

While it was true I had not planned on helping initially, I found myself working together with the four of them. As we pushed the piles of ice into small clumps, Marles would come by to melt each one. If only my talent could be so convenient; using it now would only create more of a mess. As the five of us continued, our efforts soon began to show. Though I wondered how long it would take before it all piled up once more, or how long it would take for Marles' mother to order them to once again shovel and sweep it all out of the way. Like some never-ending punishment.

The caretakers were overjoyed with the results. And I decided that this idea I'd had to pass the time may not have been the worst after all.

"Mars, you really didn't have to do that for us. But I do want to say that your fire talent hasn't faded in the slightest!" said one of them as she smiled. The rest spoke over one another almost immediately after, and proceeded to shower Marles with more compliments. While he was quite humble about the whole thing, he did not seem to shy away from their praises.

"Lyla here was the one who suggested I do this, so I don't deserve all this credit alone. And all of you put in a great deal of effort too!" I heard him say as I watched them from where I sat to rest by the mansion's doors some few ten or fifteen feet away.

I caught a few gazes peering my way for a moment before turning back to Marles. Yes, I had put in effort to help them, but I knew it would take more than helping with a few chores for them to warm up to my presence. I had, afterall, been the one to take their precious Marles from them—at least from their point of view.

Still, it warmed my heart he was trying his best to get them to like me.

They chatted with him a little longer before returning to other tasks they had to get done. Marles joined me shortly after on the cold stone and leaned on me, his cheek resting on my shoulder. He was breathing a little heavier than usual, but seemed relaxed otherwise. I was about to open my mouth and make a sly comment, but stopped short as I heard a noise coming from behind us.

The mansion's large doors began to open back up again; as they did so, we quickly got to our feet. I watched as a caretaker began to scurry towards us. She had a worried look on her face, but once she saw the state of the mansion's exterior her negative expression dissipated.

"Alrighty, Mars! Your room is all ready for you, just as you requested. If you would please follow me, I'll escort you two down the corridors," she insisted. The two of us followed her into the mansion, and soon I felt Marles' tail as it intertwined with mine. A small grin crept its way onto my face, but I kept my gaze forward.

While I had entered the mansion before, it was a truly different experience seeing things lit up and lively with caretakers rushing about and tidying the place. Most of the skylights had been boarded up to keep out the cold and ice flurries, but there were plenty of lit wax clumps neatly placed on fancy stone pillars. The dancing lights illuminated the halls in a way one might call cozy. The walls were also adorned with a plethora of paintings that I knew had to be Marles' own work; though, something about them seemed less vibrant than the paintings he had back in the dome.

After the brief walk in the hallway we finally came upon Marles' old living quarters. It was much cleaner than when I had been there months prior. The pile of cushions were more arranged instead of being strewn about, and there were no bowls with remnants of a yellow substance. Though the lighting was a little dim since none of the wax clumps appeared to be lit.

Marles took a moment to gaze at his old room before turning towards the caretaker.

"Thank you, Eris. I appreciate all of you taking such good care of things here in my absence." He smiled at her and she soon became flustered.

"It's no big deal, Mars. Why, anything less and we'd get thrown out!" She paused long enough to laugh softly. "A-anyway I'll be out of your way for now. You'll be called for the evening meal in a little while. Until then you two just relax and call on one of us if you need anything."

She lowered her head slightly and soon left us to ourselves. Once we could no longer hear her footsteps outside the room, the wax clumps became ripe with flames. Heat rose in my chest as my mouth began to grin with excitement.

"You sure know how to light up a room. How do you even do that without—"

I did not hesitate a moment before kissing him back and bringing myself closer. Being caught off guard like that was a pleasant surprise. When we broke away a few moments later, my smile grew as I caught the look in his eyes. Orange fires burning brightly as light from the flames reflected in them; it made my heart race, and I found myself craving more. But, as expected, he soon realized his own actions and stopped. His eyes went downcast and would not meet my own.

"F-forgive me, I-I'm quite tired. Y-yes that's it. My mind isn't thinking straight after exhausting myself earlier," he said, fumbling over his words. I chuckled softly.

I could believe him being a little tired from the day we had, but not to such a point that he didn't know his own actions. Though, it was possible I wasn't taking another factor into account. It must be quite taxing on him to suddenly return home like this. To face his parents and his old life.

"Oh shush you; quit your apologizing. This "tired" side of you is quite fetching, you know," I said softly as I gently caressed a path with my right paw over his chest and up his neck. Red began to slowly creep over his face as I began to stroke his cheek. "Perhaps being tired makes it easier to show your true intentions?"

Retrieving my paw, I planted a kiss on his neck. I giggled as he became completely flustered, and moved to rest my head on his chest. His heart was pounding at a rapid rate, more so than usual. I decided it would be best if I took pity on him and toned down the teasing just a little.

"Why don't we lay down a bit; you are tired, after all," I suggested before guiding him towards the cushions.

His movements were a bit stiff, but soon I found myself innocently clinging to him as usual once we laid down. Then I simply thought silently to myself for a while about the events that would unfold over the next few days, wondering if Marles' was doing the same. The peace that suddenly surrounded us both in the warmth and quiet of the room kept me from asking.

I gazed at the flickering of the wax clumps' flames as their shadows projected onto the dark wooden walls. Only after having the chance to rest again made me realize how tired I was. Being surrounded in an enclosed, moderately warm environment with Marles could put me right to sleep if I was not careful. Even my stomach seemed too relaxed to cry for sustenance.

"So we're really going to do this huh? Rob them when they least expect it?" I heard him ask, one of us finally breaking that comfortable and cozy silence.

I pondered over Marles' question for a moment before I let out a short yawn. Even though my body was tired, I was mentally wide awake from the thousands of thoughts coursing through my brain. And it sounded like he was dealing with much the same, answering my curiosity from earlier.

"That was an idea we had, but we don't necessarily have to act on it," I said as I traced my paw gently across the top of his head, watching him now. His eyes softened a bit as he glanced upwards.

"Well we're here now and we have some time for deciding," he replied sleepily as I slowly started to stand up. As I did so, I felt a tug on my tail, which made me wobble only slightly before catching myself. "It's too early to be getting up," Marles whined as he continued to gently tug my tail, apparently hoping to coax me back down.

My limbs longed for more rest, but I could not relax knowing we would have to get up again relatively soon. I bent myself to his level and crouched over him as he laid on his back.

"Didn't take you long to revert to being a spoiled heir of the Iseirre's," I joked as I brought my face closer to his. He began to pout in response to my teasing. I quickly kissed his forehead before he had time to fully react. "I'm only kidding, Marley. I know you've been tired and it hasn't been the easiest on you coming here. You're lucky we're not on a heist right now." I smiled as his expression softened.

Grinning, I managed to sneak in another kiss hoping he would not notice. Only this time he pulled me close and on top of him, and I began to giggle as he nuzzled my face. Positive giddiness filled my head from the brief, but still sweet, moment. Unfortunately, a knock coming from the other side of Marles' door cut that feeling short.

"E-excuse me Mars! I am here to accompany you and your l-lady to the dining hall!" a familiar voice declared as the door slowly began to open. Quickly, I stood up and took a step away from Marles. In nearly the same moment, Eris peered her head into the room with one paw over her eyes. I somehow managed to stop myself from snorting laughter as she obstructed her view with such minimal effort. As if that could keep her from seeing something she shouldn't, or didn't want to. She soon dropped her paw and her eyes scanned over Marles. He was still laying on his back. She then looked over towards me. "I don't mean to rush the both of you, but they are eagerly awaiting your presence."

Soon enough, the two of us were walking down the dimly lit halls. Marles seemed a little tense, but I hoped that my presence reassured him that everything would be okay. It was a brisk walk to the mansion's dining hall and soon the caretaker took her leave as we entered. An intense feeling washed over me as two sets of eyes seemed to watch my every move. As we approached the large, elegantly carved stone table, I studied the Celegon I had not seen before.

Beside Marles' mother sat who I assumed was his father. His fur was dark brown in color and his eyes gleamed a pretty pinkish-orange hue. The vibe coming from him felt nowhere near as imposing as his mate's, and more so felt as though he was bored of the situation he found himself in. His handsomeness was almost on par with Marles, but the dullness in his eyes took away from that. Turning my gaze back over to his mother, I saw that she was eyeing me coldly.

"Well, are you two just going to stand there or take a seat?" she asked. As she spoke, I tensed a little at the sound of her voice. I had gotten completely distracted by observing the pair. Looking at Marles, he too seemed quite stiff, but for reasons different than mine. We began to make our way to the table as she scowled. "Quit dallying. I would appreciate it if I ate my meal before it cools."

Once we were situated in the cushion padded wooden seats, I examined the spread of food on the table. It was hard to not get distracted by it after not having eaten much since the cold year took its course. Roasted water nymphs, exotic roots and several other goods were evenly divided among the four plates. My stomach twinged in anticipation and it took much more resistance than necessary to avoid eating it all right away. Showing interest in the food in front of me proved to be a bad call however.

"I can see you are not up to date on current social etiquettes. *Or*—are you simply incapable of introducing yourself in the presence of others? You certainly aren't much, mesmerized as you are by that paltry meal speaks for itself," she remarked as agitation grew inside my chest. Still there was no need to lose my cool over her rudeness. A simple introduction should hopefully smooth things over.

"Mother, please."

Before I could open my mouth, Marles had already spoken up in my stead. His tone and demeanor was quite firm, but as he sat beside me I noticed he was shaking slightly. Her yellow eyes narrowed as they practically pierced through me.

"What is it you're trying to say Marles? That this statusless Celegon you've brought here can't even speak for herself? This is all the reason why—"

"Ereda," Marles' father interrupted, "That's quite enough." Immediately, his mate stopped speaking. I felt as the tone of the room shifted, all of the tension releasing and easing away. I felt my heart rate slowing, and the boilings of rage tempering down.

"Please try to exercise a little restraint in your words next time dearest," he continued after a brief pause—as if trying to both ensure that tempers had cooled, and that he was being heard, "They are our guests, after all." He turned his gaze from his mate to me. "You will have to excuse her, as she is quite exhausted from all the planning. As you can likely gather, or have heard, we will be having a social gathering tomorrow night. Now then," he said with a barely visible smile, "Will you speak to us your name?"

His voice was so calm and soothing that it had taken me a moment to realize just *how* the entire tone of the room had shifted, that he had been the cause... And while there had been a tinge of irritation present in his words, he was far less aggressive than the Celegon who sat beside him. His eyes did not seem any more focused than earlier, however. In fact, he appeared even more tired than he had just moments before.

"Skyli, Lyla Skyli. Though, she's right; I'm not used to being in places like this, nor do I know current etiquette trends. Last I've heard, idle chatter isn't to start until the main host has spoken," I said as Ereda looked at me with curious eyes. Marles' father's eyes also had a particular shine to them as a faint grin plastered itself on his face.

"Well then, it seems my mate's rash assumptions were incorrect. You clearly aren't grouped in with the common rabble now are you?" he asked. I felt a sense of relief that I had managed to retain some of my social gathering knowledge, and that it was still up to speed. "But someone of good standing, that's just not you. The Skyli name is unknown to me, so one could only assume you are not from a particular lineage. Those who forge their own names and titles are those who come from nothing, or worse—abandon their birth titles. Unfortunately, things will become messy if you tarnish the Iseirre name with your blood," he finished, and I quickly saw the direction the conversation was going in. I had forgotten how much wealthy Celegons were obsessed with lineage and names.

Marles seemed like he was itching to get more words in, but I used my tail to covertly tell him I had things under control. The best thing to do was *not* lose control of my emotions, as getting angry would be letting them think worse of me. That did not mean that frustration was not building in my stomach.

"Sir, with all respect I—"

"Wilmor," he said as the smile grew on his mouth. Despite how polite he was with his silky words, it was clear I was looked down upon.

"Sir Wilmor. With all respect, my blood is just as valuable as yours." I started out with a direct, but not callous tone. Both him and Ereda's eyes grew wide at my comment and he almost seemed stunned by my next words. "We're all Celegons here and lineages can't change that. No one's bloodline makes them any more resistant to death. Though if believing that makes your lives easier, who am I to stop you? To me the importance of lineages are vastly based on ignorance and arrogance. It's a reason I renounced my—"

I stopped before I let that last bit slip out. If they knew, my words would have much less of an impact. I doubted saying that one piece would completely change their position, if at all, but I was able to say what I wanted.

"Say no more; I think I've heard enough out of you for one night. Can we please just eat our meal in peace without strife? There's no need for raised voices, especially at this hour." Wilmor sighed before finally indulging in his fine meal. That was the end of all conversation at the dining table.

My stomach felt heavy and full despite not eating hardly anything at all. Still, I forced it down as it would have been foolish to pass up a free meal. The environment severely impacted my taste buds, however. While the food was delicious, I barely noticed. Marles, too, seemed to not be enjoying his food, and I could not help but think it was my fault. I had said far more than I had intended, and now look at what had become of the situation.

Once the plates were emptied, the two Iseirres stood themselves up and took their leave without saying a word to either of us. When they were out of sight, I lowered my head and sighed. Soon something began to tug at my tail, and I instantly knew it was Marles' own. I hesitantly looked over in his direction and checked his expression. At first glance it seemed like he had his usual weak, but comforting smile that appeared every time he attempted to ease my worries and make me feel better.

He was trembling. I could tell he wanted to cry, the very edges of his eyes were damp with wet droplets barely gathering. But he was doing his best not to, My heart ached seeing him try so hard to act like he was fine when I could see right through him. Worst of all, I felt like this could have been avoided had it not been for me.

Before I could utter a word, he immediately threw himself around me and held me close. His shaking finally ceased as he held me tightly, as my body pressed comfortably against his. He held me like that for a few moments before pulling away and staring into my eyes. He'd lost the battle and I could see wet trails rolling down his cheeks, but he suddenly put on a confident grin and quickly wiped at them.

"You remember where my room is right?" he asked, catching me off guard with his abrupt change in demeanor.

"Y-yes I do," I answered, unsure of the thoughts going through his mind. While I did appreciate he did not seem upset anymore, there was something ominous about the sudden change. He pulled me in for another quick hug before stepping back a few paces from me.

"There's something I have to do at the moment. I know this is a bit sudden, but can you please make it back there without me? I shouldn't be long—hopefully before you fall asleep," he assured me with a smile before hastily dashing out of the room.

His smile put me in a good mood, at least until he'd left the room. An emptiness crept in my heart, and I hoped he would be okay wherever he was off too. Not wanting to cause a stir after tonight's incident, I followed his suggestion and headed straight to his room. Completely unaware the night was far from being over.

Very far.

Chapter Eighteen: Warmth

Quickly, I made my way back through the darker halls towards Marles' room. Most of the wax clumps were extinguished of flames. And with no skylights, the halls were almost as dark as it was outside. If I focused on getting there, the thoughts that plagued my mind would subside as they always did when I focused.

Once I pushed open the wooden door, I practically flung myself into the cushion pile. I laid there motionlessly for a bit as I pretended my head was empty of thoughts. Too bad my mind caught on fast to what I was trying to do. There was nothing to worry about as everything would turn out okay in the end. Why else would Marles smile at me like that before he left?

No, not again. Why now, of all times, did this have to happen; especially all alone like this? Using a cushion, I managed to wipe my face clear and kept at it until it stopped the flow. I was tired, that had to be what had weakened my emotions to this extent. Simply going to sleep would make things better by the next day.

As I bundled myself into a ball, I heard a knock coming from the door. I knew it was not Marles as he had no reason to knock on his own door. Before I could speak up, a voice called out from the other side before barging in.

"Mars it's me! Just wanted to let you know I'm coming in!" a cheery voice stated as the door was pushed open. As I had no time to inform her he was absent, I was soon staring into wide orange eyes. She was holding a bowl of soup in her paws that appeared to consist of a very familiar yellowish liquid. "O-oh, sorry for the intrusion. I assumed Mars would be in here at this hour," the pink Celegon apologized as her eyes began to dart nervously around the room. "I thought he might want a bowl of his favorite soup after being away from home for so long."

She continued to shift nervously from foot to foot, her eyes looking anywhere but me as she clutched the bowl tightly. A touch of sympathy brewed inside me, and I figured there would be no harm in telling her that she was free to wait here until his return.

"I'm sure he'll be back soon, why don't you just stay a while?" I suggested as she looked at me in shock.

"S-stay? With you, in Mars' room? Well, I have just finished my tasks for the day..." her voice trailed off for a moment as she continued to stare at me. "I..."

She put the bowl of soup down on a small wooden table before briskly walking towards me as my neck began to tingle. Her meek demeanor instantly changed and I simply stared back at her in bewilderment.

"Can't stand for this! You have some nerve stealing Mars away from us! Sure, you have a charm about you, but just look at Mars! Do you really feel like you're that special to just strip him away from us like that?" Her voice broke near the end, and she seemed surprised at her own sudden outburst.

I was taken aback by what she said, but I quickly grew to understand her. She soon slumped herself into one of the cushions next to me and let out a groaning sigh. "Who am I to blame you? I'm sure anyone would be thrilled to have Mars be theirs. His folks definitely won't be happy about it though, I know that for sure. Honestly, since Mars left, things have been pretty tense around here. He was the one who kept the peace between everyone and us caretakers were always treated kindly by him. Then he finally comes back with some classless Celegon, of course they'd be mad," she said as the guilt returned to my chest.

While I certainly did not steal him, clearly his leaving left a negative impact on the mansion's environment. Seeing how the caretakers reacted to seeing him again was proof enough how much they missed him. His parents, however, I was not too certain about.

"Was Marles truly happy here?" I asked as she suddenly grew stiff.

"H-happy? Living here sure beats living out there right?" Her smile was wobbly, and as she spoke her pink tail began to fidget back and forth rapidly. "Honestly how can you be so—" her voice paused as she began to examine me more closely. Her orange eyes scanned all over my light lavender fur before peering deep into my eyes. In doing so, I did the same to her, though I could not say I recognized her in the slightest. "No way... can't be..." she said softly, her eyes widening briefly as she then said, "Pura Vannril?"

My entire mind went blank for a moment as I began to process what she'd said. It was a name I had not heard in quite a while. The fact that she could recognize me even after looking so different was an astonishing feat. Though I was curious how she could pick me out in the first place. If she already knew that much, denying the fact would be pointless.

"No, not anymore. Maybe I was once years ago, but I'm Skyli now. I would appreciate it if you kept this little detail to yourself; this bit of information is hardly useful after all," I said as my insides began to tense. Just hearing that name again made me sick to my stomach.

"So you are then. I assume Mars doesn't know either," she asked as I looked down. "I used to be a fan of you Pura sisters, two Celegons born from the same egg and of pure white. It was the most bizarrely amazing thing that no Celegon had seen before. Then one day at that social gathering your eyes and tail stone—"

The door began to creak and she immediately sprang up and ran to fetch her bowl of soup. Right as Marles began to enter the room, she proceeded to trot over to him with a nervous smile on her face. His face showed clear signs of confusion as to why she was there, but he was far from bothered by her presence.

"M-Mars, so glad you're back! To celebrate, I figured I'd make your favorite cheese soup." She smiled nervously as her tail straightened with excitement when she presented him with the small bowl of soup.

"O-oh I see! Thank you Kirra for being so thoughtful," he said as he smiled back at her. I could see the telltale sign in his expression, as much as he tried to mask it for her, that he was resisting the urge to gag.

It was painfully obvious that he was not pleased with his gift, but he was trying very hard to act grateful for her kindness. Upon handing it over to him, she promptly excused herself and immediately left the room. He then turned over to me with a nervous grin before glancing at the soup and grimacing. After hastily finding a good spot to place the bowl of yellow liquid, he made his way over to me. Smiling, I jumped up to kiss his nose.

He seemed a little taken aback by my action, but not in the usual sense that would result in embarrassment. His eyes gleamed with delight and saw they possessed a certain wonder to them. My mind was filled with airy thoughts that caused me to temporarily forget about the events that happened at dinner.

"You never cease to amaze me you know," he grinned and before I could inquire further he began to kiss me.

Much more deeply and calmly than he usually did. Anytime he initiated I always felt more fluttery around him than normal, even though he would always end up a blushing mess afterwards. Soon he broke away, and I found myself staring into slightly watery eyes. I took my paw and began to dry them as he gave a slight smile.

"My parents, how they treated you was downright awful. I am so s—" I cut him off with another kiss. Though he was not very receptive this time around. "L-Lyla. To reward me for not properly stepping in more, I don't deserve it," he stated as his ears drooped. It seemed like he was on the verge of crying despite his eyes looking too exhausted to shed any more tears.

I took his face in my paws and began to gently stroke his cheeks. They were so soft and warm to the touch, I felt as if I could hardly think seriously at the moment.

"Shush, that's old news. Honestly, I was a little worried about you Marley when you went off on your own. I'm always a little actually; when you leave I worry you won't come back at times. You've seemed on edge since we got here, so let's relax and have a bit of enjoyment, shall we?" I felt as if I was losing control of my words as the feeling took over. One moment later I nipped at his neck. "This is as much my reward as it is yours."

His face immediately went red as he reached to touch the spot on his neck. He managed to calm himself soon though and shook his head.

"Come on now, do you really think I'm so gullible to fall for that? Honestly Lyla, even at a time like now you do this." He sighed, but must have noticed the confusion in my expression, because he went on. "The teasing. Whenever there's affection between us, you always shy away before things get more serious," he explained as I stared at him completely flabbergasted by his comment. It was enough to snap me back to my senses, which quite annoyed me.

"M-me? Well every time I make a move on you, you turn redder than an emeri!"

While we had been mates for a while now, neither of us had really progressed in such a way to pursue the more intimate side of romance without ending up teasing one another. Ironically, knowing how we each felt did not seem to make things easier. Perhaps it made things even worse; perhaps knowing just now strongly we felt could be intimidating at times?

"Well, you rarely get that way with me! You probably still see me the same as when we first met." He sulked as my head began to spin with confusion.

"What does that even mean? You're incredibly handsome alright? Absolutely stunning! I don't see why it's bad I see my mate that way!" I stated firmly and suddenly the atmosphere grew silent.

I had to think back on my words and I soon found myself wincing at my poor choices. A devilish smirk grew on Marles' face, one I both disliked and found quite attractive simultaneously.

"So you do find me good looking after all," He smiled as his face brightened substantially. It was like the little fires that burned in his eyes had completely dried up any traces of them being wet. I quickly turned away from him and began to try to squirm away from him, but without any real effort.

"Like you need me to tell you that. You already get dozens of compliments on the regular. Me saying that often will probably give you narcissism." I sighed as I felt him wrap himself around me. It felt pleasant, but I was still upset at myself for saying those words.

"It's quite different when it comes from you, you know," he said as his voice softened. "You're the only one I care about hearing that from."

My chest felt like it was being filled with air that sent several positive shocks throughout my body. Unfortunately, it did not take too much to become vulnerable to his affections. Though I knew the moment I went in to kiss him that he would become flustered red within dozens of seconds at the latest. Granted he was quite adorable when red. Pushing those thoughts aside, I gently grabbed him and began to kiss at his neck.

I hugged him tightly while doing so and was surprised to see how well his body was reciprocating. Soon my mouth was directed back to his and we began to kiss until my mouth grew tired, which was a first. My eyes opened back up to see Marles staring back as I could feel his heartbeat accelerate. His fur was only slightly red and not completely stained with the color. I caught myself staring almost as if I had become entranced by him and my face grew warm.

"Lyla," he paused as he began to study my face for a moment, causing my heart to beat faster. "You're just like an emeri," he murmured before nuzzling close to me. It took my brain a moment to realize what was going on and before I knew it, I had my face buried into one of the blankets. He began to chuckle lightly which did not help the current state of my face. "So this is what it feels like to be on the opposite end of things. You're quite sweet Ly-Ly."

As much as I wanted to protest, an overwhelming sense of tiredness enveloped me. I carefully repositioned myself so that my back was comfortably against Marles' front. Hearing his heartbeat resonate in my ears was always reassuring.

"Seeing me like this better not turn you arrogant." I sighed before backing myself into his chest more.

"Arrogant? And here I was overjoyed about seeing you this ecstatic about me." He faked a whine before gently kissing the top of my head.

Exhaustion seemed to consume Marles first and I could hear him faintly snoozing as I was cradled next to his chest. Sleeping was a great way to temporarily forget about all the stresses in the world. Yet, I had so many, it seemed impossible to accomplish—even while this close to the Celegon I adored most. For a while I simply held my eyes closed and breathed, but no matter how long I did I could never seem to sleep for some reason. Frustrated, I figured if I could not sleep I might as well scope out the mansion a little more.

Soon I had transferred from the warm confines of Marles' embrace, to the colder dark unlit halls of the mansion. I was not planning on staying up for too long; he would notice my lack of presence eventually. Traversing the halls was less than fun with how abysmal the lighting was. Looking around would not be very productive, but I was still full of restless energy. The thought of accidentally walking into Marles' parent's room made my insides squirm.

My tail flicked with surprise as the halls suddenly became more visible thanks to the freshly lit wax clumps. I was surprised Marles was able to awaken from his deep slumber so soon, but his senses must have been sharper than expected to detect my leaving. Turning myself around to face him, I instead met the eyes of Ereda. While initially spooked at seeing her yellow eyes, they were lacking the intensity and sharpness from earlier.

"Skyli? W-what brings you out into the halls so late at night? Guests typically stay in their rooms until the first light of the day," she said as I quickly picked up that the former hostility in her tone was no more. It was a pleasant change, but also quite jarring.

"A-ah Lady Ereda, what a surprise! To tell you the truth my mind is wide awake and I'm finding I am having a little trouble resting," I responded, trying to be polite in my tone.

There was no need in lying as it was the reason I was up, but I did think it prudent to omit the small detail of looking for valuables to snatch. Though perhaps referring to her as "Lady" was a tad too much. She continued to stare at me like she did not believe a word that came out of my mouth.

"So you took to wandering the halls in the darkness," she said, her voice trailing off as she continued to eye me. That was until a slight wheeze emerged from her lungs. She then quickly grabbed at my tail and began pulling me down the hallway. "The halls are no place for chatting like this, come now and make sure you keep up," she insisted as she loosened the grip on my tail, perhaps because she felt no resistance on my part.

I was slightly reluctant to follow her, but as I saw the flames dissipate I picked up my pace. She eventually entered a room and ushered me inside before quietly shutting the door behind her.

Immediately upon entering, the room flourished with light thanks to the numerous wax clumps that were now ripe with flames. The room appeared to be a study of some sort, with several papers stacked on shelves and tables. There were also cushions and several dishes that held small quantities of fresh fruits and roots. Aside from Ereda's presence, I felt like this room was inviting.

"Over here Skyli, why don't we chat a little," Ereda said as she sat herself down onto one of the nearby cushions. I reluctantly followed her command and soon found myself sitting on quite the comfortable cushion. She took a few berries off one of the plates and popped them into her mouth, all while eyeing me curiously. "You did not seem to eat much during dinner, have some," she suggested before tossing one over in my direction.

I caught it, but felt no inclination to eat it. It was definitely delicious but eating it felt slightly wrong at the moment. With her continuing to eye me I quickly forced it down my throat and swallowed it to avoid suspicion. This seemed to please her as a slight smile formed on her face.

"There you go, you will feel better now. The kaeberries are quite good at helping Celegons relax, I am sure once the properties kick in you will lose a bit of that tension keeping you awake. Eating them too often can cause a bit of dizziness unfortunately, so they are not reliable for when I am overburdened with social gathering planning," she explained before she stretched herself into a more comfortable position. I felt a little guarded on eating the strange berry, but seeing as she was eating some herself made me feel slightly better. "Also while you are at it, I would be grateful if you forget our initial greeting and what happened during dinner."

My ears perked at her request. There was no aggression in her tone telling me that and it felt odd. Almost as if she were threatening me without being hostile about it. Playing along with her wishes was key, however, as I would not like a repeat of what happened earlier.

"Alright, I'll forget," I said as her eyes lit up with surprise. "If you explain why I should. I would like to be on good terms with both you and Wilmor if I'm able. I'm not looking to cause any friction in your family."

She stared at me a moment before nodding her head. Her expression turned bleak for a brief moment before she began laughing lightly. She continued to grin before she spoke. I tried not to let on that I was uncomfortable.

"You seem quite perceptive, very well I will explain. To put it plainly, our treatment towards you was a sham. Wilmor and I bear no ill feelings towards you personally. It was meant to stir up Marles, as it is clear he cares very much about you," she explained as I refrained from speaking my mind openly.

If what she was saying was true, this was a sort of twisted manipulation towards Marles. It sickened me to my core at the thought, but I knew better than to anger her at this point in time. If he was not aware already, Marles would be informed of this immediately once he woke from his slumber.

"So this was meant to be punishment towards him?" I asked as she quickly nodded her head.

"Correct. And it worked just as planned. After dinner he came straight to Wilmor and I to tell us off on our treatment towards you. Been a while since he had gotten so worked up, he seems a bit different since meeting you."

The pieces seemed to fall into place now and I could understand things slightly better. He left to speak with them about their rudeness, which ended up being exactly what they wanted. From the time I had known him he had always seemed so sweet and amicable, though when a situation presented him with me facing hostility he took action. The fact that this was meant to hurt him was beyond cruel though. I could understand not being pleased with me, but attacking Marles? It made me wonder what other sick things that could have happened to him growing up.

I had to keep this conversation light so it would be best to slowly divert it into a different territory to avoid conflict. It did not mean I had simply forgiven her for doing that to her son.

"Still... as a Celegon without status, I'm sure neither you or Wilmor will approve of me being Marles' mate," I said as chuckled nervously as she stared at me with a smile.

"Was I not clear? Everything you heard from us prior to this conversation simply does not exist. A status can be achieved; you are Marles' mate. All you must do is renounce your Skyli name and transition into being an Iseirre. Then, if time will allow, you and Marles will produce heirs who will further contribute to the Iseirre name," she explained as a slight chill went down my spine.

To stop being a Skyli would be losing a part of myself I strived to hold onto the moment I got it. I would have straight up refused the idea right to her face if Marles was not in the picture. This was not my ideal living situation, but I had to consider his feelings as well. He had grown up in this comfortable lifestyle after all.

"May I have a bit of time to consider your offer? It may not seem like much, but I have grown quite attached to this name of mine," I started as she visibly tensed, then added quickly, "But much more to Marles."

Her face began beaming with delight and I felt a tad more relieved. At least telling her that seemed to temporarily satisfy her. A suspicious smirk soon donned her face as she made her way uncomfortably close to me.

"So with that little talk out of the way, how is your courtship coming along?" She grinned and I felt my stomach lurch. "Soft, playful, savory, how is he with you romantically? You cannot blame a mother for being curious of how her child behaves with the one he adores," she finished. Even as she spoke, I felt lines had been crossed.

How Marles and I were together seemed a little personal to be telling her about, especially without Marles' consent on the matter. Though saying how he turns into a blush ball would certainly get an interesting reaction. She probably just wanted to know if he was truly happy being with me.

"He's sweet. Very kind to me even when I'm not being agreeable. Always listens and takes what I say to heart no matter how arbitrary it—"

"Dear, that is good and all but I was talking about *physical* affections. Does he kiss you well?"

Our conversation lasted late into the night, getting progressively more uncomfortable as Ereda kept prodding for personal information regarding Marles and I. It did help me realize she was not as big of a threat, seeing her act quite improperly for a wealthy Celegon of status. As for Wilmor, I had yet to learn more about him. A part of me wondered if the entire conversation I just had was simply a ruse.

Chapter Nineteen: Stability

Morning light began to peek through the miniscule openings of the boarded up skylights. A small flicker hit my closed eyes which made them blink open in agitation. My body laid sprawled out across two cushions with my legs teetering over the wooden floor. As I began to stretch, a sudden sense of dizziness washed over me and my head began to throb. An unusual occurrence to happen after a night well rested.

My vision took a moment to adjust to my surroundings as I tried to blink away the blurriness. I could only focus on doing that. Thinking about other things was a challenge. I started to shake my head, hoping that doing so would help me unclog my mind. Despite the mental haze I found myself in, I could see that I was still in the room that I had had a chat with Ereda in. I must have fallen asleep. Trying to remember what we'd talked about —after she'd brought up crass topics related to Marles—was near impossible.

The headache I had made it too painful to think deeply about anything at the moment, so instead I assigned myself a simple task. Find Marles. I had not a clue what I would do after I accomplished that, but it was a start. First things first: stand upright. Simple enough.

What usually was one of my easiest early morning routines was considerably more difficult than I remembered. My limbs felt loose and my head was still dizzy, making standing a harder challenge than I had considered. Soon, I stumbled over myself, toppling down onto the wood floor before I was scrambling upright again and forcing balance—somehow. This current issue did not stop me from locating the wooden door; which ended up being a hassle to open, but I managed. I found myself aimlessly wandering about the halls, trying not to stumble over.

"S-Skyli?"

A familiar voice called out to me, but I could not remember who it was nor could I see them properly thanks to my blurred vision. A pinkish blur approached me as I tried squinting my eyes.

"Wh-what are you doing scrambling around on the floor like that?" the voice asked as I picked up a hint of concern in the tone.

I was on the floor? I could have sworn I was just standing moments ago. Maybe not all upright, but on four limbs. Sure enough, once I felt my body it appeared I was only using two, with my back legs dragging behind me. They almost felt non-existent with how numb they were.

"Ah. Pardon me, but my senses... They seem to be slightly inebriated this morning." My voice quivered as even my vocal cords found it hard to operate.

"Slightly? You've completely lost control over your own body! Seeing you squirm around like that is just everything," the voice began to chortle with laughter as I grew annoyed. Not fuming with anger, but a tad frustrated that this entire situation was happening. My brain could not even think of any retorts and I felt quite pathetic in the presence of whoever this was.

"Oh, well I suppose I can't just leave you here for others to see, as fun as that would be. Let's hurry it up. I'll help you find your way to Mars. He'll probably get a good laugh out of this," she chimed as I felt my body being lifted by a strange source. "Lucky you're lighter than you look, a little too much in fact. It would be in your best interest to eat as much as you can at tonight's social gathering. Or not. Having leftovers is one of the best perks of being able to stay here as of late."

My senses decided to give out again and I felt myself go limp. Though I was not in any pain, I was losing control of my thoughts as they slipped away from me. I could feel my tail flickering wildly about, but that was it. Eventually, I felt myself being dropped on some cushions and I tried to open my eyes again. Still blurry.

I was being nudged and my ears began to feel tingly. The next thing I was able to feel was ice cold water being drizzled atop my head. That snapped my senses right back to me. Well, my hearing and thoughts at least.

"Lyla! Can you hear me?" Marles spoke coherently as I began to protest.

"You're quite loud, Marley," I groaned as I continued to be frustrated with my clouded vision.

Aside from the faint headache, I was still functional enough to talk. At least I assumed I could. I was still woozy and some words unintentionally came out a bit slurred.

"I don't like your mother," I continued, as I laid on the soft cushions. My paw attempted to touch Marles' nose, but it failed to cooperate and landed on his thigh instead. "The reason why she was so rude—why both of your parents were—was just to mess with you! Can you believe that? I am not fond of them, Marley. Not at all."

Marles' eyes widened slightly as he listened to my somewhat garbled ramblings. Then he took a breath before stroking my head soothingly.

"That is not unlike them. I do not believe them to be bad Celegons at heart but..." He paused as he gazed down at me for a moment. "They can be very invasive. It would not surprise me if my mother overwhelmed you with all sorts of questions last night."

I quickly nodded my head in response. Yes, she did ask a lot of questions. If only I could remember half of them.

"She did ask if you kiss me well," I responded without much thought, causing Marles to go a bit red. "I told her... yes. That I love being your mate and that you brighten up my world. Quite literally—you use your fire talent all the time. If she tries to take you away from me, I may have to fight her."

Marles laughed a little before leaning down to give my face a kiss. But it was clear he had extended plans when he used his arms to lift me up for a moment.

"Come here," he beckoned, pulling me so that my head now rested against his stomach. "I won't let it come to that. But for now, I suggest you rest. You'll feel better once you wake up again."

Even though it lacked the soft plumpness it once had, it was still a very comfortable place to sleep on. His body was always so warm and inviting. I wished I had slept next to it the previous night.

It took almost an hour to recover from what I was currently going through. Despite only having a single kaeberry, the results were quite drastic in their affect on me. Thankfully, I would not make the same mistake again. Blaming Ereda would be uncalled for as she did give me a warning, though her tolerance to such things was obviously higher than mine. If only I could take back the events of squabbling around on the floor.

Since it was daytime, I could only have Marles like this for so long. Next order of business was a full tour of the mansion followed by a light meal. Kissing the tip of his nose as I pulled away, I made my way to the door and signaled I was good to go.

With the wax clumps brimming bright with flames and Marles at my side, wandering through the mansion was much more agreeable. No paranoia or constantly reevaluating my surroundings. Perhaps I was too comfortable. As we walked down the halls we passed several caretakers who were caught up with work. I then recalled that the social gathering would be held tonight, which would explain their hastiness. It sparked my curiosity as to why we had not come across any of the guests yet, especially since most should have already arrived.

"Hey Marles, the social gathering is happening tonight correct?" I asked for the sake of clarifying things. He smiled warmly at me before he briefly brushed his tail against mine.

"That's right. Why the sudden interest? Are you implying you want to spend most of it with me?" He chuckled as he began to emit a radiance of positivity.

"N-no. I mean, I suppose I can bear it seeing how estatic you seem to be about it. I was just curious about the other guests. Shouldn't most have arrived by now?" I asked, knowing that Blubelle, Ariele, Basion and Soeki were to be attending. Marles took a moment to think on my question before his face lit up with understanding.

"Aw Ly-Ly don't get my hopes up like that! Or, my bad for misinterpreting. For this social gathering, the guests were instructed to remain in their rooms until preparations are complete. Actually, it's been like this for around a decade now since a certain incident. Mother says it keeps things more orderly. Though, I suppose you and I have the privilege of roaming while the others don't. It just gives us more the chance to scope out the good spots." He grinned as I nodded in agreement.

The arrived guests were to stay put in their rooms. It was hard to imagine Celegons who were like Blubelle being quietly cooped up into a room. Being stuck in a room with Marles would not be so terrible, but being alone with nothing to do but stare at the walls would be slow torture. Blubelle's constant chatter would certainly drive the others mad. Thinking back on Marles' earlier comment took my mind off Blubelle again as a tightness began to form in my chest. A longing feeling that made me a little weak settled in.

"I'm also interested," I said, "In attending the social gathering with you, that is. We'll be together as mates, if that's what you want." I fought against a grin trying to take over my expression. His eyes began to glow as he stared at me for a moment. Then a glint of mischievousness took them over as he smiled.

"Of course, I'd be delighted to show you off to others." He smirked; in reaction, I lightly pushed his side. "Lyla, I'm only kidding. Though, it would be nice to see you all adorned—ah nevermind my thoughts."

The mansion was a tad smaller than the one we'd infiltrated back in Rimereach; however, what it lacked in size it made up for in quality. From the decor to the food being prepared in the kitchen, everything appeared to be of the finest calibur. As one of the most wealthy Celegon names in Lixion, it was to be expected. The Iseirres were surely not afraid to boast about what they had. It did my curiosity wonders to know how they managed to acquire such wealth.

My expression soon hardened at the thought. Surely nothing good. How wealthy Celegons came to rise above other Celegons, there was something unnatural about it. Some may call it envy, but it was just a feeling I had.

I knew that Lixion's culture used to be different in the decades before my birth. Back when towns had been first established. Reportedly, there had been much less monsters in the past. Back when they chose to hunt nymphs instead of Celegons. There were times I considered asking Z about it, considering most other Celegons had perished from those times.

"Lyla, is everything okay? You seem a little out of it again."

I was brought back to focus by the sound of Marles' voice. The frequency of finding myself lost in thought after continuous thought was increasing as of late. If Marles was not there to snap me out of it, I would very well be trapped in my own mind for several hours.

"You had quite a serious expression on your face. You're usually a little more perceptive of your surroundings," he said as he lightly rubbed against my side. Shaking myself, I turned to brush my face on his cheek and followed with a brief kiss.

"As should you. Though, that berry I had must have scrambled my mind a little. Lots of thoughts have been running through my mind, but I'll pull through," I said while giving him a grin. He had a look of concern on his face before he pulled me close. I was grateful that at this point in time there were no caretakers close by to see.

"Back when we met, you were always on high alert," he began.

I immediately responded with, interrupting, "I'm aware. My senses have dulled over time. I have not been a good role model for you lately."

He pulled me closer and began to examine me with his exuberant sunset eyes.

"No, no, don't say that. I like to think it means you feel comfortable enough to let your guard down knowing I'm at your side. There's a lot to think about with all that's been happening and I certainly don't blame you for getting absorbed in your thoughts. I'm always here to ease the burdens of any troubles lingering in your mind," he assured me and at those words I began to feel a pleasantly warm feeling. "How about we share a meal? I'm sure that would help with clearing your mind for a little while at least."

The Iseirre mansion's kitchen was practically swarming with caretakers preparing food for the night's social gathering and morning meals to deliver to the guest Celegons that patiently waited in their rooms. Even with all the ruckus and orderly chaos that ensued, Marles was able to get some freshly made muffins and some berries from the caretakers. I felt worried for them; all the preparations seemed to have run a few of them ragged. Remembering that they were preparing for a social gathering. I idly wondered how hard Marles' mother worked them for such an event.

After acquiring food, the two of us relocated to a less busy part of the mansion and proceeded to eat in peace. Instead of going back to his room, we found a nice area in one of the hallways that was accompanied by a very cozy wooden seat. Biting into the warm muffins caused a bit of stream to escape and trickle up my nose. There was no way I would deny that gourmet food was quite pleasing to all senses. The few muffins were gone within minutes, leaving our stomachs devoid of hunger pangs.

"How surprising," I started as I licked my paws clean of remaining muffin crumbs. He looked over with a curious smile, awaiting what I had to say. "I recall you protesting against eating muffins when I last tried to share them with you, is all."

I half expected my comment to make him go flustered upon remembering that event. It did to a brief extent as his eyes lit up with surprise, but they soon softened before he began smiling again.

"I did do that, didn't I? Well that was then and this is now. Don't worry, I won't gorge myself and tarnish my figure. Especially not after what you said to me yesterday." He grinned before grooming his face.

And there it was: an egotistical nature brewing in his heart induced by vanity. I was responsible for this, I know, but I still felt undecided on this new version of Marles. How long before his sweetness in entirety gets replaced by hubris? Perhaps a little over exaggerating, but it could very well be a possibility in the future.

"S-Skyli? Lyla Skyli? Here? Lyla, Lyla! Long time no see!"

My muscles tensed. I knew that voice. It was one I did not care to hear, at least not until a little while later. Boundless amounts of bubbly energy engulfed me as she hastily approached, tail flickering around excitedly. As abrupt as she always was, something about seeing her again made me smile—internally, that was. She seemed vibrant, alive and well.

"Oh... you're still alive, I see," I said in a tone of light disinterest, only to see her expression become horrified.

"Y-you're really going to say that to a friend you haven't seen in forever? Well! I for one am happy to see you again! You too Mar—"

She stopped mid sentence to examine Marles. He looked back at her, bearing a charming smile. Her brain seemed to be processing a great deal of information. To stop Bluebelle's chattering point blank too quite a lot.

"By the Sacred Spirit, you're hotter than the flames of fire!"

"Blubelle!"

Shockingly enough, it was not I that chastened her this time. Instead, that came from a usually soft spoken Celegon, who by his own action had quickly made his presence known. His pinkish eyes appeared to glower as he used his paw to direct Blubelle's eyes off of Marles by gently turning her head. The indigo furred Soeki had arrived on the scene to hopefully quell Blubelle's madness.

Before I could offer to thank him however, he quickly began to hug Blubelle. This felt oddly familiar, watching two Celegons embrace alongside Marles. Though, I felt very uncomfortable watching them display these things right in front of us. Despite having a mate of my own, I still held the same values as before.

"What have I told you about openly flirting with other Celegons? Forget running off when we're supposed to stay put, you know how I—"

"You have nothing to worry about dearest, he just surprised me, is all!"

I was not surprised to find out the two of them were mates, but I certainly did not foresee it. With their contrasting personalities, I wondered if there was a bit of friction. Thankfully, that whole exchange ended rather quickly. Soon enough, with things now cleared up between the two mates, Soeki was in on the conversation. It took me a little bit by surprise how vocal he seemed to be compared to when I last saw him in Tarrina Town.

"Apologies for how she reacted. Once we heard of your description from a caretaker, Bells wanted to reunite with you right away," Soeki explained and I grew curious as to why a caretaker would have told them that.

"You mean *those* descriptions? If it was not for her saying light lavender fur, I would have never guessed she was talking about Lyla!" Blubelle spoke up with a huff as my interest was increased.

"Blubelle," I started as unease settled in my stomach. "Please continue and don't hold back on those little details."

Just by looking at Soeki's face, I could tell that these were most likely not nice things. Marles seemed a little uneasy after glancing at my face, almost as if he were guilty of something.

"So this caretaker came in to deliver us some breakfast, but she seemed a little out of it. She couldn't stop laughing, so I wanted to know what was so funny! So naturally I used my charms and convinced her to tell us. She told us that early in the morning a really idiotic Celegon was stumbling around in the halls like a fool because she got her mind wrecked on these exotic berries. Then I asked for a description of this Celegon since they would seem like a treat to meet in this fancy place, and she described you perfectly."

So it was that caretaker who was the one who saw me staggering in the hallway. It made sense, considering how rude she was to my weakened state. Getting angry would be pointless as the situation had passed and would be confirming that entire event to Blubelle and Soeki. Neither of them seemed pleased about the news, which meant they had not changed their opinion of me regardless. Marles however seemed weighed down by guilt, possibly because he could not do anything to stop Kirra from telling them that.

"Sorry, let me apologize for Kirra's behavior. She's always been a bit of a jokester and tends to over exaggerate things. Lyla was feeling a little unwell this morning, but you know as well as I do how perceptive and quick she is." Marles lowered his head as my brow knit in surprise.

Even as witness to that, and the fact he could have embarrassed me, he chose not to. I suppose although he had grown a little vain, he had kept his kind heart. It took a lot of strength to avoid snuggling close to him after he spoke.

"Of course! The Lyla Skyli I know would never lower her guard enough to do that," Blubelle proclaimed as Soeki simply nodded his head. Blubelle then took a moment to pause and glanced towards Marles as a mischievous gleam coated her eyes. "Sir Iseirre, if it's alright with you, may I whisk Lyla away with me back to my room?" she asked as Marles' eyes sparked with curiosity. "Without Soeki of course."

Soon I found myself being dragged down the halls by a rambunctious light blue Celegon. Surprisingly, she had yet to talk my ears off as we dashed down the hallway. It was very likely she had things she wanted only me to hear. It made me wonder how thin the walls were here, considering Marles' room was slightly isolated from the rest of the mansion. Once the door was slammed shut behind me, Blubelle began to giggle wildly. Oh the things she had to say.

"Lavender, I can't believe you never told me! Even though I thought we were close," she whined as I began to mentally sigh. It was clear she was referring to Marles and I being mates, though it was hypocritical considering her relationship with Soeki. "Pura Vannril, what a story this turned out to be. Your fascination with Iseirre makes much more sense now!"

My stomach clenched up into tight knots. That rumor spreading caretaker was behind this too no doubt. While a name is just a name, ties to that one were best left severed. Blubelle was not inherently malicious; though, her knowing that name was dangerous for my livelihood as Lox Lavender.

Chapter Twenty: Adorned

Vannril. The name was not particularly well known for having riches in the circle of the wealthiest Celegons of Lixion. They had enough orbs and food to be mostly worry free on those fronts, but lacked a large estate. What they did have was me. Me and my sister.

Our coming into this world had been especially unique. Two Celegons to hatch out of the same egg and to be born of pure white with no other coloring. A Celegon to be born of a solid color was extremely rare. Z was the only other I knew of. If there were other cases of twin Celegons emerging from an egg before, I have never heard of it before. This phenomenon was what brought fame to the Vannril name well enough to be invited to the social gatherings of the wealthy.

Essentially, we were used by our particular circumstances to elevate the Vannril name. The Pura Sisters everyone called us. I shared that name with my sister until I met Alise. Then I became Lyla Skyli and Lox Lavender, Pura Vannril was no more. I had hoped my changed appearance would rid me of that name for good.

Blubelle stared at me with an expression I had never seen from her. Instead of a playful or mischievous look in her eyes, there was a more serious undertone that sickened the atmosphere. If she were scheming something particularly dangerous, I would not hesitate to break whatever ideas she had as they came to fruition. At the same time this was Blubelle, my most reliable informant. Would she really use my old name against me in hopes of dragging me down?

"Blu, why don't we talk things through before you start jumping to conclusions," I started as I began to piece together the words I said. My uneasiness was quickly picked up on as expected of someone like her.

"Conclusions? You are Pura Vannril, or one of them at least. You aren't fooling me Lavender; maybe you have that Iseirre fooled, but not me."

Her voice was coarse and full of bitterness. Just the sound of it pricked my skin the wrong way. The bubbly, cheerful tone that annoyed me to no end had long diminished. It almost felt as if someone was impersonating her as this was not the Blubelle I knew. Arguing against her case was not an option, but negotiating was.

"Alright. If I am Pura Vannril as you assume I am, what will you do with that information?" I questioned as she cocked a grin. As an informant, Blubelle could either spread that information rapidly or only to a select few of Celegons. Why she would do that eluded me, but hopefully she would give a reason.

"Two gold orbs," she stated as a smile plastered over her face. My fur raised at her insinuation I pay her to know something so simple. "Time's are rough. What can I say, Lavender? I know you have some on you."

I glanced at my satchel that had remained loosely fastened to my side. Even without checking I knew I only had two gold orbs left, including one of sentimental value. If I used other orbs to substitute the value of another gold one, I would be nearly out of them for spending.

"The same goes for me. I can spare you *one*," I said as my tone became firm and her eyes pierced me with irritation.

"Just let the Iseirre's take care of you for now. What do you even need orbs for anymore?"

Blubelle tried her best to sound intimidating, but at the last word her voice broke. My eyes widened as she began shaking despite attempts to stabilize herself. Tears dampened her fur as she could not stop them from staining her face.

"L-Lavender, y-you don't n-need it. B-but I-"

Her voice squeaked as she continued to shake uncontrollably. Regardless if her actions were deceitful or not, it was clear that she reeked of desperation. No Celegon would resort to tears if they were not. As someone moderately close to her, it hurt me to see her in such a state. My body tensed as she practically threw herself on me, sobbing. I took my paws and gently caressed her back, hoping it might soothe her once more into a functional state.

"B-Blubelle? What's gotten into you to behave like this?" I asked as she continued to sob uncontrollably.

"I-It's over, L-Lavender."

After a few minutes, I was able to calm her down enough to the point she could talk coherently again. Her body still trembled from fears that lingered in her mind. She swallowed a lump in her throat before she proceeded to tell me what happened.

"I-I'm sorry Lavender, for earlier. When you're cornered it's only natural to resort to the quickest options to survive no matter how dark they are right? As an informant, I could easily leak out that part of you to the Celegons here. But I'm also your f-friend. I don't want to do this, but you have to understand how limited my opinions are here," she spoke in a serious, but empathetic tone as I shot her a look of understanding.

"But what has you so riled up to stoop to that, Blu? I know that the cold year has been tough, but surely Soeki and the others have been taking care of you as one of their own while you stay with them," I reassured her. I knew they had a moderate amount of wealth due to Ariele's monster slaying profession.

"This is different from just orbs and food, Lavender. In the end, even if I did use that information against you it would not be enough. I pride myself on being one of the best informants on Lixion, but that comes with a burden. Let me phrase things blankly, have you heard the word *Pythera* at all in your travels?" she questioned and I felt my blood freeze.

Z. He said that word to me when we last met. The species that would end the Celegons. Blubelle caught sight of the look in my eyes and began to sigh.

"So you've heard the rumors too. Well, unfortunately they aren't just rumors."

She could not be more serious at this moment. There was no possible way that she and Z had met and planned this entire charade just to scare me; though, if they did it would make for a well done prank. My posture loosened as I looked into her steadfast deep blue eyes. No, Blubelle may be a jokester and a thief, but she would not make up these types of lies.

"I've heard that word, yes. But rumors are simply rumors without solid evidence," I said calmly, hoping it might soothe her. Blubelle transitioned herself to sit on the large cushion atop the wooden frame bed in the room.

"There have been multiple sources about these... creatures. While I've yet to see one with Ariele's team, they do exist. From what I can tell, fighting against them is pointless. They hit you with what's described as vines that come out of their sides, then you watch as the same happens to your comrades—completely immobilized. Lavender, if they're real then—"

I found myself embracing her to keep her from crying again. Me comforting her like this, it made me reminisce when Alise comforted me when monsters surrounded the dome. It took everything I had to not tremble while doing so. Showing her that I was afraid would only worsen her fears.

"Do Soeki and the others know about this?" I asked while continuing to hold her to lessen her shivers.

"N-no. I've kept this to myself. If they knew, it would only cause distress among the group. Ariele is strong, one of the most powerful Celegons I've seen. You should see the way she uses plants to thoroughly decimate her..." She stopped, sighed, and said, "Against one of those *things,* I'm afraid even she would be outmatched." Blubelle then pulled away from me and slid backwards onto the blanketed cushion.

I thought to myself before a faint smile rose to my face. She appeared to leave out a small detail.

"Maybe alone that is. But while you're here, keep in mind that there are lots of us if one decides to show up on the mansion's doorstep. And that's *if* they manage to get past the barrier that keeps out monsters. I might not be exceptionally talented in combat, but Marles and I have fought plenty of monsters before so we'll definitely be around to help just in case. So don't worry so much alright? Let's just kick back and enjoy this prissy social gathering for what it is." I grinned and my words appeared to perk her up slightly.

"Perhaps I won't attempt to extort you for money after all." She smiled before mulling things over in her head. "By the by, what brought you here? We haven't really gone over that yet have we Lavender?"

From one discussion to the next, I filled her in on my plans for Iseirre mansion as well as events that happened upon my arrival. We had an information exchange of sorts as she told me about specific events during our time apart. Most of it was hardships she faced during the cold year, but there were also certain details that stuck out. It appeared as if she had gotten a lot closer with her traveling partners and hearing about how she bonded with them warmed me a little. Over the course of the conversation, it seemed like Blubelle was returning to her usual peppy self.

"So both of us have found our mates then. What a lucky coincidence, don't you agree?" She grinned as I let out a nervous sigh. "That being said, Iseirre has changed since I last saw him. How do you manage to keep your eyes off such a specimen?"

Her playful smirk had returned. It would only be a matter of time before I tired of her mannerisms, but I vastly preferred this Blubelle to the former. Soon I found myself mindlessly replying to her without considering my words.

"I don't," slipped out of my mouth before I could stop myself. But I was quick to say, "I don't stare at him all the time if that's what you're insinuating. We're a bit too busy to be idly ogling each other, even before this cold year made things more difficult." Though, by her expression it was clear she was not buying it. Then her eyes lit up with newfound knowledge of another slip up on my end.

"Before the cold year? You both got cozy with each other then? That's so sweet!" her voice crooned as I tightened my jaw.

Luckily, a knock and Soeki's voice calling for her came from the other side of the door, causing her to lose focus. Blubelle quickly sprang to action, exiting the room momentarily to talk to her mate. She soon returned, however, closing the door behind her and leaving Soeki outside.

"Lavender since the social gathering is tonight, how about I help you get ready?"

The last thing I wanted was to have Blubelle put the ornamental ribbons on me. Knowing her, they would be way too tight for my liking. This was also hours before the social gathering would start, so it would be pointless to get ready so soon. The only thing I was tolerant of wearing was my satchel, which had gotten quite battered over the past few months. Still, I held my mouth shut and did not protest as she walked over to a wooden storage closet, fumbling through to find what she was looking for. The thing she held high consisted of much more material than ribbons.

It was a large piece of dyed cloth, big enough to wrap around a thin Celegon's body. The dark purple color of it was quite eye-catching; it was also probably quite expensive for the plants needed to make it that shade. Such garments were only seen at the most wealthy of Celegon mansions; selling that to the right Celegon could net a fortune of orbs. Though, definitely not during the cold year. Blubelle approached me with it while bearing a massive smile on her face.

"No. Hundreds of times no. I'd much rather you attach ribbons to me than trap my body in that thing." I grimaced as she began to frown.

"It's not that bad, I promise! I've already tried one on earlier. It's silky soft! It seems as if they are providing everyone who attends the social gathering a basic one, but I did sneak out a while ago and caught glimpses of ones that have lots of lace and patterns too! Come on Lavender, if you wear this we can match. Well—sort of! And you can't deny that the color really suits you!" She beamed as I continued to sulk at the idea of putting it on.

True, I suppose it did match my eyes and tail with its purple hue. But what if it restricted my movement in some way? If an emergency happened I would be hindered by its material. Plus, it would make me stand out; at least ribbons were more subtle.

"It's sure to catch Marles' eyes."

. . ⚓ . .

After Blubelle finished adding ribbons to my ears, the ensemble was complete. She had not been lying to me when she had said it was not downright uncomfortable. I could still move freely to some extent, though using my wings would involve stripping myself of the pullover.

My wings.

I had not used them in such a while except for the occasional practice thanks to the cold year. Though, as a result, I felt as if I had become even swifter in my terrestrial movements.

"See, I knew it would look nice on you!" Blubelle smiled as I tried to look at myself. Apart from the purple ribbon on my tail and the limited view I had on the cloth wrapped around my torso, I could not see a huge upgrade in my overall appearance.

"If you say so," I said as I went along with her antics. She soon grabbed my paw and practically began to drag me towards the door. "W-wait, where are we going?" I stammered as I tried to resist being pulled around.

"Don't you want Marles' opinion too?"

Unlike the last time she'd brought him up, I was less than reluctant to go along with her wishes. My feet were dragging across the room's reddish brown carpet as she hauled me over to the doorway. Something seemed to click inside my mind that told me not to let him see whatever Blubelle did to me. My body shuddered as another knock came from the door, quite louder than last time. At least Blubelle let go of me as she skipped on over to open it.

"Skyli, what—what are you wearing?"

Ereda stared at me from the door opening before rushing in to examine me up close. I knew it! Blubelle must have done something to make the outfit look off in some bizarre way.

"These accessories are for the *guests*. You must come with me right away, we will clothe you in more suitable attire after Wilmor gets a few words in from you," she said before swiftly taking hold of my arm. She pulled me along so fast I had no time to say my farewells to Blubelle.

This all felt vaguely familiar. Being forced into different locations, often too fast for my preference. I put up with it as I did back then, but I could not wait to be done with it all. The fast paced and proper life of the wealthy was something I could never grow accustomed to. After a minute of darting down the halls, we had reached the room Wilmor was currently residing in.

I followed Ereda into a large spacious room filled to the brim with fancy wooden furniture as well as stacks of papers lined neatly on several shelves. In the middle of the room sat Wilmor who was sprawled over a low wooden table, tail tip covered in an herb based ink as he used it to scribble out words on once-blank paper. His ears twitched as we approached and his eyes briskly darted upwards before returning to his paper. Soon, I felt Ereda's presence leave my side and disappear from the room, allowing Wilmor and I a moment alone. Once she was gone, he lifted his head up from the paper and started sighing.

"Skyli, why on Lixion are you wearing that?"

His tone was questioning, but not imposing in the slightest. He seemed weaker, more tired perhaps than the previous night. Definitely not in the mood to start a verbal fight. Though I did not want to annoy him by waiting too long to answer his simple question.

"A... friend of mine wanted to dress me up," I replied as his eyes lit up with interest.

"Friend? Interesting that an acquaintance of yours is one of our guests this evening. Ah—drat I'm out of paste. *Stupid complimentary favor messages.* Skyli, I hate to be a bother, but would you bring that small plant over?"

He pointed to a tiny black plant that sat in a pot on a shelf to the far right end of the room. I quickly made my way over and had to leap into the air to grab it, but otherwise it was a simple task. Handing it over to him, I was surprised to see his mouth break into a small smile.

"Thanks, I appreciate it. If only I had a bit of psi talent, it would make getting my materials from over the room so much easier. Unfortunately, all I can seem to do is this," he stated as the pink stone in his tail began to glow.

I noticed that his smile resembled Marles'. It took me quite by surprise, as he'd seemed bored the last time I talked with him. A few black leaves on the small plant began to swell until they became plump squishy ovals that fell off the stem into Wilmor's paws. He then squished them into the round dish beside him on the table and drained each one of inky juice. His brown paws were stained black as a result and I was surprised to see him begin to gleefully lick away the black substance that colored his paws. If not for the slightly refreshing smell, I would have gagged because of how similar it looked to monster blood.

He dipped the sharp end of his tail into the ink and continued to scribble out words in a quick, but elegant way. Watching him write almost made me forget about the reason I came to this room. It seemed like he had as well, considering his focus shifted almost entirely back to tailwriting.

"Ereda told me that you wanted to have a word," I spoke up. His tail stopped suddenly, and it appeared mid-writing. I was slightly concerned at the nature of this conversation given how sudden his action was, but when I saw his eyes my tension loosened.

"She did? Let me recall. I may have mentioned that I would like to see you before the social gathering, but not for a particular reason. Oh that's it," he began as he quickly finished up his writing. He looked over towards me with a faint smile as he began to recollect his thoughts. "Dinner. I would like to apologize for your experience at last night's dinner personally. I believe Ereda already gave you a rundown on the details, but I wanted you to hear condolences from me as well," he went on as my stomach started to feel knotted. "You have nothing to worry about, it's that son of mine who needs to learn a thing or two. Running off without notice—it especially gave our caretakers quite the scare."

My heart sank again as I was further reminded of that life changing situation. While I did not agree with their controlling methods on Marles, I felt as if they did care for him a great degree. True, I had not known them as long as I had Marles, and I did not plan on knowing them any more deeply, but I knew all that I needed to know. My own mother, back when I ran off and was taken in by Alise, did she worry for me? I already knew the answer to that.

"But enough about him," Wilmor finished with a sigh before focusing his gaze on my outfit once more. "Ereda will have something more fitting for Marles' mate than those clothes. You will find her in our room if you want to have a say in what style you would prefer. I... still have so many of these to finish before this evening, so I'm afraid I will not be able to talk much until then." He let out another sigh as I nodded in response.

I soon left afterwards and began to search for the room Ereda was supposedly in. Though, I would have much rather found out where Marles had gone off to after our separation. Here I was—back to following orders from someone else; I had to remind myself to just endure it and stick it out for a little longer. Then Marles and I would be on our own once more. Hopefully with lots of supplies to last out the rest of the dreadful cold year.

"Skyli, there you are. I was just about to send someone to fetch you."

Though... after it's all over, what then?

"Sorry for making you wait; Wilmor and I just finished our chat."

With Blubelle's news, would there still be a Lixion like the one before the cold year?

"So, which one of these strikes your fancy for this evening? There's lace, patterned stripes, dots and plenty of others."

But as long as Marles and I could survive it, I suppose that's all that really mattered.

"That one. It's... perfect."

Right?

Chapter Twenty-One: Nostalgic

Lace and ribbons. Someone decorating my figure with such novelties.

Almost felt like that time fourteen years ago. It was...

"C-can you please be gentler when tightening certain things?"
Painful. Absolutely painful.

"No can do, Skyli! We can't take risks with anything slipping off. If such a thing happened you would be seen as disgraceful. You wouldn't want that to happen would you?"

Ereda helped me choose a nice turquoise outfit that would later wrap tightly around my form, though it did have an embroidered gap in the back that had room for my wings to emerge if I desired. It was of the finest material, adorned with great quantities of lace and silk; all things I could care less about, but she was happy so I acted like I was pleased. She had to get ready herself with the help of a caretaker, leaving me to do so with the assistance of this one. That pest, Kirra.

"Wait, shouldn't you know that already? Sure you aren't wearing all white, but ribbons are a delicate matter and should be fastened carefully and tightly," Kirra lectured me as I resisted saying unkind words in retaliation. "Geez, can't you consider how I feel about this? I was tasked with helping you of all Celegons to get ready when I could've been helping Mars. That would have been much more satisfactory," she went on as I held in a sigh.

Making any conversation with her would likely backfire on my end in some way. I had to admit, though her treatment of me was blunt and rude, I did appreciate that she was straightforward with her feelings and easy to read. In fact, if I played my words carefully I might even be able to get on better terms with her. Not enough to have her consider me an ally, but at least lessen the chances that she would spread more news of Pura Vannril to others.

"I assume you weren't able to switch tasks with Marles' designated helper?" I asked.

She scoffed. "Of course not. Everyone here adores Mars. Helping him get ready is the closest anyone can get without crossing any lines. Though, I suppose you wouldn't know, as his mate you're able to get close to him in ways no one else can." She sighed as she pulled the lace around my waist a smidgen tighter.

I could empathize with her feelings as I once had someone I looked up to, but was unable to get too close to as they kept a distance. While it was not Marles, I understood the feeling of wanting to share a bond with those you idolized. Since coming here, I felt like I had little alone time to spend with Marles. As selfish as I wanted to be, perhaps they deserved more time with him too. I could be selfless, at least for a little while.

"Hey Kirra? What if I was to avoid Marles for a portion of the social gathering?" I suggested as my ears began to be pinched.

"Then you'd be an awful mate undeserving of Mars!"

"Now hold on. What I mean is, I'll leave him be to give you and the others more time to catch up with him."

There was a pause as she came around to the other side of me and looked me directly in the eyes. She held an aggressive demeanor before she eventually turned away to sigh.

"I do appreciate you offering that, but have you forgotten that we're caretakers? We'll be entirely too busy for the whole of the social gathering and then some. As much as I hate to say it, you should be the one who makes sure Mars has a good time by being by his side. Hm, tell you what! If you keep that offer open after, then maybe you're not as bad as I thought." She grinned as I began to smile along with her.

After the social gathering we would have no reason to stay here. Even if I insinuate something that might not come to pass, it would surely put her in a better mood at present. Sure, we would be fed and taken care of, but I could not stand this environment. At some point I had to meet up with Marles so we could reassess our plan. If we robbed them, if we stayed, or simply left—I could not decide that without Marles' input.

It was time. Time to head out into the large dining hall. It would be too cold to have it outside, so improvisions were made. I began to walk briskly down the hallway alongside several of the guests who were practically frolicking in their fancy outfits. How many of their smiles were fake, I wondered. It made me long to see Marles' smile once I met up with him there.

The path to the dining hall had been decorated during the time everyone was getting their ribbons and whatnot assembled. Flowers of blues, violets and reds spread across the wooden walls intertwining together like wild vines. Considering most flowers had gone into temporary hibernation during the cold year, I could only assume the use of plant talent was involved in perking up the flowers to make them seem lively. They carefully avoided the wax clumps, for in their fragile condition they would have easily burst into ash if too close to the flames.

Upon entering the dining hall itself, I briefly stood in amazement at how peculiarly lit up the room was. There were wax clumps centered on each table atop thin, stone slabs that Celegons gathered around. The tables each had fancy cloth that coated the wood, really drumming up the wealthy social gathering atmosphere. Because of how spacious the room was and the clumps only being on tables, it was a bit dimmer than I expected, but still quite easy to see the surroundings. As Celegons began to take seats at the many tables, I wondered where I should go.

Scanning the room, I found Marles was nowhere to be seen. Wilmor and Ereda seemed to be overwhelmed with conversation at their table. Seeing everyone be able to talk freely must have meant the Iseirres had already said their initial greetings to the first wave of guests, which made me relieved I had one less thing to worry about. I then saw Blubelle among Ariele, Basion, and Soeki, all of whom seemed to be enjoying their reunion. After our earlier conversation, I felt reluctant to intrude on their group. Socializing among wealthy Celegons was not my forte, but I would manage for the night.

"U-um excuse me, but are you perhaps looking for a table to sit at? If you'd like, perhaps we can join one together?"

The voice was familiar and my head glanced towards the source. My eyes widened as I instantly recognized the pink eyes and yellow fur. Reene. Seeing her again in a place like this was almost nostalgic. No doubt she did not recognize me; how could she? Last time she saw me was several years ago when my appearance was different.

"Thank you, that's a great suggestion! I think I'll take you up on that. It's a pleasure to meet you, Lady Hune." I bowed my head slightly. I watched as her eyes lit up upon reaching mine. A moment, only a moment it seemed like she may have known who I was. It caused a flash of my memories to come rushing back.

"I just can't believe it's really you! Pardon my rudeness, I just never thought I'd get to meet the Pura sisters in the flesh like this! Pura Vannril, I just want to let you know how ecstatic I am to meet you—and you too, Pura Vannril! We seem to be close in age too if I'm not mistaken, this makes our meeting even more grand!"

"It's a pleasure to meet you too, Lady..." she paused as she had, thank goodness, not the slightest idea of who I was.

"Skyli."

"Well it's a pleasure to meet you, Lady Skyli... huh?" She stopped in her tracks as her eyes continued to examine mine. "We have never met before, have we, Lady Skyli?"

There was no point in saying yes as it would only breed confusion. Still the chance that she might remember me somehow struck me in an enchanting way. I certainly did not miss most of my past, but she was linked to how I first met Alise. Not to mention, a Celegon whose interest in me dove deeper than just being something exotic and rare. Lying to someone who showed me genuine kindness was something I had no intent in doing however.

"We have. But I didn't get to introduce myself properly last time," I explained as she nodded her head in understanding. Perhaps now she would get to know some of the real me.

We were soon situated at a table as more and more Celegons began to flood their way into the spacious area. It was honestly astonishing how many there were; they must have been invited from all across Lixion. Chatter soon broke out across the table, much to my dismay, but I managed to keep up a facade like I did at past social gatherings. The only Celegon I was genuinely interested in talking to was Reene, as for the others I could care less about forging meaningless bonds that would fade away after this event ended. Every so often I would glance away to see if Marles had entered, only to be disappointed when he was nowhere in sight.

"Is something preoccupying you Lady Skyli?" Reene asked me as I quickly turned my focus back to the center of the table.

"Apologies, my mate seems to be running a little late is all." I chuckled as her eyes lit up with excitement.

One thing I remembered about the younger Reene was that she was one of the Celegons who constantly dreamed of finding her future mate. Her reactions to me having one was quite entertaining, and reminded me even more of how she was when we first met.

"You have one? That's so sweet. I hope to find my own someday. What's he like? You must tell me!" Her enthusiasm practically pierced through my being.

"Well he's..." my voice trailed off as I began to lock eyes with the very Celegon I was talking about. In a matter of moments, he swiftly made his way over to the table with a grin on his face.

"There you are! Sorry I'm a little late. Preparations took a little longer than expected."

He always put in effort to keep himself well groomed, but tonight he was particularly eye-catching. Male Celegons typically only wore a ribbon around the end of their tail and spared the extra accessories, so I was surprised to see he opted to go above and beyond wearing an outfit of his own. More specifically, *that* outfit; the one I saw him wear many years ago at my last social gathering as a Vannril. It was bright and had mixes of sunset colors intertwined with lace and stripes. Despite being flashy, it brought a lot of attention back to his eyes.

"Lady Skyli, you mean to tell me your mate is..." Her mouth was partially agape as she stared at the both of us.

The other Celegons at the table seemed intrigued as well. Marles turned towards her and shared a small smile.

"Lady Reene, it's been a while hasn't it?" he asked as she became flustered quite like she had when she had been years younger. Though, she quickly composed herself and soon nodded her head as she returned his smile. Then she turned back towards me.

"I'm glad you have a good one, Lady Skyli. Take care of each other now," she said as she encouraged me to stand and go to his side.

As I stood up, my chest tightened; I felt as if every set of eyes in the room were looking this way. I tried to avoid catching any of their direct gazes as best I could by directing my focus towards Marles, but that created another set of problems. My chest was filled with fuzzy feelings, which were not well combined with my other emotions. It worsened when he used his tail to guide me to a new table by entangling it with mine. While I would much rather look at him than anyone else in the room, this was bound to have an effect on my face.

Soon I felt a new tug on my tail coming from a different direction. The tugs increased as we passed through the gaps of the many tables, and soon I found myself completely halted by the tugging force. My eyes traced for the source to see that a pink aura was faintly glowing around the base of my tail, the culprit which prevented me from going further. A use of psi talent no doubt, but from who? My thoughts were soon answered as a figure smiled over at me from the table to my right.

"Everything alright Ly—"

Marles froze as he stared at the silver furred Celegon with green eyes. Despite using her talent to hold my tail, she seemed very fixated on Marles. Her tail was well hidden under the table to hide the glow, but I could feel she was the one immobilizing me.

"That's enough, Lady Clain."

His voice was firm, but not raised in a way to alert many of the guests. She continued to smile sinisterly as I felt my tail's movement return.

"Now, now, Iseirre, no need to be so formal. Or harsh for that matter. I simply thought I'd try to catch your attention after not seeing you for so long. My, how you've changed since then," she said in a softer tone, though I could still sense an air of deviance in her voice.

Marles was quick to shut her down; however, his way of doing it was at my expense. He gently nipped at my neck for a brief moment before looking back at her shocked expression. As surprised as I was, seeing her smug face reduced to horror made me forget his brief open display of affection. At least to the point I was more embarrassed for her than myself. That feeling did not last long, as once again eyes began to look my way—now more than ever. How Marles was unfazed by it all was a mystery to me.

I had assumed that for the social gathering we would be sitting at his parents' table, but to my surprise we headed for the one Blubelle sat at. Her eyes caught us quickly and sparked with interest, though there was a faint dullness about them.

"I was wondering when we'd see the both of you," Ariele said as she pointed over to two conveniently empty cushions at the table. "Blubelle kept insisting that we should save you seats."

Blubelle simply nodded in response, and I could tell she was trying to fight the urge to appear morose and worry anyone. Perhaps she still needed more time before she felt like her usual self. My eyes caught Soeki slipping his tail close to hers, which seemed to provide a bit of comfort to her.

"Now, when are these meals going to be brought out? I can't wait but a minute longer," Ariele said as her tail bobbed back and forth in anticipation.

"The meals will be brought out shortly. Everyone looks to be seated now so the caretakers will—ah there they are," Marles smiled as we watched a group of caretakers sweep into the room carrying many dishes in their arms.

They were quick on their feet to place down a variety of dishes on each table in a timely manner. I caught a glimpse of Kirra placing down a plate full of roasted roots a few tables away from us. She spared me and Marles a brief glance before returning to her duties. Her expression was more focused than anything, though I wondered if deep down she was still thinking about our previous conversation.

In a matter of moments, our own table was getting attention from caretakers who started placing several dishes in front of us to choose from. My nose was overwhelmed with exotic scents and I could only imagine how much Ariele was restraining herself from diving right in. Proper social gathering etiquette requires that the host give a speech before mealtime commences. This was different from the introductory speech that allows small talk. I had nearly forgotten how many words had to be said at these events. For Ariele and all the other hungry Celegon's sakes, I hoped that it would not be too long.

"Attention! Attention everyone who has gone out of their way to come here for this wonderful night!"

The voice unfortunately came from Ereda. I prepared myself to be in for a long drawn out speech that lasted long enough that all the freshly prepared food grew lukewarm.

"Again, I thank all of you for managing to come here even through such weather conditions. The cold year has brought many a misfortune upon us. But as it stands, you are all here now so let us forget about the hardships of the outside. Let me start by telling you about the lovely meals that the Iseirre caretakers have prepared. They consist of exquisite—"

Ereda went on explaining the exotic and luxurious items included in the dishes, going into great detail that they were acquired despite Lixion's harsher conditions. Every so often my eyes would glance towards Ariele who looked hungrier by the second, bored listening to Ereda rant about the food in front of her. Hearing these long, and often meaningless, speeches was yet another reason I dislike social gatherings. I suppose that was the price to pay for gourmet food in a lavish environment.

After what seemed like forty torturous minutes of my time being wasted, it was finally time to eat. Ariele could not wait a millisecond more to begin grabbing assorted goods from plates and piling them in front of her as she was quickly followed by Basion and Soeki. A few more dignified Celegons from other tables gave some disapproving glances that made me smile; this was the table I wanted to be at. Blubelle, however, seemed to lack an appetite. As focused on her own food as she was, Ariele was quick to state her mind.

"Kid, I swear if you don't eat any of this food," she stated between mouthfuls. "You'll take on the role of *bait*."

Ariele's words were said in a serious and almost sinister way, but Blubelle seemed more confused than worried.

"But Ari, that's *already* my role," Blubelle responded as Ariele began to think to herself. That was a pretty fitting role for someone like Blubelle, not good at fighting but great at making noise to attract monsters. Still, I could not imagine how she put up with being in such a dangerous position; surely she complained.

"True, it is. So, eat your food and Basion will take the role of bait," Ariele suggested as Basion gave her a shocked look.

"I will? Oh, fine. I'll do it if Blubelle eats until she absolutely can't anymore." Basion sighed as Ariele sported a triumphant grin. Blubelle seemed pleased with those terms as well, and soon enough she began chowing down roasted water nymphs.

"Skyli, this is the best thing I've tasted all—" She stopped mid sentence as other Celegons from nearby tables began glaring at her for the loudness of her voice. "Y-year," she said more quietly as I smiled.

Chapter Twenty-Two: Vannril

With Blubelle's chaotic energy restored, things began to feel just a little more normal. It almost felt as if I was not at a social gathering, but at an inn surrounded by good company. Aside from these outfits, the time we spent together like this was reminiscent of back when we first met. We bantered and shared many stories from our time apart. In this huge dining hall all I could see was this table, filled to the brim with delicious food and Celegons I was on good terms with. Uncharacteristic of me it might have been, but I missed this.

The collective food on our table was gradually diminished thanks to six hungry mouths. As much as I enjoyed it, eating any more of it would probably cause me to get sick from overindulgence. It was a problem most Celegons did not have the pleasure of experiencing. Marles was the first of us to stop, which was unsurprising as he had had this luxury more than any of us. Even Ariele was starting to slow down in her consumption.

"You two are done already? There's still so much left," Ariele said as she put another seasoned roasted root into her mouth. I hoped that she would be able to keep everything down after eating so much.

"No more for me. If I eat any more it would probably bloat my stomach, and this outfit is already plenty tight enough." Marles chuckled as he pawed at the top of his outfit. "Besides, I want to be sure I'm swift enough for dancing later."

It did not occur to me that this dancing activity would happen prior to coming here. Neither Ereda, Wilmor, or the caretakers mentioned such a thing would be present at the social gathering. I knew dancing was a common thing, but not every social gathering had one. I had assumed I would have been informed, at least before I had put this outfit on. A lump felt like it was forming in my throat, but swallowing did nothing to make it go away. The others, save for Ariele, appeared to be pleased with the news—especially Basion.

"R-really? Well isn't that a wonderful surprise, isn't it, Ariele?" Basion chimed, practically beaming through Ariele with his contagious smile. She seemed quite indifferent to the act of dancing, but still humored her trusted partner.

"Um, sure whatever you say. The free meal was the best part of this, but I suppose I could leave a little room in my stomach for your dancing," she replied, much to his delight.

Blubelle also seemed noticeably excited by the idea of dancing with Soeki, while he seemed a little unsure. Dancing was not something most Celegons did, as they did not have time to waste on a thing that did not bring better odds of survival to their lives. In fact, I was surprised at how excited the two of them were about it, as common Celegons were not usually taught how to dance. Not for social gatherings they would not be attending. Yes, it was an activity that mates could do with each other, but dancing at social gatherings was a different category entirely.

"Have you danced at a social gathering before, Basion? You seem awfully excited about this," I said as his brown eyes continued to glisten with excitement.

"Nope! But I've always wanted to. Now I finally can with Ariele!"

So none of them aside from Marles and myself had any real experience dancing before. This was not something I should have been too concerned with as it did not affect me, but I could not help but worry about them. Thanks to the countless lessons I had had to endure as a child to ensure my form and poise were top notch, messing up was the least of my worries. Dancing the way that was expected of me, it had been a while; though, I was sure I could pick it back up easily. Still, they saw it as something fun and enchanting. For me, it was something I could not do; I had been forced to dance so much during my time growing up that I grew to loathe it, as well as the eyes on me as I performed. Because, in the end, it was a performance.

"Are you up for dancing, Lyla? We'll most likely have to as my parents would probably get fussy if we didn't. I'll admit it has been quite a while since I have, so I might be a little shoddy at first." He smiled nervously before subtly stroking my paw. I must have been deep in thought as that caused my heart to race more than it normally would have.

I was not particularly thrilled at the thought, but going against their wishes would only cause unnecessary friction. Having everyones' eyes on me, even if there would be more dancers than just the two of us, churned my stomach. A dance with Marles in private could be quite romantic. Most likely, he shared the same sentiment; however, I could not refuse to dance with him now knowing what was at stake.

"I'd love to dance with you, if that's what you're asking. Only with you though. I wouldn't have any enjoyment if I was to dance with someone else," I told him honestly as I used my tail to graze his back. It was true, dancing with anyone else would be thrice as dreadful as an experience than it would be already.

His face reddened slightly before averting his gaze, which accelerated my heartbeat. Though it was not a long duration, it excited me that I was able to get him a little flustered. If not for the countless Celegons around us, I would have gotten closer and leaned on him. Thankfully, the others were still caught up in the idea of dancing and paid that little chat between us no mind.

Most other Celegons had grown bored of the idea of stuffing themselves long before our table. It was shortly after I noticed this when the caretakers returned in a swarm to clear the tables of uneaten food. They seemed to move faster this time around than when setting out the food. Perhaps had been given permission to feast on the leftovers once the social gathering had ended.

Once the food was cleared from the room, they came back again to politely ask Celegons who sat in the tables centermost in the room to stand from their seats and to wait to the sides of the room until the tables were repositioned. A few of them left the room entirely as they probably knew what was to come, one of them including the Clain Celegon from earlier. They took the tables and began to relocate them so that now there was a decently spacious area in the center of the room no longer obstructed by objects. Kirra and a few others stood in the cleared area as the rest continued to transport the remaining tables. Their tails began to glow and soon several glowing figments of light began to waft through the air, with several colors all clashing together in harmony. A display not attainable without psi talents. Just looking at all the colors sparked my heart with excitement.

Ereda stood herself up next which lessened that excitement. Another speech was going to come into play.

"Bringing the meal portion of the night to a conclusion, it is time to begin our dancing event. Since there will be no dancing under the stars tonight, we have improvised and provided you with these psi illusions as a lovely compromise. As formality dictates, all guests must partner up and head to the center of the room. However, in light of recent events it has come to my understanding that not everyone is feeling up to it and tonight's dancing event will be purely optional. As some of the guests have already, feel free to retire to your rooms for an early night if your mood fits that criteria," Ereda announced as my ears perked up.

I felt an immediate release of pressure knowing it was at least optional. Perhaps I would be able to sit this one out knowing that others would be doing the same. Then Ereda added a few extra words.

"In other news, I am pleased to announce that my son Marles has recently returned home. Not only that, but with a mate of his own. So as a celebration to his return, I think that it is only fair if the two of them put on a display of their dancing before everyone else joins in," Ereda declared as my heart sank.

Optional for everyone excluding Marles and I it seemed. This put a lot of eyes on Marles and I even before we rose to our feet. Walking to the center of the room like this gave me flashes of when I performed with my sister. We would do synchronized dances together, and do them so well that watchers would not be able to tell the two of us apart. Looking the exact same in appearance definitely helped. This time I would be dancing with Marles, however.

He gave me a few glances which silently told me he knew I was not the most eager to do this. Still, this did not stop either of us from heading to the room's center as instructed. More eyes followed us as they waited to see what we were capable of. I tried not to look at them, but a few glances stood out. Especially Blubelle's expectant eyes. Marles pulled me closer to quietly whisper something in my ear.

"Are you ready for this?"

My mouth resisted letting out a scoff in response. He should have already known, not like my answer would change the outcome. I gave him a subtle nod as a slight grin appeared on his face.

"I hope you don't mind if *I'm* the one leading you this time."

A second later I found myself being escorted in a dance I had never seen before. It took me a moment to observe his movements; once I could, things progressed smoothly. The mindset that carefully calculated where I would step was not present for this dance. Instead I put my faith in Marles who guided my form throughout the process. Once I stopped worrying of messing up or being exact, the entire exchange was quite a lot of fun.

As serious as the event was supposed to be, Marles could not stop smiling as he directed my movements around the open space. The interactions between us felt akin to two young Celegons playing with one another in a safe space, free of worry, and focused on pestering each other. And pester me he did. Several times he had pulled me closer unexpectedly and snuck in several playful nicks with his mouth on various areas around my upper body.

Almost if we were lost in time, I had not realized that several minutes after we started dancing that other Celegons had joined us. It felt like mere moments since we began, but I suppose becoming entranced in an activity can confuse the mind making it lose track of time. Marles noticed this as well and took this as an opportunity to pull me closer again. Not to tease or kiss me, but to just hold me closer than before and continue to gently dance with me. I used my tail to caress his back for a moment before leaning into his chest.

The material of the outfit he was wearing itched my face a little as I leaned against it, but the pros outweighed the cons. His heartbeat was happy and calm which further soothed my nerves. My eyes wandered to the other dancing pairs. The first to catch my gaze were Blubelle and Soeki who were both clueless, but having a good time nonetheless. Then I saw Ariele and Basion. Basion was trying his best to lead while Ariele attempted to follow, but it was clear she was struggling to keep up.

Ereda and Wilmor were also dancing together. My eyes widened as I briefly saw their faces nuzzle for a quick moment before they pulled away. When I had seen them before, they hardly appeared affectionate with one another despite being mates. I turned my focus back on Marles before he grew curious of why I was looking away and embraced him tightly. As much as I possibly could without hindering our dancing.

"You seem to be enjoying this more than I thought," Marles remarked before he spun my body around.

"It does help to have a dance partner know what he's doing," I said before my mind thought of how the others were dancing. "No. It helps because my dance partner is *you*. So yes, I'm having a wonderful time."

His eyes lit up more as the sunsets grew ecstatically vibrant. It seemed like he was leaning in to express more affection before I was gently pulled away from his grasp. Jerking my head behind me, I saw that it was none other than Wilmor. Ereda had also transferred herself to Marles' side, much to his surprise.

"Hello again Skyli, mind if I have a turn with you?" Wilmor asked as he guided Marles and I apart with Ereda's assistance.

My eyes shifted to Marles briefly as he gave a hesitant smile before turning towards Ereda who began chatting him up. The vibe I got from him seemed friendly enough, so I was not too worried about the possibility of him insulting my dancing.

"You dance remarkably well for someone who would rather not be here."

I spared him a confused glance as he gave a slight grin.

"No need to look so startled. All I'm saying is, it takes one to know one. I've never been one for these types of events myself, but you grow tolerant of them with time," he stated before averting his gaze to look at Ereda.

She looked happy with whatever she was relaying to Marles. On the contrary, Marles looked like he was being lectured by her which I hoped was not about our dancing.

"Well I'm sure it helps to have such enjoyable company," I said as I gestured towards the pair of them. His eyes gleamed in response as he gave her another brief glance.

"It's been almost fifty years now, well forty-eight to be exact."

I tried to resist looking shocked, but my eyes gave me away. I knew that wealthier Celegons often lived longer as they lived in safer conditions, but it did not occur to me that his parents were that old. It was true that Celegons stop changing physically after reaching maturity, but these were high numbers. He quickly caught on to my thoughts before speaking more.

"Yes, forty-eight years since I've known her. I was thirty-seven years of age at the time. We did not immediately click when we first met, but with time soon we both realized and started sneaking off together," he explained as his expression warmed.

"Sneaking off?" I questioned as he gave a slight nod.

"Believe it or not, Ereda was once a caretaker here. When she started working here, I grew intrigued by her before I knew why. My father thought it to be a passing interest and disapproved of me being so social with her at the time. The connection between my parents was quite instant, so I assumed it was a lack of understanding on his part," he explained further as I put the pieces together.

It was hard to imagine Ereda as a caretaker, but now knowing that softened my opinion of her as she came from humble origins. Learning more about the two of them would make it harder to steal from them, however. Unless I uncovered more unsavory news like what they did to Marles. Then, it clicked that Wilmor had mentioned his parents, but it was clear they weren't around. I wondered if Marles had ever been able to meet them.

"I see, I suppose instant connections were a more common occurrence in the past? But your parents... are they—"

"Deceased? Yes, a few decades ago. In fact, only after their partings was I able to properly move things along with Ereda four years after I met her. It's not a memory I look back on fondly, but it bothers me less and less every passing year. Our mansion here, well it was not always protected by the filters. Monsters infiltrated and their lives as well as many others were lost."

Now I wanted to steal from them less. Perhaps I would target one of the pompous guests instead. That Clain Celegon came straight to mind. Wilmor's eyes grew slightly frazzled as if only now he realized all the information he spilled to me.

"H-how very rude of me to tell you such foul things. The point of this evening was to relieve ourselves of such harshness, yet here I am informing you of that which you needn't know," Wilmor said as he bowed his head in apology before I quickly reassured him.

"N-no, don't feel that way. I'm glad you trusted me enough to tell me this information. Knowing helps me feel closer to the Iseirre family because of it. I've learned a great deal about Marles since meeting him, and it's nice getting to know his blood family and caretakers. Even though I disagree with how you both treated Marles when we arrived, I don't think that makes either of you bad Celegons."

He appeared taken aback at my last sentence, but soon smiled once he realized what I said as a whole. Before passing me back to Marles, he had one more thing to say to me.

"Marles is lucky to have such a Celegon as his mate."

The words he said, though short, cut deep into my heart as I gave him a small smile. Then he traded me away to Marles so that he and Ereda could dance together once more. Ereda gave me a slight grin as well, which made me wonder what their conversation was like. Before I could ask, I was pressed into a tight squeeze by Marles.

"A little touch-starved are we? It's only been a few minutes Marley," I whispered to him with playfulness in my tone.

"Minutes? Feels like hours to me. I've been starving all day, like I can't get enough," he softly replied as my ears quivered with excitement.

A warmness spread across my insides and my face as I returned his embrace. As we continued to dance, I felt like I was on air. The night would continue to go on like this, peacefully, until a certain Celegon called out my name.

"Sk-Skyli!"

A panicked voice cried out as all heads in the room began to turn towards the source. Marles and I immediately stopped dancing as the room was soon filled with gasps and muffled shrieks. My entire body had tensed before I even turned towards the source, almost as if I already knew what their eyes were looking at. There was the pink Celegon Kirra with crimson blood dripping from her left side as she crawled on the wooden floor. She held her paw over the open wound in an attempt to lessen the bleeding, but it seemed to be pouring out too fast.

While most of the other Celegons were stunned at the sight of her, Marles and I raced over. I removed the outfit I was wearing as fast as I was able. Underneath was my satchel that I managed to hide quite well prior to putting on the outfit. There was an emergency emeri inside that I quickly crushed. I then began applying the juices to her open wound. She looked over at me and I tried my best to tell her with my eyes she would be okay as I continued to treat her. Her orange eyes grew desolate and more bleak by the moment.

"Y-you better h-hurry. She's awfully impatient."

Chapter Twenty-Three: Favor

A surge of silence fell across the room as she spoke those words. Whoever did this to her was waiting outside for *me*? For a Celegon to attack another like this, if this creature was a Celegon at all, the situation must have been dire.

As I held the emeri in place against Kirra's side, my mind began to wander. This could not have been Z, could it? On multiple accounts that deduction seemed wrong. For one, Z was male. He was unusually erratic the last time I saw him, certainly not himself, but would he go as far as to harm another Celegon? I could not think of anyone else who would come here for me, however. Even those I had stolen from, they would not have harmed Kirra as a result of my actions.

Waiting around and wondering would be the worst thing I could do in this situation, as the assaulter had the potential of doing the same to others. To ease everyone's minds, I decided to go to where 'She' was waiting for me. Using my tail, I directed Marles' paws to the emeri as I removed the pressure my own were providing to it. His eyes lit up with worry as he watched me stand.

"Kirra, I know you're wounded, but do you have the strength to tell me where 'She' waits?" I questioned as Marles' fur began to bristle while others in the background were quick to voice their fears.

"Whatever did this to Kirra can do the same to you. At least let me tag along with you," he interjected as Kirra's weak eyes widened.

"N-no! She h-hates Mars. You'll b-be attacked on sight. She t-told me to tell you that as well. Only Skyli is p-permitted to see her," Kirra stuttered between coughs as Marles applied more pressure to her wound. "She awaits you at the m-mansion's front entrance. Just outside."

This being, whoever she was, seemed quite violent to resort to such extreme measures to make sure Kirra relayed that to me. Threatening Marles, even indirectly, was also something I would not let slide. I was by far not the most skilled in combat. But my ice was something I could subtly prepare without arousing suspicion, especially given the cold and snow outside. Most of the other Celegons were still paralyzed in fear of what could be waiting, but a few stepped forward. A smile formed on my face as I recognized those who approached me. Even if one of them was Blubelle, who I heard only runs from dangerous situations, I was touched.

"If Marles can't go, we'll be tagging along right behind you! Whoever did this to her won't get past us, if they happen to get through you," Blubelle beamed. While I appreciated the thought, there was a sinister undertone in the latter part. She was definitely bold to say that; perhaps she had grown since tagging along with Ariele.

Ariele then walked forward as she nudged Blubelle's side. Her arms then crossed and her dark blue eyes gave the impression that she was ready for a fight.

"Whoever this is seems to want Skyli. They probably won't be pleased to see a group closing in behind her. That's a good way of escalating things. Sorry Skyli, but we'll be following from a good distance. Enough to hear if things turn sour, but it's up to you to hold your own until we get there," Ariele stated as I gave a nod. This was frightening, but pushing those thoughts aside, I knew I had to be quick about it.

Turning towards Marles, I briskly nuzzled against his face before pulling myself away and dropping on all limbs to run. My feet scampered across the wooden flooring of the dining hall until they met the soft carpet flooring of the hallways. The carpet felt as if it was slowing me down. And as I had no time to lose, my back ached and soon my wings were speeding me across the halls. When I spotted the large wooden doors of the entrance, I retracted them—albeit too fast. If not for my reflexes, I would have tumbled across the floor. Pushing open one of the heavy doors, I was met with cold gusts; my eyes squinted in response.

Though the winds were harsh, I was at least able to see decently. The air was not coated with ice flurries as it often was at night. Sitting close by the mansion's entrance was a Celegon who had pale fur with subtle green tints. But that was not what my attention focused on the most, although for my safety it should have been. On top of the once pure white small snow pile that had gathered, there was a coating of crimson. New ice flurries had already begun to cover it, but it was still quite fresh and new. My nose picked up the scent of Kirra's blood.

My eyes had a hard time looking away from it; there was just so much. The trail led to the doorway I emerged from. I had not noticed, but there was most likely a trail from Kirra dragging herself across the carpet. There was also blood leading to the Celegon before me, who soon turned to face me after noticing my presence. I was unable to look them in the eyes. All I could focus on was their paws and tail, both drenched in Kirra's blood.

"My stars... It's really you."

The voice that came from her made me sick to my stomach. It was not particularly obnoxious, but there was something off that made my fur bristle. My eyes soon forced themselves off the blood and into the speaker's eyes. Cool, grey, and almost white. Eyes that I used to see all the time. They were soon filled with tears as the Celegon slowly approached me.

"Stay where you are!" I ordered as my tail flung itself behind me and out of her view. It grew colder than the outside air in preparation to fight off the Celegon in front of me if I had to. Her eyes widened and then softened, surprising me. Still, I didn't let my guard down. "Why have you requested for me and why did you have to violently attack one of the caretakers here to make sure I was to come to you immediately?" I asked, demanding she answer right away.

Instead of telling me immediately, her eyes became flooded with tears. Part of me wondered if this reaction was in response to guilt setting in for fatally wounding one of her own kind, possibly wondering if she had killed the victim.

"But, Pura—it's *me*. Don't tell me you've forgotten," she whimpered and realization struck.

"*No...*" left my mouth as I slowly backed away from her as she continued to approach. At this point questions should have been filling my mind to the brim. Though, all I could really think about was maintaining a safe distance from her.

"I've been tracking you for a while now, learning many things. It's natural you don't go by Pura Vannril anymore, after you left the family. I don't blame you though; it fell apart all too fast. Father's passing took quite the toll on mother, we both knew that. She lived many years after you left though, barely. Until the cold year. I was just tired of dealing with her, always crying all the time. I was patient, but even I have my limits."

My body was quivering at this point and she took notice. She blankly smiled and her eyes seemed to show no emotion.

"It was over surprisingly quick, she didn't even harden her bones," she stated as her bloodied tail began to swish back and forth. It was an emotion I could not comprehend. "If she really wanted to live, she would have struggled."

"H-how could-"

I bit the side of my both to stop it from trembling. I forced my body to ready itself just in case. I had to remain calm.

"You killed her. You took her life, just like that. A life that was not yours to take. That's Lixion's one rule. Do you even realize what you've done? Is it not apparent to you that our numbers are already in a constant state of decline?"

I began to walk closer to her, same as she was trying to do to me moments ago. This time, she was the hesitant one. I should have been scared. Or be crying about how she killed her own blood. My own blood.

"What did it feel like? What went through your mind as you cut her down? Better yet, how do you feel right now? Wounding Kirra like that must have given you quite the rush, huh? And now you can't stop and wish to continue the process you started by killing your blood sister, is that right?"

She had completely frozen up. It was as if just now, she had come to realize what she had done. Her dull eyes watered as she looked down at her paws, almost as if she was shocked to find them stained with red. She looked over at the ice flurries that had already gone to work at covering up her mess.

"I..." her voice trailed off as drips fell down her face. "Monster. I'm a monster. Though instead of eating them I just... put them to permanent rest," she said as her voice softened. She looked over at me as the tears had stopped. "I relished every second. But understand that I didn't come here with the intention of doing the same to you."

My insides squeezed, but somehow I managed to force a smile across my features. In some bizarre messed up way this all felt very nostalgic. Perhaps too much. She had been lost to her own madness a long time ago, and I was surprised I did not fully realize it until now. Memories came back in flood.

"I know you didn't."

Far back to when I was small, for as long as I could remember, I was afraid of my sister. She used to frequently stain my white fur with red with her claws, though never to the point of fatal damage. As our white bodies were considered precious and valuable, this of course made our mother furious. Dual siblings received dual punishments, though nothing physical to avoid further damaging our coats. I never protested, not once, to whenever she wanted to 'decorate' my fur—as she would often say.

As with my mother's treatment, I grew tolerant of whatever my sister did to me. Anything to avoid more conflict. I never knew then, but she was unwell. Corrupted by something that must have creeped into her brain long ago. However, she was still my blood, and I empathized with her pain. Even if there was nothing anyone could do to help her.

"There's something coming. A creature with a large tail and snout. It's dark green with yellow streaks. It's coming here. No. *They* are coming here," she whispered as she looked me in the eye with a fearful expression.

Before I had time to react to her obscure statement, it was already happening. Vibrations of hard and heavy feet that pounded through the layer of ice flurries resonated in my ears. It was definitely not a monster; the body sounded and felt sturdier, and the weight seemed to me proportionally different. Monsters often ran wild, with their claws scraping against the ground. Whatever was coming here had careful and organized movements.

My fur bristled as I firmly took hold of my sister's arm and used all my strength to squeeze the both of us through to the other side of the mansion's door with minimal pulling. Once inside, I let go and quickly pulled it shut. From the corner of my eye I could see colors that belonged to familiar Celegons just further down the hallway. After taking hold of her arm again, I darted down the hall frantically in their direction. It was clear they were disturbed by the sight of her fur, but I had to do everything I could to tell them that there were more dangerous matters coming into play.

Many of them began speaking out at once, probably about the blood on my sister, but I did not pay attention to a single word. We had no time to discuss the assault, as disrespectful as that was. For a moment, all I could do was lock eyes with Blubelle as mine became blurry. This was not the time to let my guard down, but my body did not give me a choice. The voices stopped once they saw the state I was in as I tearfully approached Blubelle. Her eyes grew terrified, almost if she knew what I was going to say.

"They're coming. The Pythera. I-I heard them coming," I practically sputtered as my mouth started to quiver too much to allow me to speak properly.

There was a brief uncomfortable silence that lingered in the air. This was followed by confusion and fear. Some of them were unsure of what I was talking about, while others like Blubelle knew. Blubelle's eyes seemed to be in complete shock, but she soon closed them and began to breathe.

"So this is it then. There's no way we're going to make it out of here."

Several others looked at her in disbelief, including Ariele. Others seemed to have already given up by the looks in their eyes. Ariele began to scoff before using her tail to modestly whack Blubelle's back. The dullness in Blubelle's eyes was replaced with surprise. She stared at Ariele and opened her mouth to protest. Before she could, Ariele was quick to talk over her.

"Listen up, you. I don't know what this Pythera is, but it and possibly its buddies are heading this way as we speak. No matter how strong these creatures are, they are still creatures that can be fought off. You may think you're weak, but you had enough energy to snap at me just a minute ago. That means you still haven't lost the fight in you just yet." Ariele gave a slight smirk and Blubelle's eyes seemed to glimmer. Though her small smile fell when she remembered a devastating detail.

"If they manage to hit us with their vines, we'll be paralyzed."

Ariele took a moment to think as the others began whispering to themselves. Blubelle's ears drooped as chatter between Celegons turned bleak. I had no reason to doubt her. These creatures would be dangerous if they touched us. It was a false confidence. But even on false pretenses, it was what everyone needed to hear right now to remain motivated enough to stay alive.

"We're Celegons. More evasive than any monster or nymph can dream to be. All we have to do is not get hit. We're fast and that makes up for your lack of strength. It's a fact that's kept many of us alive for years. Our talents can be used at range; as long as we keep our distance and are perceptive of their movements, we can survive. Plus, there are many of us gathered together. If we hurry, we can tell the others back at the dining hall before it's too late and come up with a strategy," I suggested before grabbing onto my sister's arm once more. "You're coming too. Once we survive this we'll figure out a proper way to deal with you."

The others bore skeptical looks at the Celegon I held onto, but as we needed to hurry there were no objections. As we raced towards the dining area, my ears listened carefully for the heavy steps of the Pythera. Our small group reached our destination, only to find a few Celegons remaining. The Iseirres, and the others I could see cowering under tables and the like. I rushed over to Marles whose eyes locked on to the bloodied Celegon at my side.

"Where," I started as I gazed about the cluttered dining room. "Did everyone go? We all—we all needed to be here."

Wilmor soon walked over to us after an attempt to comfort Ereda, who appeared to be in a state of shock. She was seated next to a table on the floor. His eyes looked hopeless as he started to explain.

"One of our guests 'sold out'. Following the incident with Kirra, one of our caretakers found a scrap of paper near the garden's entrance and came in here shortly after you left. The contents of that note—It doesn't matter." He shook his head, and then continued, "The contents made it clear that the guests here are no longer safe. Most of them had attempted to flee or seek refuge, but those creatures that the note describes should arrive any minute now." As Wilmor finished, he shivered slightly.

All of the Celegons in the dining hall looked far from eager to fight off such creatures, but if any of us had a chance of survival it needed to be done. Marles looked incredibly worried on multiple accounts, but otherwise appeared mentally stable enough to help in fighting them off. No, the reality of it was, most in this room would probably not survive. But I needed to, Marles needed to, and I was sorry for everyone else. There would be casualties and, if worse came to worse, we would have to escape during the chaos.

Letting go of my sister's arm once more, I spoke a speech I knew would get a lot of them off their tails.

"I'll be blunt with the lot of you. If you continue cowering like this, paralyzed in fear, these Pythera will get you. When they do, they will physically paralyze your body and then do who knows what. I don't blame you for cowering, but I beg of you to snap out of it! If all of us work together using our talents, we at least have a chance. You're all wealthy Celegons. Aren't your riches worth fighting to stay alive for? Or will you simply sit and let your lives be taken from you?" I questioned as a few of their ears perked up.

I was never one for saying things to boost morale, but perhaps reminding them of what they stood to lose would help them come to their senses. A few of them came out of hiding and got to their feet, but were still noticeably shaken. Ereda shook herself as she slowly trudged over to reunite with her mate. At that moment my ears perked up, though not from any words. Heavy footsteps began to stomp on the carpet flooring of the hallways, and I heard the sound of something being dragged as well.

Panic arose in many Celegons and some immediately went back into hiding. Those who remained began to distance themselves from the entrances to the dining hall as we waited for the Pythera to come. My tail grew cold in preparation for the fight that would commence in a matter of moments. Other tail stones began to glow as well from across the room. I looked at Marles one last time before a Pythera made its way into the dining hall.

My ears had previously picked up the sounds of at least four pairs of heavy feet walking down the hallway, but so far only one had entered the room. Very tall, the being had to crouch down a little to fit under the doorway. Though definitely smaller than the biggest of monsters, it was bigger than Malypsi; at least double their size. Two thick sturdy legs with hard bottoms walked into the dining hall as a large heavy tail slithered across the floor where the creature's back legs would have been. Teal eyes with golden slits scanned the room and all of the Celegons in it.

"Tidings. Looks like we missed the little event you Celegons put together."

His voice was calm, yet thick and heavy almost to the point it was hard to understand him. As I watched the Pythera's jaws open, I saw that he possessed no teeth. Instead, there was a large yellow tongue that filled his narrow mouth. Though he posed no threat in the moment, the vibe that he gave off was eerily curious—as if he was carefully watching our every move. His gaze seemed hyper focused on my sister, specifically the bloodied parts on her fur.

"You. Come here."

His demeanor became demanding as other eyes moved to glance towards her. Part of me wanted to grab her, but she soon began to mindlessly walk over to where the intimidating creature stood without a fuss. Why was she not afraid? I was. That petty reason was why I did not have the strength to stop her. She looked up at the large creature whose yellow tongue slipped from the confines of his mouth.

He lowered his neck slightly, allowing his long tongue to reach her paws. I watched as he took a long taste of the red substance that had dried onto her fur as a shiver went up my tail. His slits began to morph into circular pupils, which could only mean he relished the taste. It made sense that creatures other than monsters found our blood delicious, but this did not feel right. It felt like he was degrading us. In an instant, the vine-like things that were described to me emerged from the creature's sides and struck her down.

"Such a delicacy would be wasted on the beasts of this world. Our queen was right about this, of course," he said as his vines began to stroke at my sister's limp body. "She died. Because of one of your kind. Now we will carry out her last wish and see it through. I'm sure that she would not mind if there were a few *casualties* to pay for what happened."

He soon lifted one of his heavy feet and before my eyes had time to process, a crunching sound filled my ears. I could not bring myself to look at what he had done; I knew that if I did, I would be too scared to move. *Do everything you can to not get hit. Survive.* This is what I told myself before launching a blast of ice directly into the eyes of that awful creature.

After that, everything became a panicked blur. The Pythera let out an almost deafening hiss that rattled my ears and rendered me temporarily uncoordinated. Heavy floor vibrations closed in on all entrances to the dining hall, and I found myself ascending to the ceiling to get a clear view of the current situation. Other Celegons had similar thoughts and rose upwards as they took flight, but we had greatly underestimated the range of the Pythera's vines. One by one, they were knocked down by the vines along with the faint sound of cracked bones as they finished their descent.

Some of them had managed to leave the room, however. My eyes scanned the floor for Marles to see him carefully using his fire talent so as to not set the entire mansion ablaze. There was no way I could save everyone. The Pythera were just too strong, swift, and resistant to talents. But Marles, I could save him. I could save both of us. That was all that mattered. My eyes burned as I took a dive and flew towards him before snatching him away.

Squeezing tight, I ascended the both of us into the air briefly as I sped toward the exit. It took a lot of strength, but I managed to transfer both our bodies out of the chaos infused dining hall. He could chew me out as much as he wanted once we were both at a safe place far away from these beings. Call me a coward, a deserter of our friends, his family, his old home. As long as we survived I was able to put up with the consequences of my actions. Things would be bad for a bit, but they would get better. I told myself that over and over again.

Until I was hit.

My wings immediately retracted and the both of us began to roll and tumble onto the hallway's carpet. I did not hear anything break. And despite losing my sense of movement, I felt a burning sensation of where the vines slashed at me. There was also a soreness from falling. Marles, thankfully, did not appear to have been hit in the process. He quickly scrambled over to me with a horrified look on his face. He should have left me there and gone back to save everyone. Instead, he scooped me up before racing down the hallway as fast as his two legs would allow him.

I tried to open my mouth to talk to him, but it would not open no matter how hard I tried. All I could do for the time being was breathe through my nose, barely blink my eyes, and try to think. I could not even harden my bones for protection, which was a terrifying thought after what had happened to those other Celegons. A part of me wished that I could not think at all in this situation and simply regain consciousness once this was all over. *Please, just let this be another one of my vivid dreams.*

I squeezed my eyes shut as Marles ran past a Pythera in the hallway. With how precise and quick their vines were, I assumed he could not possibly get by while carrying me. Though, that one's focus seemed to be on another poor Celegon that was not so lucky. It allowed us to slip by unnoticed. Marles continued to rush until we came across a familiar door. He briefly set me down to open it before carrying me inside.

Soon I was placed on a cushion and watched as Marles used the sharp end of his tail to cut into his arm. In a desperate attempt to restore my movement, he took some blood in his paw and gently pried my mouth open before drizzling it inside. My tongue began to regain movement, as did my mouth a few seconds later. It was not instant, but soon I was able to speak again once my tongue had thawed from paralysis. Marles' eyes lit up with delight once he saw that the blood was restoring my senses, though he still seemed a bit shaken from earlier events.

"Y-you're going to be o-okay. We b-both are," his voice stuttered before he nuzzled into me. He then pulled away before removing his social gathering outfit as I imagine it had been a hindrance to run in. "I promise. We'll make it out of here alive and t-then," he continued as his voice began to break. "A-and th-then-"

"Marles."

My words got his attention, but my gesture brought life back into his eyes. There, in the room with us, were a few other Celegons attempting to stay hidden from the Pythera that lurked about outside. Three I did not know and two were recognizable. There was Clain as well as a small yellow Celegon I had not seen at the social gathering. Upon closer examination, it was indeed Annazie who was related to Reene Hune. A sickening feeling lurked in my stomach seeing Reene herself was not with her.

Clain appeared to be allowing the child to cling to her, but seemed too out of it to offer proper comfort. Annazie took interest in us as she gazed with big, watery, orange eyes. All of them looked terrified or willing to accept what was to come. My hope of survival, too, had been drained. At least until my eyes traveled upwards to the familiar skylight I had entered through many months ago. Perhaps hope would not be lost after all.

"The skylight above. We need to use it to escape," I strained myself to say, my body still weak and suffering from paralysis. The others turned their heads upwards.

The skylight had been covered by thick monster pelts and wood to prevent the cold from getting in, but it would be easy to remove once Celegons flew up and started hacking away at it. They seemed hesitant, but two soon flew up and began to frantically remove the blockage preventing easy passage through the skylight. The debris fell down below and soon cold air began rushing in from the outside. The three Celegons left without hesitation, leaving just Clain, Annazie, Marles, and myself. Though Clain soon shoved Annazie away before standing and sparing a glance at Marles.

"Farewell, Iseirre," she said abruptly before dark blue wings emerged from her back and propelled her upwards.

Annazie dejectedly began to open her own pinkish wings before giving me another look. She may have only met us once, but that must have been just enough for her to worry for our safety.

"Don't worry, we'll make it out of here somehow. Go along and fly to someplace safe. I'm recovering fast, so I'll be able to fly us out soon," I lied to her, hoping she would leave before the Pythera discovered the room.

Instead, she rushed over and attempted to lift me from the cushion I laid on. Her efforts, while endearing, were in vain as no way a Celegon of her age would be able to lift something almost double her size. She tugged and tugged, but my body would not lift further than an inch at most. Tears welled in her eyes as she continued to try with all her might. Then, something truly astounding happened.

All three of us began to be lifted into the air by some unseen force. We ascended and found ourselves above the skylight with Clain standing nearby. She walked over to us and heaved an exhausted sigh.

"Last time I do you a favor, Iseirre."

Chapter Twenty-Four: Together

Even now, the ice flurries continued to fall. After the escape from Iseirre mansion. After Clain went missing. After miraculously discovering I was with an egg. After Annazie.

Too much, it was too much. I wish they would stop. But day after day, they continued to pile up higher around Lixion. More and more white masses while the suffering lingered on. Why must they keep polluting our lands?

The aftermath of escaping the massacre at Iseirre mansion had added stress on all of us. Once we got to the roof of the mansion, thanks to Clain, we were hopeful. Despite the mansion being surrounded by several of the awful Pythera, we managed to evade them by ascending far enough in the air. Their eyes watched us, but they made no effort to follow a few escapees. The Celegons left inside the mansion would do. The ones we abandoned.

We survived. That should be all that mattered, right? Clain acted like she was about to die from overexerting herself bringing Marles and I to safety, but she was still alive. We all were in our small group, and things stayed that way until she went missing a little over a month past that event. Without a word to anyone, the Celegon who had helped us escape capture was gone.

It had been obvious that she was unwell when she'd been staying with us. Stricken by a grief none of us could relate to. That is what possibly led her to do something so foolish as to leave the safety of the dome one night. The reality was, the weather was terribly cold and stormy with heavy flurries. No one wanted to waste energy to search for her as it was her choice to leave.

After Clain's disappearance, there was less food to split between the three of us. That was a benefit at least. The ice flurries raged on outside, but in our dome there was a comfortable peace. Together, we lied to ourselves and pretended that things would be okay for around two months. Then something unexpected happened; I was with an egg.

Celegon fertility rates had always been low for as far back as it goes. How I was able to carry a child of my own under such terrible conditions was beyond my understanding. There was no specific mating ritual done for an egg to start forming, unlike with monsters and nymphs. It was simply an unpredictable outcome after Celegons became mates and shared blood. Most would call the event a blessed and fated day, but to me it was nothing more than a burden I did not wish to carry. It would either kill me or, worse, I would watch it die.

The egg growing inside me caused a lot of pain and amplified problems that already plagued our lives. Weaker and weaker I became, and more sensitive to the cold and hungrier as the developing egg sapped up my energy. I still forced myself to do needed tasks, much to Marles' chagrin, even though I felt sickly exhausted afterwards. Him and Annazie both worried a lot for my condition, which only irritated me more. Being a burden who was not strong enough to help out did not rest easy on my conscience.

One day, he and Annazie left to forage and persuaded me to stay in the dome. I was upset at not being able to help that day, but otherwise fine. Come nightfall, and Marles returned with no berries and no Annazie. She was gone... and I did not need to question what had happened by the look on his face. Another casualty of the cold year. Her passing took an especially large toll on Marles, who had to experience it up close. It hit me hard as well, but I had to pretend to be strong to keep his head above water.

Marles' presence helped me hold onto my decaying sanity. Though it was not enough. No matter how long he held me in the night, the moment he let go my mind became flooded with terrible images and thoughts. Of Pythera, Celegon bones cracking, Annazie's demise, and this egg inside of me. I felt guilty and on edge whenever I was away from him, which I often was as he had to forage food for the both of us. This caused me to form a self loathing mindset, hating myself for not being strong enough to go outside and help most days.

At Marles' request I seldom left the dome. Despite my dislike at not doing anything that would prolong our lives, I was content with sleeping the majority of the time. My body needed to so it could conserve the little energy I had. Another two months had passed before we knew it. I was even weaker then, but I had long grown tired at staring at the same surroundings every day all day. What I needed was some fresh air, even if it was frigid and detrimental to my health.

When Marles returned home that night, I begged him to accompany me outside if only for a little bit. My desperation to go clearly hurt him as he only wanted to keep me safe. Still seeing me in such a state had softened his heart. He was reluctant, but we did as I requested the following morning.

Then I saw Blubelle.

The ice flurries had piled so high that they reached almost past our bipedal waists. We still pressed on however, even though Marles constantly glanced at me with concern. Eventually we reached a small clearing with little trees to navigate through. It was then my eyes laid upon a peculiar sight. Trudging over to it, my eyes widened as I saw what it was. The ice flurries had covered most of the body, but I could see sky blue fur blowing lifelessly in the cold breeze.

Still alive, I see.

My eyes soon burned and then felt as if they were freezing over as trails of my tears stained my face, becoming ice. Soon, I felt my stomach knotting as if I was about to vomit. Thinking about her caused me to sob uncontrollably. Every other time I saw her she was always so lively and vibrant. It hurt to know that I would never see her like that again.

A part of me knew that it was not even her corpse. She was back at the Iseirre's. I saw it happen. But my mind never got a proper chance to process it all. Everything from that point forward felt like a never-ending nightmare. Marles took hold of my side before I could get any closer.

"Lyla, please don't look. Just come here." He sighed before pulling me in close and averting my eyes from the situation.

I dampened his chest with silent tears as warmth began to surround me. My body fell limp and he gripped me tighter. Memories of Blubelle began to flood my mind. They were wonderful, irritating ones. Even so, I felt nothing but pain remembering them. I had not wanted to leave her there to perish. Everyone at Iseirre manor, I apologized for not sticking around to fight. Again.

More months passed after that, and I had not gone outside since. The egg was still inside me and had grown even more. I felt like it would be ready to emerge from my body in as little as a few weeks. I could only stay awake for a few hours at a time then, from not having enough to eat and the egg becoming more demanding. Once it was finally out of me, I could help Marles—who was looking worse for wear.

He had offered me most of the food he found, which was not a lot, to prioritize my health as well as our future child's. As a result, he had grown quite thin; probably as thin as Z was or possibly more. It pained me to see him like that and I pressured him to eat when food was available. Still looking out for me, that was a rare occurrence. I was afraid that he would die of starvation before this infernal egg was expelled from my body.

I should not hate my egg, but I did not want it to be the cause of Marles' death. My heart longed for Marles far more than any egg and I openly admitted to myself that it was selfish of me. We could make more eggs, but Marles' life was not as replaceable. If this cold year would only cease. Then food would be plentiful for Marles and our young.

Marles was currently resting next to my side, shivering under the thick blanket we shared. Although he disliked his heavier appearance in the past, I think if he had it now it would do him well by keeping him warmer. The egg in my lower abdomen appeared to be doing a good job of keeping itself warm at the cost of my energy and well distributed body heat. Marles was curled close to my stomach as that was where the heat was. My mouth formed a weak smile before bending myself to kiss the top of his head.

While both of us were weaker physically, I always had the strength to be affectionate with him regularly. Even if he was incredibly tired, he would reciprocate my advances as much as his body was able. His face stirred and he gently opened his sunsets; which had been duller in color from lack of nutrition, but were still a delight to see each day. He leaned up to kiss me, careful to not put any pressure on my stomach before pulling away.

"Morning already?" he questioned before caressing my face.

"Oh-n-no. I just wanted to kiss you, is all. Definitely not time for you to be going anywhere," I said as he let out a relieved sigh.

My ears picked up the sound of his stomach making notices, starving for food. I felt guilty that for the past few months I had been entirely useless for gathering food. I had been taking and not giving a single thing back to Marles, save for affection.

"We still have some berries that you found the other day right? You should be the one to have breakfast this morning," I told him before gently gently poking his far too skinny stomach.

I knew that there were not a lot, but some were better than none. Not enough to make him feel substantially stronger, nor enough to put any weight back on his bones. Just enough to make his stomach stop screaming and feel just a tad healthier for a brief period. More than anything, I wanted Marles to feel better and make a recovery.

"Won't you and our egg be hungry? There isn't a guarantee I'll find any food today," he said and I was quick to deny being hungry.

It was a lie, but there was no convincing Marles to eat otherwise. My stomach was only slightly peckish, and I was sure that egg would be fine if I took breaks every now and then from consuming. Once it was out, aside from having to keep it warm, it would no longer be sapping away my energy.

"Hm. Alright then, I suppose I'll have a little bit to eat," he said before stretching out and leaving the warm confines the blanket provided.

I shifted my body to the spot he was previously occupying as I waited for him to return. It was cooler than my spot, which made my heart sink. He must have been conserving energy, as without it he would surely perish in the ice flurries outside without his fire talent. Regardless, it still pained me greatly in how many ways he was affected by all this.

He returned shortly with a measly amount of berries in his paws. They were incredibly small and not at all ripe, but at least they were edible. Once the cold year ended, berries would grow faster and bigger than the ones we had been forced to live off of for months. Thankfully emeri trees were not too impacted by the cold weather. Most monsters had long since gone to sleep for the cold year, so at least there were less chances of monster related deaths.

Marles began popping them in his mouth much to my delight. His body seemed eager to swallow them down and get the nutrients into his system. But before his throat could force them down, he leaned over to kiss me. Picking up what he was trying to do, I preemptively turned myself away. Only he slinked around to the other side of me and pressed against my mouth.

"M-Marles st—"

It was already too late. I felt two of the five berries enter my mouth and slide down my throat involuntarily. My body must have been so hungry that it practically swallowed them without a second thought. Frustration brewed inside me, directed at myself for indulging and at Marles for offering. While it was a considerate gesture, it was a poor move to make. Three miniscule berries would barely provide him with any energy at all.

"I told you I would be fine without food today," I growled as Marles' weak grin brightened.

Despite snapping at him, which I have done a lot more in the past few months, he never retaliated. Not even the tiniest bit. Instead he would just smile at whatever I said and try to comfort me. I was sure he had bitter things to say building up deep inside, but he never let them out.

"Lyla," he said before nuzzling closer to me. "You don't have to lie for my sake. I've told you this time and time again. I'll be okay. L-Lyla, please don't cry, I didn't mean to upset you. I promise that I'll eat lots more once you no longer have to provide energy for our egg. You are doing such a great job. I know it's been hard on you, but I know you are strong and will pull through."

His words were so warm and kind. Though I felt as if I did not deserve any of them. I wished the roles were reversed and I was the one providing for him. At least then I would have felt like I was paying back my debt. The memories of Iseirre mansion still haunted me.

The sound of the Pythera entering the dining hall, of bones being crushed, they were sounds I could not empty my brain clear of. Worst of all, I ran. I selfishly took Marles away from the scene before a Pythera could do the same to us. Everyone who did not make it out was gone, no doubt about it.

"I can't rid my mind of what happened months ago. The memories torment me, as they should as I ran away like a coward. My sister... she did awful things, but no one deserves that horrific fate. I just stood there and didn't even try to stop her. And then there's Blubelle, your parents—"

"Lyla, we've been over this. None of that is your fault, it's just an unlucky chain of events we found ourselves in. The Pythera had been planning to come; not just to the mansion, but to all the towns of Lixion. So please don't berate yourself for this. Some of our friends may very well still be alive," his voice trailed off as he wiped my wet face with his paws. "There are still other Celegons out there. I can't tell you how many the Pythera have taken, but we are most definitely not the only ones left on Lixion. If we are, then we can make this *our* world. Ah—sorry, perhaps I was a bit insensitive. The world might be a little emptier, but I'm sure we'll come across other Celegons eventually."

No matter how much he wiped, the tears kept coming. So much that my eyes started to burn. Yet I could not stop. He was so kind; why did he have to be so kind all the time? His optimism only made my heart ache more. Not once had he broken down since all of this happened. But he was so sad and I could sense it through his smiles. He could not cry because he felt he had to be strong for my sake.

"Why don't you ever cry? Your overwhelming positivity is tearing me up inside. Like you don't even acknowledge these awful events that have passed—"

"I do—"

"No. You bore witness to them and yet... I'm always the one crying. All the time. I'm just crying now. All these awful things and you don't even acknowledge the possibility of those we care about being dead merely because we didn't see it happen. Your parents, the caretakers—you haven't said a word about them since we left. You know that I worry about you and care for you very much. I don't want you to feel like you have to hold all this pain in."

My mouth quivered as I closed my eyes. Again, I went overboard with my emotions. Saying this to Marles would not solve anything. It would not miraculously change the past, rendering the horrible events to have never happened. A bitterness swelled in my heart as I realized I regretted saying those words to him. Once an action was done, it was set in place for all eternity.

"Lyla, come here," Marles calmly stated as he pulled my body into a tight embrace. "Do you really not feel like you deserve to feel grief after everything that's happened?"

My stomach churned. He could see right through me, as usual. His breathing became unstable as he gripped me tighter. A wetness caressed my neck as it fell down my back. Now what had I done; I made him feel like he had to cry.

"Of course I've been affected. But I know things will get better; after all, you're still here with me. You've always been so strong, stronger than I've ever been. Lyla, I want to live. I want to live in this world with you no matter how bad things get," he said before his voice broke and he sobbed into my fur.

I held him tightly, as tightly as I possibly could without smothering the egg in my stomach. He was right, we would make it through this. Our egg too. We would all get to see the light of Lixion after the cold year passed. Where happy memories could be forged.

In a few more hours Marles would go outside again and not return until nightfall. Until then, we huddled together underneath the blankets to share warmth. For now, he was with me. Safe. If only we could sleep our way past the cold year as monsters do.

Time passed as the egg inside me continued to grow. Marles would return every night as promised and occasionally bring a few berries back from foraging. Most of the time he would come back with nothing. But he always brought himself home. That was what mattered most.

The night finally came when the physical burden was expelled from my body. My egg, I grew to love it much more now that it was no longer a part of me. It was mainly purple with tints of oranges and greens on its outer shell. More importantly, the year of carrying it was finally at an end. Now Marles and I could take turns venturing out and he would finally get his much needed rest.

The following day I urged Marles to stay with the egg while I braved the cold and scoured the area for forage. I was worried he would protest because I was still a bit weak. But to my pleasure, he seemed grateful that I was so eager and full of energy. He kept the egg warm in my stead as I went out and scanned various places for food. As reckless as it was, I even used my wings in hopes of covering more ground. It was not terribly windy. Much to my surprise, I soon gathered over fifteen wild fruits. I was thankful, even if most of them were quite dinky.

Marles was going to be thrilled when I brought everything back. I planned to insist he stay home for the rest of the cold year as we waited it out together. I needed to support him as he had supported me. There was no way I would let him outside until he had gotten better. With my wings I bet I would be able to gather many things daily, more than he could just by walking.

When I returned, I surprised him with my large haul of fruit. That was enough to convince him to stay home for the next few times I would go out to find more. Though, on that day I admitted to going a tad overboard; perhaps to the point of overexertion. But it was fine. Marles and I had food that would satiate us again.

• • ᢀ • •

My heart and stomach had never felt more full than it had in those recent days. Vibrance had returned to my eyes with newfound energy as I went out nearly every day to gather a hearty amount of forage. Yes, it was still cold, and yes, we had not seen another Celegon in a good long while. But we were thriving. I no longer resented my egg either and greeted it warmly everytime I came back. The only thing I could hope for was the ice to go away by the time my child took their first breath of air.

Marles' gaunt body was finally starting to heal and fill out around his bones. Since I would often bring back plenty to share, there were no longer any objections or telling me I needed it more. With some of his strength restored, I apparently had it in me to start playfully teasing him again. We were both healthier than we had been in a while, which was definitely a factor. Having fun with him like this really made me realize how much life was worth living.

"How can you say such things Ly-Ly?" Marles pouted as he averted his eyes from mine. "In front of our egg too? Must you always go through such lengths to embarrass me?"

My smirk widened as I approached him. I tried to hug him, but he turned his back towards me in distaste. So I opted to rest my head on his back instead.

"You simply take me too seriously darling. I don't see how you are so worked up with me calling you an old nickname. *My Muffin~*."

Despite his scowling, he did not protest when I latched myself onto him. It did not take long before he turned himself around, allowing me to snuggle my face into his chest. It had gotten slightly more comfortable to lean against as it now had a tad more padding, but if I pressed too hard I could easily feel his bones with little effort. I gave him a tight squeeze before kissing him and pulling away.

"To think you would start calling me that again. Whatever happened to calling me handsome? I know I haven't exactly been in top form, but I have missed being the object of your attention. I know, it's probably vain of me to say things like that," he said as he closed his eyes to hide from mine.

"Darling, it's not vain to think that. Well, maybe a little," I started as he gently sighed. "Times have been harder. Granted, things are starting to look better, and I haven't been able to give you the verbal praises you require. Both of us used to be exhausted every day and only now are we really starting to recover. It's because of that I have a longing desire to mess around with you like I always have. I care for you most, you know, so I'm glad to see you doing so well."

He pulled me in for another embrace which I quickly accepted. This feeling, I wish I could hold onto it forever. To an extent I could, but eventually the warmth would fade away. Like a fire that needed kindling. You never forget the warmth, not completely, but memories can never fully replicate what once was. So I never truly wanted to let go.

I then glanced into his enchanting eyes like I always ended up doing. There was so much energy in them, like he was ready to tackle any problems the world threw at us. Of course I was happy. He was better and would continue to get better, yet this subtle sadness filled my being. I knew what he was going to say. I had no right to deny him of what he asked, for that would be hypocritical.

"I have been feeling better, that's true. You've been working so hard gathering food for the both of us. Don't you—"

"You sell yourself short, Marles. For most of the past year you've been out there every day, putting in as much effort as you possibly can to provide for us. I want to do my part as well, you know? Just—just let me take over provisions for a couple more months—"

"Lyla."

It would not be right. Not to keep him cooped up in here day after day like I had been. Yet I was so determined to keep him safe regardless. I wanted to protect both of them. Just a little longer.

"Darling, I know you're hesitant to let me go back out there, but you need to have a little more faith in me. You are finding us lots of food, but you regularly come back exhausted from overdoing it. This is a team effort, and as the best of the best our work should be divided fairly. So I can't just be lazing around here every day. I love you, Lyla. So let's do this together like the proper team we are."

Marles was persuasive, but even more than that he was right. So the next day I let him be the one to trek into the cold outdoors while I stayed home and provided warmth to our egg. I missed him soon after he left, as always, and found myself humming a tune to the egg next to me. Some Celegons have memories of sounds they heard before they hatched, so I figured I would give it a try. I was never one for songs, but familiarizing my child with my voice would be a good practice.

Singing and humming, I caressed its shell as I waited for Marles to return. Perhaps I should entertain myself by telling my egg a few stories. I knew quite a few good ones that the underdeveloped mind might be able to enjoy.

Chapter Twenty-Five: Pinnacle

Patience is a virtue. I remember hearing that quote from someone long ago.

It was a saying that I held true to during my time as a thief. Thieves must be

patient when waiting for the opportune time to strike. But what about love?

There are also phrases that it is patient, kind, and free of envy. Whoever strung together those quotes clearly has never been in love at all. Being patient can cause you to lose the one you love to something you could have prevented if you had intervened sooner. Kindness, while it was good to show affection, too much can soften and weaken both sides. Then there is envy. How is it possible to be free of envy, knowing that the Pythera are thriving while the Celegons have lost nearly everything to them?

Marles never came back. Yet I could not bring myself to despise him for it even though I should. I never wanted him to go, but I allowed it. Now he is gone. Now I have nothing.

My eyes glanced over at my egg, warmly wrapped beside me and encased in blankets. No, I still had my unhatched child. Even so, I felt incredibly alone with no one else for comfort. The only reason I looked after it so well was because one day it would hatch and bring forth a new Celegon into the world. Hopefully sooner than later, as the loneliness I felt was eating away at me day by day.

I had not set foot outside the dome since Marles' departure, which was around two weeks ago. Staying in the same place in hopes he would return. At first I was just a little worried after a few days passed. Perhaps he found others or so much food it would take a while to bring it all back. Or he just took a nap in the white powder. If I went out to look for him, not only would I be leaving our egg unattended, but if he came back he would be worried about my whereabouts. But that was not the case as he never came back.

My food stores had run almost completely dry, down to the last few berries left. Staying here longer was becoming less of an option, as the life of my child would be jeopardized if I could not be there to assist. Since getting weaker would lower our odds of survival, so I had no choice but to travel to a new location with the dome. Marles would not come back. I had to repeat that in my head dozens of times to convince myself to go through with the new plan without him.

Before I left however, I spoke to my egg. There was no way of knowing that my time outside could be the last chance I had at living. With that in mind, I had to tell my egg one more story, like I did every day. Even if they could not hear my words, if there was a chance, it would be good of it to remember the potential last words of its mother.

"Hello, young one. Hm, I still can't get over how weird it is to not be able to call you by a name yet. But one day you'll forge your own name just like I did. Of course, you are always free to ask me for suggestions. If I had the right to name you, I would call you Steluna. Or perhaps Lokiir. We don't know what you'll turn out to be after all.

"Though enough about that, how about a story? This one continues off from the last Lox Lavender adventure. I will warn you, however, this one is particularly dangerous. The infamous Lox Lavender finds herself cornered, trapped in enemy territory as she fears making the smallest sound could blow her cover. Even though she is afraid, her bravery helps push her through and she begins to navigate through the forbidden mansion..."

After I finished, I made sure the egg was bundled up as snugly as possible to prevent heat from escaping and kissed its shell. Slinging my satchel across my back, I made plans to travel far away and cover as much ground as possible. It would not be easy to brave the cold alone, but I had little choice. Either I do this for the both of us, or we both perish. The latter hardly seemed fair to the little one who had not even had their chance to leave a mark on the world.

The coldness of the outside was particularly unforgiving that day. An ice flurry storm, though mild, was a piece of work to navigate through. Thankfully, my agileness in the elements had not softened despite staying indoors for the past two weeks. My back ached as I tried to push through the storm and squinted my eyes to see. It was far from recommended to fly during such gusts, but doing so would not kill me.

Even in this blinding storm, my eyes were able to detect a berry bush a little while after flying. I eased myself down as gently as possible. Though they were hard and bitter, stuffing them into my face would satiate my hunger for the time being. I plucked all that I could to store for later before ascending once more.

Most trees had long since gone barren of leaves, but there were a select few that managed to keep their leafy coats. Seeing how some trees kept theirs and others lost them made me think of all the monsters who had entered a deep sleep for the cold year. For every tree that lost its leaves, I wondered if an equal number of monsters had gone to sleep as well. And for the plants that remained leafy, those represented all the Celegons still surviving out there. Marles would have said something like that.

Several hours soon passed and the sky grew dark, signaling me to return to my egg until the next dawn. I found an ideal area to set up for the night before I excitedly entered my small home. Almost as if it was built into my memory permanently, I expected to see Marles there with his body warming our egg. Of course, he was not. It was an illogical thought to have as my dome had been stored in my satchel until now. Wishful thinking and missing him made me conjure false expectations.

After slipping off my satchel, I went to check on the temperature of my egg. It was faintly warm, not yet cold. A few months after an egg is laid, the Celegon inside becomes strong enough to generate its own heat. This would not be enough to keep it warm on its own, especially not during cold years, but it would buy me more time to go out and forage. Wrapping myself around it underneath the covers, I began to envision the moment it would begin to hatch.

If I listened closely with my ear against its shell, I could hear a faint developing heartbeat coming from the other side. It was very light, but hearing it temporarily made my heart feel full and relaxed my worries. As long as I looked after this egg, it would one day hatch into my child. Knowing that gave me a fraction of hope. I had another nice story to tell it tonight as well.

"And after another successful heist, Lox Lavender was victorious. Her satchel was filled to the brim with all kinds of riches she had stolen from yet another pompous Celegon. Just what will she do with all her earned spoils? Of course, she'll save a large chunk for herself. But she is also generous. If she ever spots a Celegon in need of food, she'll offer them some as good Celegons always look out for one another."

Shortly after I finished, my body ended up drifting off in the warmed blankets. I had forgotten to store the food I had gathered into the jars, but they would be fine in my satchel for the night. My stomach was a little hungry, but I could eat in the morning. Yes, I could do this. Just repeat the same process for a couple more months until I got to see my child. Then things would get a little brighter.

Since Marles had been gone, my vivid dreams had progressively returned. Several times I woke up from something particularly horrifying, not able to sleep afterwards. All of them had taken me to places I had never been to before. In most of them I was alone. The ones with strange creatures, those were the worst as they tried to frighten me. *Child, please hatch soon and may your presence help me combat the dreams.*

· · ⌘ · ·

Morning after morning, more days passed and I was able to survive. Sometimes I practically scraped by on food, but I managed. The world outside wasn't showing any signs of getting warm enough to melt ice. My egg still has a heartbeat, though. Soon, it would hatch into my child and I would finally get to see another Celegon again.

Occasionally, I would hear movement coming from inside the egg. I admit I had not been keeping track of exactly how much time had passed, but eggs hatch around one year after being laid. The fact that I could now hear movements meant that it should not be too far away until I could meet my child. The egg had grown warmer on its own as well, signifying that the child inside was healthy and sustainable.

Loneliness was never an emotion I thought would matter to a Celegon like me. Of course I missed my Marles, that was a given. But everyone else?

Gone. Aside from the one husk I saw buried in the flurries with Marles months ago, I had not seen another Celegon alive or dead.

With no Celegons around, there would be no one to steal from. No, I would have everything to myself. I would, of course, share equally with my child once the time came. I had to stop thinking like this, so selfishly. With no Celegons there was no Lixion. Only monsters.

It was time to be brave like the Lox Lavender I told my egg stories of. For all these months, we had been avoiding towns and other places Celegons have been known to gather. Pythera had come to invade, and no doubt towns would be the most unsafe spots to be in. But I had not seen anyone in so long, perhaps the Pythera got what they came for and left the remaining few alone. So I set the course for none other than Tarrina town.

Of all Celegon towns, it was one of the largest in terms of structures. There had to be survivors left. Seeing wax clumps illuminating in the night would be a pleasant sight as well. Anything other than the color white.

No longer protected by the trees of the forest, I focused my gaze out at the tundra. My eyes could faintly see Tarrina town in the distance, though with the ice flurries my vision was slightly obstructed. A shred of hope clawed at my heart as I ascended into the windy sky. It would not take long at all to fly there and my anticipation only propelled me along faster. There had to be at least one.

In the tundra there were no trees to soften the breeze, so flying was a bit difficult. But I persevered as light ice began to pelt my fur. It was nearly sunset, and I had to make it to a safe location before dark. Tarrina town was always most vibrant at night, so I would be making it just in time. Perhaps the inn would still be running and I would be able to book a room for the night.

My heart began to flutter as the town grew closer. Not out of excitement, but fear. The closer I got, the more I wanted to turn back. I tried my best to convince myself that there was no point in cowering after how far I had come. My gaze turned towards the ground I was flying over to distract myself from what I was getting into. Thick with powdered ice, the tundra looked like a quick death.

Eventually I had to land; I did in that same spot Blubelle and Ariele dropped me off long ago. As my feet touched the icy ground, my gaze fixated upward at the town I would be scavenging through. Tarrina town. It did not look as majestic after being torn to icy ruins. My instincts were screaming at me that I would die if I entered. Since when do I listen to those anymore?

It was quiet and windy; no other Celegons appeared to be present. Most of the stone buildings had collapsed and merged into each other with ice coating it all. The remaining structures that still stood were worse for wear, as if they had not been maintained in months. The damage did not seem like it was done by the Pythera, but simply neglect. No one had been around to care for the town and it gradually wasted away.

Any hopes I had of seeing another Celegon dissipated as I scoured the remains, looking for anything alive or of value. As the sky above darkened, there were unfortunately no wax clumps to illuminate the once beloved Tarrina town. Food that I found was rotten and there were no orbs in sight. Even the inn had fallen to despair with its walls too holey and no longer comforting.

There was a place I still had to check. No chance a Celegon would be there, but a chance they still would be. Carefully stepping over a few sharp fallen rocks, I navigated my way to that spot. A fair chance it had been reduced to rubble like most of the town, but I owed it to him to at least check it. Turning a few more corners, I stepped into the location I recalled it to be in.

Decimated and destroyed. Ice had taken most of it, but if I dug underneath the cold, thick layer, I could see a few vines that used to hang between the walls. As I touched them, my mind grew sharp. Vines. They were still here. Weak from the cold, but still somehow surviving. Looking around, the other flora that he brought to life was still around, just barely scraping by.

Grabbing hold of some, I felt tears sting my eyes. Marles once told me that those with plant talents can keep the plants they grow alive as long as their hearts continue to beat. These plants were weak, but still surviving in this cold, harsh weather against all odds. He had to be still alive, perhaps captured by the Pythera like countless others. I gently kissed the plant before putting it back on the ground.

How could I have been so clueless? The plants he had cared for back in the dome were still surviving even with my limited ability to care for them. If I could only use his plants to track him somehow. As I glanced around the rest of the area, something else caught my eye. I was certain I was hallucinating as there was no logical explanation for why one would be there.

A Celegon egg was nestled in several blankets near one of the collapsed buildings. It was not mine, for it was safe in the compacted dome in my satchel. This egg was mostly dark blue in color with tints of yellow. There was a fair chance that whatever was inside was long dead from the cold. Cautiously, I approached it to touch it with my paw. It radiated with heat and life.

As I returned my paw, I glanced around more to see if there were any Celegons nearby. No Celegon would simply abandon their egg in the cold like this. Unless they needed food and the town was the only safe place they knew of to shelter their egg. It would be wrong of me to transfer someone else's egg inside my dome. Then another idea popped into my head as I opened my satchel.

In a matter of time, I had retrieved my own egg as well as Marles' red scarf and a blanket from my dome before slipping the tiny form back into my satchel. The scarf had lost his scent long ago, as it had been months since he had last worn it, but it would do well in keeping my egg warm for the time being. I bundled the both of them up with more blankets before I admired my handiwork. Both eggs would stay pleasantly warm while I went on a search for the lively egg's parent. If they happened to return before I found them, they would be obligated to stay put until I returned. Before I left, I figured the two of them could use an introduction and perhaps a quick story.

"Well now, aren't you two just a pair? If all goes well maybe you'll grow up to be close friends. You really can't get enough of those these days. Treasure them well and be kind to them. But always give it to them straight. Also pestering them and being a nuisance might cause resentment.

"Now, you are new but I'll give you a rundown on all of the Lox Lavender tales I have disclosed thus—"

Heavy footsteps began to vibrate off the ground. My body flinched as I remembered the vibrations. It was something that was permanently etched in my mind. They had found me. I was careless and now I was to be captured.

My eyes glanced over to the two eggs. They were hidden well enough, safely encased between chunks of the fallen walls. I knew that I had to leave.

If I stayed, they would simply search the area until they found me and the eggs. At least this way they would have a chance, even if it was a slim one.

For what might as well be the final time, I touched the warm shell of my egg. Unfortunately, I had no time to tell it another story. Though if it could hear me all this time, I hope that they found them enjoyable. Perhaps I would be able to tell them more stories in the future. Now it was time to fly.

Speeding my body upwards, I ascended over the wall and made a beeline for the vibrations. It was already too late as they had seen me. If they were intent on capturing another Celegon, they would undoubtedly not rest until they had completed that task. So my only option was to fight. Even though I had no hopes of winning against the likes of them.

My tail grew cold, colder than the outside air and right as I locked eyes with one of the two to target, I was falling. So soon huh? I hoped I could at least land one square in the eyes with a mess of ice—do some damage. At least I could say I tried. Contrary to last time I was hit by those vines, I felt little fear as I fell from the sky.

Whenever it felt like I might be approaching death, time seemed to slow and my hearing was enhanced in that I could hear my own heart beating in my chest. Adrenaline had a similar effect, though in this instance I felt entirely calm. Possibly a side effect from the vines. I did not fear my fate. My body had lost its will to fight back, as did my mind. There was no point in trying anymore. But I would not say I did not have the best time during my life. Life was cruel and unforgiving, but there were good parts to it too. And those good parts are why most strive to keep on living.

Do most Celegons' thoughts race through their mind before death? That must be what is happening, because I feel like I have all the time in the world to think and yet I have not hit the icy ground yet. I suppose when I do, that will be the end of me. Considering I cannot move at all. Why am I not scared of this? I have a child that I need to raise and make sure they grow up okay in this world.

No, that does not matter anymore. I should focus my last thoughts elsewhere. Maybe about what orb variation my remaining strength will take the form of after I die. The tales go whenever a Celegon dies, their remaining power is transferred into an orb; which shows up on the bank of the body of water closest to them. It sounds a bit ridiculous as there is no proof of that, but it is an interesting thought. If it were true, I imagine for aesthetics mine would be a white orb.

Marles, I would want my last thoughts to be of you. I am certain that you are still alive, if so I apologize if my death causes your soul grief. Now, what memory of you should I think back on as my last thought? Oh yes, that one. What a lovely memory to recall before my mind goes blank.

It was really you who was the iridescent one Marles.

Epilogue

I began to stir on the cold hard floor I had been resting on. Though, no matter how much rest I got, I always woke up weaker; more so as the days went on. The only hint of rejuvenation I got was from a single emeri. I had not eaten one in what felt like a month.

Opening my tired eyes, I stared vacantly at my bleak surroundings. Every color I could see was grey or black, and it was all made from stone or a material called steel. I had been in a cell, as the Pythera called it, for a few months now. Somehow I was alive, but just barely. The temperatures inside were cooler than Lixion even without a breeze.

I had little knowledge of the world outside, other than it was called Hisera. The building I was in seemed to hold Celegons like myself captive. The Pythera did not appear to want to kill us, but rather use and study us in the harshest ways I could ever imagine. Mainly, the extraction of our blood. That, and a lack of a consistent diet of food from Lixion and emeri, was making me weaker no doubt. Weak, but still conscious enough to think; which was what I did with most of my time now.

I had lost the strength and will to try escaping ages ago. While it was true I was in a cell, the gaps were big enough for Celegons to easily slip through. Several times I escaped and ran down the cold, strangely lit hallway. That was until a stationed Pythera would—with ease—whip out their tendrils, as they called them, and strike me down and render me paralyzed for several hours. This had also resulted in an immediate forced blood donation on my end as punishment. I was lucky enough to learn this earlier than others, who had died from losing too much.

These days I often spent my time simply thinking and reminiscing about old memories. Days of flying, engaging heists, Marles, and freedom mostly.

Lately I felt I had been getting better at conjuring up new events in my mind that I could get lost in. Though, no matter how vivid they became, nothing could replicate Marles' warmth in this cold cell. I missed him most of all.

Every week, or thereabouts, I had received a 'visitor' at my cell. A Pyther; one who seemed slightly younger in terms of personality, but just as big as the rest. He would occasionally come to random Celegon cells and sometimes stop by mine. Nothing helpful was exchanged, but his visits at least reminded me I could still talk. Vian, his name was; I assumed he held importance in Hisera since he was allowed to walk freely and talk to any Celegon of his choosing. He also had a blue fluffiness at the top of his head and tail tip, which was strange as the other Pythera lacked any sort of fur or hair on their bodies.

Lately, even my mouth exhausts easily, so I wondered if I would be able to give him proper responses next time I saw him again. I had to do everything I could to conserve energy, even if it meant lying on the awful floor for days on end. My stomach was so hungry and the pain was constant, but I grew used to it. Part of me even accepted that I was going to die here. I was even getting hallucinations caused by my weakening mind.

"Lavender, get up."

Z's voice. What an awful thing to hallucinate. Anyone else would have been more preferable. Even Blubelle. How I had grown to miss her. *Still alive, I see.* I told her that all the time as a joke, and now look where it got her. Though, I suppose hearing from Z again would not be the absolute worst. I would give anything to know that a Celegon I know of was still alive out there.

"Little Lavender. Skyli. Lyla. Lox. Get up."

He probably would have nothing good to say to me though. Still holding a grudge over me that I had gotten along better with Alise than he ever could. Never would we manage to see eye to eye, no matter how nice I was. He was infuriating.

I blinked as I stared at the steel wall in front of me. Nothing was there, as expected. For some reason a pain filled my heart. Why was I sad about hallucinating? If anything, it was a better way to pass the time. Going mad was my only sanctuary in a place like this.

Blinking away the blurriness that was forming, I saw that an emeri was on the floor just inches away from my mouth. First voices; now I was seeing things? How fast was my maddening going? I weakly reached out to touch the imaginary fruit as I felt it in my paw. My eyes widened and I quickly sprung up to crawl over and devour it in one gulp. It was real, the metallic juices I had not tasted in far too long were now rushing down my throat.

"Now will you get up? We don't have a lot of time."

My ears twitched as I heard his voice again, much clearer this time. I was hesitant. Hesitant to turn my body around and see nothing there. An uncomfortable feeling began to swell in my chest until I finally summoned the courage to do so. A Celegon of all black was standing just inside the cell a few paces from me. The feelings in my chest began to come out through my eyes and trail down my face.

My body practically stumbled over itself as I approached him. It had been *so* long since I had seen him, so long since I had seen any Celegon, only hearing their screams or catching swift glimpses. I was desperate to know if he was real or not, and I leapt up to hug him. Gently, as I reminded myself of how frail he was. His fur was bristled and coarse, but it was indeed him.

"I... appreciate your gesture, but we really should get moving. We're a little strapped for time," he told me as he slipped himself away from my grasp.

I was reluctant to follow him when he walked through the bars. After being thrown back in here a few times, leaving again made me skittish. A part of me had simply convinced myself that this entire event was not real, which bolstered what little courage I had summoned and needed to escape. After slipping through, I followed him as he led me down the dull hallway.

Any moment now, and we'd be done. I was sure we would be hit by the tendrils of the Pythera stationed to guard the cells, but no matter how far we proceeded I had yet to see a single one. The other cells we passed still had Celegons shuddering inside, however. My conscience told me to tell them to climb out and escape with us, but my feet kept moving. Z did not seem particularly interested in anything else other than finding the way out, which he appeared to know with how precisely he navigated through the massive hallways. Until he made a comment that made my mind go into a brief state of grief.

"After we collect your egg from this place we're getting off this awful planet. It's not too far, the place where they keep Celegon eggs."

My egg that encased my unborn child. Memories flashed of when I had left it next to another and wrapped them with all the warmth I had, including Marles' red scarf. Z must have thought that I had kept the egg by my side until I had fainted from exhaustion in the ice flurries one day. It did not surprise me that he knew I had an egg at all, but it still hurt to think back on that day. Though it pained me to tell him that I had abandoned my egg, as I assumed I would not have much longer to live, going along with him on this would be cruel and slow down our escape.

"My egg isn't here," I stated as he continued to walk briskly, as if he did not hear me. "I... left it with another back on Lixion. Then I collapsed during an ice flurry storm, far enough so that no Pyther could track where it was placed."

Z heard me this time as his movement was halted completely. A string of guilt coursed through me. I could practically sense the emotions seeping from his being.

"You couldn't even protect your young. No matter, I've still made up my mind that I'm going to get you off this world."

His words were harsh, but spoken in a calm manner. I already felt guilty enough about not being strong enough to see to it that my egg hatched into a healthy child, but his word cut. I, like many times before, began to wonder what could have been if I had been strong enough to keep it safe and by my side. These thoughts snapped others back into the forefront of my mind. Though my strength returning definitely played a part in that too.

"I may have failed as a mother, but as a mate... Marles. We have to see if Marles is locked away here in one of these cells. There's a chance he is and we can find him if we just—"

"That's enough, Lavender. You know as well as I do that he's gone. No use searching for someone who isn't here. Before you try arguing with me, remember that I am well acquainted with the area of this world. I-I'm sorry, Little Lavender, but we need to keep moving if we want to survive."

Gone. He could not be, there was no way my mind would accept it. My heart ached with the thought of leaving him here. I trusted Z, as much as I held a mutual dislike for him, I trusted him. Still, Marles being gone was something that had to be incorrect. For both his sake and mine, he had to be alive.

I resumed navigating the strange dark hallways with Z in the lead. Looking down the length of them, they appeared dark; however, as we walked down further, they brightened with light—as if they were lighting our way. Everything in this large place looked so similar too; I wondered why the Pythera did not make an attempt to add decorations or landmarks to make navigation easier. I grew curious about the world outside of this structure.

"Will we be outside soon, Z?" I asked as we continued to traverse the cold bleak halls.

"No. The outside air is far too toxic for beings like us to breathe. Just trust me and keep following; talking like this will only slow us down," he responded, and I pondered on that.

If we would not be able to go outside, how would we be able to leave this place? It also chilled me to know that the air outside was not breathable. Not being able to breathe sounded like an incredibly painful way to go.

Continuing to follow him, I spotted a Pyther lying on the ground. Not dead, but appeared to be severely weakened. Their eyes followed me and Z as we scampered on by. I had not the slightest idea of what was going on with them, but I decided to keep my questions to myself until Z let me know I could speak. I would get answers out of him eventually if I prodded enough. Soon, Z stopped in his tracks and stood in front of an odd steel plated door.

It appeared to be sealed tight by some strange Pytherian contraption. He stood tall on his two back legs and stretched himself to examine these strange symbols that were grouped together in a rectangular form on buttons. They were the Pythera versions of numbers. I recognized a few of them; they looked incredibly similar to the ones on my dome's control buttons. I felt an uncomfortable realization as I made the connection.

Z could not reach the buttons because of how high up they were, but with the wave of his tail, he used his psi talent to push a few in. As he did, I noticed he looked visibly more pained; even using a talent was taxing on his body. The buttons he'd pressed began to glow blue and the steel door began to slide away, granting us passage. The room behind it somehow felt even more frigid than the hallway we came from. My eyes lit up at all the colors and blinking lights that were in this new area I had not seen before. This room was filled with lots of strange technology I was both impressed with and afraid of.

As Z went on to operate a device in the room, my eyes wandered and soon locked themselves on something transparent. Approaching the clear barrier, I examined what could only be a fraction of the area outside this building. I saw a dark sky; it was illuminated with thousands of stars, but no moons. Looking downwards, I saw an area barren of any plant life or water; it was just colorless dirt and rocks as far as my eyes could see. I flinched as I felt something tap my back.

"Ease yourself; it's only me. In Hisera, their world is barren and lacks the many natural resources we have on Lixion. Though the Pythera don't seem to mind the barren scenery. Where they live and stay is in fact far underground, filled with lots of their Pytherian technology. The surface level structures are where they store things acquired from other worlds, while at the planet's core is where the Queen... well..." he said, trailing off. After some hesitation, and I wondered about that, he continued, "It's where they have their base of operations." As he explained, I examined the outside area more. "Not that that information is important to either of us at the moment, since we aren't heading for the core. Come on, I have a pod ready for us to escape in."

He walked over to a large piece of strange technology; though, I supposed *all* of it was strange to me. It vaguely reminded me of a dome, but the entrance and the exterior were far bigger. It also had many other objects attached to it I had never seen before now. Before entering it, he picked up a sizable pack; I could smell provisions inside of it. Seeing it made me clutch my side, where my satchel used to hang close to my waist.

The area inside was enormous, but far less cozy than a dome. Everything was coated in steel, buttons, or transparent glass that made the outside visible in various places. I sat myself down on the cold flooring as Z began to fiddle with more buttons. Soon, I began to feel heat radiating from somewhere, like the dome-like structure was heating itself up to a comfortable level. My energy quickly faded away from me despite my efforts to stay conscious. I gave in as I curled myself up into a ball and pressed my head against the now warm and vibrating floor.

I stirred as I felt something soft and weighted being draped across my back, but I was too comfortable to open my eyes. From the soothing rumbling, to the warmth caressing my body, I felt lulled into sleep. And just as soon as I had dozed off, I was waking up—overwhelmed by terrible, frightening images that never seemed to cease. I shivered as I glanced around at my surroundings; while many things had changed, nothing bad appeared to be happening. Pushing aside the nightmares, I gazed in wonder at what I saw outside the glass partitions.

As I gently touched the cool glass with my paws, I stared at thousands of stars in the black abyss. Some were closer than others, which was as equally fascinating as it was terrifying. We were far beyond the barriers of the sky if we were able to see things like this. There were also rocks that floated off in the distance—and if I squinted, other worlds? I backed away from the viewing glass and decided to examine the rest of the vessel since some of my energy was restored. Z was sitting on a Pyther sized cushion along with several buttons close by him.

He appeared to have faint hints of terror in his eyes as I approached him, wide with fear like had just seen something monstrous, but he quickly snapped out of it once he saw me coming closer. He then pressed a button that closed all the openings to show the abyss outside our vessel and turned his body to face me. There was a relieved smile on his face and I mirrored it. It took a minute for me to realize that this was real and I was a prisoner of the Pythera no longer.

"You woke up just in time. I just finished navigating this pod through a space hole. If you woke up a moment sooner, you would have seen some frightening things," Z said with a sigh before reaching over to grab his large pack.

Before I could question what a space hole was, my eyes lit up to see my trusty satchel in his paws. Sure it was just a satchel, worn and begging to be replaced, but it was also a memory of Lixion. Not only that but it had some weight to it. Peering in, I saw that all of my items appeared to be intact and safe. My dome too, it had many of Marles' paintings within that I could now hold onto forever.

"I know you probably have lots of questions, and I promise you I'll answer them later. But for now I must rest."

He curled himself up and began quivering as his body coaxed itself into sleep. I went over to grab the cloth that had been thrown on me earlier and put it over his torso. In spite of my previous nap and insatiable curiosity, I climbed up on the large, sleek black cushion and sat close to him. Laying my head down without falling asleep. Just thinking like I did back in that cell, only now I had another Celegon to talk to as well as a chance to live again.

A sense of safety enveloped me as Z slept by my side. Perhaps this situation could help us learn to get along so we could survive together. Though with Z's health issues, it would definitely be harder; even now, he was shivering from whatever plagued his body. But he was tough. He'd survived this long, after all, and had proven to be more than tactically useful when he'd helped me escape. The question was, when would we both lose ourselves to our damaged hearts?

I had not a clue about Z's mate; even Alise had never spoken of her to me. For all I knew, she could have been dead already and he was barely keeping himself together. Marles was definitely alive though. I was still sane; weak, but mentally functional. Perhaps once we were in a better situation we could return to Lixion and find Marles and our egg. I would find them. Both of them. And they *would* be alive.

That would be my pinnacle of perfection.

Lyla's narration has concluded.
The Celegons will return...

Don't miss out!

Visit the website below and you can sign up to receive emails whenever Razz Vernicus publishes a new book. There's no charge and no obligation.

https://books2read.com/r/B-A-QQSDB-KBOBD

BOOKS 2 READ

Connecting independent readers to independent writers.

Milton Keynes UK
Ingram Content Group UK Ltd.
UKHW030845190824
447134UK00008B/619